CROW
TALK

ALSO BY EILEEN GARVIN

The Music of Bees
How to Be a Sister

CROW TALK

A Novel

EILEEN GARVIN

DUTTON

DUTTON

An imprint of Penguin Random House LLC
penguinrandomhouse.com

LIBRARY OF CONGRESS CATALOGING-IN-PUBLICATION DATA

Names: Garvin, Eileen, author.
Title: Crow talk : a novel / Eileen Garvin.
Description: First edition. | New York : Dutton, 2024.
Identifiers: LCCN 2023044667 (print) | LCCN 2023044668 (ebook) |
ISBN 9780593473887 (hardcover) | ISBN 9780593473900 (ebook)
Subjects: LCGFT: Novels.
Classification: LCC PS3607.A782894 C76 2024 (print) |
LCC PS3607.A782894 (ebook) |
DDC 813/.6—dc23/eng/20231011
LC record available at https://lccn.loc.gov/2023044667
LC ebook record available at https://lccn.loc.gov/2023044668

Printed in the United States of America
1st Printing

Book design by Nancy Resnick
Title page art by paseven/Shutterstock.com

For Margaret,
who taught me to listen

The language of birds is very ancient, and, like other ancient modes of speech, very elliptical; little is said, but much is meant and understood.

—Gilbert White

1

NESTING SITES

Where a bird determines to locate her nest is the key concern in establishing home territory. Oftentimes the nesting site may be inspired by natural boundaries—such as field, fen, shrubsteppe, pond, or lake.

—*G. Gordon's Field Guide to the Birds of the Pacific Northwest*

Mary Frances O'Neill was a young woman of many firsts. First in her graduate school class in the University of Washington's avian biology program, she was almost certain to graduate with honors. She was also the first female student in the history of Hood River Valley High School to earn a full ride to UW for academics and not sports. She was the first member of her family to complete a bachelor's degree, let alone a master of science. And she was also the first woman in the history of the family—O'Neill on her father's side and Healan on her mother's—to reach the advanced age of twenty-six without becoming a mother. This last, it should be noted, was not an accomplishment universally admired by her kin, many of whom wanted nothing more for her than a marriage with a nice local boy and a steady job at the county.

On this September day in 1998, Mary Frances, who almost everyone called Frankie, was not thinking about her academic, professional, or romantic future. She was focused entirely on getting to June Lake, where she hadn't been in more than a year.

The truck puttered along the Old BZ Highway north of the Columbia River, hugging the banks of the White Salmon River as it
twisted and turned its way through the great dark woods. It was a
difficult road, but Frankie knew it by heart—every curve and corner,
each patch of rough pavement, and all the road signs, which grew
fewer as the highway climbed up into the remote corner of the Gif-
ford Pinchot National Forest. Here was the bridge at Husum Falls
where flashing white water tumbled over the double drop into the
river. There was the wide gray face of the dam that held back the
once-wild flow of the White Salmon River. She knew which shoulders would be crowded with kayakers shuttling the whitewater run
and which would be thick with fishermen casting from the sloping
banks for fall steelhead. Then came fields stretching out on either
side of the highway giving way to thickening woods as the road
climbed toward the little jewel of an alpine lake tucked high in the
forest at the foot of Mount Adams. Frankie cracked the window and
listened to the rush of the river and the crash of the falls as she
crossed the bridge. A kingfisher keened along the riverbank and a
Steller's jay chattered a machine-gun reply. She'd driven this road
countless times over the decades with her parents, her brother, her
grandparents, and her cousins. This solo trip was a rarity and one
she'd been looking forward to for months—clutching it like a lifeline,
if she was being honest.

Her thoughts drifted as the trees flashed by, and she forced herself to think of practical concerns—the checklist of supplies she'd
brought for her trip, the potential change in the weather during this
transitional month of September, and the hour of sunset, which was
the most important question of the day. Like most people who frequented June Lake, the O'Neill family never ran the boat after dark.
Driving at night was to risk running aground in unseen shallows or
colliding with old deadhead logs—remnants from the forest's timber heyday—that could surface unexpectedly. And even in summer,

the weather could change quickly on the lake. Since the boat was the only way to reach the family cottage, it was a key consideration. Frankie glanced at her watch and at the sun now far above the west shoulder of the mountain. She had plenty of time. The knot of anxiety in her chest loosened a bit, and she leaned back against the cracked leather seat.

Traffic thinned north of the dam. A logging truck blew by trailing the sharp, sweet tang of freshly cut trees. After that she had the road to herself. It took more than an hour to reach Mill Three, and a light rain began to fall as she pulled into the marina parking lot.

Mill Three was one of several small logging towns unimaginatively named by the Cooley Lumber Company in the 1920s. The once-thriving settlement was now just a wide spot in the road with a gas station, a post office, and a shabby park next to a small marina where the O'Neills docked their boat. The communities of Mill One and Mill Two had long been reclaimed by the woods, and those who remembered them were all dead.

Frankie cut the engine and looked out over June Lake at a view that seemed unchanged in her more than twenty-five years of coming here. The dark green water caught the muted sunlight that slanted through the clouds and undulated without breaking. Large ponderosa pines and Douglas firs grew close together here all the way down to the water's edge. The empty halyard on the flagpole slapped in a nearly indiscernible breeze, and the weathered cedar docks rose and fell gently in the shifting water. A mourning dove cooed from within the branches of a big oak, and an osprey chirped sharply from its perch on a piling. Frankie climbed out of the truck and looked up the long, narrow lake. Mount Adams rose to the north with a ring of clouds circling its shoulders, heavy with new snow. Frankie zipped up her sweatshirt and turned toward the dock. The marina was almost empty this time of year, as most people pulled their boats out after Labor Day. An old Century Raven bobbed gently against her lines in one slip. Someone, probably Patrick or maybe Hank, had repainted her name on the side, bright yellow against the black wooden hull. *The Peggotty* had been named by Grammy Genevieve, who'd been a great lover of Dickens and thought *The Peggotty* called to mind *David Copperfield*'s unfussy, practical, and dependable heroine.

Only two other boats remained—a sleek Sea Ray and a battered red Hewescraft. The former belonged to one of the other families and the latter functioned as a water taxi and cargo boat. With no road access to the homes on June Lake, the summer residents were dependent on boats to haul people, food, and supplies up the long stretch of water. Some might have found the remoteness of the place an inconvenience. But for Frankie, June Lake had always been the calm center of the universe. It was a comfort to be back here where she felt most herself—a girl at home in the woods and falling in love with birds for the first time.

The sun struggled with the clouds, and the top of the mountain disappeared. The osprey chirped and then circled, dove, and snatched a fish from the water. Frankie shouldered her backpack and carried a load of boxes down the dock. She pulled the cover off the boat, and the Philippine mahogany decking gleamed in the low light of the cloudy afternoon. She smelled the faint scent of varnish and a knot rose in her throat. Refinishing the woodwork was a tedious annual undertaking that her father had always completed in fits and starts. She could picture him here, sanding, wiping the wood clean, brushing on varnish, and reading a tattered detective novel between coats. She dropped her gear in the boat and turned away from the image, returning to the truck to unload the rest of her supplies. In the boat she opened the faded red leather hatch to negotiate with the carburetor. *The Peggotty* could be cantankerous and hadn't been driven in months. Eventually the engine sputtered to life and the instrument panel on the dashboard lit up like a memory of Christmas. Frankie let the engine hum in neutral for a couple of minutes. She cast off and pulled away from the dock as the rain increased. The spattered windshield reflected her lanky frame and short dark hair. She pushed her bangs out of her face and flipped on the wipers.

Frankie's father, Jack O'Neill, had taught both of his kids to drive the summer Patrick was twelve and Frankie was eleven. She'd been thrilled about the prospect of getting behind the wheel, though Patrick hadn't seemed to care much. When his lesson was over, he went back to his stool in the dock store and the book he'd been reading. But it was different for Frankie. She could recall every detail—the feel of the polished wheel under her hands and the timbre of her father's voice as he explained the function of each dial on the instrument panel. He showed her how to affix the navigation lights and how to change the wiper blades. How to gas up, where to add oil and coolant. He demonstrated the art of drifting the boat in neutral, forward, and reverse. How to gauge the effect of the wind when landing and leaving the dock. He explained right-of-way, safety, and man-overboard scenarios. He quizzed her until he was satisfied and then put the keys in her hands. Frankie adjusted the choke, turned the key, and coaxed the engine into a stuttering neutral. "Gotta be patient with the gal," Jack had said. "She's older than your old man."

That day Frankie pulled away from the dock and puttered toward the center of the lake. Once she was clear of the log boom, her father nodded at her, and she eased the throttle forward. She watched the bow plow through the liquid green and accelerated until the boat came to plane. "That's my girl!" Jack yelled over the sound of the engine. He settled into the passenger seat and put his feet up. After that, Frankie became the de facto driver of the family, which suited her just fine. It was Frankie who ran her dad back and forth to the marina. Frankie who picked up supplies in Mill Three for Grammy Genevieve's store. Occasionally she drove other residents down the lake when the water taxi wasn't available or picked up their friends at the marina. They gave her big tips, but she would have driven for free.

Her love for the old boat had never left her. Now, in the increasing rain, she felt her heart lift as *The Peggotty* cut through the water at medium throttle. If it wasn't exactly joy she felt, it was a lightness compared to the weight on her chest, the tangled mess of feelings she'd been carrying around for months.

The trip from the marina to the north end of the lake took nearly two hours. The water was fast and flat, and Frankie leaned back, steering with one hand. She took the middle channel, watching for deadheads and other debris that came down off the mountain with fall rains. The breeze carried the clean scent of water and evergreen, damp earth and woodsmoke, and blew her hair around her face. She gazed at the high cliff line along the east side of the lake, which marked the boundary of the Confederated Tribes and Bands of the Yakama Nation. When she passed Arrow Point at the halfway mark, she noted the still waters of the small cove there. The blue light of the glacier on Mount Adams glinted in the rain, and the Windy River was a thread of white tumbling down the south chute of the mountain. She slowed at a large tree-covered headland that shouldered its way out into the lake. Rounding the corner into the sheltered cove of Beauty Bay, Frankie felt her heart crack wide open as the houses came into view. The ten Cape Cod–style cottages retained the genteel charm of the 1930s, when they'd been built. Painted in soft hues of blue, green, and yellow, the cluster of houses looked like a toy village from a distance. The summer homes had been owned by the same families for generations and maintained in their original style. The houses and the sandy beach were separated by a long, elegant stone seawall that had been built by Italian masons lured away from the WPA program building Timberline Lodge on Mount Hood. Green lawns ran from the seawall to the porch of each house. It was the perfect spot for the clutch of summer homes, but it was also the only location that would have worked on June Lake. The south bank belonged to the unincorporated community of Mill Three. The sheer cliff of the west shoreline was impossible to build on, and the eastern side belonged to the Yakama Nation.

In the 1960s, the Magnusen family, newspaper scions of Seattle, had made noise about wanting to build something more modern but had never followed through. None of the other families saw fit to change anything. So as the years passed, the houses, their wooden docks, and the elegant stone seawall endured. The trees grew tall and broad. With no automobile traffic, the birds and wild creatures flourished here.

The O'Neill family, scions of nothing, had gained a foothold at June Lake thanks to the mysterious machinations of Frankie's grandfather, Ray O'Neill. Ray had emigrated to America in the 1930s along with thousands of Irish who'd crossed the Atlantic looking for a better future. Her devilish grandfather, with his sunny disposition and gift of gab, had landed in Hood River and talked his way into a job as an errand boy for Charles Stevenson, the local timber baron. On the Stevenson payroll, armed with his bright blue eyes and genuine love of people, he charmed everyone from the town housewives to the gruffest of lumberjacks and the small coterie of businessmen who controlled the then wild corner of Oregon. And if they didn't like his stories and jokes, those men appreciated Ray's talent for procuring the best Canadian whiskey during Prohibition. When Prohibition ended, Ray opened the River City Saloon in Hood River. The thirsty lumberjacks and rivermen patronized the tavern along with local law enforcement, who'd always been among his best customers.

The origins of the cottage were murkier. Ray never confided the full story, not even to his wife, Genevieve, but it had something to do with a backroom poker game with the developer of the Beauty Bay Resort, which had gone from investment scheme to full-blown boondoggle and eventually resulted in the construction of these few summer homes along the lakeshore.

Whatever the case, when Frankie's father, Jack, was just a boy, Ray had gained possession of the caretaker's cottage and the seasonal employment that came with it. Much smaller than the other lakeside homes, the O'Neills' cottage was a compact single-story perched on a rocky outcropping above the lake—a location deemed subpar by the developer. Jack and his sister, Dorothy, spent summers at the lake with Genevieve. Ray came up during the week, leaving the tavern in the hands of Hank Hansen, the responsible young Dane he'd hired. And when Jack married Judith and had his own kids, they'd spent summers there too.

Frankie couldn't remember a time in her life without the lake, the snug cottage on the cliff, the stretch of wild woods, and the constantly changing face of the dark green water that mirrored the mountain, snowy through summer. She and Patrick grew up helping their grandparents with the dock store and doing maintenance for the summer people. Now, glancing up toward her family's place, she could almost see her grandparents waving from the lookout, though they had been gone for some time.

The rain intensified as she neared the shore. The wind churned the lake into a rough chop and pushed the prow of the boat. Frankie nudged her way into the shelter of the dock, landing with practiced ease. She tied up and stood for a moment taking in the silent houses. Birds flitted through the trees, and a pair of slender deer disappeared into the woods. Retrieving a dock cart, Frankie pulled her cargo to the bottom of the trail.

In the 1980s, Ray had installed a small electric trolley for Genevieve, who'd begun to tire of the steep climb. Frankie and Patrick had made a game of racing up the adjacent trail as their diminutive grandmother chugged up the hillside on the trolley. Now Frankie sent her books and supplies up the trolley and walked to the top of the headland as the rain darkened the air around her. At the summit, a large boulder marked the border between the woods and the cottage, its craggy green shoulders gleaming with wet moss. The pale yellow clapboard cottage was tucked in there like it had grown out of the forest floor. The back door stuck slightly as Frankie unlocked it and shouldered it open. She stepped into the mudroom and breathed in the familiar scent of woodsmoke, lemon, and peppermint. She found the breaker box in the dark and flipped on the power. The overhead light snapped on and cast a warm glow on the bottle-green walls of the low-ceilinged kitchen.

There sat the deep sink her mother had bathed her in when she was a baby and the ancient Wedgewood stove that had been the origin of Genevieve's wonderful baking. She could almost smell the ghost of an apple pie, the hot sugar and cinnamon of sticky buns and quick breads. The refrigerator, a squat white box that dated from the 1950s, hummed to life. Frankie carried her perishables in from the trolley and put everything away. In the living room, she pulled kindling, paper, and logs out of the woodbox and soon had a fire blazing. She stood in front of the woodstove warming the backs of her legs as she considered the room. The couch and two armchairs had come from Bergen's Furniture in Portland—far fancier than anything the O'Neills could afford. The Bergen family owned one of the cottages and gave Ray and Genevieve these castoffs back in the 1950s when they were refurbishing their lake house. Forty years later, the O'Neill family continued to refer to them as the "new" couch and chairs. Her grandfather's record collection was shelved near the couch and his old turntable perched between a pair of speakers. A large wooden coffee table dominated the seating area and was strewn with books, magazines, a cribbage board, and a half-completed jigsaw puzzle.

Frankie had always felt comforted by the beloved cottage, but now her scalp prickled. She felt the edges of something nameless but threatening and familiar. She pushed it away and returned to the business of unpacking.

The first bedroom exhaled a cold draft as she opened the door. The room was lined with white beadboard and furnished simply with a double bed, two bedside tables, and a dresser. This room had belonged to her grandparents. The other belonged to Judith and Jack and was also simply furnished. Frankie knew she'd sleep on the porch, like always, but stored her pack in Genevieve and Ray's old room.

Outside the rain had lightened. Pulling the nonperishables off the trolley, Frankie carried them to the root cellar. She hesitated outside the adjacent pump house, then opened the door and flicked on the light. Standing in the doorway, she breathed in the familiar scent of her father's world: sawdust and turpentine, the tang of cold metal, and the faint, eternal smell of cigarettes. She scanned the room, taking in the workbench, the stool she'd perched on to talk to her dad while he was working, the postcards tacked to the walls. Everything was the same, exactly as she'd left it, she told herself. But before she finished the thought, she knew it wasn't true. Nothing was the same at all and there was nothing she could do about it. She'd told herself coming up here alone would be a good thing, but it only made her feel lonelier and more adrift than she'd been all summer—all year, if she was being honest. For everything had begun to unravel last Thanksgiving, hadn't it? She felt the now familiar stab of panic in her belly.

She turned to shut the door and flicked off the overhead lights. In the waning daylight, she glanced up at the rafters above the workbench. She could almost see the glint of the bottle there, feel the cool glass in her hand, taste the heat of it, the burning in her throat, and the blessed forgetfulness that would follow. But no, she wouldn't. She would not.

She pulled the door shut and went back into the house, crossed through the living room, and stepped onto the screened-in sleeping porch. Two enormous ponderosa pine trees grew close together just off the house. Their tops moved in a breeze that was undetectable below. Down at the water, the wind had dropped, and the lake lay flat. In the diminishing light, it shone like a dime.

Frankie lowered herself onto the daybed that had been hers since she was a child and pulled off her boots. Leaning back, she stretched her long legs in front of her and gazed up at the understory of the big pines. She closed her eyes to listen to the roll call of the woods.

The drowsy *yank yank yank* of a nuthatch.

Bell-like peeping of goldfinches.

Tok tok tok tok tok of a downy woodpecker.

The eponymous *chicka-dee-dee-dee-dee* of the chickadees.

"Oh dear me!" cried the golden-crowned sparrow.

And out of the deep woods behind the house came the *Ha! Ha! Ha! Ha!* of the crows. Always the crows.

Listening to the bird chorus almost made her want to get to work—a feeling that had eluded her for some time now. Work, which had been her mainstay, had disappeared with everything else. But she was tired, just so tired. She stayed where she was, listening to the familiar avian symphony around the little house.

Birdsong, wind in the trees, the rhythmic lifting and clanking of the dock in the waves, the water lapping the shore. Sounds as familiar as her own breath. It was a comfort to hear them, as she'd hoped. But the feeling wouldn't last; she already knew that. The last weeks of effort to get here had felt, briefly, like she was moving toward some solution. But now she knew it had all been a distraction—vacating her apartment, selling her books, distilling her belongings down to her backpack and several boxes, and catching a ride home to Hood River with a field team on their way to Bend. It was all just a way to keep herself from thinking about the impossible corner she found herself in. Everything she was running from rose in front of her here at this beloved old place. Because she was not a girl at home in the woods and falling in love with birds for the first time. She was twenty-six, homeless, and staring down a host of uncomfortable new firsts in her life.

She was unemployed and unemployable. She was facing potential legal action. Bereft of friends and allies, she was out of options, out of ideas, and out of places to go.

Her throat caught and she tried to find her breath.

The rain began in earnest again, and she could hear the light patter on the metal roof. She scooted down until her head lay on the pillow. She'd just rest for a minute or two and then she'd get to work, she thought, closing her eyes.

The rain was a living thing. In her mind's eye she could see it moving through the woods like a beaded curtain, down the hillside, across the meadow, and over the sleeping bodies of deer there. In a rain like this they would curl their dun-colored bodies deeper into each other's flanks, mothers and yearlings and new fawns all burrowing together. The rain would travel over the pitch of the roof and down to the lake itself, dimpling the surface of the water like pebbles thrown by the hand of an invisible giant.

The thought of the sleeping deer made her feel so lonely. She ached to talk to her father, the one who always helped her figure things out.

She fell into a fitful sleep. She saw Jack O'Neill standing by the back door of the cottage. He shrugged on his red-and-black plaid jacket, smiled reassuringly, and beckoned her to follow. But he disappeared into the woods, and she lost sight of him. The path became dark and unfamiliar. She was lost on her home ground and didn't know which way to go.

2

BIRDSONG

The world's birds exhibit an astonishing range of beauty and complexity of voice.

—*G. Gordon's Field Guide to the Birds of the Pacific Northwest*

Anne Ryan had always taught her students that the key to any successful composition was a simple question: What emotion drives the piece? For any work to come off as genuine you had to understand the feeling at its very core. Was it love? Betrayal? Playfulness? Longing for home? If that central idea could not be conveyed to the listener, then the composer had failed. Or one could blame the performer, she codded them to get a laugh. But truly, whether you began with lyrics or melodies, the same principle held fast. Human emotion was the cornerstone of any successful piece, and especially with traditional choral music.

Anne herself had always begun with verses, naturally drawn to the origin story at the heart of a song. The words came first, in a flash, the narrative laying itself out in front of her like it had just been waiting for her to pay attention. Katherine, by contrast, began with the tune, saying that the melodies came out of the noises of the everyday world around her. She told Anne that when they'd been first-year composition students at Trinity College in Dublin. She said the songs threaded their way into her brain when she was on the bus, walking along High Street, or amid the din of St. George's—the corner pub they'd frequented since the beginning of their first term at university.

Anne, who needed complete solitude to work, couldn't imagine that. *"How do you find music in the sound of Fat Phil hollering at Peter Hanrahan to bloody fecking score already?"* she'd asked Kat, glancing at the corpulent bartender, who was just then gesticulating at the football game on the telly.

Fat Phil had seen them looking and, tugging his shirt down over his belly, called them a pair of bloody harpies and asked what they were looking at, which set them snorting into their pints. In any case, Anne's and Katherine's contrasting approaches to composition were something they'd always loved to talk about. However, it had been quite some time since Anne had tried to write anything, or even talked about writing, for that matter.

Now from her spot on the picnic bench, Anne listened to the activity around her and wondered what tune Katherine might have heard in the racket of downtown Seattle. There were layers of overlapping noise at the small park near Pike Place Market—the droning horn of the approaching ferry, the clang of the passing cargo rail, and automobile traffic crawling along the viaduct high overhead. A truck beeped in reverse at a construction site across the street, and children called to their mothers from the playground. And under all of that, the worried murmuring of pigeons bustling about on the pavement near the benches. What song might Kat hear?

Anne glanced toward the playground, where Aiden sat at the bottom of the slide with his book open on his lap, tracing the illustrations with one small finger. The wind tousled his auburn curls, which matched hers exactly. None of the other children seemed interested in the slide, so she didn't call to him to move. She knew he was lost in his beloved storybook. No harm in that.

A plump crow alighted on a telephone pole next to the ferry terminal, then leaned forward and dropped something from its shiny black beak. Another crow landed near and repeated the motion. Mussels, Anne decided, as she watched a third glossy bird tug a shell off the pier, fly up to a pole, and drop its booty into the street. The birds remained perched, gossiping among themselves, as cars began to disembark the ferry. When the last car had departed and the lane was clear, the crows swooped down to gobble up the bits of mussels cracked open by unwitting commuters. Anne chuckled with admiration.

Cheeky buggers, she thought.

A little girl began hauling herself up the slide ladder one rung at a time.

"Sweetheart, come sit with me," Anne called. "Someone else wants to slide down now."

Aiden didn't look up, though she knew he could hear her.

"Come on, now. I'd like one more game before we head home, if you please."

Aiden continued to ignore her. The little girl, now at the top of the ladder, turned and called something to her mother. Anne pulled out a package of Fig Newtons, which she unwrapped noisily.

"I guess I'll just have to eat these myself, then," she said.

Aiden shut his book and came to her, as she guessed he might. He sat on the bench opposite and stared at the biscuits expectantly with dark green eyes that matched her own.

"Oh, now you want my company, do you?" she teased. "What kind of a boy has to be bribed to sit with his mam?"

Aiden looked away and smiled faintly. Anne passed him the deck of cards.

"It's your deal, dearie."

She watched him lay the cards in neat rows on the picnic table. Her gran had bought the memory game at the store that sold Irish-themed trinkets, blankets, and Aran jumpers to Americans coming over to "find their roots" on the island where Anne's family had lived for generations. Anne could picture her counting out the loose pounds and pence that she'd collected in a tea tin and telling the clerk about her great-grandson in America.

When the cards were all aligned, Aiden folded his hands in his lap and waited for Anne to begin. She flipped over one card and then another.

"Ah! The harp and the leprechaun. You must watch out for this fella," she said, tapping the picture of a little man in a green jacket and trousers. "He isn't always kind. Remember the story of Snow White and Rose Red? That horrible little man got his beard stuck in a log, didn't he?"

Aiden turned over two cards of his own. The claddagh and a clover. No match there.

Anne flipped over the harp again and the Celtic knot.

"The knot is for loyalty, faith, friendship, or love," she read aloud. "The Celtic knot can be a gift between lovers."

She turned the cards face down again and watched her son scanning the table methodically. She saw his father's face in that thoughtful look—Tim Magnusen, the man she'd married.

As a girl she'd sworn to remain single. "Marriage is legalized servitude!" she'd told her parents during secondary school, mostly to needle her mam. This was not an accurate characterization of Margaret and Matthew Ryan's marriage, as everyone knew Margaret wore the trousers. But daughters will rile their mothers. Gran chided her and Margaret regarded her with a cool stare.

"Don't fret, Mam," Margaret said to her own mother. "Saucy Annie here will understand someday."

As Anne had grown older and her friends paired off, singledom came to feel like a strangely acceptable fate. She dated the odd bloke at Trinity, but there was no one special. She got on well enough with her male classmates as friends. But by the time she'd graduated, a solo life had begun to feel inevitable. It didn't seem like such a bad thing, though Kat had taken to calling her "Sister Anne." Kat, who was forever snogging some new man. She wouldn't mind it, she told herself. Living alone would allow her all the time in the world for her music.

Then, six years ago, she and Tim Magnusen had become lovers— a completely unexpected development. They'd met at a fundraiser for Cornish College of the Arts in December of Anne's first year teaching there. His family's newspaper was a sponsor for the event, which had attracted a fair amount of attention for its evening entertainment, a Grammy award–winning jazz ensemble. Anne hadn't understood what modern jazz was until that evening and quickly found she didn't care for it. She stood outside the performance hall where she'd volunteered to run the silent auction. Kat had scolded her in her last letter, saying she needed to get out and meet people. But Anne soon realized that silent auctions were self-serve events. No one had any questions, and she had no idea how to strike up a conversation.

The ensemble was well into its first set when she decided to leave. Her feet were killing her in the regrettable choice of heels she'd worn—cheap knockoffs she'd hoped would make her look more sophisticated among the urban Seattle crowd. She grabbed her bag and coat and was about to leave when Tim appeared and began to browse the auction display. She sighed, put her things down, and leaned against the wall to wait. When he got close enough, she told him to please let her know if he had questions.

He had a nice face, she thought. She shifted from foot to foot and forced herself not to look at her watch as Tim carefully studied the offerings: pottery from a local artist, a weekend at a Vashon Island B and B, dinner for two at Jazz Alley—things like that. Later, when he knew her better, they'd laughed about how visibly irritated she was, wishing he would hurry up and leave so she could too.

"I was trying to work up the nerve to ask you out," he'd confessed. "You're a little intimidating, you know? All that red hair and that accent."

"I was completely shattered!" she reminded him. "You try standing around in heels for an evening and see how friendly you feel."

Tim had bid on tickets for a play at Seattle Rep and then asked Anne what she thought of the ensemble. She knew she should lie, as she was representing the college. But she didn't.

"Honestly? Sounds like a secondary school band warming up in the back of a cement lorry."

Tim laughed with surprise.

"Okay if I quote you on that for the paper?"

"You bloody well may not," Anne replied coolly.

He'd asked her if she wanted to get a drink at Serafina. She decided to say yes, mainly because the idea of waiting for the bus in those shoes seemed impossible just then.

"Alright, then," she said pulling on her coat. "But I'm up early tomorrow, so I really do just mean one."

True to his word, he'd run her home after the one drink. The following week, he found her number in the school directory and left her a message at work. Why did she call back when she was safe at home and in perfectly comfortable shoes?

She remembered calling Katherine, who was still in Dublin then, and telling her about Tim. How just one drink had turned into something more. It felt like a confession, and oh, how her friend had screamed down the phone.

"I do NOT believe it! After all your big talk!"

Anne took the slagging off. After all, it was true she'd sworn she'd rather chew her own arm off than date some pompous American. In her defense, she reminded Katherine, she'd made that proclamation late in the evening of her going-away party and should not be held accountable for a word she'd said after her second pint.

Now Aiden had found the knot's match.

"Well done, sweetie."

She passed him half a Fig Newton. He set it aside for later, always one for delayed gratification.

A crow flapped lazily across the park and landed in a tall pine near the picnic table, muttering and fluffing its wings. Anne glanced up at the big evergreen. There were no trees like this at home. And though Ireland's skies were rainy, they had texture and movement to them. The first flat gray winter in Seattle had nearly done her in. She would never have stayed if it weren't for Kat. Her friend sent long, newsy letters on blue airmail paper, recounting her romantic escapades, and assured Anne she was not missing anything. She described trying to find work with her small ensemble at weddings, private parties, and holiday gatherings and her unsuccessful attempts to land a teaching position. The country was flailing under the leadership of the Fianna Fáil party and shaken by intermittent bombings. Katherine joked that she could always join a convent and sing in the choir if things got bad enough.

"Room and board, at least? But truly, Ireland does not need another unemployed musician, my darling," she'd written. "Stay where you are and try to enjoy yourself!"

So Anne had stayed, and she'd discovered how much she loved teaching. She and Kat continued to write together—Kat scoring melodies and Anne sharing lyrics. She loved seeing Kat's handwriting on thick envelopes, ripping them open to reveal the latest tape, hearing her dear friend's voice as she said "hiya" and then explained what she'd decided to do with the arrangement. The sound of Kat's hands touching the piano keys as she began the tune.

Aiden grabbed her hand and pressed it to the deck of cards.

"Sorry, sweetie," she said, flipping over two cards. The leprechaun again and the banshee.

"Oh, the banshee! She's the sad lady. Remember her? The banshee wanders the moors at night and cries for her lost love," Anne read from the card.

She'd felt like a banshee herself after discovering she was pregnant one bleak February day. In lighter moments, Anne would refer to her pregnancy as "when I come down with our Aiden," in her thickest brogue, which always got a laugh from Tim. But that dark afternoon at Planned Parenthood hadn't been the least bit funny.

The kind nurse asked if he could call anyone for her, and Anne shook her head. He gave her the number of a counseling line and a pamphlet on abortion services. She'd walked down Broadway in a cold rain and called Kat from the first pay phone she could find, crying her eyes out.

Kat had been her practical self. Straightaway she'd asked what Anne wanted. And Anne didn't hesitate. She wanted that baby. It wasn't about religion either. The Ryans were lapsed Catholics and Anne had no qualms about abortion. It was something else and so unexpected. She was more certain of it than anything in her life before or since. Everything in her yearned toward the idea of this tiny beginning within her. Though it would mean moving back home with her parents and surrendering the opportunities in Seattle. She could handle the village gossip and her parents' disappointment. The baby was what she wanted. She'd laughed, and Katherine had too.

"But man, is your da going to be raging!" Kat had said, which made them laugh harder, though it wasn't really funny.

She'd asked Tim to meet her at Café Paradiso. She'd never forget how handsome he looked as he came through the door of the café that day, his light blue shirt freckled with rain, his short, sandy hair dampened. His eyes found hers as he crossed the room, and she thought how he would never look at her like that again—so easy and pleased to see her. After all, they'd only been dating since Christmas. He was surprised by her news, but when she'd made it clear she was keeping the baby, he said he wanted it too. He kissed her and asked her to move in, which she hadn't expected at all. But his enthusiasm won her over, so she agreed to give it a try. What a strange time— getting to know him when she was at her absolute worst. Exhausted yet not sleeping. Starving and unable to hold anything down. Furious one minute and laughing the next. Her small frame ballooned, and she hogged the bed. But they'd managed and they genuinely liked each other, then loved each other. Despite their differences, perhaps because of them, they made each other laugh. Like the day Tim, trying to brush up on his Irish English, had referred to her underpants as bloomers. Anne had nearly wet herself laughing.

"*Bloomers!*" she'd howled.

Aiden considered the cards methodically and Anne didn't rush him. The crow hopped down from the tree and perched on the lip of the garbage can and pulled out a McDonald's bag. Dropping it on the sidewalk, the crow began to feast on limp fries and pickles. A breeze picked up and rustled the greasy paper.

Aiden glanced toward the bird and slipped down off the bench.

"*Crack-oh!*" said the crow and hopped away as Aiden retrieved the bag and placed it in the trash bin. Idiosyncratically tidy was her boy. Anne sighed, stood up, and took him by the hand.

"Thank you, love," she said. "Let's go wash our hands. Might as well go potty too."

The air was cool inside the low stone restroom. Aiden went into a stall and carefully shut the door. Anne washed her hands, looked at herself in the mirror, and grimaced. Not a stitch of makeup. I look like an old woman, she thought. She pulled her scarf out of her bag and tied it in her hair. Leaning back against the sink, she watched little sparrows flit in and out of the open grates near the ceiling.

Aiden emerged from the stall and stood on tiptoe washing his hands while humming the ABCs. The daycare staff had taught him this, and he was ever faithful to it. The melody was the same as "Baa, Baa, Black Sheep," which Anne had learned as a child.

"My, he's thorough, isn't he?" a voice said.

Anne turned to see a woman and her child waiting to use the sink. It was the little girl from the slide.

"Oh yes, he is. A regular hand-washing champ," Anne said, smiling.

"Well, we're happy to wait until he's all done!" the woman said with false cheer.

Anne felt a stab of irritation and forced a smile. She knew if she rushed him, he'd only start over at the top of his ABCs. No point in trying to explain.

"Hi," the little girl said to Aiden. "I'm Cora. I'm four. What's your name?"

Aiden ignored her and reached for a paper towel and dried his hands. The little girl stared. Her mother whispered something.

"What's retarded?" the little girl asked.

The woman reddened and refused to meet Anne's eye.

"Let's go, sweetie," Anne said, and they went out into the sunshine.

The breeze had blown the cards across the table and onto the ground. Aiden gathered them and handed them to her one by one.

"Thank you, love. We can play again later at home."

They walked, zigzagging around Lake Union to avoid the steepest hills on the way to Fremont. It was over three miles, but her boy didn't tire. He marched next to her on his sturdy wee legs, refusing to hold her hand. At busy intersections, he grabbed on to the strap of her shoulder bag—a compromise, she supposed. When he moved ahead of her on the sidewalk, she noted his purposeful gait, this independent creature, and marveled at the fact that they had once shared her body. It seemed impossible that Aiden had just turned five.

When they reached the apartment, he took off his rainbow-colored sneakers and lined them up on the shoe rack. Waiting for Anne to shed her shoes, he placed them next to his and ran into the living room and snapped on the TV.

"What did we say about TV, dearie? After dinner, okay?"

He stiffened with frustration but turned it off and went to his record player. He set the needle down in the middle of the record, locating the very start of "Annan Waters," which had been a favorite tune of late. He'd been playing it for weeks now. She encouraged him to listen to the rest of the record, which he did from time to time. But the repetition seemed to soothe him when he was feeling edgy.

Though he had an odd habit of never letting the song finish, pulling the needle off at the same spot near the end.

"Let's let it play through this time, shall we, sweetie?" Anne said.

Aiden crossed his ankles and leaned over the record player and didn't reply. Anne closed her eyes and felt the prickle of rising tears as she went to the kitchen. She sat at the table and pulled out her notebook. Flipping to the back, she found scribbles from her last wrecked attempt to write a song. When was that? "March 3, 1997," she'd written. Almost eighteen months ago.

Aiden had started the song over again.

Oh, Annan Water's wondrous deep.

He let it play through the three verses and into the last chorus. The song built and swelled, and Anne willed him to let it play through to the end. But just at the peak of feeling, Aiden picked up the needle and started it over. Anne gritted her teeth in irritation and laughed at herself.

Maddening child, she thought and crossed to the stove to put on the kettle.

If she'd asked her students about the emotional core of this particular song, they'd probably have said love and loss. The lover riding the moors, the horse in fear of the roaring water, the swimmer losing his strength. But this just showed how words failed. The anatomy of grief was too much to translate into words. You could argue that all lyrics failed, really. Words alone could not express the emotion that remained trapped inside a bruised and broken heart. That's why the story always needed a melody to go along with it. For this song, it was the querulous rise at the end of each phrase and the call of the uilleann pipes that expressed the sorrow words could not. Without that music, the story alone was a broken and incomplete thing.

Broken and incomplete. How she felt now, how she'd felt this past year and a half. She listened for a sound from the living room.

"Would you like a cup of chocolate, sweetheart?" she called to her son and waited.

Say something, Aiden. Anything. Please, she thought.

The needled lifted off the record and the song began again.

In her mind's eye, she saw Katherine at the airport—black hair and blue eyes, yelling goodbye and waving madly as Anne entered the boarding bridge, calling out to her and blowing kisses that flew up into the sky and disappeared.

3

THE CHICK

Human intervention may be said, in such cases, to disrupt
Nature's balance.

—*G. Gordon's Field Guide to the Birds of the Pacific Northwest*

Once upon a time there was a little cottage in the woods where a
man and a woman lived. They loved each other very much and
though they dearly wished for it, they had no children.

One day an old crone appeared at the door with a baby girl in her
arms. Would they care for it, she asked, the little changeling? They
loved the beautiful baby like she was her own.

One day the woman went to the crib and the baby was gone. A
large bird perched on the windowsill, and it sang at her sweetly, and
then it flew away.

4

TERRITORIES

Song is a valuable tool in the proclamation of territorial boundaries.

—*G. Gordon's Field Guide to the Birds of the Pacific Northwest*

⁓ ⁓

Frankie awoke slowly to the sound of the dawn chorus. She lay still and listened as the forest ticked awake around her. An osprey chirped somewhere over the predawn waters of the lake. The bossy honking of Canada geese floated across the bay. Down on the beach, sandpipers trilled as they scurried through small waves. The liquid twittering of wrens among the ferns grew louder as the light strengthened. Mournful coos of doves, brash clamors of northern flickers, and the melodic interjections of thrushes swelled gradually to a kind of symphony. A crow cawed emphatically, and another replied.

Frankie had first read about the dawn chorus in *G. Gordon's Field Guide to the Birds of the Pacific Northwest* when she was seven years old. The book explained that the morning song was not some random musical happening, but rather a process for marking territory. The birds who sounded off earliest were those perched higher in trees and therefore saw the sun first. Some people reasoned that those with larger eyes sang earlier. And the birds continued to sing for other reasons at all hours of the day. Territory, mating, brood rearing, protecting the young—it was all communicated in song. As a child, Frankie understood the practicality of this explanation but found it somehow lacking. There was something more there, surely. It was her first ornithology class that taught her the power of wondering, of seeking an answer beyond what was accepted as true.

"Why else might birds sing?" Dr. Tandy had asked. "Besides finding a mate, marking territory, or communicating with their brood?"

Her classmates had shifted uncomfortably and looked down at their notes as if they expected answers in college, not questions. Frankie raised her hand and tried to think of the right word.

"Um, announcement?" she'd said. "Something like 'Hello, friends and neighbors. Here I am'?"

Dr. Tandy had cocked her head, regarding Frankie with piercing blue eyes.

"Exactly, Ms. O'Neill. And what else might be going on there? Don't be afraid to ask the question just because you don't know the answer."

Frankie hadn't been afraid to ask questions after that. She'd been surprised to discover that she was good at asking new questions and seeking their answers, at least when it came to science and especially to birds. Who'd have thought it? Lanky Frankie O'Neill was good at something. For although she'd landed at UW on a full academic scholarship, Frankie had felt like an impostor when she arrived, as if she were there by accident or someone pulling strings. She'd spent her whole life in a small town politely waiting her turn and moving to the back of the line, embarrassed by her height and apologizing for taking up space. In grade school she did her homework during lunch and in high school ate alone or in the company of the ham radio club members, who tolerated her presence because she was quiet and knew how to fix things. She wasn't used to standing out or leading the pack. But it took only a couple of weeks at UW for her to realize it wasn't a fluke. She belonged there.

Now Frankie looked out the screen of the sleeping porch into the

still-dark woods surrounding the cottage. The house faced northwest, so the morning sun would take some time to appear. Here in
the shadow of the woods, the dawn chorus lasted longer and built
more slowly. She closed her eyes and listened as the smaller birds
joined in. Chirruping robins, twittering tree swallows, peeping goldfinches, zinging hummingbirds, and a covey of quail calling *"Chi-
ca-GO! Chi-ca-GO! Chi-ca-GO!"* as if they were all late for their
train.

Frankie swung her feet to the floor and stretched. She'd fallen
asleep in her clothes the night before and now wryly congratulated
herself for saving time. She pulled on her boots and walked out the
screen door and around the side of the house to the woodshed.

Three crows perched on a downed pine and regarded Frankie as
if she'd interrupted a very interesting conversation. She noted the
duller, browner feathers of the small one—a lone fledgling with its
parents, she guessed. Moving slowly so as not to disturb the birds,
Frankie retrieved the ax from the shed along with an armload of
logs. The morning air was chilly, and she warmed up swinging the
ax. The wood was dry and split with a satisfying crack. The crows
muttered among themselves, watching her, and then moved off into
the woods, yawping conversationally.

Sunshine scattered the clouds and her thoughts cleared. It had
rained all night, slowing just before dawn when Frankie had startled
awake from a series of images. Judith's disapproving face in sharp
relief. Davis Grant walking away from her at the spring symposium.
Father Brash on the altar with his hands raised. Past events and
dreams were all tangled together, and she did not try to sift through
them.

Inside, she kindled a fire and looked down at the water, which lay
flat and placid under the white face of the mountain. The tarnished
hands of the old wood and brass barometer pointed to "Change." A
wind line moved across the silver water of the lake like the breath of
a large, unseen creature.

The battered orange coffee pot chugged and wheezed, and Frankie snapped on the radio. It had only ever picked up one or two stations, and now the sound of a Debussy piano concerto wound through the room, comforting and slightly scratchy. She recognized it as one Grammy Genevieve had loved. She sat at the kitchen table and pulled out her manuscript. "Family Ties: The Role of Pair Bonding in Habitat Rejuvenation for the Spotted Owl."

She flipped open the folder that contained the comments from the most junior members of her thesis committee—Dr. Wood-Smith and Dr. Andreas. Frankie knew their suggestions would be easy enough to address, mostly because they fell in line behind her advisor, Dr. Davis Grant. And Frankie's thesis was mostly Dr. Grant's idea. That fact had been made clear during their meeting the previous winter quarter—the start of everything falling apart.

If she'd told her father about it, he would have threatened to call Dr. Grant himself. Jack would also have called Dr. Grant a horse's ass. He might have jokingly offered her a job at the tavern, then more seriously suggested she call Samuel Ortiz, her old boss at the Forest Service. He would have hugged her and told her how sorry he was, which would have made her feel both better and worse. But her dad hadn't said any of those things because Frankie hadn't told him what had happened between her and Dr. Davis Grant.

She stared down at her committee's editorial letters without seeing the words. She'd read them so many times, she practically had them memorized. But the weight that pressed down on her heart made it all seem pointless and impossible.

There was the unmistakable drone of a motor then. Frankie strode to the lookout, and her binoculars revealed a boat piling through the lake—the old Hewescraft water taxi. Frankie pulled on her windbreaker and descended the twisting trail to the dock. From behind the wheel, Jerry Sewell doffed his hat in greeting, his wild gray hair blowing in the wind. "Mr. Water Taxi Man," she and Patrick had called him when they were kids—until the day he invited them on a trip up the lake. He'd let Frankie drive and Patrick managed the manifest as they handed off the cargo to a fishing guide at a far dock. On the way home, Jerry shared the cookies his wife, Marilyn, had sent along and told Jack they were fine workers when he dropped them home. He was just Jerry after that.

As the red boat slid in just behind *The Peggotty,* Frankie caught the bowline and tied it off. Jerry stepped out with the stern line, beaming at her through his shaggy beard.

"Hello there, young Frances!" he called.

He came down the dock, spry as ever, though he was older than her parents, and clapped a hand on her shoulder. In his work pants, flannel shirt, and WSU Cougars hat pulled down over his wild gray hair, Jerry seemed ageless.

"We heard you'd come up the lake. A bit late in the season, isn't it?" he said.

"You're one to talk," she said. "Why aren't you at home watching football?"

He pulled off his cap and ran a hand through his hair.

"You're right! I should be working on my dream team," he said, laughing.

He gestured to the west side of the lake.

"Cooley is doing a cut near Osprey Creek, and they hired me to provision the camp for the month. Running supplies up and such."

He pointed his hat up the seawall.

"And I'm dropping off some groceries for the Magnusens. One of the sons is coming up for a bit. Tim Junior, I think."

Frankie followed his gaze to the Magnusen house, set off by itself on the far end of the bay. She tried to think of something polite to say and failed.

"Oh," she said.

Jerry laughed.

"I guess you expected to have the place to yourself. You O'Neills usually do outlast the rest."

His face grew somber, and Frankie turned away to study the cargo in his boat, which included several boxes of dry goods.

"That's all for Tim Magnusen?" she asked.

Jerry blew air through his lips and surveyed the pile.

"Most of it. I don't know what it's for. I don't ask questions. I just run the meter."

He began to unload, and Frankie brought a pair of carts down the dock. Between them, they shuttled four loads up to the house. Jerry chatted away about his daughter and her grandchildren, who had recently moved back from California to be closer to Jerry and Marilyn.

"Smart as a whip, that little girl. I'm not so sure about the boy. His little sister does all the talking for him."

Jerry's familiar prattle was soothing as the radio, and Frankie was grateful for it, knowing he wouldn't expect her to say much.

The Magnusen house sat apart from the rest as if aloof like the family that inhabited it. Over the years, Ray, Jack, and then Frankie had done maintenance for the Magnusens, who were unfailingly polite and paid promptly. But while the other families became friends, inviting the O'Neills to their barbecues and children's birthday parties, the Magnusens resided on the other side of an invisible line of class and money. The present Mr. Magnusen, Tim Senior, was the third generation to own the house at Beauty Bay and, Frankie knew, the third to run the Seattle newspaper.

Frankie pulled a cart of nonperishables to the root cellar, unlocked the door, and pushed it open with her knee. The air smelled cold and metallic. She unloaded the boxes and returned to the front of the house to help Jerry lift a rowboat off the porch and carry it to the beach. As they walked back down the seawall, Frankie listened to Jerry talking about the logging company contract and felt a growing irritation at the idea of Tim Magnusen at Beauty Bay.

"Did Mr. Magnusen say when Tim was arriving?" she asked as they reached the dock.

Jerry pulled off his gloves and tossed them in the boat.

"Soon, I expect, given that they sent me ahead with food. Oh, heck! I almost forgot your mail and messages. Donna asked me to bring it up."

Donna was the postmistress of Mill Three. She could be counted upon to forward mail and take phone messages, if somewhat begrudgingly, as Beauty Bay was too remote for a phone line.

Jerry pulled a stack of envelopes and magazines off the dashboard of the Hewescraft along with a paper plate covered in aluminum.

"This is from Marilyn for you. Brownies," he said, looking shy.

His discomfort made her want to look away, and Frankie forced a smile.

"Tell her I'll swing by and say hi before I leave."

"Sure thing, kiddo," Jerry said. "You keep an eye on the weather. You know it can change real quick up here."

He gave her a quick hug and started to say something else but shook his head. He pulled away from the dock, looked over his shoulder, and raised a hand. Frankie watched the red boat disappear around the headland. Long after it was out of sight, she could hear the engine, persistent as a mosquito in the dark, echoing across the water.

She felt that heaviness on her chest like a hand pressing down. She pulled off her boots, dangled her feet in the water, and shivered. She should go for a swim and wake herself up, she thought. She remembered long days swimming in the cold alpine lake with her brother and her cousins, the countless hours she'd spent jumping off the dock and climbing out to help unload a boat or sell snacks to fishing guides and their clients. She yearned for those summer days of the past where work and play bled together. But that was all so long ago. She pulled her boots on and walked up to the house, intending to review her committee's editorial letters. Instead, she dropped her mail and the brownies on the kitchen counter and went back outside.

She followed the trail behind the house up through a sunny meadow and paused at a small circular platform ringed with vertical slats of weathered wood. Grandpa Ray had built the hunting blind in the 1930s for Beauty Bay homeowners. However, since pheasant, turkey, and deer were in season long after most families shuttered their houses, it was never used much and quickly forgotten about. Over the years, the cedar had weathered and grayed, so it blended into the woods around it. Moss climbed the legs and crept into the interior. Frankie took it over the summer she was seven. Her father had given her *G. Gordon's Field Guide to the Birds of the Pacific Northwest* for her birthday, and she spent hours sitting in the shelter of the blind watching the avian visitors pass through the meadow. It was her father's idea to record her sightings on the slats of the blind itself. You could say that Frankie did her first fieldwork in 1979, recording the species she'd seen on the soft gray cedar slats in Magic Marker. She ran her finger along the lists she'd made over the years, which climbed higher as she'd grown taller, though her childish scrawl hadn't improved much. The last year of record, 1996, had been sparse. She'd hardly been home at all that summer, as she was deep into her fieldwork for her master's. There was no entry for 1997.

Recalling the crows from that morning, she pulled a pencil out of her pocket and wrote "1998," then "3 crows: 2 parents and 1 juvenile." It felt satisfying to document that, like some sort of official record of return and belonging. She climbed out of the blind and set off through the woods listening to the resident birds that hadn't yet migrated for the season, or would not, like the crows. Walking the familiar curves of the path felt like a homecoming and buoyed her heart. Deeper in the woods, a far-off sound arrested her movement and she felt uneasy. She listened again but heard nothing and kept walking.

The question of Tim Magnusen's arrival was soon answered. From up in the woods, she heard the growl of an engine on the lake below. When she got back to the house, her view from the lookout revealed the large Sea Ray tied up behind *The Peggotty*. It was a fifty-two-foot, two-deck fiberglass monstrosity that the family upgraded every year or two. Mr. Magnusen named each new boat *Peace-o-Heaven* and had the name painted on the bow in gold. Jack O'Neill, prone to colorful hyperbole, had always referred to the Magnusens' boat as "Moby Dick," or in more colorful moments, "Magnusen's Big-Ass Sea Ray."

The bow and stern lines were secure and the fenders out. This relieved Frankie of the neighborly obligation to run down and catch the boat and make small talk. It was bad enough that he was here at all. Let Tim Magnusen do whatever he'd come to do and leave her in peace.

A person climbed out of the boat and set a cooler on the dock. Small framed, with curly red-gold hair, Frankie thought it was a child. But then the figure turned and revealed a woman about her age. The woman glanced at the houses on the bay and then back to the boat. She zipped up her windbreaker and stepped toward the gunnel of the Sea Ray. Frankie waited for Tim to emerge, but he didn't appear to be in any hurry to disembark. The woman sat on the cooler, leaned against the piling, and waited.

This was not Tim's sister, Crystal Magnusen—a year older than Frankie and all blond hair and bangles. Frankie remembered the single time Crystal had invited the O'Neill siblings to one of her parties in high school. She and Patrick had watched, amused, as the girls grew screamy drunk on wine coolers at the bonfire Frankie built for them. They all ended up in the water—some skinny-dipping on purpose and others falling in. Crystal and her friends were disappointing. Frankie had expected them, as city kids, to be more sophisticated.

The woman tipped her head, and as her gaze swept the ridge, Frankie blushed and stepped away from the lookout, feeling like she was spying. She went inside, poured herself some coffee, and returned to the kitchen table.

She pulled open her notebook and tried to read but found herself distracted. Waves hit the beach and the dock clanked against the pilings. Grammy Genevieve's wooden wind chimes tok-toked in the breeze. Frankie realized she was waiting to hear the voices of Tim Magnusen and this woman, who must be his wife, as they walked up the dock. Half an hour later she returned to the lookout, and the woman remained sitting there. What the hell was Tim Magnusen doing aboard the boat? Not engine trouble, she hoped. She swore softly to herself as her mind followed that possibility. If the *Peace-o-Heaven* had a mechanical problem, she'd have to ferry Tim to Mill Three to use the pay phone. And the marina repair shop was closed for the season, so getting anyone out to fix it would be unlikely. So she'd be stuck taking Tim Magnusen and his wife down the lake to their car, and perhaps coordinating a tow for the boat, which would mean getting a crew up from Hood River or Bingen. She groaned. The last thing she wanted was to be drawn into a maintenance adventure with the neighbor.

Crows called from behind the house and the wind switched and blew down off the mountain. There was movement below. The woman, standing, was clapping her palms lightly and singing. Her voice was high and sweet, and the song carried up the cliff to where Frankie stood. She listened, unable to catch the words. There was something familiar about the melody.

She heard a man's voice and the singing stopped. Tim Magnusen strode down the dock toward the woman. He crossed his arms over his chest and gestured at the boat. His voice drifted up the hillside.

". . . going to wait out here all night?" he asked. He sounded annoyed.

The woman walked toward him, and Frankie could see she stood more than a foot shorter than Tim, who'd retained the lithe athlete's build Frankie remembered. The woman reached up and put a hand on his chest. Her voice rose and fell as she spoke. Tim's face relaxed then and he dropped his arms and turned toward the beach. The woman called after him, and he stopped and turned back to her. His face lit up with laughter at something she said. Then he walked up the dock, his footsteps echoing off the water.

The woman returned to the cooler and resumed the song and the soft clapping. A spark bloomed in Frankie's chest, a feeling of deep, inexplicable longing. The woman stood then, and a small figure climbed down out of the boat. Blue jeans, red sweatshirt, and the same auburn curls as the woman. A little boy. The child dragged a backpack out of the boat and stood in front of her. He spun in a circle, raised his hands in the air, then brought them down and clapped three times. The woman mirrored his motions, still singing. Then she lifted the pack onto his shoulders, and they walked up the dock together toward the seawall and out of sight.

Frankie returned to her notes feeling relieved that she wouldn't need to interact with Tim Magnusen and his family. Later, when she was heating a can of soup for dinner, she realized she was humming the tune she'd heard the woman singing. What was it? Familiar and mysterious at the same time, it haunted her, twisting in and out of her mind all evening as she fell asleep to the sound of the wind in the great trees above the house.

5

FLIGHT PATTERNS

Every species exhibits a distinct array of habits and behaviors that are activated by specific stimuli.

—G. Gordon's Field Guide to the Birds of the Pacific Northwest

Anne dug her toes into the cold sand and listened to the waves lapping the shore, wind in the trees, birds in the woods behind her. Her
eyes found Aiden, who was sitting in the sand near the green water
of the lake. Above him, the clouds were white thumbprints across the
blue sky. It was a beautiful, quiet morning and, after all the prepara-
tion to get away from the city for a couple of weeks, should have felt
restful. Instead, Anne felt acutely aware that she should be elsewhere.

What would she have heard on a typical September morning on
her way to work at Seattle's Cornish College of the Arts? The hiss of
tires on damp pavement, the airy sigh of bus brakes, or someone hollering down Broadway—piss-drunk, mad, or simply late for the bus.
The far-off horn of the train approaching the station downtown. The
urban bustle of Seattle was not something she'd particularly liked
when she'd first arrived six years ago, but she'd grown so used to it
that she missed it now or at least felt its absence. Was that the same
thing? she wondered.

Normally she'd be in class at this hour teaching Choral Composition I to the incoming freshmen. Or, more likely, she'd be running late to class, having stopped for an emergency coffee at Vivace. Cup in hand, she'd rush down the sidewalk under the broad canopy of chestnut trees outside Kerry Hall, where the large choral classrooms were located. She'd hear someone practicing scales on the grand piano, an opera student warming up, perhaps the pulsing throb of bass from the jazz wing and the traffic jam of a horn section tuning. She'd probably stop in the middle of the sidewalk as she often did, arrested by the cacophony of overlapping sounds, the beautiful accident of music, the ever-changing soundtrack of Cornish. Then she'd be truly late, and slinging her bag over her shoulder and with an apology ready on her lips, she'd hurry inside to greet the new gaggle of young musicians who'd signed up for her course.

But she was most definitely not doing any of that, not this morning and not this semester, as she was officially on leave. That leave had started at the end of spring, but she felt it keenly now, not being there the first week of school. After so many years tied to the academic calendar, first as a student and more recently as an instructor, it was strange to have so much time on her hands on what would normally be a busy fall day.

A plump crow settled atop a piling near the stone seawall with something in its beak.

A second bird landed near, jostling the first.

"*Hoak, hoak, hoak,*" said the new arrival.

The first crow dropped its prize, and the intruder snatched it up. A chase ensued with a third and then a fourth bird joining in the playful pursuit.

Aiden had commandeered a dock cart and was pushing it back and forth on the beach in front of the house. The soft sand hindered the cart's movement, but that seemed to be part of the game for Aiden, who was perfectly absorbed in the activity. Well, that was something. Wee heathen didn't look the least bit tired. Neither one of them had slept well. Aiden was uneasy the first night in a new place and felt the need to check things. Last night he'd climbed out of bed repeatedly and pattered down to the living room. Anne followed, knowing she'd find him peering at the stack of CDs lined up in a tall case there. They were not in any particular order—classical and rock thrown in with jazz and fifties pop. The lack of care with which her in-laws approached their music collection made her anxious, and that made Tim laugh at her. Next thing you knew, she'd be alphabetizing the spice rack, he said. And she laughed too, because she'd already done that.

Aiden had become attached, for some inexplicable reason, to Grandma Christi's Barbra Streisand CD, a double album of all Barbra's biggest Broadway hits. Anne knew he didn't want to listen to it or take it out of the case to look at. He just seemed to need to know it was there. Well, he'd taken it out one memorable time. Last Fourth of July, Christi had left it in the player on repeat for hours. The stereo only held four CDs, so it was Streisand, Vivaldi's *Four Seasons*, Bobby Darin, and the Oak Ridge Boys all bloody day. Anne gritted her teeth each time the cycle started over, and her suggestion that they change the music was lost amid the overlapping conversations of her in-laws and their offspring. At midday, she switched out the CDs with Ella Fitzgerald, Ravel, Debussy, and Nat King Cole. That offered some relief, though Christi eventually put the Streisand CD back in the rotation without comment.

Anne never needed to hear "Some Enchanted Evening" again in this lifetime. And not just because of the repetition. That July night she bolted awake to the song and raced to the living room to find her small son contentedly rocking from foot to foot in front of the stereo. He didn't respond to her scolding or his grandfather's when Tim Senior appeared in his bathrobe and threatened a spanking. Aiden had allowed her to lead him back to bed with an air of quiet resignation. The rest of the weekend, he'd steal over to the stereo and just touch the CD cover, then go back to whatever he'd been doing.

He'd done the same last night. He'd touch the Streisand CD case with one small finger, whisper something to himself, and scuttle back to bed on tiptoe. Anne followed him, tucking the blankets around his narrow shoulders each time and returning to her room with Tim across the hall. Just as she began to doze off, she'd hear Aiden's small feet in the hallway and follow him back to the CD collection and back to bed. Over and over it went. She knew from experience that nothing—not scolding, restraining him, or pleading—could stop it. His fixation was like a little tempest. It would boil itself up and wear itself out. Around 4:30 a.m. she surrendered the idea of sleep and went into the kitchen to make tea. The lake came to light as the sun rose over the hillside at the back of the house. The water went from black to silver to shimmering green. Aiden stayed in bed for a couple of hours more, and Tim appeared later, stretching and crowing about how well he slept at the lake house.

"Well, I feel like I've been run over by the lorry that is your son," Anne said wryly. "Looks like you're on breakfast duty, love."

Tim was taking forever in the kitchen, but this was a rare opportunity to sit still in the morning and she told herself to try to enjoy it. She could hear him banging around like the Anglo-Norman invasion was afoot, not pancakes and eggs. She glanced at the house behind her. It was a beautiful old place in many ways. The exterior reflected the elegant era in which it had been built. While the adjacent homes retained their charming screened-in porches, her mother-in-law had had theirs deconstructed ten years ago, wanting a more modern look. The couches and chairs scattered about the patio matched the interior decor of the house, a sort of beachy casual that looked like it came directly from the Pottery Barn catalog, because it had, and was far too purposeful to convince. Nothing about Christi Magnusen was casual. Christi liked new things and redid her Seattle home completely every three to five years. The lake house had escaped notice for as long as a decade, partly because Christi came up so rarely now that her children were grown and, Anne assumed, because of the inconvenience of the location.

She closed her eyes and listened to the morning air around her— gossiping gulls, wind in the trees, waves lapping the shore. The cart's wheels squeaked in the sand and the dock clanked in a gentle wake. An unseen crow rattled and cackled in the woods.

Anne thought of her childhood home and how the island would sound in the morning—larks singing out of the heather, the neighbor's cows lowing. The wind murmuring and whistling as it blew down the bluff and hummed sorrowfully along the power lines. Whenever she walked to the dock to fetch her father, she'd hear the sea crashing against the foot of the cliff and the crying of gulls, which were not unlike the gulls here. Near the harbor, the water-washed stones of the beach rattled and hissed under the pull of the outgoing tide. There was the clamor and clang of the boats in the harbor and the sound of men's voices, her father's among them, calling to each other as they came in with the day's catch.

She opened her eyes. Now her lovely boy had seated himself next to the cart. A crow landed upwind of Aiden and squawked.

"Wok! Wok! Wok! Wok!"

Aiden turned to the bird, then back toward the lake.

Tim appeared behind her and dropped a kiss on her head.

"Last batch is on the griddle," he said.

He sat in the low chair next to her. Another crow had joined the first and was pacing about in the wet sand near where Aiden sat with his hands tucked inside his life preserver. A third, smaller crow flew down and joined the other two. The biggest crow hopped sideways and fluffed its wings, croaking. The smallest crow laughed a call and Aiden watched them.

Anne told Tim about the crows' chase and those she'd seen at the ferry terminal in Seattle dropping mussels on the ferry off-ramp.

"Clever, don't you think?"

Tim frowned at the birds, which jostled each other.

"Maybe smart, but they're also trouble. There's a big flock living near Phinney Ridge by the zoo. The 'Zoo Murder,' everyone is calling it. They've become a nuisance, and the neighborhood association is pestering the city to do something about it."

"Nuisance how?"

"You know—roosting in trees, crapping on cars, making lots of noise."

Ironic that the same neighborhood that took such pride in its lovely collection of caged animals would begrudge a gathering of wild birds, Anne mused.

"You know how people are," Tim said. "They want their wildlife curated. I think we'll do an article soon. Maybe when we get back, you and Aiden can wander by the zoo and collect some ideas for me?"

She felt a flash of anger. Was he trying to help her fill her newly empty days?

Now Tim was talking about the paper. His father and the board wanted to expand into other parts of the region. That was why they'd come up to the lake. Partly anyway. Family time, yes, but Tim Senior had also asked his eldest son to evaluate the new potential markets—Portland and Ashland in Oregon as well as Spokane and Richland in eastern Washington. Spokane was actually bigger than Seattle until the 1930s, Tim was saying.

"The population now is about 185,000, but it looks like there's lots of room for economic growth, mainly in tech and healthcare."

The smallest crow yanked the tailfeathers of one of its companions, which squawked in complaint.

"They have an opera house in Spokane and a proper symphony," Anne said. "Patrice took the graduating class to a workshop out there last fall."

"Well, the arts are never really part of the financial picture, you know," Tim said. "So much of that stuff is run on grants and donations from the wealthy. It's small potatoes. Dad wants to look at core markets that—shit! The pancakes!"

He jumped up and ran into the house.

Aiden tiptoed up the beach toward the crows. He was getting so big, losing his baby softness and becoming such a sturdy little boy.

Tim reappeared.

"Disaster averted," he said. "Your breakfast awaits, my queen."

He pulled her up with both hands. Down the beach, Aiden had nearly reached the crows, which watched him closely but hadn't moved.

"Aiden! Time for breakfast, son!" Tim called.

The birds considered Tim, but Aiden did not. Tim called again, and still the boy didn't respond. Tim sighed and strode down the sand toward him. Anne tensed and moved to follow but stopped herself.

At Tim's approach, the crows lifted off and flapped down the beach. Aiden watched them go and ignored his father. Tim squatted down next to the boy and said something. Aiden tipped his head back and smiled. They came back across the sand together, and Anne's heart heaved with relief.

After breakfast Tim went into the sunroom, which he was using as an office, promising to work only until noon. Anne and Aiden went back outside to the beach. Aiden had brought his wee book of fairy tales and paged through it for a time. Then he found a garden spade and began filling the dock cart up with sand. When Anne tried to join in, he made it clear it was a game he wanted to play alone. She returned to the chair and tipped her hat to shield her face from the sun. She pulled out her notebook and her syllabus from last semester and put on her glasses. Her department chair, Patrice, had suggested she use her leave to consider any changes she'd like to make to her core classes. Anne looked at her notes for the course she'd intended to teach this fall before her leave had been scheduled. *"Amhráin Aoib-hneas, Cumha, agus Lullaby*: Songs of Joy, Lament, and Lullaby," she'd called it. The syllabus promised to introduce students to the Irish language as well as various classic ballads from the last three centuries.

Her mind wandered as she looked over the pages. If the lake felt warm enough, she wanted Tim to take Aiden swimming later. The boy loved water and they spent hours at the local YMCA in Seattle. But it nagged at Anne that he hadn't learned how to swim properly, just as she hadn't as a child. She'd berated her mother about it her first summer home from university after discovering that most of her classmates had learned as children.

"And how would we have gone about that, exactly?" Margaret had asked. "Toss you off the pier with a quick Hail Mary?"

Her parents couldn't swim either. Most locals couldn't, and all of them fishing families. It exasperated her. It was true that the rough waters of the island were inhospitable. All the more reason one should know how to swim, Anne argued. She'd taken lessons at uni as a first year. Hearing the instructor's lecture on hypothermia, she'd thought of her fisherman father.

"At water temperatures below four degrees Celsius, you've no more than fifteen minutes to exit the water," the instructor told the class, pacing the pool deck, as they stood shivering in the shallow end.

Da surely knew that, though, didn't he?

She'd passed the swim test on the first try but never felt relaxed in the water. Tim had grown up with his own pool and agreed that Aiden needed to be a confident swimmer. She watched Aiden tip the cart over on its side and empty the sand back onto the beach. He stood next to the one exposed wheel and spun it with the flat of his hand.

She blinked, growing sleepy in the warming sun, and tucked her glasses in her pocket. Her notebook flopped shut in her lap. Aiden righted the cart and pushed it along the wet sand near the water. The wheels sank in the damp, and he pulled it backward onto higher ground. He crouched low, picking up rocks and stuffing them into his pockets. He glanced at her and away. Her heart filled and ached. She wanted to scoop him up and cuddle him and bury her face in his soft little neck and cover him with kisses. But she wouldn't. She couldn't. She knew better than to try that. Not now.

Aiden straightened and looked up the beach. Anne followed his gaze to the crows hovering on the light breeze above the waterline. Their wings caught a thermal and they rode it, adjusting their bodies ever so slightly to hang in place.

Her thoughts drifted to her classroom, her students sitting around her at the piano, sunlight streaming in through the windows. A song threaded its way through her brain.

Oh, if I was a blackbird, could whistle and sing.
I'd follow the vessel my true love sails in.
And in the top rigging I would there build my nest.
And I'd flutter my wings o'er his lily-white breast.

She heard her students join in with harmony. She heard Gran's voice. Then Katherine's.

She fell into a doze listening to the cart moving back and forth in the sand and the waves lapping the shore. The teasing squawk of the crows.

It could have been a minute or an hour. She didn't know, but she jolted awake to a different sound, her heart racing and her palms sweating. Up in the woods behind the houses, the sound repeated, and the earsplitting echo of gunshots rebounded off the hillside and over the water. The crows voiced a chorus of complaint.

"Karr! Karr! Karr! Karr Karr!"

Anne struggled to her feet and moved toward her son. The cart was on its side, a small pile of rocks neatly stacked on top like an elegant cairn, a milepost, a way marker.

But Aiden was nowhere in sight.

6

THE NESTLING

Now the nestling must enter the world all on its own, piercing the shell from within. Not even the most attentive parent can help with this moment of emergence.

—*G. Gordon's Field Guide to the Birds of the Pacific Northwest*

Once there was a queen who had a baby who cried and cried and would not be comforted. "Oh, how I wish you would turn into a raven and fly away," the queen said with impatience. In a flash, the baby changed into a large black bird and was gone, and the queen wept and her heart broke.

Once there was a king who had six sons, and a witch turned them into wild swans. When their little sister grew up, she went to look for them and discovered their hidden cottage deep in the woods. At sunset the swans flew down to the little house and turned back into her beloved brothers. If she were silent for seven years and knit them each a shirt imbued with her tears, she could break the spell, they said. She lived her vow of silence and others accused her of being a witch. And the little sister would not speak to save herself from dying by fire. But the swans flew down and she cast a magic shirt over each one and they changed back into her brothers, and they freed her.

Once there was a crow and the crow said, "I am not really a black crow, but an enchanted prince, who has been doomed to spend his life in misery because of a curse. If you only liked, you could save me."

Once there was a boy and he broke all the things and they said he was a very naughty, very naughty boy, and he wanted to change into a bird and fly away into the woods and disappear.

7

THE FLEDGLING

In the forests of the Pacific Northwest, birds surpass all other creatures in their variety of songs and calls.

—*G. Gordon's Field Guide to the Birds of the Pacific Northwest*

Frankie sat at the kitchen table willing herself to concentrate. She'd been reading the same sentence repeatedly without retaining its meaning. The begging call of a juvenile crow behind the house kept pulling her mind away from the text in front of her. She couldn't very well blame the little bird, though. She'd been distracted long before the hungry little corvid had started its racket.

"Ah-eh! Ah-eh! Ah-eh!" the bird called.

The morning had not gone as planned. The plan had been to sit down and dig into her manuscript revision in a direct and organized manner. She'd pulled out all her notebooks, relevant reference articles, notes from her committee, and the master copy of the thesis manuscript itself. She poured herself a cup of coffee, sat down at the table, and considered the revision outline she'd sketched back in the spring: 1) Read through committee's suggestions. 2) Review relevant data sets. 3) Reread studies in support of thesis. 4) Research abstracts of newly published studies focused on spotted owls. 5) Meet with committee for advice on next steps.

She'd ticked most of these items off the list already. However, the last had been impossible for reasons she couldn't let herself think about just now, but she told herself it wasn't entirely necessary anyway. Regardless, the best hours of the morning had passed, and she hadn't written a word. She stared at the blank page of her notebook not knowing where to start.

The young crow renewed its call behind the house. Its nasally complaining was interrupted by urgent contact calls between its parents, who were likely working frantically to satiate the hungry youngster. The juvenile's call changed to a gargling, and Frankie knew that meant one of the parents was tucking food down its ravenous little throat. The birds fell quiet.

Frankie pushed her notebooks aside and pulled a dog-eared paperback toward her. The well-worn cover of *G. Gordon's Field Guide to the Birds of the Pacific Northwest* communicated the miles it had journeyed since Frankie's seventh birthday. She'd received it from her father at her birthday breakfast at this same kitchen table all those years ago. Frankie had carried it through the woods that summer, and when the family returned to town in the fall, she tucked it in her book bag every morning. During the long school year when she missed the lake, the woods, and the little cottage, the book was a comfort. Over the years, *G. Gordon's Field Guide* had made its way to her high school locker and her college dorm room. Out in the field, to the graduate school lab, and now back to the cottage. Though the information within had long been superseded by ornithology and biology textbooks in her studies, it was a talisman, a touchstone, a reminder of where she belonged.

She flipped to the back of the book. The pages marked "Field Notes" were full of cramped, childish handwriting. She'd begun her first official bird journal the very day she'd received the book from her dad. "Cliff swallow, May 26, 1979" was the first entry. She remembered trying so hard to write neatly because the book was special. But by June of that same year, and midway down that page, her careful printing had given way to her typical loopy scrawl and the entries included sketches, doodles, and illegible notes. She'd run out of room quickly. It was then her father had suggested the slats of the bird blind for her recordkeeping.

She flipped to the section on the common crow, *Corvus brachy-rhynchos*. She glanced at the photos, noting the difference between adult birds with their glossy black wings and dark eyes and the juveniles, which were small, duller in plumage, and blue-eyed.

"*Corvus brachyrhynchos* is a large, chunky, ebony bird whose feathers can appear purplish in strong sunlight. Bill and feet are also black in color and quite dexterous. The tail is fan-shaped when the bird is in flight. Often gregarious and curious, crows prefer diverse habitat: woodlands, farms, fields, lake shores, towns, and dumps. Range: Year-round in the contiguous lower forty-eight, summers across Canada, excluding coastal British Columbia."

She scanned to the section on brood. Eggs ranged from blue-green to olive green and numbered from three to seven per season. Both mother and father took turns incubating the eggs, a process that lasted eighteen days. Young remained in the nest for four to five weeks and continued to be fed by the parents after they'd fledged. Juvenile crows remained dependent upon their parents in this way for months.

She thought of the young crow behind the house and wondered what was on the menu this fine morning.

"Food sources include grains, fruit, insects, small invertebrates, reptiles, mammals, carrion, refuse, and eggs and young of other birds," she read.

Crows were dedicated omnivores. The entire corvid family was, including ravens, jays, magpies, and nutcrackers. They were all part of Nature's janitorial staff, cleaning up roadkill, carrion, and garbage. Frankie appreciated their role in eliminating waste, though some found their scavenging behavior disgusting.

She recalled her fourth-grade teacher reading Poe's "The Raven" aloud in the sleepy hour after lunch. Frankie had been a little in love with Miss Duncan, who had apple-red cheeks, a blond bob, and the rosebud lips of a fairy-tale princess. Frankie remembered her voice, singsong and hypnotic in the drowse of the afternoon classroom, sunlight slanting through the windows and the sound of the fifth-grade PE class outside. Frankie followed along as Miss Duncan read.

"'Tell me what thy lordly name is on the Night's Plutonian shore!' / Quoth the Raven, 'Nevermore.'"

Mindy Osterbach raised her hand and announced that crows were a sign of death and bad luck.

Frankie was annoyed at the interruption of the poem, but Miss Duncan nodded.

"Yes, that's right, Mindy. That's called symbolism in storytelling, remember? Now, who knows what a group of crows is called?"

She paused for effect, and when nobody raised a hand, she stage-whispered, "A murder!"

Mindy squealed and buried her head in her arms, and the other girls imitated her, all but Frankie. Miss Duncan scolded the girls and the boys jeered.

Frankie raised her hand.

"Yes, Mary Frances?"

A raven, *Corvus corax*, was not a crow. Crows and ravens were in the same order and family, but a very distinct species of bird, Frankie wanted to say. And if you wanted to get specific, a group of ravens was called "an unkindness." As for crows, "murder" was only one name for a group of crows. They were also called a muster, a parcel, a congress, a cauldron, or a cabal, according to *G. Gordon's Field Guide to the Birds of the Pacific Northwest.*

"Yes, they *do* eat baby birds, Mindy," Miss Duncan was saying—shuddering and forgetting she'd called on Frankie.

Frankie put her hand down and regarded her teacher. She wondered if Miss Duncan knew that cute, bright-eyed chipmunks were more likely to eat baby birds than crows were. Or that Tibetans and the Canadian Haida People left the bodies of their dead for birds to eat. She'd read about that in *National Geographic*. At first it seemed sort of shocking, especially the pictures. But when she thought about it, it didn't seem weird at all. People were animals and people ate animals. Why shouldn't animals eat dead people? But Miss Duncan went back to Poe, and Frankie didn't say any of those things.

She remembered wishing Mindy would like her, though she was so mean on the playground—excluding Frankie from four square and making fun of her clothes, which were often Patrick's hand-me-downs. Why did she care about being excluded from the birthday party when Mindy was so awful? Patrick had asked when he found her up on the garage roof crying. She couldn't explain it then or now. She certainly hadn't gotten better at friendships, she mused.

She'd spent a lot of time with adults as a child, a consequence of her father owning the tavern. The regular customers of the River City Saloon, who called themselves The Irregulars, were some of her first friends. There was Old Joe with his big gray beard, who liked riddles and puns. He came in with Billy, who worked at the library and brought books for Frankie. Nils and Clarence played bluegrass music, and there was Maxine, who dressed like a man and whom everyone called Max, who often brought her fiddle. They'd remained an important part of Frankie's life as she'd grown older, always insisting on buying her a drink when she came home to visit. They wanted to hear about school and her life in Seattle. As did Hank, of course. She loved Hank best. Hank Hansen, her father's best friend. She should go see him next time she was in town. The idea cheered her.

The young crow called again from behind the house. Frankie glanced at the old barometer, which pointed halfway between "Fair" and "Change," and went outside. The trees swayed in the breeze and the sun ducked behind a cloud. She slung her binoculars around her neck, grabbed her sweatshirt from the mudroom, and pulled the door shut behind her. It squeaked as if scolding her for procrastinating. She ignored it and struck off up the hill.

The trail wound up through a large stand of cedar trees and circled around the meadow, a tangle of ferns and late-season Shasta daisies. The leaves of the huckleberry bushes had bloomed red and hung thick with berries. Frankie picked a handful as she passed and popped them in her mouth. She climbed into the bird blind. From there the top of a large cedar tree was just visible at the apex of the hill. Her heart warmed at the sight of the beloved old giant. She glanced at her watch, calculating how long it might take to summit. Quite a while, she knew, depending on how many trees had fallen across the trail. But she had time, didn't she?

She walked with purpose now, noting the coolness of the air and the sun winking behind the clouds. Just east of the meadow, a pair of small tamaracks lay across the trail. Frankie stopped and lifted them clear. As she continued, the fallen trees grew bigger in size, and she was forced to step and then climb over. She evaluated them as she went, knowing she'd need to bring up the chainsaw to clear the trail. Windfall was a natural part of the annual cycle at the lake. June Lake's location between the base of Mount Adams and the Wishram River Gorge caused strange thermal pockets that drew the wind in from odd angles. Unpredictable storms boiled through during winter and uprooted trees like Tinkertoys. Frankie had learned to run the chainsaw at the age of twelve and loved the annual task of trail clearing with Jack and Patrick. It was a chore meant for spring, she thought, as she clambered over a big pine, though she knew nobody would have completed the task this year, and she hadn't been to the lake for two summers.

She dropped down to the other side of the big tree and a gust of cold wind struck her neck. The temperature had dropped considerably. Up along the ridgeline, purple thunderheads had gathered into a substantial mass. She felt the first cold drops of rain then, hitting the backs of her hands and her bare head. She shivered and then she felt something else—the unnerving sense that she was being watched. The hair on the back of her neck stood up and she swept her gaze along the woods in front of her. Something moved off to her left.

The June Lake woods were full of wild creatures. In her lifetime, Frankie had seen all manner of large mammals—black bears, mountain lions, bobcats, foxes, and coyotes. Mountain lions were the only creatures she worried much about. The others were keen to avoid contact with people. But the big cats were unpredictable, intelligent hunters, and these woods made the perfect habitat. Twice in years past, Frankie had had this sensation of being watched and seen a mountain lion. Both times, the cats perched high on the limb of a big tree and watched her, unblinking, motionless, perfectly calm. Frankie had made herself appear as large as she could. Then she slowly backed down the hill, keeping her eyes on the animal's eyes, ready for any movement and not turning her back until the cat was well out of view.

But the shape she saw moving into the trees now was not feline. It was human, and Frankie had the uncanny sense that he knew he'd been seen. She caught a glimpse of the man's face and noted the rifle over his shoulder. She'd run into people up here before, but very rarely. Occasionally she'd meet a group of Yakama women harvesting camas root. Once they'd stopped to chat and Frankie asked questions about how they preserved the roots. She'd been intrigued by the plant and simultaneously aware of the discomfiting fact that the Beauty Bay Resort had belonged to the Yakama Nation until about one hundred years earlier.

But this was different—someone hunting here out of season.

"Hello!" she called. "Hey there!"

The figure disappeared into the woods, and she couldn't shake the feeling that he'd heard her and pretended not to.

The rain came down harder now, and thunder rolled overhead. Struck by the cold, Frankie turned and jogged down the hill, careful to keep her weight back so she didn't slip. Thunder rumbled and lightning flashed ahead of her. When she was about halfway down the hill, she heard the report of a shotgun. Once, twice, three times.

Her heart raced and hot anger shot through her body. Shooting in her woods.

She moved through dripping trees and wet sword ferns as quickly as she could. As the view opened in front of her, she could see the storm moving south toward the marina and down to Hood River. She spotted the smoke curling out of the chimney as the full force of the cold hit her. Her cotton sweatshirt was soaked through, and her jeans were heavy with water.

Peeling her clothes off in the yard, she ducked into the outdoor shower. The hot water bored needles into her cold flesh. The rain dripped from the eaves in a beaded curtain, and she heard the begging call of the young crow again. As she turned off the water, a cold wind gusted through the clearing. She pulled on her robe and hurried into the house thinking about the man in the woods, the gunshots, and what she should do about it.

The door was ajar, which was strange, because she was sure she'd shut it. She stepped inside and looked around the small room. Her books and notebooks were where she'd left them, but the chairs had been pulled away from the table and lined up in a neat row facing the bookshelf along the wall. Strangest of all, there was a small figure stretched out on the chairs—auburn curls and red sweatshirt. It was the boy from the dock. Frankie thought he was asleep, but as the door squeaked shut, his eyes flicked toward her. He moved his gaze to the low crossbeams of the ceiling.

"Hi there," she said and paused. "Are you okay?"

Again the child's eyes darted toward her and away. Frankie set her boots down on the shoe rack and noticed a small pair of tennis shoes placed neatly just inside the back door. They were red, yellow, and green. The toe of one shoe said "Right!" and the other said "Left!" She wondered how he'd gotten separated from his parents. She stepped closer.

"My name is Frankie. Did you get caught in the rain?"

The boy began to hum and put his fingers in his ears. Instinctively Frankie stepped back. She waited in silence, and he quieted. Time ticked by and the cold air chilled her bare shins.

"Okay. Well. I'm just going to change clothes. I'll be right back."

The boy didn't move or respond. Frankie crossed to the guest room and shut the door. She pulled dry clothes out of her pack and dressed hurriedly. She toweled her hair and combed it with her fingers. When she returned to the living room the boy hadn't moved. She wondered how old he was. Five, maybe? He'd taken his fingers out of his ears and was twisting them together, braiding and unbraiding them. She could feel his small animal energy fluttering about the room like a trapped bird.

"So . . . are you staying down at the big house with your mom and dad?"

No response. Was he deaf? No, not deaf. He seemed to hear her voice. There was a crack of thunder, more distant now as the storm rolled down the lake. The boy jumped and gasped. He was scared of the storm. Of course he was.

Frankie eased toward him.

"It's okay," she said. "The storm is going the other way now."

She waited a few seconds.

"I'm Frankie," she said again. "I knew your dad when he was little. What's your name?"

The boy's lips began to move, and he had something in his hands, which he turned over and over. Frankie eased into his field of vision and gave what she hoped was a friendly wave. He didn't look at her, but for a moment, his hands paused their frantic movement. Then he blinked and resumed the flicking of the object in his fingers.

Frankie didn't know many children, but years of observing wild creatures in the woods and the lab had taught her about animal fear. She knew an animal could panic when out of its habitat or in the field during tagging. She'd seen birds go into shock when handled roughly by students. Some even died. Small humans were likely also sensitive, she mused. She pushed her damp hair out of her face and moved over to the woodstove. She stoked the embers and added a log. It snapped and crackled as the fire caught. Glancing back at the boy, she saw that his hands had stilled, and she could hear him humming. Frankie could remember how it felt to be little and afraid. She crossed to the kitchen and pulled Grammy Genevieve's copper pot down from the wall.

"I think I'll make some hot chocolate," she said aloud.

She pulled milk out of the refrigerator, put it on to simmer, then whisked cocoa and sugar with hot water before blending it in. The kitchen filled with the smell of warm chocolate. She pulled a pair of mugs off the shelf and poured the chocolate. The boy's attention flickered toward her.

"I think I'll go sit by the fire," she said, not looking at him. "It's warmer over there."

She set the mugs on the coffee table in front of the woodstove and grabbed a pile of books from the kitchen table. From the couch she could see the rain dimpling the lake, which was navy blue under the gray belly of storm clouds. A flash lit up the southwest end of the lake, but there was no audible thunder now. Once the rain let up, she'd walk the boy home.

She glanced over her shoulder and saw he hadn't moved. She opened *G. Gordon's Field Guide to the Birds of the Pacific Northwest* and, remembering how she'd enjoyed being read to, began to read aloud.

"The American crow is listed as a Species of Least Concern by the National Audubon Society. Of the more than two thousand species of birds making their homes in North America, American crows are one of the few that do not migrate and subsist year-round on diverse food sources."

She wondered about the juvenile crow she'd heard in the woods that morning. It would spend the winter with its parents sustained by the food sources they located in the snowy woods. What ingenious ways had they developed to survive the cold weather? she wondered.

The sofa creaked as the boy slipped up next to her. He kept his gaze low, and his small hands cupped the thing he'd been flipping— a feather. She heard him humming softly and she turned back to the book.

"The American crow's range covers the contiguous United States, most of Canada, and southern Alaska. *Corvus brachyrhynchos* has an approximate breeding population of twenty-seven million."

Frankie pushed the mugs toward the edge of the table. Patrick's had a bright red fox on it. She'd always liked it slightly more than hers, which was adorned with a smiling green pig. The boy curled his small hands around the fox mug and brought it to his lips.

Frankie kept reading, listening to the water drip off the eaves, the crackle of the fire, the boy humming softly.

"Crows are diurnal in nature but are known to sound alert calls and also 'mutter' and 'babble' at night," she read.

The rain had stopped completely now. Glancing at the clock, she saw it was nearly 3 p.m. His parents must be frantic. She'd need to find some way to get him back down the trail without scaring him. Or she could leave him here and walk over to the Magnusens' alone. Which was better? She heard a noise then, faint at first, but persistent. She braced herself, listening hard for the sound of gunshots. But the sound was coming from below the house, not up in the woods.

The boy put the mug down with a thump, sat up straight, and looked right at Frankie. She was startled by the force of his green eyes and bright smile. He jumped down and ran to the door.

Frankie heard it again. A faint sound growing louder but still muddied by the moaning wind.

The boy threw open the door, grabbed his little shoes, and without a backward glance, he was gone.

8

ALERT CALLS

Instinct follows simple stimulus in the bird's world. As such, what might seem like mother love is nothing more than a deeply ingrained automatic response.

—*G. Gordon's Field Guide to the Birds of the Pacific Northwest*

Anne searched the beach around her and the waterline below her for the small figure of her son. She looked at the cart on its side, the small cairn of rocks piled there. Something moved at the far end of the seawall where the boats rose and fell in the growing shore break. She started forward, but it was only a large bird, a solitary heron stalking through the shallow waters near the log boom. It rose now, pterodactyl-like, and flapped slowly across the beach and out of sight in the light patter of rain. The sun had disappeared, and the sky was a canvas of gray.

She ran to the water's edge and scanned the lake for Aiden's red-and-blue Snoopy life preserver, also willing herself not to see it. The green water had grown turbulent with whitecaps under the strengthening wind. She hurried back to the cart and looked in the sand for some clue as to which direction he'd gone. The ground was a patchwork of his small footprints, her own, the hooves of deer that came down in the night, and the crows that had landed and left.

He'd been right there in front of her. Right there! Where could he have gone?

She stood rooted next to the cart and heard the report of the gunshots in her mind. She wanted to run or yell Aiden's name or go get Tim. Or all three at once. But she couldn't move. She willed herself to speak, to act, and could not. She felt cold all over. Both there and not there. She felt herself falling away, leaving herself, shutting down.

Time bent and folded. She saw her mother then, holding Aiden in her arms the one and only time Anne had taken him home to the island to see her family. Margaret Ryan recounted the story of how Anne had gone to have tea with the mermaids. It was an old story and one Anne had heard dozens of times. There was fear in Margaret's voice, but to Anne, who hadn't felt the danger then, it was a pleasant, if strange, memory. She couldn't have been more than four. She remembered hurrying down to the docks clutching her stuffed kitten. She had something she urgently needed to tell her father, though she never could recall what it was. The other fishermen were accustomed to the sight of Matthew Ryan's fire-haired wain tripping down the gangway by herself, and they might have called hello, but she didn't remember that either. She recalled seeing her father's boat, *The Kestrel*, not quite having landed, and was chuffed to beat him to the wharf. Eager to reach him, she broke into a run and dropped straight into the water of an empty berth.

The cool, dark sea enveloped her in a tight embrace. There was the shock of falling, but she wasn't afraid. Sunlight streamed down through empty berths in the wharf. It must have been undulating fronds of kelp she saw there, but in her child mind it was the waving hair of the beautiful mermaids. They sang and held out their hands, and Anne stayed the whole afternoon, and they had a tea party with the kitten. They taught her to sing a lovely old air and she couldn't wait to tell Gran about it. Those activities had been rudely interrupted by her rescue.

"It was poor Robert Cleary pulled you out," Margaret said, looking over Aiden's downy head at her daughter. "Could barely swim himself. Took years off the poor man's life and you chattering away about the pretty ladies singing under the water."

"Good Christ, Mam! You'd think I'd drowned then," Anne said, trying to make light of it. "I can swim now anyhow. No thanks to you."

Margaret looked at her only daughter with piercing gray eyes and said nothing.

Gran turned her teacup in her hands.

"*Níl aon anacair anama ann go dtí go mbeidh leanaí ag duine,*" Gran said.

There's no anguish of the soul until one has children.

Oh, Anne understood that now, didn't she? The thought brought her back into the present terrible moment, the rain coming down, the empty beach. She willed herself to focus, scanning the area around her for some sign of Aiden. Where had he gone to?

She jumped as a crack echoed down the hillside. Another gunshot? The rain increased and moved in a sheet across the lake. Then Tim had her by the arm and was pulling her into the shelter of the eaves. Surely Aiden was with him. Tim draped a towel around her shoulders and scanned the patio.

"Where's Aiden?"

Her heart plummeted.

"I don't know! He was right there! He's vanished!"

She pointed to the overturned cart and Tim took her shaking hand in his.

"It's okay, Anne. We'll find him. He can't have gone far."

Tim was good under pressure and rarely got overexcited. He was steady when things got stressful, like when Gran fell ill and Anne couldn't fly home because she was eight months pregnant. And the day of her review at Cornish when she would or would not be offered a permanent position. When she went into labor when they were at the movies. He was unflappable.

"It's only a rainstorm, Anne. He'll probably come running in any minute now."

"But, Tim, I heard gunshots!" she said.

He shook his head.

"No, the sound carries in strange ways up here. It's fine."

"But—I'm bloody sure, I—"

Only now she wasn't sure of anything at all.

"It was just thunder, Anne."

But that was cold comfort because Aiden was so afraid of thunder. At home a storm would drive him inside the apartment and into some cozy corner of his own making. Surely, he was inside somewhere. Tim told her to check the house and he'd look around the outbuildings. Anne flew through the rooms of the first floor, calling her boy. She checked the window seat Aiden favored, behind the curtains where he liked to hide with his little book, and the eating nook in the kitchen, the sunroom, then up to the rooms of the second floor. She found nothing but his absence in the silent house.

Tim met her at the sliding door to the patio and shook his head. He grabbed raincoats from the closet and waited for Anne to pull on trousers and boots. Then they hurried off together down the seawall, calling their son's name. At each of the houses, Tim stopped to circumnavigate the quiet and shuttered buildings, looking for any inviting corner that might entice a frightened five-year-old boy. Anne paced in a parallel line along the shore close to the water, dreading that she would see him there.

The rain came down harder and a cold wind blew off the lake. Anne wiped the water out of her eyes. She told herself this would be over soon, that he was tucked in out of the rain nearby. Any minute he'd come running down the beach and into her arms, his bright curls wet with rain. But he wasn't there. He wasn't anywhere. Thunder cracked and rolled overhead. Where could he have gone?

Tim pointed to the house closest to the dock and Anne ran toward the gangway.

"I'm going to check the boat!" she called to him and sprang down the dock. But there was no sign of Aiden in the cozy bunks of the family boat or in the small wooden craft that belonged to the caretaker's family. She swung around and raced back toward Tim, and her heart stopped at the sight of the red-and-blue Snoopy life preserver half-submerged in the dark shallows of the lake.

In slow motion she plunged into the cold water up to her knees. She reached for him, and only the life preserver came free of the water. She scanned the area between dock and beach and did not see Aiden's small form. The cold lake hadn't claimed him, then. She sobbed with relief and stumbled onto the shore. Tim yelled, holding something up. Aiden's fairy-tale book. He pointed up the hill.

"Maybe he went up to the O'Neills'," Tim said.

They climbed the steep, slippery trail calling their son's name.

Anne began to bargain then with a God she wasn't sure she believed in. She'd be a better mother. She'd be a better person. She'd do everything right this time. Just please, please, please give her the chance. Let him be safe. Let him not be frightened. Let him come back to her. Please.

Nobody tells the truth about having children, Anne knew. People congratulated you and said how lovely and isn't that just grand? Being a parent is the best thing that ever happened to me, they said. My child is my biggest accomplishment, my greatest pride. They were all bloody awful liars. Nobody ever admitted that being a mother is an epic of failure. There were just so many opportunities to fail: when your baby won't eat, or sleep, or stop crying, or has a rash, or has a cold, or won't look at you, or won't speak to you. Or stares at his hands and won't respond when you say his name. Or screams inconsolably for some unknown reason. Or worse things. Or when you take your attention off him for one minute and he vanishes into thin air.

So many things had surprised her about becoming a mam. Having the baby wasn't the half of it. As hard as it had been to carry him and go through labor, that all seemed like a lark after he arrived. The hunger, thirst, and exhaustion were nothing. That first year she was completely overwhelmed with the weight of loving him—his wee hands, the joy on his face each morning, the heft of his tiny sleeping form on her chest—it all undid her. She felt like her heart was a giant exposed wound that would never heal.

"There's just so much to worry about," she'd wailed to her mother at the end of that visit home to the island when Aiden was a baby.

Margaret laughed but her eyes were bright with tears.

"Oh, sweetheart. It's going to be grand. Don't you worry."

Anne wiped her streaming eyes.

"So it gets better, then?"

Margaret shook her head.

"No, love. It doesn't. It only gets worse!"

And they both laughed as they cried, for what else was there to do?

There's no anguish of the soul until one has children.

So many new emotions came with motherhood. Wonderful and terrible, intense and exhausting. Nobody told you that. Nobody told you the person you'd been before would disappear completely. Who was that carefree girl who stayed up late drinking and carousing and had big plans? Nobody explained that being a mother turned your heart inside out and that the person you were before was a clueless eejit. Nobody mentioned that for every mistake you made there was no learning from it, because you'd just repeat it in a different and possibly worse way. Maybe that's why you had to have more than one child—so at least you could screw up differently and your offspring could share the burden of having a terrible, awful mother.

"Please let him be safe," she begged someone, something. "I can do better. I will do better."

But even as she said the words, she didn't believe them. She didn't deserve another chance, did she? Because this wasn't the first time she'd failed Aiden, her one and only. She'd had dozens of opportunities these last eighteen months. And she failed him over and over again.

Tim strode ahead calling Aiden's name. Anne stopped to catch her breath and realized she was muttering aloud.

"Please," she said.

Tim, hearing her, turned back to look. Up on the hillside beyond him a spot of color appeared on the trail. A flash of red against the slick brown earth. The spot grew into a shape and the shape became a body, a person moving toward them. Then he was there, her dearest one, her maddening child, her perfect boy. He descended the trail, his dear, wee frame tripping down the hillside like he was coming back from tea with the Queen. He brushed past his father and walked to Anne. She sat down hard against the bank and reached for him, hoping he would let her hold him. Her tears mixed with the rain streaming down her face. Aiden sat in her lap and held up a glossy black feather. He tucked his head under her chin and leaned into the curve of her body. She closed her eyes and rocked him lightly and heard him humming a little tune. She forced herself to hold him gently, her arms loose around his small, precious little body.

"Oh, Aiden, love. You'll be the death of me," she said quietly.

Tim gave a short laugh.

"That makes two of us. Think I just got my first gray hair," he said.

Aiden reached up and took the book from his father and tucked the feather inside it.

Back at the house Anne took a hot shower while Tim ran a bath for Aiden. They ate an early dinner of grilled cheese sandwiches and tomato soup. Anne did the dishes and Tim built a fire in the large stone fireplace. He popped a film into the VCR, an old Disney movie called *Dumbo*, which Anne hadn't seen before. Aiden wanted to sit with his face pressed close to the screen, but they coaxed him back to the couch, where he perched between them briefly. Then he moved to stand slightly apart, rocking to the music and flicking the feather in his fingers.

Then the lullaby, the imprisoned mother elephant caressing her baby through the bars.

"Good Christ, Tim!" Anne yelled and threw a pillow across the room.

"Sorry! I forgot about this part," he said and fast-forwarded the movie past the terrible scene of the mother elephant being separated from her baby.

"Trying to cheer me up, are you? What's next? *Sophie's Choice*?!"

They were laughing together, their shared dark humor. It helped to end the day like that, to put some space between now and that time that he was lost to them. Short as it had been, it would forever stretch long and terrible in her memory.

Tim pulled her close and she leaned into his shoulder. He took her hand and idly twisted her wedding ring. It had been five years that spring—their marriage a bigger surprise than her pregnancy.

For though they'd agreed about the baby, they hadn't discussed marriage. Their legal union was inspired by a hiccup with Anne's work visa. US Immigration insisted she renew it midsemester, which would mean returning to Ireland. Being so close to the end of the year, it wouldn't make sense to return if she left then. She'd have the baby at home and she and Tim might have gradually lost touch. But he proposed on a beautiful April evening. And in the romantic urgency of the moment, she'd accepted. They'd gone to the courthouse the next day and celebrated with dinner at Place Pigalle at Pike's Place Market. Anne had murdered a braised lamb shank and a crème brûlée and stole sips of Tim's wine. It had been great fun.

Tim's family had not shared their giddy joy. At his parents' house the following Sunday, Anne felt like she'd been called to the head matron's office for a uniform violation or smoking in the girls' toilet. Christi Magnusen made it quite clear she was not thrilled to have accidently acquired a daughter-in-law.

To her credit, Christi had tried. Robbed of the opportunity to throw a grand wedding for her eldest, she'd held a baby shower for Anne at the Four Seasons Hotel tearoom. It was a nice gesture, only Anne didn't want a baby shower. Her family couldn't afford to travel from Ireland, and the do was a lopsided affair of Christi's friends, Tim's sister, and a couple of Anne's friends from Cornish. It was an uncomfortable afternoon and just the start.

The Magnusens were big on tradition—Sunday dinner, holiday celebrations, birthdays, and the like. Anne soon realized she wasn't being welcomed; she was expected. And when pushed, she balked. Like when she skipped a boating day party. She was trying to wean Aiden and didn't want to chitchat with a bunch of yachties while breast milk leaked into her bra pads.

"For the love of Mike!" Anne yelled, replaying Christi's phone message for Tim. Christi had called to ask if everything was okay and said everyone missed her at the party. "You'd think I murdered the patron saint of boating!"

Tim laughed then, but Anne often felt her mother-in-law's eyes on her. It seemed Christi was waiting for her to make some colossal mistake. Something awful and unforgivable—like losing track of your child by a lake. Your child who could not swim. Your child who could not call for help.

Tim never asked her how she'd lost sight of Aiden. And she didn't tell him about the feeling on the beach either, that cold paralysis, and how similar it had been in May at the graduation ceremony. Because she hadn't told him then either. That night she'd simply said she was ill. She didn't know how to explain it, or maybe she just didn't think he'd understand. It wasn't his fault. She did love him—though there were so many gaps between them that seemed to be widening more all the time.

If only she could write. She might be able to capture her feelings and examine them like butterfly specimens pinned to paper. Drafting the lyrics could help her articulate what was happening to her—to her mind, her heart, and her marriage. Her music had always sorted her, helped her understand her life. But her music had deserted her now.

She looked at Tim watching the movie about the young elephant finding his way. He was right there, wasn't he? But with everything she couldn't tell him he might as well be a thousand miles away.

9

IMMATURE HUNGER

Often a bird's most powerful survival skill is the readiness to flee.

—*G. Gordon's Field Guide to the Birds of the Pacific Northwest*

Once there was a crow and the crow was very thirsty. The crow came upon a tall pitcher full of water and the water looked clean and cool. But the crow's beak was too short to reach the water and the crow did not have any hands to tip the pitcher. The sun grew hot, and the crow grew thirstier and wished someone would come along and help. But nobody did.

After a while, the crow saw pebbles lying near and had an idea. It dropped the pebbles one by one into the pitcher until the water rose high enough and the crow had a nice long drink of cool water.

"What a clever crow I am," the crow said. It was no longer thirsty, and it flew away.

Once there was a little crow and it did not know how to swim. "Why should I swim when I know how to fly?" asked the crow. And the crow flew away and left a feather as he went. It was a magic feather and anyone who held it could fly too.

Once there was a little crow and he was a clever crow and the clever little crow could talk and sing. But nobody seemed to understand what he was saying.

10

CONTACT CALLS

After the young fledge the nest, the family relationship ends for many species. But some overwinter with their parents and return with them to their natal grounds in spring.

—*G. Gordon's Field Guide to the Birds of the Pacific Northwest*

The chainsaw bumped against her leg as Frankie walked off the hillside. She'd cleared a dozen downed trees before quitting for the morning. It was satisfying work and, though she was loath to admit it, a convenient distraction from her thesis. The morning had begun as the previous one had. She'd sat down with every intention of getting to work on her revision and had failed to make any progress. But then again, the distractions had multiplied. She'd lain awake half the night, her mind whirring with all that had happened—the poacher in the woods, the sound of gunshots, and the peculiar boy in the cottage. After breakfast, she decided to hike back up into the woods to see if she could find evidence of the shooting. She took the chainsaw along and cleared the trail as far as the spot where she'd seen the man. Just off the path there she found discharged shotgun shells and muddy boot prints. She tucked the shells in her pocket and scanned the woods but saw nothing. She knew she'd have to call the sheriff and the Yakama Nation agency office next time she went down the lake.

As she descended the hill her thoughts returned to the boy, Tim Magnusen's son, and his intriguing strangeness. From the lookout she'd seen him reunited with his parents and didn't feel any reason to go talk to them about it. She'd give the Magnusens their privacy and hope they'd offer her the same.

As the roof of the house came into view, Frankie heard the call of an eagle.

"*Haliaeetus leucocephalus*," she thought and remembered Dr. Tandy's voice in the darkened lecture hall. Her petite professor's head bobbed as she advanced the slide projector to a close-up of a bald eagle.

"*Leucocephalus* means white-headed and *Haliaeetus* denotes the eagle family," Dr. Tandy said. "This big raptor has been the symbol of the US since the 1780s—a suggestion of Benjamin Franklin's, by the way."

Dr. Tandy went on to explain how the number of bald eagles had plummeted to a few hundred in the 1950s, their reproductive success inhibited by the pesticide DDT. But *Haliaeetus leucocephalus* was a success story in recovery. A recent study showed that its numbers had rebounded following the banning of that chemical. Some estimates put the current breeding population at about three hundred thousand.

"That happened during your lifetimes. It's not something to take lightly," she said and advanced the slide. "A true success story of the conservation movement."

The student next to Frankie slumped in his seat muttering. Frankie recognized him from the first day of class when she'd heard him talking with his friends.

"My pledge brothers said she's fucking ancient. Easy A," he'd said then, smirking.

Now he yawned openly.

"Oh, it's Friday, isn't it?" Dr. Tandy said, running a hand through her short white hair. "I nearly forgot about Bird Bingo! Anyone know the name for a grouping of eagles?"

Frankie raised her hand.

"Ms. O'Neill?"

"Aerie, jubilee, or convocation," she said.

"Well done, Ms. O'Neill."

The frat boy next to Frankie crossed his arms.

"Who cares?" he mumbled.

Frankie suppressed a laugh. By now this guy understood that it was a common prank among fraternities to recommend Tandy's class to freshmen. Dr. Tandy was anything but doddering and had a fierce agenda of acquainting her students with as many common species as possible during the fall quarter. Visual identification of one hundred birds and their classification would be part of the final. Given that there were ten thousand species of birds in the world and two thousand in North America, one hundred birds wasn't much, she'd said almost apologetically. Frankie remembered this kid swearing when he'd heard that. Dr. Tandy had made the announcement the day after the deadline to change or drop classes. Over the years, Frankie had seen many students with the same attitude as that frat boy, including some in sections she'd TA'd. They puzzled her. Why were they at college if they didn't want to learn?

Frankie stowed the chainsaw in the pump house and, as she emerged, caught sight of the eagle flying low. It was one of the family she'd seen fishing just south of the dock for the past few days. Breeding and chick-rearing was a time-intensive undertaking for these raptors. Incubation took thirty-five days, and the young didn't fledge for ten to twelve weeks. It made sense that the family unit was a tight one. The parents and young would likely stay together through winter. They might spend the season here at the lake or migrate slightly south to the confluence of the Columbia and Hood Rivers.

There was at least one nesting pair near the cottage every year. That first summer after college, Frankie told her dad what Dr. Tandy had said about their nests—six feet in diameter and weighing up to a ton.

"A ton," Jack had said, looking up at that year's nest and marveling. "Stick by stick too. Industrious little bastards, aren't they?"

The eagle called overhead, and something scuttled down the path in front of Frankie. It was a little crow—recently fledged, from the looks of it. Any closer and she'd have stepped on it. The young bird didn't move but huddled lower and regarded her with a cocked head. After beginning their lives as pink-skinned, featherless dragons, baby crows open their eyes after a week and begin to grow the downy fluff that precedes their feathers. The eyes of the young are a striking blue, and their mouth interiors bright red. This one had brown feathers and its eyes were still blue. Frankie scanned the trees for the parents and did not see them. She crouched down and looked at the little bird. It tipped its head and rasped at her.

"Hey, little buddy," she said. "Where are your folks?"

A crow this age could not fly well. It was common for fledgling crows to alight on the ground and wait to be fed while their parents foraged. It struck Frankie as a poor strategy given that the babies were exposed to ground predation. She wondered if the parents had been scared off by the eagles and if the little bird had any siblings nearby.

The woods were damp from yesterday's storm and the sun had not penetrated the clearing. Frankie shivered, then gave the bird a wide berth as she walked to the woodpile. She gathered an armful of logs and observed the baby crow as she passed. He looked like he needed a good preening, that was certain.

She thought again of Dr. Tandy, who'd included the crow in her class.

"The American crow, *Corvus brachyrhynchos*, is another highly successful species."

Dr. Tandy's slide had shown a pair of crows, the larger one grooming the other.

"This is an example of allopreening, which is common in many species. At its most basic, this is hygienic behavior—chiefly removing mites, dust, and dirt and facilitating feather shape and regrowth. But it is also clearly a show of affection and bonding. Now, can we assume this bigger crow is a parent?"

Frankie raised her hand.

"It could be a parent or an older sibling," she said.

"Correct, Ms. O'Neill. Crows are cooperative breeders. Older siblings help raise new broods and remain in close proximity to their parents for the length of their entire lives," Dr. Tandy said. "Family is the key social unit of the crow."

"A round of robins!" she said, advancing to the next slide—a close-up of a clutch of robin's eggs. "There's a myth that robins represent those who have departed this life. 'When robins appear, loved ones are near,' the saying goes."

Eagles and crows and robins. These were some of the hundred Dr. Tandy had taught them that semester. Classification and trivia and history—she mixed it all together. Frankie had loved Dr. Tandy's Bird Bingo, which offered extra credit on Fridays. A charm of goldfinches. A descent of woodpeckers. A rafter of turkeys. A jar of nuthatches. The name of Dickens's raven (Grip), the origin of the ravens in the Tower of London (late nineteenth century, but opinions differ on the exact year), and what kind of bird inspired Mozart (a starling).

You could see that Dr. Tandy was simply delighted by the world of birds and wanted to share that delight with her students. Younger faculty laughed at her behind her back. But Frankie loved her class, and she sensed something under their derision. Dr. Tandy hoped to breed curiosity and investment in conservation, even among non-science majors like the mumbling frat boy. The rest of Frankie's tenured professors, including her advisor, Dr. Davis Grant, seemed focused on competing with their colleagues. Maybe they envied her enthusiasm?

Family is the key social unit of the crow, Frankie thought, observing the little bird. It looked a bit dazed and like it could use its family just then. She gazed around for the parents or siblings that should be feeding it and didn't see them.

"Good luck, little one," she said, and carried the wood inside.

While she kindled a fire she thought of the social unit of her own family. Judith certainly hadn't seemed to miss her when she'd left for college, but what a scene the day Patrick moved out! You'd have thought he was leaving for Greenland instead of the west side of town, the same zip code. Judith sobbed as he stood next to his car, and Patrick patted her back and promised he'd come home for Sunday dinner, which was the next day. Frankie rolled her eyes at Patrick and their father soft-shoed down the driveway humming "Oh, Danny Boy" under his breath. Judith had snapped at them both and Patrick smoothed things over, as he did.

Oh, Dad, Frankie thought now as she stoked the fire. Pushing Mom's buttons.

The house warmed as the fire perked along and Frankie returned to the kitchen table and the work at hand. Her excuses were exhausted for the time being. Behind the excitement of the previous day lurked the problem that had dogged her all summer—the issue of graduation.

There was no denying the stark facts of her situation. Since last spring the chair of her thesis committee—Dr. Davis Grant—had thrown up every obstacle in her path to graduation. He'd ignored her emails and avoided her in the department hallways. When she made appointments through the department secretary, he canceled them. Dr. Davis Grant, whom she'd once called Davis with a familiarity that seemed impossible now, was also her boss and had fired her from the lab. Not only was she cut off from the lab resources, but she'd also lost her income. The worst blow of all was that Dr. Davis Grant had been her mentor through undergrad and grad school. Her friend, she'd thought all these years, almost like a father to her.

She remembered the first time Davis and his wife, Rebecca, had her over for dinner to their comfortable house near Lake Washington. Frankie had felt awkward—all elbows and knees, not sure which fork to use, embarrassed that she hadn't brought a hostess gift like the others had. But Rebecca was so kind, and Davis had drawn her into the conversation, praising her fieldwork and research. He'd respected her, she thought, all that time, and she'd looked up to him. That made everything so much worse, the way he'd cut her loose.

She'd been scheduled to defend in May, but Dr. Grant's actions had made that impossible. Now she had to try for a December graduation. At summer's end, finances exhausted, she'd decided to come up to the lake to complete her manuscript. She'd make the revisions suggested by her committee and submit it by the end of September or early October at the latest. After that, the next move would be Dr. Grant's to make, as she'd have fulfilled her obligations. Surely once she'd submitted her thesis, the systems in place would move things forward. She could imagine herself at her defense, standing in front of the committee while Dr. Grant glowered at her and asked her hard questions, trying to trip her up. She'd seen him do it to others who fell out of his favor. She'd just never expected to be on the wrong side of Dr. Davis Grant.

She returned to the copy of her manuscript that Dr. Andreas had annotated and read through his editorial letter. Of her three committee members, Dr. Andreas made the most superficial comments. He had questions about the way she formatted her data sets and asked for some minor clarifications regarding the maps and territory grids she'd included. That information came from Dr. Grant's research and would be no trouble at all.

She worked swiftly, making notes, and the morning fell away. The sun climbed higher in the sky and the little house eased out of the shadow of the woods. By late morning, the room had warmed up considerably. Frankie pushed through all of Dr. Andreas's comments until she felt she had responded to each point. Returning to the material felt comfortable and familiar. Maybe this wouldn't be so hard after all, she thought.

The eagle called, right behind the house this time. Frankie opened the back door and scanned the trees for it. The enormous raptor dropped from the sky in front of her and nearly touched down on the path near the young crow. It was stunning to be so close to the magnificent bird. She felt the rush of air from its powerful wings, which could span up to eight feet. The eagle startled when it saw her and gave a shrill *"Klee!"* and rose into the air. The little crow scuttled into the shelter of a sword fern.

The eagle flew around the front of the house in a wide circle, returning to the back. It swooped down, ignoring Frankie, and grazed the ferns just above the little crow. Then it soared back into the air to prepare for another pass. Without thinking, Frankie pulled off her sweatshirt, tossed it over the bird, and scooped it up into her arms. Stepping inside, she placed the little crow gently in the deep kitchen sink. She lifted the sweatshirt off slowly, and the fledgling didn't move. It blinked up at her out of glassy eyes and opened and closed its beak mutely. Frankie cupped the bird in her hands and did a brief exam. The soft, warm body felt miraculously light in her hands. She turned it over and looked at the small feet, slightly darker than the brown-black feathers, and the dark gray toenails. The little bird regarded her out of its blue eyes. Its slight frame pulsed with a thudding heart and rapid breath. As she'd noticed before, some of its feathers were rumpled and broken. But the real problem was the right leg. She considered the anatomy of the small limb—particularly the tibiotarsus. It was bent in the wrong direction. She lowered the bird back into the sink and set Grammy Genevieve's old wicker laundry basket over it. Then she hurried out to the pump house. She saw the eagle there, perched high in a mountain ash tree, waiting. It gazed down at her, a huge, gorgeous specimen.

"Sorry, beauty. No crow snack for you today."

She dug around in the pump house, grateful for her father's treasure trove of junk, and found a Popsicle stick and a roll of narrow electrical tape. Back in the house, the young crow was quiet. She lifted the laundry basket away and examined the leg, moving slowly so as not to alarm the fledgling.

Frankie always enjoyed handling birds. A dozen or so resident owls cycled through the lab but lived at nature preserves. Too injured to fend for themselves, the beautiful creatures now served science and public education. But they were wild animals and Frankie retained a healthy respect for them. Doing physical exams, weighing them, and drawing blood, she'd learned to hold them firmly but gently. A small crow like this did not have the beak and talons of an adult spotted owl, but Frankie approached it with the same care.

She turned the young bird in her hands and marveled at its lightness—all hollow bones and feathers. She looked at the leg, then set the bird in the bottom of the sink. She snapped the Popsicle stick in half to form a splint and strapped it into place with tape. She released the fledgling and it hobbled away from her. The splint wasn't perfect, but it was the best she could do. The effort of moving to the other side of the sink seemed to exhaust the little bird. It rested there and closed its eyes.

Crow babies this size ate at least every hour, so this little one could be starving. She retrieved a set of tweezers and an eyedropper from the bathroom and opened a can of tuna fish. The little bird perked up, nodding at her, and opened and closed its beak. Frankie presented the dropper, and the fledgling gulped the water down. Like the Tin Man coming back to life, it bobbed its head and croaked. Using the tweezers, she fed it bits of tuna. The little crow ate and hobbled closer, seemingly ravenous. When it had eaten a quarter of the can, it fell into a doze. Frankie tucked one of Grammy Genevieve's soft old aprons around it for warmth and replaced the laundry basket over the sink.

She pulled out her notebook and, out of force of habit, jotted down her observations about the encounter with the baby crow—date, time, temperature, and the episode with the eagle. She noted the state of the injured leg, her remedy, and possible causes for the injury. She

wrote down the calls she'd heard over the past few days: juvenile begging, parental scolding, contact calls, and now this soft sleeping noise
emanating from the sink. She knew she shouldn't keep the bird inside
for long. If it couldn't survive after a short intervention, it wasn't
meant to. Intervening at all would be condemned by many of her
colleagues, but she'd acted on instinct and what was done was done.

She returned to her manuscript revision, keenly aware of the other
life in the room. Her bruised and lonely heart felt undeniably cheered
by the idea of the little creature convalescing in the sink. She laughed
at herself, but since there was no one else around, what did it matter?
She worked through her notations and listened to the sound of the
little bird sleeping. Its soft churring was a whisper in the quiet.

She thought of the little boy then, whispering to himself and pretending not to see her when she first came in the house. It seemed
strange, though she certainly didn't have much experience to go on.
Frankie was not comfortable around children. Though all her cousins had children now, their progeny at family events felt like an invasion by a small foreign army. Frankie didn't understand how to play
with them and found them noisy and startling.

"Are you a mommy or a kid?" her cousin Jeff's daughter had demanded two summers ago, puzzled as to why she didn't want to play
dress-up. Frankie hadn't known what to say.

Maybe the Magnusen boy was afraid, but wouldn't he cry or ask
for his parents or at least tell her his name? By the time she was four,
she'd known her address, her parents' phone number, and even the
number of the tavern by heart. The boy had seemed to retreat inside
himself, though he could hear, she was sure. And the way he looked
at her before he left, almost conspiratorial. What was that all about?

She was grateful that the problem had resolved itself. She wasn't
interested in seeing anyone else or getting drawn into neighborly
small talk with Tim Magnusen and his family. But she wondered idly
about Tim's red-haired wife. Was she anything like his sister, Crystal, or his mother, Christi?

Christi Magnusen was tiny, tan, and eternally blond. When everyone else wore shorts and T-shirts all summer, Christi favored linen pants, low heels, and gold bracelets. Frankie felt like Paul Bunyan around her.

The summer before Tim started college, his mother managed to bring up his acceptance to Yale at every opportunity. The way Christi Magnusen talked about it, you'd think she had something to do with it.

"You know my Tim, he's starting at Yale," she'd say to the O'Neills or one of the other summer residents, any chance she got.

They'd heard it so often that Patrick had perfected an imitation of Christi that made Frankie howl. When she came into the store for a pack of gum or a can of Tab, Patrick would raise an eyebrow, shrug a shoulder, and silently mouth, "My Tim? He's starting at Yale." Frankie would have to leave the store to release her laughter.

Had Tim's wife gone to Yale too? she wondered. She chided herself for caring. It would be fun to gossip with Patrick about it at any rate.

After about an hour, the little crow roused itself and began to make a weak begging call. Frankie rose, fed it, and gave it water. It ate another quarter can of tuna and then another. It was moving around more easily following its nap, and throughout the day it grew stronger and louder. The little crow began testing the splinted leg tentatively at first and then hop-waddling. The Popsicle stick made a clicking sound against the bottom of the sink. The fledgling made a jaunty little move and gave a demanding squawk. She laughed.

"A little bowler and you'd look just like Charlie Chaplin," she said.

The baby crow attempted to preen itself but became worn out by the effort. Frankie took the laundry basket away and considered the leg splint. It might help to shorten it, she thought. She carefully unpeeled the tape, removed the splint, snipped it shorter, and replaced it. She set the fledgling down gently and noticed a few stray pin feathers bent and broken. Slowly, she smoothed them down with two

fingers. The little bird seemed to like it. Frankie swaddled the bird
in her sweatshirt and held it lightly in the crook of her arm. It felt
warm against the inside of her elbow. She passed her thumb and
forefinger along its small head and ruffled the feathers gently at its
neck. The bird made that little churring sound and it vibrated against
the skin of her arm. She smoothed the feathers down and the fledgling nodded off.

"There you go, Charlie Crow," she said, placing the baby crow in
the sink and tucking her grandmother's apron around it again. A
strange feeling settled over her, and she realized it was contentment,
a feeling that had eluded her for quite some time. How she'd missed
working with her hands.

Frankie knew that half the reason she was a good scientist was
simply because she didn't mind work. She wasn't looking for a nine-
to-five job like so many of the girls in her dorm who had majored in
business, marketing, or communications. Even nursing students could
count on a defined schedule. But Frankie didn't watch the clock. When
she put her mind to something, she was all in. She just kept going
until the work was finished. She'd learned that from her father.
Whether they were felling trees, doing maintenance for summer
people, or hauling kegs up and down the stairs at the River City
Saloon, O'Neills worked. That was self-employment for you, Frankie
supposed. She worked hard for the Forest Service for a full year between high school and college, and she'd taken the same attitude at
the lab. It also helped that she was handy and didn't mind getting
dirty. That's why Dr. Grant had hired her in the first place, to clean
cages and catalog equipment for his owl studies. By her sophomore
year she'd joined the field crew, which was mostly graduate students,
and was running the summer field squads by the time she started
graduate school herself.

She did a lousy job tracking her hours. So much of what counted
as work was simple pleasure for her. Driving the lab truck into the

dark woods of the Mount Rainier National Park was when Frankie felt most herself. She'd roll down the window on a cold morning and watch the sunrise bloom above the snowy cap of Rainier. Hiking up into the old-growth Douglas fir, hemlock, and cedar forests to look for nesting sites was a meditation. Hours would pass in what others would think of as silence. But Frankie was listening. For any sound of owl or prey of course, but also the constant and shifting symphony of the woods. Up there the wind played through the branches of the trees, pushing them this way and that. Under the musical peeping of goldfinches came the querulous scold of a pine squirrel. Early mornings at camp or late in the evening, the coyotes chattered at each other through the dark woods. Thumping feet of rabbits telegraphed warnings in their burrows. Lying in her tent at night she might hear a deer snorting just outside or a porcupine chewing its way up a young sapling. None of that felt like work.

Most people didn't understand, but her dad did. Jack O'Neill understood her passion for her work, if he didn't understand her thesis. She remembered trying to explain it to him last Thanksgiving as they'd sat outside in the garage. Judith was a tornado in the kitchen, and everyone had cleared out while she finished dinner.

Frankie was working on her data sets and trying to explain to her father how her work connected to Davis's.

"Um-hmm," Jack said, listening as he dug around on the workbench. He located a quart bottle of whiskey behind a stack of Sears, Roebuck catalogs.

"There 'tis!" he said.

He sat down across from his daughter and passed her the bottle, which was about half full. It was cool in her hand as she twisted the cap off.

"Jameson!" she clucked. "And I thought you were a Bushmills purist."

Her father laughed.

"Don't tell Old Joe or I'll never hear the end of it."

He pulled a pack of cigarettes out of his shirt pocket. Frankie tipped a small, warming drink down her throat.

"Thanks, Dad," she said, handing the bottle back.

Jack lit a cigarette and leaned his chair back on two legs. He offered Frankie the pack and she shook her head.

"Reformed, are we?" he teased, and she rolled her eyes.

"Newsflash: Cigarettes are actually bad for you, Dad."

"Says who?"

"Oh, just the surgeon general of the United States. And everyone."

He laughed and ran a hand through his hair. Once black like her own, it was more salt-and-pepper now, which made her feel unaccountably sad. She took a cigarette out of the pack and tucked it in her pocket.

"So Dr. Davis Grant wrote his whatsy-hoosy—"

"Dissertation, Dad. Don't act like a country bumpkin."

"His dissertation," Jack said, with false gravity. "And now twenty years later, he's still getting money to study the same damn thing?"

"No!" Frankie said, exasperated. "Well, I mean, kind of? But you make it sound like a racket! Look—"

She pushed her notebook across the table at him and drew a diagram.

"Dr. Grant helped establish the importance of old-growth forest for the survival of the spotted owl, which was groundbreaking at the time. He was one of the experts consulted by the Audubon Society in their lawsuit against the Forest Service. You might recall how that decision went over around here."

Jack chuckled.

"Oh, I remember. 'I love spotted owls—deep fried!' Wasn't that the bumper sticker they sold at Windmaster Corner? Oh, and 'Save a logger. Kill an owl.'"

"You'd remember better than me, Dad. So anyway, he got funding to study how the owls were recovering after the government placed limits on logging old growth. The spotted owl is important because it's an indicator species. So, how well it's doing or not doing gives us a larger picture about forest health in general."

"Like Larry Bird and the Indiana State Sycamores," Jack said.

"Sure, Dad. Like Larry Bird. When was that?"

"In 1979! The NCAA tournament? Oh dear, I have neglected your education," he said.

"There's still time, Dad. So, anyway. After Davis established himself as an expert, he kept studying owls and now his graduate students continue by looking at various elements of their habitat. Things like food sources, water tables, other keystone species. My piece of it is to look at pair bonding—what conditions result in strong populations."

Jack nodded and blew smoke above his head.

"And then what? After your dissertation," he said.

"Dad, I'm a master's student. It's just a thesis."

He waved a hand.

"But what's next for you?"

Frankie sat back in her chair.

"Well, then, hopefully I'll do my own doctoral work. Not at UW, probably."

She didn't tell him about the opening at Oregon State University in Corvallis, which was closer to home, just two hours away from Hood River. She wanted to wait until she'd applied.

"Dr. O'Neill! I wish your grammy could see that," Jack said, and his eyes grew bright.

"Well, someday. I hope," she said, embarrassed by his uncharacteristic show of feeling.

Jack cleared this throat and stubbed out his cigarette.

"So. You'll be done in May, then?"

Frankie nodded and could almost hear his next question—why

not come home for a bit and work at the tavern next summer? She hated saying no to him, but she didn't want to come back to Hood River. She glanced at her watch and stood.

"We should go in. Mom said she wanted dinner on the table at three or—"

"She'll flay us all," Jack finished.

As they walked across the yard, Frankie looked up at the underside of the old oak tree dwarfing the little house. The gutters were choked with acorns and leaf debris that needed to be cleaned out before it snowed. She'd do it that weekend before heading back to Seattle. And help paint the basement at the tavern. And the rest of the list of things Patrick had confided in her that needed attention. It would have embarrassed their father if either one of them had brought it up, so they'd agreed to take care of those chores while he was at work or at Hank's annual post-Thanksgiving poker tournament.

But Frankie hadn't done any of those things. Thanksgiving weekend had not gone as planned. She thought of that moment, crossing the yard under the great old oak, and looking at her childhood home, the house her grandfather had built. She wanted to go back to that moment, knowing what she knew now. She'd do everything differently. She'd change the course of things, choose different words, interrupt the conversation that caused her family to explode. But she couldn't now. They'd done what they'd done and said what they'd said, and nothing could change it.

Frankie pushed back her chair and rose to look down at the lake. The cottage was silent except for the crackle of the fire and the sound of her own breath. She was so accustomed to being alone that it took her a while to realize she was crying.

The moon was rising over the right shoulder of the mountain, and she was stunned to stillness by the beauty of it. It was a harvest moon, a great orange globe climbing clumsily into the sky. The moon cast a glow over the snowfields on the south-facing slope of the mountain. Frankie had watched this same moonrise for her entire life and the beauty of it still shook her.

The little crow stirred in the sink. The Popsicle splint scraped against the porcelain and there was a rasping caw of hunger that grew louder. Frankie turned from the moon and abandoned her sorrow. After all, Charlie Crow needed tending. There was work to do.

11

BOUNDARIES

Birds will defend their territories fiercely from members
of the same species. However, many large birds—such as
corvids, owls, and eagles—will tolerate numerous small
songsters in their midst.

—*G. Gordon's Field Guide to the Birds of the Pacific Northwest*

Anne watched the morning light bloom slowly over the lake from her
perch at the kitchen counter. On the far shore, a thick mist crept
down out of the trees and spread into the ravine below like the ghost
of a waterfall. As the sun made its way over the hill behind the house,
the mist broke apart and dissipated. A few insubstantial clouds
streaked the skies pink and orange before disappearing into the
bright blue sky of what Gran always called "second summer."

Anne sipped her tea, feeling jittery and tired. Aiden, who'd grown
accustomed to the rhythms of the lake house, had slept through the
night. But Anne remained alert, listening for any sound from his room,
her body bracing for action. Neither she nor Tim had revisited the
topic of Aiden's disappearance in the storm. But Anne couldn't stop
thinking about it—waking from a doze on the empty beach, the cast-
off life preserver, her failure to watch him. Was Tim thinking about
the same things? He'd wandered before—to one of the neighbor's
apartments and once, terrifyingly, out into their Seattle neighborhood in the middle of the night. But both Anne and Tim had been

equally to blame those times. Blame. Was she keeping score or worried that Tim was?

Now, while Tim and Aiden slept, Anne checked the pastry dough she'd begun the night before. The smell of warm yeast rose as she turned the dough, gave it a fold, and covered it with a towel. She mixed up a batch of scones and slid them into the oven. Eyeing Christi's generous double oven, she pulled a frozen roll of shortbread dough out of the freezer and sliced it into thin rounds. They browned nicely and filled the house with the smell of butter, sugar, and lemon. All the recipes were Gran's.

"With respect, I don't see the point, Mary," Katherine had said to Gran. She sat on the kitchen counter watching Gran pull a heavy tray out of the old oven, drumming her bare heels against the cabinet. Anne had brought her friend home from uni for the bank holiday weekend, and Mary was teaching Anne to make proper pastry.

"Why not just pop down to the shop and buy a packet of biscuits? Why spend hours fussing about in the kitchen when you could be out doing something fun?"

Katherine was the eldest of six children and Anne knew that in the chaos of the O'Faolain household there had been no time for dreamy afternoons of baking. Katherine had grown up changing diapers, helping her mother get supper on the table, and chasing her siblings to bed.

In her youth, Gran had volunteered with the WAAF in France during World War II and came back with a talent for pastry. Gran passed Katherine a plate.

"We don't have a bakery on the island, dearie" was all she said.

Katherine sank her teeth into the hot croissant and groaned.

"I take it all back," she mumbled with her mouth full. "Don't ever leave this kitchen, Mary. Please. For the love of Christ."

Gran tsked but smiled at her.

Anne loved baking with Gran, but she didn't keep it up at uni. For one thing, her bedsit only had a small toaster oven. For another, there was so much to do in Dublin. Music in the pubs and cafés. Concerts in the market, at the park, and at the university hall every weekend. The practice rooms were full of aspiring musicians of all stripes, and visiting artists came on a regular rotation. Anne wanted to stuff her brain with it, pass it all through the sieve of her senses. Her plan for Trinity had originally been practical—to get her teacher's license and eventually teach closer to home on the west coast. But at Trinity she'd fallen hard for music. She wanted to listen and perform and write. Music had completely taken over her life. It was everything. It was who she was. What had happened to that girl? she wondered now. And why had her music deserted her? So much had happened since then.

Aiden's bare feet tapped the floor as he tiptoed into the kitchen. She turned to greet him and kept her arms by her sides, resisting the impulse to hug him tight.

"Hello there. How's my young man this morning?" she asked.

A smile played about his lips, and he looked away. She turned back toward the counter and pulled a cooling rack out of the cupboard. Her son sidled up next to her and leaned his soft weight into her side. She put an arm around him lightly and he moved away. She closed her eyes against hot tears. Aiden crossed the room and climbed into the window seat with his book. With the little volume of fairy tales propped on his pajamaed knees, he looked like any five-year-old boy on holiday in the morning.

Tim came up behind her and slipped his arms around her waist, leaning down to bury his face in her hair. Anne turned to embrace him and felt his body still warm from the bedclothes. His familiar physical presence was a comfort and made things feel okay between them.

"It smells amazing in here," Tim said, kissing her cheek. "You've been up with the elves, I see."

Anne shook her head.

"Oh, not me," she said. "It was all Suzy."

Tim laughed, as she'd hoped.

"Oh, Suzy," he sighed. "What would we do without her?"

Suzy was a long-running joke. During the first months of their cohabitation, when Anne was newly pregnant, it had become abundantly clear that neither one of them excelled in the domestic arts. Tim, because his mother had hired people to cook and clean for the family, hadn't learned to boil an egg. Anne had been an only child with two working parents and was expected to look after herself but also had a grandmother living just over the wall who helped with the household chores.

They'd fought about it one morning after Tim tripped over a pile of dirty laundry in a rush to get to work. He'd suggested in a not very nice way that Anne find time that weekend to run a couple of loads of laundry.

"I've done my washing, thank you very much!" she said, also running late and also crabby. Her pregnancy had advanced to the point that hardly any of her clothes fit and she was faced with wearing the same pair of fat pants for the third day in a row.

"I've spent more than enough time in the basement with Hippy Dave!"

Anne had learned not to linger in the basement laundry room after one of their neighbors had discovered she was a musician. When he saw her in the elevator with her hamper, he'd fetch his guitar and try to enlist her in a jam. Bob Dylan and the Stones mostly. She'd tried to be polite and told him she wasn't into that kind of music. Dave had so persisted that now she took the back stairs to the basement.

"And I did the linens and the towels, thank you very much!"

"Well, what about that?" Tim gestured to the overflowing hamper. "What's all that?"

Anne crossed her arms and stared up at him.

"That, my friend, is your own fecking problem," she said coolly. "I am not Suzy Fecking Homemaker."

Tim's frown disappeared and he squeezed her tight, laughing.

"You're my fecking problem, you Irish terror!"

That's how they fought—fast and furious and then it was over. Tim had done his own laundry and they shared the responsibility of grocery shopping, cooking, and cleaning. The apartment was less tidy than either one of them preferred, and when one of them grumbled about it, the other would suggest they call Suzy.

That's the way things had been before, anyway. They were in strange new territory now that she was on leave. She looked around the spotless kitchen, the piles of freshly baked goods, the rising tray of pastry. Suzy Fecking Homemaker was exactly what she felt like just now. Bloody hell. And as for arguing, she preferred those furious exchanges to the polite restraint they'd adopted lately. She pulled away and poured him a cup of coffee.

"When are you heading down the lake?" she asked.

"After breakfast," he said. "I have a few calls to make and I'll probably stop at the marina store to pick up a few things if they're open. I'll be back after lunch. Why don't you and Aiden come with me?"

The timer dinged and Anne turned toward the oven. She pulled out the scones and demurred, saying she'd promised Aiden a walk in the woods after breakfast. Was it a lie, an excuse, or a bargaining chip? Did it matter? Tim let it drop and she was grateful.

"I'll stop by the post office while I'm down there," he said.

He didn't say more, but Anne wondered if he was thinking about the assessment from the University of Washington Department of Pediatrics, which neither of them had mentioned since their arrival at the lake. They'd been expecting a response for weeks now, but it hadn't arrived. At home, she'd dreaded the sight of the postal truck each day and was dismayed to learn their mail would be forwarded up to Mill Three. The thought of the report from UW sat like a stone in her belly.

Later, as Tim pulled away from the dock, she waved with false cheer. And as the boat receded into the distance, she felt both shame and relief at being alone with her son.

Aiden scampered away from her back to the beach and shed his life preserver on the grass. Her breath caught as she remembered pulling it from the shallows of the lake water. But he was following the rule they'd impressed on him: If he was on the beach, in the water, or on the dock, he had to wear his life preserver. Pulling it off on the grass was within bounds. She couldn't scold him for doing as they'd asked, now, could she?

Aiden paused at the foot of the cliff. The red trolley that had been there the day of the storm was absent. Anne recalled how Tim had found Aiden's precious book tucked in there out of the rainstorm. It made her smile now. Practical little vagabond protecting his precious storybook.

Aiden eyed the track climbing up the hillside. And in a flash, he was clambering up the adjacent trail.

"Aiden, wait, love!" Anne called, but he didn't slow.

She dropped the life preserver and hurried after him, breathing heavily by the time she reached the top. There sat the caretaker's cottage, a cheerful yellow one-story house tucked under the trees like something out of a fairy tale. A plume of smoke curled out of the chimney and twisted through the trees. At the back, a laundry line was hung with flannel shirts and work pants. Aiden had alighted in the little red trolley at the top of the tracks.

"Aiden, time to go now. This isn't our house," Anne said, her voice low, glancing at the back door to the cottage.

He ignored her and kicked his feet against the seat. Anne tried to coax him away, saying it was time to go back to Grandad Tim and Grandma Christi's house. Aiden giggled and twisted away from her. Her frustration rose and she heard Christi's voice in her head. *"Who's in charge of whom, Anne?"* She closed her hand around Aiden's wrist and tugged him toward her. He resisted, and when she let go, he sprang out of the trolley and ran toward the house. She chased him, now furious at herself. She knew better than to try to grab him.

"Aiden Matthew Ryan Magnusen! You come here this instant!" she hissed.

He'd reached the door by then and had both hands on the knob, twisting it back and forth. His brow was furrowed in concentration and when the door opened in front of him, he fell back with such surprise, Anne would have laughed had she not been angry.

The young woman in the doorway looked down at Aiden and then up at Anne. She was tall and thin, with short dark hair that she pushed out of her face with one hand. She wasn't smiling.

"Oh, hiya!" Anne called, waving a hand, and then, "Bloody hell," under her breath.

She moved quickly to close the space between herself and her son. She stood behind him and resisted the urge to grab his shoulders.

"So sorry to disturb you! I'm Anne Ryan, Tim's wife," Anne said, trying to catch her breath.

She gestured in the direction of the trail. The woman didn't say anything, and her face was blank. Anne felt the weight of the silence between them, the heavy pause where it was the other person's turn to speak. Aiden ducked under her arm and skipped back to the trolley and clambered onto the seat. The woman crossed her arms, glanced at Aiden and then back to Anne.

"Erm, this is my son, Aiden, and we were just out for a walk, and he decided to come up the trail."

The silence was unnerving.

"Sorry—I don't know your name," Anne said, feeling desperate to fill the quiet. "Tim told me your family are the caretakers? But we've never met."

The woman uncrossed her arms and blinked.

"Oh. Sorry. I'm Frankie. Frankie O'Neill."

Her voice was low and quiet. She brushed her hair back and held out her hand. Anne shook it, wanting to laugh at the awkward formality.

"Pleased to meet you, Frankie. I'm so sorry to disturb you. This rascal son of mine!" she said and forced a laugh.

Frankie looked at the boy, then back to Anne and down at her own attire, which Anne realized consisted of men's boxer shorts and a jumper with "UW" emblazoned across the front.

". . . wasn't expecting anyone," Frankie mumbled, her face flushing with color.

Anne began to move toward the trail.

"Well, it's lovely to meet you, Frankie. Perhaps we'll come back some other time when its more convenient and pay you a proper— Aiden!"

The boy flew between them and bolted into the cottage behind the tall woman. Frankie turned slowly to look after him and then back to Anne.

"I'm so sorry," Anne said, moving toward the doorway. "He doesn't—he won't. If I could just—"

Frankie stepped aside to let her in, and Anne felt a barrage of familiar and impossible feelings—maternal concern, shame, frustration, and deep down the urge to laugh at the absurdity of the situation: chasing her child through the house of a complete stranger.

Aiden was standing in front of the sofa and Anne crossed the room to him. He was paging madly through a book on the table with a fierce sense of purpose. She crouched down next to him and spoke quietly in his ear, trying to keep her voice calm.

"Aiden. Sweetie. This is not our house. You need to knock first and wait to be let in. It's very impolite to barge in. Remember what we talked about with Mrs. Silva?"

She could tell he was listening, though he didn't look at her. His fingers slowed over the pages, and he stood stock-still. Before she could react, he ran across the room and out the door, slamming it shut behind him. Frankie, who'd followed Anne into the house, looked surprised. There was a furious knocking at the door, and when Frankie opened it, Aiden bolted back inside and dashed to the coffee table, smiling triumphantly.

Anne began to laugh great, heaving peals of laughter. She knew she shouldn't, which made it harder to stop. He looked so pleased with himself for finding a work-around. Wait to be let in, she'd said. Little conniver. Hands on knees, trying to catch her breath, she struggled to pull herself together. Oh, what must this poor woman think of them both?

The door clicked shut. Frankie O'Neill smiled faintly.

"Excuse me a minute," she said.

She went into another room and pulled the door closed. Anne, swallowing her laughter, sat on the couch next to Aiden and touched his curls lightly with one hand. He had the book in front of him open to a series of photos—crows and ravens and rooks. His face was now a picture of contentment. She dropped a kiss on his wee head, and he shifted away from her.

"Young man," she murmured. "What am I going to do with you?"

The coffee table was strewn with books, a deck of cards, and an unfinished cribbage game. A pair of floral armchairs framed the view, and two cozy beds were tucked in on the screened-in porch. Out the front windows, Mount Adams loomed over the navy-blue waters of the lake, and a skein of geese skimmed the water, honking as they landed. The fire crackled and popped in the woodstove and the wind played through the big trees in front of the house. It was so comfortable and inviting.

Frankie returned wearing trousers and a flannel shirt. Her hair was damp and her face slightly pink.

"Would you like some coffee? I just made some."

Anne followed her to the kitchen. There she took in the deep farm sink, a battered old stove, and a diminutive refrigerator. The kitchen was painted a warm bottle green, and the rest of the room was bordered in cream-colored wainscot. A bookshelf filled one entire wall and a series of framed photos adorned the opposite. A long table divided the kitchen from the living room area and one end was covered in books and spiral-bound notebooks. The doors to what she assumed were bedrooms and bath were closed.

When she turned back, Frankie was watching her and frowning.

"Bit of a mess . . ." she said faintly.

"Oh, I think it's lovely," Anne said. "So warm and comfortable. It reminds me of my grandmother's place."

Frankie handed her a mug and glanced at Aiden, still bent over the bird book.

"Is it okay that he's looking at your book?" Anne asked.

"Yes, it's fine," Frankie said.

They sat at the kitchen table, and Frankie pushed aside a large stack of journals.

"Sorry about all this. I'm sure things are much neater down at the Magnusens'."

She sounded embarrassed.

Anne recalled the last family trip up to the house when Christi had enlisted her help in tidying the already tidy drawers and cupboards.

"That's one word for it," she said dryly. "Christi runs a tight ship."

Frankie smiled faintly and asked how long they were up for. Anne found herself explaining about the newspaper expansion and Tim's research on other markets. Frankie nodded politely, but Anne could tell she wasn't terribly interested in plans for the Magnusen media empire. She wasn't either, if she was honest.

"And you? Do you—work? Or are you mostly busy with—" Frankie gestured toward Aiden.

Anne's face grew hot. People often assumed that the wife of a Magnusen would never work outside the home, as Christi liked to put it.

"I'm a musician," she said, "and a teacher at Cornish College of the Arts in Seattle."

"Oh," said Frankie, sounding surprised. She leaned forward on her elbows. "What kind of musician?"

Anne turned her cup in her hands.

"Traditional Irish music," she replied. "I'm a singer by training and I teach voice and composition at the college."

"Irish—I thought so from your accent. My grandfather was from Ireland. From County Kerry."

"Really?" Anne said, feigning interest. Here we go, she thought. The story about how the family went over to find their roots and all that. Visited the graveyard and read the church records. How it felt like a part of them belonged there. Then they bought their sweaters and headed back to America.

"You been over yourself, then?"

Frankie shook her head and frowned.

"We never had money for a trip like that. My grandfather went back once, I think, when he was young. When his mom died."

"Yes, I know. It costs a mint going between here and there," Anne said.

She glanced at her son, still absorbed in the book on the coffee table and whispering to himself.

"What about you? How long will you be at the lake? Tim said you were probably shutting things down for the season."

Frankie's eyes traveled the length of the table over the books and notebooks piled there.

"I'll be closing up the house in a couple of weeks, I think," she said slowly.

Anne sensed she didn't want to explain further. Frankie was looking at Aiden again.

"You're sure it's okay? Your books?" Anne asked.

A strange look crossed Frankie's face.

"Yes, it's just . . . Aiden came over the other day," she said slowly, and stopped.

Anne's body flushed with shame, and she braced herself.

"Oh, I'm so sorry. What did he—did he come in the house? Did he break something?"

She thought of Mrs. Silva standing in the hallway in her bathrobe with dripping hair, furious. "You need to teach that kid some manners, Mrs. Magnusen!" she shouted.

"I want to replace it if he took something or—"

"No, he was fine," Frankie said.

She explained that she'd come back to the house during the storm and found Aiden there. He was perfectly well-behaved, she said.

Anne couldn't speak.

"We had hot chocolate and looked at some books. I was going to walk him home when it stopped raining, but then he ran outside. I saw you all on the trail together and I didn't want to . . ." She trailed off. "Sorry. I should have come out and explained," she finished.

Anne laughed with disbelief and turned to look at her son.

"So, you came up and had a nice cup of chocolate, did you? Made yourself right at home, you cheeky monkey?"

Aiden did not turn, but from the tilt of his head, Anne could tell he was listening, and she would wager he was smiling. She turned back to Frankie and tears rose in her eyes. The fear of having lost him lived in her body.

"Thank you so much," she said, trying to keep her voice level. "We were down on the beach and I . . . He's afraid of thunder."

Frankie looked uncomfortable and glanced away.

"It was nothing. I never lock the door, and I'm glad he came in out of the rain."

There was a strange sound from the kitchen then, a sharp and rasping squawk. Frankie pushed back her chair and stood.

"Excuse me a second."

She lifted a wicker basket off the sink with slow and careful movement. Another squawk, louder and demanding this time. Frankie half turned to Anne.

"It's a little crow. Do you want to see?"

Anne stood and Aiden flashed between them. He moved in close to Frankie, who used an eye dropper to dribble water into the beak of a bright-eyed little crow. Anne could see it had some sort of splint on one leg. The bird stopped drinking to look up at them, then resumed.

"Anne and Aiden, meet Charlie Crow. He's got an injured leg," Frankie said in a low, steady voice. "But mostly I think he was just hungry and thirsty. I'm fattening him up to get him back to his family."

Aiden curled his small hands over the edge of the sink and leaned closer to the little bird.

"Careful, Aiden," Anne said.

"He's fine," Frankie said quietly.

The bird sidled sideways, the splint clicking against the sink. Frankie set down the water and the dropper and picked up a pair of tweezers.

"Aiden, will you please pass me that can of tuna?" she asked in that same low voice, not looking at him.

"Sorry, he won't—" Anne started to say, then watched, dumbfounded, as her son pulled the can toward him with both hands and held it up to Frankie.

"Thank you, Aiden," Frankie said, and explained in the same steady voice that crow babies like this one needed to be fed every hour or so. And after he learned to feed himself, he would spend the winter with his parents and his older siblings and likely the next few years until he started his own family. So, it was very important he get back to his family quickly.

Aiden leaned in as Frankie fed the little crow. At her request he took the water and dropper and set them aside. Anne struggled to compose herself. When was the last time he'd taken directions from anyone? Even his parents?

After a few quiet minutes, Frankie put down the can and the tweezers.

"Okay, little buddy. I think that's enough for now. See you in a bit, Charlie Crow. Say goodbye, Aiden."

She replaced the wicker laundry basket over the sink and turned back to Anne, smiling. Aiden returned to Anne's side and twined a small hand around her wrist, then let her go. Her heart flipped over, and she could barely trust herself to speak. She pulled her hair off her neck and forced a smile.

"Well, that was lovely and so interesting. Thank you for the coffee, Frankie. We'll let you get back to your day. Please pop on by the house while we're here."

She knew she sounded abrupt, but if she didn't get away, she'd start to cry in front of this stranger. Frankie stood in the doorway watching them as Aiden hopped up into the trolley and off, and then scrambled down the trail as nimble as a mountain goat.

What to make of it all? Who was this strange, quiet woman who drew Aiden so? Aiden, who did not want to be touched, who didn't speak, who didn't respond when spoken to. Aiden, who lived in his own little world.

She thought of the questionnaire from the University of Washington Department of Pediatrics, the written part of the assessment Dr. Shelley had asked her and Tim to fill out. Information about Aiden's home life to provide context for the clinical assessment. That bloody long list of aggravating questions.

"What activities does your child enjoy doing alone? With others? How does your child behave when meeting new people?"

She thought of Aiden holding up the can of tuna fish like some precious thing, an offering, a prayer, a magic token of understanding.

12

THE JUVENILE

A nest offers shelter to incubating eggs as well as young
and vulnerable hatchlings—a crucial feature for survival.

—*G. Gordon's Field Guide to the Birds of the Pacific Northwest*

Once upon a time a king banished his twelve sons deep into the forest. Their little sister journeyed a long way to find them, and they
lived happily together. One day she unknowingly picked enchanted
flowers that turned her brothers into ravens. "Is there no way to save
them?" she cried. An old crone said, "You must be dumb for seven
years and may not speak or laugh and you might free your brothers."

Once there was a man who loved his youngest daughter best.
When he asked what she wanted as a gift, she said a singing, soaring
lark. He bargained for the bird, but accidentally promised his little
daughter to a fearsome lion in exchange. The lion was really an enchanted prince and he and the daughter loved each other. But then he
changed into a mourning dove doomed to fly the world for seven
years, dropping feathers. She could free him if she followed and gathered them up and saved them.

So many children got lost or enchanted. So many had brothers
and sisters. So many seemed to change by accident. So many went
hungry. A boy knew what lost felt like. He didn't know what brother

or sister felt like. He knew what it was like to feel hungry, although he never had to say anything. His mother seemed to know, before he did, that the tight squeezing in his belly was hunger. At times eating seemed to make the hungry feeling worse so he didn't eat. He could manage the feeling when it was small, but not when it got away from him. When it grew big and pressed him down.

There were many things he didn't understand. But there were many things he did know. He knew stories, so many stories. He knew about those lost and enchanted and hungry children. He knew about the leprechaun and the banshee and the selkies. He knew his ABCs forward and backward. He knew his phone number and his address by heart, as well as his parents' names, though he never said them out loud.

He knew the scent of his mother from another room. She smelled of roses, black tea with milk, sunshine, and green, green grass.

He knew the middle key on the piano in his mind and the sharps and flats that his mother's voice climbed up over like the stone steps to the top of the tower at the park when she practiced her singing. Only she didn't do that anymore. Not for a long time now.

He knew his father's footstep in the hallway early in the morning and late at night. The jingle of his keys in the door and the sound of his voice as he talked on the phone in the kitchen.

He knew where to find the second verse of the third song on the B side of his favorite record.

He knew that the stickers on the ceiling of his room were meant to look like stars. When he lay awake at night staring up at them, he thought of the real stars outside and wanted to go out and see them. But he knew if he did—finding his way out the apartment door, down the stairs, and into the cool night air—his mother would cry. The first time he'd tried that, there had been so much noise, flashing red and blue lights. The sound of the siren had made him scream and scream and his mother thought he was hurt, and he couldn't tell her that it was the siren and the lights that hurt.

Another time he'd tried to look for the fireworks in the night sky at the lake house. That time his grandfather found him standing at the edge of the lake and scolded him. He said it wasn't polite to wander around other people's houses in the night and that he mustn't be naughty or he'd get a spanking.

He often thought about the stars at night and the fireworks. He wondered where the stars went during the day. He wondered where the fireworks waited between July Fourths when they shot up out of the lake. He wanted to ask his mother about that. If she didn't know the answer, he was certain she would help him suss it out. Or at least tell him it was a very good question to ask. She thought he was very sharp. Very, very clever. Clever as a fox. She told him so all the time.

So many questions. As many questions as there were stories.

A boy just didn't know how to ask.

13

THE CONGRESS

Many birds undertake long and arduous annual migrations extending from the northern hemisphere to the southern. Others, however, pass their entire lives within the boundaries of their nesting grounds. These are known as resident birds.

—*G. Gordon's Field Guide to the Birds of the Pacific Northwest*

The bright tang of autumn air seeped in through the truck window, which Frankie had cracked to clear the foggy windshield. A mist clung to the great fir trees that lined the Old BZ Highway, and the tires hissed over the wet pavement. She spotted a single crow winging its way south over the river where it curved and twisted in a parallel line to the road.

Researchers have long understood the value of seasonal migrations. Of North America's two thousand species of birds, a significant portion make an autumnal trek from the Northern Hemisphere to the Southern and back. The rewards are clear—increased food supply, warmer temperatures, and the opportunity to mate.

But the American crow, Frankie knew, didn't migrate. Not in the long-distance fashion traditionally understood as migratory, anyway. Some in the far north would fly slightly south in winter, but most stayed close to their natal grounds. The same was true for its cousins, the fish crow, the Hawaiian crow, the northwestern crow, and the

Tamaulipas crow. These close relatives adhered to their own home grounds of the US East Coast and southern coastline, the Big Island of Hawaii, coastal British Columbia, and the Gulf Coast of Mexico, respectively.

Frankie reflected on this commonality and glanced again at the crow. It looked to be a more willing traveler than she, from the easy movement of its wings. Though hardly a migration, her unwelcome journey had been spurred by a letter from the law offices of Schmidt, Whittaker, and Weatherby.

The letter had come in the stack of mail Jerry had brought on his way up to the lumber camp the previous day. He was in a good mood because the Cougars had beat the Huskies. Frankie didn't care about football, but since she was as close as he was going to get to a Huskies fan, she took the ribbing for his sake.

The pile of mail had included some books on loan from Suzzallo Library and a couple of ornithology publications. When her eye fell on the slim envelope, her heart jumped. Maybe it was from Dr. Grant or from OSU in Corvallis. Her stomach dropped when she realized it was from the law office, and she'd put off opening it. Though she'd expected this missive, seeing it in print was a shock.

Patrick had sent a note too. Sitting on the couch facing the lake, she opened that one first and read her big brother's cramped left-handed scrawl.

Howdy Frank—

You probably got the letter from Weatherby's office by now. I know you aren't going to want to come into town for this, but they need all three of us there. Mom doesn't want to put it off any longer, and I think it would be best for us to get it over with. I'll buy you lunch. See you on Friday, little sister.

Patrick

She dropped the note on the table and looked at the books strewn about. Aiden Magnusen had left *G. Gordon's Field Guide to the Birds of the Pacific Northwest* open to the section on corvids. She pulled the book into her lap and remembered the birthday her father had given it to her. It had all begun then—her love affair with birds. Every time she'd learned something, she couldn't wait to tell her dad. Those early summers in the woods with the birds and then her college classes and graduate school fieldwork. Her dad loved her bird talk. He would have enjoyed hearing about Charlie Crow. But she hadn't told him about Charlie Crow, and she knew she wouldn't ever tell him. There were so many things she hadn't told him and never would be able to. Because her dad was dead.

A wave of grief washed over her. Jack O'Neill in his rumpled clothes and mussed hair, his corny jokes, the comforting sight of him standing over the stove on a Saturday morning flipping pancakes. Playing poker at Hank's. His twinkling eyes and his corny songs.

"Lydia, oh Lydia, say have you met Lydia? Lydia the tattooed lady!"

She recalled the last time she'd seen him, that Friday after Thanksgiving at the bus stop. He hugged her hard and kissed her on the cheek. He told her he was so proud of her, so very proud. As she hugged him back, Frankie noticed for the first time that she was slightly taller than he was, and her heart ached. She boarded the bus and Jack raised a hand and turned away, put his hands in his pockets, and walked down the empty sidewalk toward the tavern.

That was the last time she'd ever seen her father. She didn't go home for Christmas break or Saint Patrick's Day, which was a big deal at the River City Saloon. She said she had to work, and nobody pressed her. So much to regret—not going home for the holidays. Not staying another day that Thanksgiving weekend. Not asking the driver to stop. She should have climbed off the bus and gone back, told him not to worry about what Judith had said. She'd hug him and tell him how much she loved him one more time.

But she hadn't done any of those things. She'd gone back to Seattle and buried herself in responsibilities, real and imagined. Fall

bled into winter and then spring. And one night last April, her
brother called to tell her that Jack O'Neill, their kind, incorrigible,
irresponsible, and delightful father, was dead.

She came up against the impossibility of it all then, the finality of
his death. Her eyes traveled along the far wall, which was covered
with family photos. She paused at the one from 1975, the first summer she could remember. The four of them were crowded together
on the little red trolley. Patrick and her father sat on one side and
Frankie perched in Judith's lap on the other. Her parents were so
young then. Judith, her dark hair in two braids, looked like a girl, and
she was younger than Frankie was now. Patrick was reaching toward
whoever held the camera, and her father's face was split in a laugh.
Another wave of grief fell heavy on her body.

Every morning for the past five months had begun with the same
realization. *Dad is dead.* She recalled his funeral. A parade of faces,
friends, family, and near strangers. Every condolence fell like a blow
on her shattered heart. Now this summons from the offices of Schmidt,
Whittaker, and Weatherby for the reading of her father's will.

She sat on the couch and let the fire die, not caring that the room
grew dark and cold. She knew she should eat, but she wasn't hungry.
She just couldn't move. It was the clamoring of the fledgling that
finally roused her. Charlie Crow had grown stronger, and she'd
moved him from the sink into the bathroom tub. He had plenty of
room to stalk about in there on his strengthening leg. She'd filled
one of Grammy Genevieve's hummingbird feeders with water, which
he managed nicely. He was eating on his own too—tuna fish and
chopped apples from Grandpa Ray's tree. Satiated, Charlie fell asleep,
and Frankie felt strangely comforted by his quiet sleeping noises.

In the morning she made sure the little bird had food and water
to last the day and then headed down to the dock. The sun was just
coming over the east ridge as she untied *The Peggotty* and motored
down the lake. As the air warmed above the water, the lake steamed

like a bowl of soup. A kingfisher clamored along the shore, and a pair of eagles floated on the thermal overhead. Frankie motored through the mist and watched the snowy face of Mount Adams grow pink in the sunrise. The beauty of it was some ballast against the dread in her heart. When she landed at the marina, she saw the mail boat tethered to the dock but no sign of Jerry.

Now in the truck, she glanced at her watch and reluctantly accelerated. Their appointment was at 11 a.m., and she'd make it on time, but just barely. She drove the curving highway along the White Salmon River and across the Hood River Bridge. The wind was up, and a barge churned through whitecaps in the wide channel. The west wind gusted and buffeted the truck as she paused to pay the toll.

She parked in front of the Hood River County Courthouse and saw Patrick on the front steps. He was wearing a white button-down shirt and a red tie with dark slacks. Patrick had completed his associate's degree at Mt. Hood Community College and, now clerking for Judge McGuiness, was the first of the O'Neill cousins to land a white-collar job. The sight of his familiar face made her want to cry. But O'Neills didn't cry; not in front of others, anyway. She tried to make a joke instead.

"Look at you, Dapper Dan!" she said.

Patrick leaned down to hug her.

"Not looking so bad yourself, Lanky Frankie," he said.

She glanced down at her rumpled pants and nubby cardigan. Patrick was more fastidious about his attire, like their mother. Frankie took after their father, who wore a timeless uniform of khaki and cotton. She folded the cuff of her sweater to hide a hole.

"Thanks for coming," Patrick said.

"Better than being hunted down by Mom," Frankie said, trying to keep her voice light.

She saw Judith then, standing inside the open doorway of the courthouse. Frankie thought of that old photo of her family on the trolley, her young mother's face, Judith's hands clasped around her own plump baby hands. She felt a surge of longing and moved toward Judith. As she leaned down to embrace her petite mother, she breathed in the smell of her familiar perfume. Judith patted her on the shoulder and stepped away.

"Hello, Mary Frances," she said. "You're looking well."

Frankie's heart plummeted at the rebuff, familiar though it was. She searched her mother's face for a trace of that young, smiling girl but did not find one. Her voice left her then, as often happened around Judith.

"Well. Peter is ready for us. Let's go in," Judith said, and walked away from them across the foyer.

The meeting felt surreal. Judith sat ramrod straight with her hands in her lap as if Peter Weatherby was reading a new parking regulation and not the contents of her husband's will. The language was arcane and confusing, and Frankie's attention wandered. She looked out the window and down Oak Street. She remembered the logging protests there, and the Earth Day celebration where she'd first heard Dr. Davis Grant speak about the interconnectedness of humans and the natural world.

"We are not separate from the environment. We have a responsibility to do less harm. Conservation is on the vanguard!" he'd said.

That was the first she'd ever heard about conservation biology and the beginning of her interest in ornithology. The inkling of an idea that she could have a career in science.

"It's a matter of pro tempore for the limited liability company Jack created," Peter was saying as Patrick nudged her. Peter peered over his glasses.

"I take it he discussed this all with you, Judith?"

"Yes. My understanding is that the three of us make up the LLC membership, but I'm the sole directing member," Judith said.

"That is correct," Peter said.

He outlined the simplest terms: The house and all its contents went to Judith. So did a small life insurance policy that would pay out $50,000. Jack had left the lake cottage and *The Peggotty* to the three of them in equal shares of the O'Neill Family LLC. The rest of his assets, such as they were, were also divided among the three of them. It wasn't much, just a few thousand dollars. But he had not left any debts, Peter was saying.

"As for the matter of the tavern, Judith—" he began.

"Let's not muddy the waters, Peter," Judith interrupted. "That's a conversation for another time."

"What about the tavern?" Frankie asked.

Patrick elbowed her and shook his head. Judith didn't acknowledge that she'd spoken. She signed the paper Peter slid toward her as calmly as if she were buying a car. It was like that day at Hennessy Funeral Home. Frankie had been mostly silent and only spoke up once when Dean Anderson was discussing the price of the coffin.

"Didn't Dad want to be cremated?"

Judith silenced her with a withering look, and Patrick had shaken his head at her then too.

Peter's secretary made copies of everything, and then it was over. The O'Neills stood together in the weak fall sunshine in front of the courthouse. Frankie looked at her brother and mother, her diminished family. This seemed more momentous somehow than the funeral, the three of them there together alone. She wanted to acknowledge the moment, but then Judith was talking about her clients and a closing she had the next day. As if it were just a regular day. And Frankie's heart folded closed. Patrick suggested they get lunch. Now that felt impossible. She was relieved when her mother said she didn't have time.

"Are you heading straight back to the lake, Mary Frances?" Judith asked.

"I was planning to. Why?"

"I could use your help with some things at the house this afternoon," Judith said.

She looked away and then back at Frankie.

"Some of Dad's things."

Frankie nodded slowly.

"Sure, Mom. I can stay and help. I need to go to Patrick's office, and I'll be over after."

Judith thanked her and walked away, raising a hand in farewell.

At his office, Patrick helped her carry his old computer and printer down to the truck. Frankie was grateful for the loan. She'd be able to type up her revisions at the cottage instead of waiting to use the computer lab on the UW campus.

Her brother tipped his face into the autumn sunshine and stretched his arms over his head.

"How are things up at the lake?" he asked. "Getting cold?"

Frankie told him about the windfall she'd been clearing from the trail and about Tim Magnusen's family.

"Big Tim and Christi too?"

"No, just Tim Junior and his wife and kid," Frankie said.

"Seems weird they'd be up there after Labor Day," Patrick said.

Frankie rubbed her chin and leaned against the truck.

"I just hope they don't need anything. I wasn't expecting anyone else to be up there, you know? I like the quiet."

Patrick's face dimmed.

"You shouldn't be alone so much, Frank. I worry about you," he said.

She assured him she was fine.

"Makes it easier to write and I'll be done soon. My thesis is due at the end of the month."

"Well, it's nice of you to help Mom today," he said. "I'll stop by after work, okay?"

"Sure," she said. "Or maybe we could meet at the tavern? I haven't seen Hank in ages."

If Patrick came to the house, Judith would dominate the conversation. But Judith wouldn't want to go to the tavern because she never wanted to go to the tavern. But Patrick would feel bad that their mother would feel left out. Frankie read all this in Patrick's doubtful look, and she waved in surrender.

"Fine. Just meet me at Mom's."

"Great. I'll bring dinner from Grace Su's," he said.

As she drove through town, she went a block out of her way to pass the tavern. The familiar face of the River City Saloon looked sad and quiet with the blinds drawn and the "Shut!" sign on the door. The tavern was generally open by noon, and she wondered if Hank was short-staffed. She decided to stop in and say hello before she headed back up to the lake. She hadn't seen him since the funeral.

The tires crunched over gravel as she pulled in the driveway of her childhood home. The old house sat under the reaching branches of the oak tree, and Frankie felt a surge of familiar feelings. Love and longing, resentment and claustrophobia. Judith was not home yet, so Frankie took the spare key from under a flowerpot and let herself inside.

The house was cool and dark. She flipped on the lights and went into the kitchen. It smelled faintly of lemon furniture polish and toast. She got a glass of water and saw a note from her mother on the counter. Judith had evidently been and gone.

Mary Frances,

1) *Box all sweaters, good long-sleeve shirts, and good slacks for the Santa Ana mission.*
2) *Box everyday wear for St. Vincent de Paul's in The Dalles.*
3) *Take all remaining items to the transfer station.*

I'll be home by dinner.

Thank you,
Mom

Judith had left the address for the mission and blank checks made out to USPS and the Hood River transfer station, suggesting that she also expected Frankie to drop off boxes at the post office, St. Vincent de Paul's, and the dump.

Frankie felt stung and then stupid. She'd assumed that whatever help her mother needed was something they would do together. It might offer some sense of comfort. But Judith clearly had other ideas and business elsewhere. Heartsore, Frankie rose and went into her parents' bedroom. The room was small and neat with a double bed that Grandpa Ray had built with a matching bureau and bedside tables, all constructed of warm Douglas fir he'd milled from trees up at the lake. Judith had left several large cardboard boxes lined up against the wall.

Frankie took a deep breath and opened the door to the closet. Reaching in with both hands, she pulled out jackets and shirts on their hangers. She tossed them on the bed to sort them, and her breath caught. There on top was her dad's buffalo plaid jacket. The red-and-black wool was frayed at the cuffs and had been patched along the collar more than once. Her father wore it constantly and even to special occasions—weddings, baptisms, funerals, and formal parties. Judith hated the old coat, which only seemed to increase Jack's affection for it. Frankie ran her hand down the front of the jacket and tugged a piece of paper from the breast pocket. She stared down at the worn ticket stub from her college graduation ceremony three years ago. She recalled how Jack's face had shone as he rang the bell at the Blue Moon Tavern, where they'd gone for drinks after she'd walked across the stage with the graduating class of 1995.

"A round for the house! My girl just graduated! The first in the family!"

The room of strangers cheered, and her father raised his glass to her, so proud.

Frankie sat down hard on the bed and pulled the jacket into her lap. Outside a gust of wind blew a confetti of leaves across the yard. It had started to rain, and a small flurry of sparrows alighted on the freshly wet earth.

She ran her hand along the arm of the jacket and was overwhelmed by memories—Jack teaching her to drive the boat, Jack pulling a beer for her at the tavern, and Jack standing with her in that same windswept yard almost a year ago at Thanksgiving. The task now before her was impossible. She rose, hastily rehanging everything, and folded the plaid coat over her arm. In the kitchen she scribbled a note to her mother saying she was sorry she hadn't had time to help after all and she'd call soon.

She climbed into the old truck and sat for a moment, unable to move. The detritus of her father's life was strewn about the cab. Ragged receipts, coffee cups, and worn work gloves littered the bench seat. On the dash was a note in her dad's familiar scrawl. "Pea gravel, 4 x 12s, Judith's birthday!!" it said. This last was underlined. Frankie leaned back against the seat and closed her eyes. Hank had been the one to go get the old truck after the accident. She yearned to see him now, but she knew she could not. Not in this state.

She drove through town and crossed the bridge over the river. It was so raw, so final. She would never hear his voice, the sound of his laugh. She'd never hear him singing as he swept the tavern floor or hear him say "How's my girl?" when she walked in the door. Or feel the rough scratch of his morning stubble as he hugged her. Never. And Judith's coldness made it worse.

It all felt impossible. She couldn't feel so much all at once. Her mind tilted toward the idea then. Just one drink, a small whiskey. Just to quell the feelings, tamp them down, and get a hold of herself. It was a neat and tidy solution. Two fingers of mind-clearing Bushmills. Then she could get to work and finish her thesis. She could get her life back on track and move on. As she drove north on the highway, the idea settled there and soon it was all she could think of—the bottle in the rafters of the pump house, the one she should have emptied the first day, the one she'd told herself she wouldn't touch.

The afternoon sky darkened. Brake lights flared in front of her just past the little town of BZ Corner, and a service truck blocked the road. It was changing a flat on a big logging truck, and there was no room to squeeze around. The flagger walked back to Frankie, and she turned off the engine.

"It's gonna be a while, I'm afraid. Lug nut's stripped and the som' bitch won't come off," he said, taking a drag on his cigarette. He looked at her then and flushed, having mistaken her for a man.

"Sorry, miss," he said.

"Can I bum one of those?" she asked.

He shook one out of the pack and lit it for her.

"Get you moving as soon as we can," he said and walked away.

Frankie smoked fast, waiting. She looked at her watch, calculating how long it would take her to get to the marina and up the lake. On a gloomy fall day, it grew dark long before sunset. By the time the road cleared and she made it to the marina, it was after 6 p.m. She loaded the computer equipment into the boat and cast off without stopping to evaluate the growing strength of the wind. All she could think about was getting to the pump house and feeling that cool bottle in her hand.

By the time she'd reached the main channel, it was clear she had no business being out on the water. The waves increased as the north wind blew down off the mountain and tumbled across the bow. The wind pushed the little boat around like a toy in the lake's current. Frankie knew if she tried to turn around, she risked being broad-sided and swamped. If she could just reach Arrow Point, she could anchor in at the small cove there and wait out the storm.

Rain lashed the windows and Frankie peered past the frantic windshield wipers, straining for any landmark to gauge where she was on the lake. Had she passed Arrow Point or was it ahead of her?

She couldn't recognize any features around her and knew all she could do was push on. She eased the throttle forward, trying to get the old boat to plane, and it crashed over each oncoming wave.

In the fallen gloom, she crept along, trying to maintain a position in what felt like the center of the channel. She'd be safest from deadheads there, those sunken remnants of the timber industry that could resurface unexpectedly. She resisted the temptation to hug the shoreline, that unfamiliar territory where a shallow bottom could be the end of the prop. And if the engine died, the boat could get beaten up along the cliff in the powerful waves. She thought of Fred Timmons and his son caught in a fall storm like this one and their boat capsizing. They'd found the son clinging to a dock that had broken free and washed up against the foot of the cliff. Fred's body hadn't been recovered for days.

She stopped looking at her watch because time seemed to have stopped. *The Peggotty* crashed along, wave after wave, banging down the long channel of June Lake. Frankie heard her pulse in her ears and the sound of what she realized was her own voice.

"Almost there. Almost there," she chanted. "Good girl, *Peggotty.*"

Then, in the darkness, she saw the unmistakable mass of the headland outside Beauty Bay and knew she'd almost arrived. The relief she felt sent a spike of adrenaline through her body. A wild laugh escaped her throat just as she felt a great thud against the hull. The engine stalled and the boat bounced as Frankie lost her footing and fell, hitting her chin as she went down. She was back on her feet in a flash and saw the deadhead bouncing madly through the wake, lit by the stern light.

Regret descended on her then in an almost physical weight—all she could have done differently. She could have stayed in Hood River and faced Judith or gone to Patrick's. She could have slept in the truck at the marina and waited for daylight. She could have turned around as soon as she'd seen the wall of clouds to the north. She'd been thoughtless and stupid and there was nothing to be done now.

A large wave set rocked the stalled boat sideways, and she struggled to keep her feet. The wind shrieked down the channel, and
Frankie felt her desperation turn to calm. She remembered her father's voice that long-ago day learning to drive.

"Gotta be patient with the gal, Frank. She's older than your old man."

She took a breath and cranked the key. The engine sputtered to
life, and she eased the choke out. Feeling the boat underway, she
wrenched the wheel in the direction she sensed the dock was. It was
completely dark now and she could discern no difference between the
water and the landmass she knew was in front of her. She slowed to
a putter, peering into the blackness, looking for any way marker—
the outline of the store, the pilings, the log boom.

Suddenly the dock flooded with light, and she could see every
inch of Beauty Bay lit up from end to end. She could have cried with
relief as she passed into the shelter of the log boom. Two yards in the
other direction and she'd have been on the rocks.

In the falling rain, she saw Tim Magnusen striding down the
dock. And as a wave set bore her forward, she threw the boat in reverse to slow her momentum. Tim caught the bow and pulled her in.
Her hands shook as she tried to toss him the bowline and dropped it
on the first try. It wasn't funny, but she barked a laugh. She climbed
shakily over the gunnel and tied the stern, never so grateful to be on
dry land.

"Wow! What a ride!" she said, her voice shaking. "Thanks for
catching me!"

Adrenaline coursed through her as she looked at Tim Magnusen
and saw he was furious.

"Jesus Christ, O'Neill! What the hell were you doing out on the
water?" he said.

A wave of cold washed over her scalp. Fear, relief, more fear. Nau-
sea surged through her. She sat down hard and threw up over the
side of the dock. She sat up feeling faint and looked up at Tim. He

had every right to be angry, because a boat in distress was everyone's responsibility. She'd have been furious too.

". . . lucky I saw you out there," Tim was saying. "I came down to check the cover on the boat."

He reached down and helped Frankie to her feet. She straightened up and faced him. She was almost as tall as he was now. She remembered that summer he'd left for college. Christi and her bragging.

"My Tim. He's starting at Yale."

Frankie took a deep breath and started to laugh. Long, loud peals of uncontrollable laughter. She couldn't help it, and the harder she tried to stop the more impossible that became. Tim looked irritated and said since she seemed okay, he was going in. He started to walk away and turned back.

"You're bleeding," he said over his shoulder. "Your chin. Jesus, O'Neill."

Frankie, weak with laughter, waved a hand at him. She pressed the cuff of her sweater to her chin and watched him lope up the dock and down the seawall to his house. Then she reached up and turned off the dock lights. The waterfront plunged back into darkness. The only light came from the Magnusens' house, which looked warm and cheerful in the rainy night. Frankie glanced up toward the cottage, where she could see the faint light of the sleeping porch winking through the trees.

The storm was moving up into the woods, and the wind gusted against her body, damp from the rain. She pulled the canvas cover over *The Peggotty* and checked to make sure the computer was snug in the freight compartment. Then she climbed up to the house on quaking legs. She stripped outside and stood under the hot water of the shower until she stopped shaking.

Inside she dressed and started a fire. She checked on Charlie Crow, who was asleep on the folded towel she'd placed in the tub. She told herself to get to bed. She told herself to make a cup of hot chocolate. But the other voice was still there, tinny and insistent in her ear. After the day she'd had, she deserved a break, a bit of relief. Just two fingers of whiskey to help settle her mind and help her sleep. She pulled on her Dad's jacket and went to the pump house. Reaching up into the rafters, she found the bottle—cool and angular against the skin of her hand and the golden liquid glinting in the soft light of the pump house. She cradled it in her elbow and took it in the house.

The bottle promised so much, like always—comfort, ease, relief. And like always, it failed to deliver. One glass became two and then another half. Then better top that off, and once more. Might as well just finish it off now. For a brief time she felt elated, then a familiar numbness descended. Later the room spun, and she was sick. She didn't know what time it was—no longer night, not quite day. She dragged herself to the kitchen and drank a glass of water. The pounding began in her head, along with the voice again, now telling her what a loser she was for giving in. *"Won't you ever learn?"* it asked.

She leaned against the sink and looked around the little house, overwhelmed with a yawning sense of absence. The photos of her kin hanging on the wall showed everyone smiling at her out of the past. Nearly all of them were gone—long dead or otherwise absent. Frankie recognized then the feeling she'd been trying to name that had dogged her since she arrived. It was as familiar as her own name. It was part of her, her invisible companion. It had been with her for as long as she could remember and always would be. It was loneliness— plain, simple, and complete. She crawled into bed and fell asleep as the wind and the rain battered the dark woods behind the house.

14

DISTRESS CALLS

Species with close physical resemblances are more easily distinguished by voice than plumage, markings, or coloring.

—*G. Gordon's Field Guide to the Birds of the Pacific Northwest*

Composition, at its most practical, is a layering of pieces of musical anatomy. Melody, harmony, timing, phrasing. Before it's plotted out on the staves, it has a kind of physical architecture to it. At the core, there is some mechanical action of pulling the pieces together, a kind of fascia. Then there's the narrative, which has its own construction of verses, bridges, and choruses. All those elements are easily seen on the page by performers when they're looking at a piece for the first time. But the actual emotional interpretation—the thing that excited Anne most—that happened off the page. Yes, a composer could guide the concept with the suggestions offered in the staff—lively, slowly, with feeling—but usually that was just a word or two, not a mandate, not a clear directive. The emotional interpretation came from the performers themselves, guided by the director, who was influenced by the composer. In this way, composition was a collaboration between what was written and what was unwritable—the ephemeral, the elusive, almost magical transmutation of music. Between living singers, a director, and an absent or even dead composer. It was an ongoing conversation that began from a single flash of inspiration that was grounded in a specific moment in time and carried on into the future indefinitely whenever the piece was performed. This creative inter-connectedness is what Anne tried to convey to her students. It all began from the singular moment the composer began. She wanted them to understand how wonderful that could feel—that joy, that spark, the flow of being immersed in the mysterious creative process.

She sat at the patio table and stared at the empty page of her notebook, remembering how she'd explained this to her students again and again. Often, they looked back at her like they had no idea what she was talking about. But how do you actually start? they'd ask. She'd laughed then, which she meant as a sort of playful encour-agement. And now she understood why some of them squirmed and others looked like they'd wanted to smack her. Because for the last year and a half, the blankness of the page in front of her made her feel like she'd never written a single bloody song in her life. That no one ever had. That the very idea was as impossible as trying to fly.

Her head ached and her eyes watered. A head cold on a sunny September day, no less. She leaned back in her chair and looked at Aiden. Lying on the patio in his swimming trunks and Spider-Man T-shirt, he spun a cushion on his slender shins. Earlier Tim had tried to interest him in a swimming lesson, plunging into the lake and thrashing around expertly while Aiden sat in the sand wrapped in a towel. Tim had tried to draw him in with his enthusiasm, but the boy wouldn't budge. As much as Anne wanted him to learn to swim, she didn't blame him. The water was simply too cold. The lake had turned its heart away from summer and it was impossible to con-vince Aiden, or her, otherwise. Yet Tim had persisted.

"It feels great! You'll warm up once you start moving around!"

Anne, laughing, told him his lips were blue.

"You're hypothermic, love! Not thinking clearly."

He'd given up then and gone in for a shower. She watched Aiden in his new game, spinning the pillow a full turn on his knees with his hands, kicking it high in the air, and catching it on his shins. He wore an absorbed and happy look.

Glancing down the seawall toward the dock, she saw the red water-taxi boat pulling away. The driver had been chatting with Frankie for some time and now headed west across the lake. It was too far away to make out her face, but Anne saw Frankie turn and look down the seawall toward the Magnusens' house. Anne thought of the other day, Frankie's curious manner, the baby crow, and her patience with Aiden. She leaned forward and raised a hand, but Frankie had turned away and started up the trail. She wondered what Tim had said to her when he'd helped her land the boat. He'd been cross when he came in the house shaking the rain out of his hair.

"Of course I wasn't rude, Anne," he'd said. "I just told her what she already knew. It was a stupid idea being out on the water in that weather."

When she'd asked Tim about Frankie's family, he'd been vague.

"Fine, I guess. They're reliable, you know. They do good work."

But as neighbors, Anne persisted. As people.

Tim looked annoyed and frowned.

"I don't know. We never hung out much with Frankie and Patrick. Doing different things, I guess. Their grandmother was sweet. She was a tiny little thing. She gave us stuff all the time—jams and things. And their dad!"

He laughed, his face lighting up.

"Funny guy, but Jesus! Trying to repair things with old parts he'd saved. Anything to save a dime or spare a trip down to Mill Three. And that boat!"

He gestured toward the dock.

"It's ancient. Frankie shouldn't be out on the lake alone in that old thing. They should have bought a new one years ago."

Anne listened to him, silently fuming.

"Maybe they couldn't afford one, Tim," she said.

He rolled his eyes. It was an old argument.

"That's not what I meant, Anne."

He backpedaled, but she knew it was exactly what he meant. Though Tim was not overtly materialistic like his siblings, he could never know what it was like to grow up without the comfort of ready cash as Anne had done. As most of her friends had done. She let the matter drop.

Now Tim came out of the house, his hair damp from the shower.

"Feeling any better?" he asked, squeezing her shoulders.

"I'll live. I think I'll have a lie-down if you don't mind."

"Sure. I've got some boat chores. Aiden can help me."

His eyes traveled to the boy lying on the patio, and Anne braced herself. Tim didn't like Aiden's odd games no matter how much they contented him. Spinning, flicking, rocking—he discouraged such things.

"Aiden, put the pillow back, please, and come here."

Anne could hear him fighting to keep the edge out of his voice, and Aiden didn't respond. Spin, spin, flip. Spin, spin, flip. The striped pillow went round and round.

"Aiden, come here, please. Daddy has some chores for you to help with," Anne said.

The boy remained absorbed in his activity as if he were alone, not an arm's length away from the people who loved him most in the world.

"Aiden—" she started, and Tim silenced her with a look that reminded her she'd promised not to interfere. She felt a tightness in her throat as the seconds ticked by. When Tim spoke, his voice had changed, purposely low and casual.

"Well, I guess I'll just have to do it myself," Tim said. "I'll go get the electric drill and the screwdrivers—"

Aiden caught the pillow, popped to his feet, and marched over to his father. Tim laughed, and everything was okay. Saved by the boy's obsession with mechanical things.

As they walked away together, Aiden cradling the extension cord in his wee arms and Tim carrying the toolbox, they looked like a typical father and son, and her heart felt easier. It lightened the weight she felt between Tim and herself, the heaviness they didn't talk about. Ever since her in-laws had insisted on the bloody assessment from the University of Washington, she'd been on edge. Tim tried to convince her that it wasn't a big deal, but the longer they waited for the results, the less inclined she was to believe him. After she and Tim had filled out the long questionnaires, she'd spent weeks that summer in the freezing corridors of the research center while the behavioral specialists had one-on-one sessions with Aiden. Those sessions had seemed interminable but were nothing compared to this excruciating wait.

She went inside and lay on the couch, dozed but could not sleep. She pulled out the novel she'd been reading, but it made her head ache to look at the page. At one point she considered checking on Tim and Aiden at the boat. But no. She'd agreed to this, letting the two of them be on their own, letting Tim try to connect without managing the situation. She'd agreed to those terms, and she knew it was the right thing. Even so, it was hard. Aiden had so rarely been away from her these past months since her leave began.

She thought of Frankie then, and the little crow, and wondered how it was convalescing. She'd hoped Frankie might come by and say hello. As she looked around the carefully curated living room, her eye fell on the coffee-table centerpiece—a collection of perfect seashells and starfish glued to a mirror shaped like an old sailing vessel. Ocean seashells and starfish at a lake house. She was almost certain her mother-in-law had purchased it at Pier 1 in Seattle. Seeing that, she realized that Frankie O'Neill would never drop in on the Magnusen family to pay a neighborly visit. But Anne could go to her.

She pushed herself off the couch and went into the kitchen, pulled out flour, sugar, salt, butter, the mixing bowls, and an apron. What would she make? She thought of the cottage, the warm little room with its low ceilings and crackling fire, the comfortable disorder of the living room and the deep, capable kitchen sink. It reminded her of Gran's place. Irish soda bread, she decided. Simple and nourishing. A nice neighborly offering.

She started a yeast sponge, then measured the flour, whisked in salt, sugar, and soda. She mixed it into a dough, rolled it, and turned it in an oiled bowl to rise. It was a satisfying chore, and she realized her headache had gone. By the time Tim and Aiden came back from the dock—her son first and her husband a few minutes later—the smell of rising dough filled the kitchen.

Aiden scampered past her and clambered into the window seat with his book. She crossed the room and leaned down to kiss him. His hair and clothing held the scent of fresh air.

Tim followed bearing an armful of mail, which he sifted through at the counter.

Anne tried to keep her voice casual.

"Anything interesting?"

"Mostly work stuff. Here's a letter from your mom," he said, passing her a blue airmail envelope. "Junk mail. Oh, and looks like there's something here from UW."

His voice changed slightly when he said that, and Anne shuddered. She watched him open the thin white envelope and pull out a sheet of paper, willing herself not to snatch it out of his hand and read it first or tear it to pieces. She turned toward the oven and slid the bread inside. Tim dropped the letter on the counter.

"Just a notification that they received our questionnaires," he said. "And that they're reviewing Dr. Shelley's data. Probably playing catch-up from summer vacations, I expect."

She could hear Tim trying to keep his voice light, as if it was nothing at all, just a small thing they were waiting for, like a dental appointment. Not some kind of edict that could change their lives completely.

She felt a flare of anger in her belly remembering the questionnaires. The University of Washington Department of Pediatrics had requested that each parent complete one separately. At the time Anne had scoffed that it seemed excessive, but a shadow flickered across Tim's face. That had been the first inkling that they were of different minds about their son's behavior.

Anne had sat down with the forms that very night after Aiden had gone to bed. The sooner this inquest was done, the better, she thought. She'd listed his food preferences and noted that he had no allergies. She detailed his sleep patterns and sleep disruptions, potty training, and documented with pride that he hadn't had an accident since he was two.

The form asked about attachments to routines and objects. She balked at the question, as if attachment were a bad thing. Begrudgingly, she made a note about his storybook that had been a favorite talisman for ages. Every child had special things. She felt like they were trying to catch her out. The questionnaire just got worse from there.

> Please describe behavioral issues such as tantrums, screaming, pushing, hitting (self and others), biting (self and others). Please note any general anxieties and worries (articulated or suggested).
>
> Please explain any episodes that have involved hospitalization of patient or others and use the page below to describe in more detail.
>
> Please note any episodes that have involved social services or law enforcement.

It went on like that for pages and pages.
Sweet Mother of Jesus, she thought.

> What activities does your child enjoy? What people does your child have special relationships with? Does your child

enjoy any favorite games? What activities does your child enjoy doing alone? With others? How does your child behave with others?

"Crikey! On this page they're actually calling him a child! Isn't that lovely?" she said.

Tim kept his eyes on the tennis match he was watching and didn't laugh.

"They're just trying to help, Anne. Maybe try not to take it so personally?"

She bridled then.

"Not take it personally that people think we don't know what's best for our own kid?"

Tim sighed, came to the table, and reached for the forms.

"Why don't you take a break?"

She shook her head.

"I've nearly finished," she said.

What the forms didn't ask, what nobody asked, were things like: Please describe how it feels to be unable to comfort the person you love most in the world. Please describe the depths of your failure as a mother and a human being.

She hadn't read Tim's answers and she didn't know if he'd looked at hers before he mailed them back. That had been weeks ago, and the waiting hung over them. The letter sat on the counter for the rest of the day, and Anne refused to read it or move it. After a while it was gone. She pulled the soda bread out to cool, fed the sourdough starter, then brewed a pot of tea. She took a cup to Tim, who was reading through the stack of mail from work, and he thanked her. She leaned down and kissed him, reminding herself that they were together in this.

Aiden had pulled several CDs down off the shelf. Blessedly not the Streisand collection.

"Want to play some music, love?" Anne asked. "Just not too loud, please."

Aiden clicked the power button and Anne watched him carefully load a CD into the tray—a collection of children's songs. He lowered the volume and scooted close to the speaker.

Mary had a little lamb,
Little lamb, little lamb!
Mary had a little lamb
Whose fleece was white as snow!

She sat at the counter and read the letter from her mother, which was as newsy as ever. With the length of her social commentary, you'd think Margaret Ryan lived in midtown Manhattan and not a small island village off the west coast of Ireland that had two pubs, one church, and a greengrocer. Father and the deacon were at odds over the design of the new baptismal font. Laney McPhee was engaged to be married to that young John from Killybegs, and it looked like it would be a May wedding. Old Thomas Murphy had passed, God rest his soul, which was a shame as there had been plans for his centennial birthday. Lastly, someone had been stealing milk off the doorstep once or twice a week. Margaret had complained to the milkman, James, who'd confessed she wasn't the only one to report such a thing.

I'm of a mind to undertake a stakeout, which your father says is a daft idea. Since he leaves earlier than James arrives, it would fall to me. So don't be surprised if you read about me cracking the village milk thief.

Anne chuckled, imagining her mother sitting in the dark in her dressing gown armed with a broom and a flashlight waiting for milk-stealing hooligans. Probably just a hungry newsboy, she guessed, or her own da just taking the piss.

Aiden had replayed "Mary Had a Little Lamb" and was now starting it for the third time.

"Let's let it play through to the next song, love," she said, and turned back to the letter.

Margaret asked about her job, and Anne's stomach dropped, then further as her mother wondered if she might be coming home that fall. Anne could picture her sitting at the kitchen table, pen in hand, trying to work out how to ask without asking.

Margaret wrote that there was to be a memorial Mass on All Souls' Day at Trinity in November. The O'Faolains were organizing it in recognition of the Good Friday Agreement. She would be happy to meet Anne on the mainland if she was of a mind to go.

Hugs and kisses to my grandson and to yourself. Please give my regards to Tim. All my love, Mam.

Anne put the letter aside. She felt a host of feelings rise in her chest and she pressed them down. She wrapped the soda bread in a clean tea towel and poked her head into the sunroom.

"I'm going to run up to Frankie O'Neill's," she said. "I'll take Aiden with me."

Tim looked up from the binder he was reading.

"That's nice of you to take her something," he said. "You know, when you were asking about her family, I'd forgotten about her dad."

"What about him?" Anne asked.

Tim rubbed his eye with the heel of his hand.

"He died this spring. It was quite sudden, I think."

Anne remembered Frankie's stricken look when Anne had asked her about her family.

"Oh, how terribly sad," she said. "How old was he?"

"Not that old. Maybe fifty-five?" Tim said.

She thought of her own parents and felt a deep pang of home-sickness.

Tim had returned to the document he was reading.

"Right. Well, I'll be back shortly," she said.

Aiden was letting the song repeat again.

Followed her to school one day,
School one day, school one day!

At the suggestion that they go see Miss Frankie and the little crow, he snapped off the CD player and bolted for his shoes.

Maybe all children were predisposed to repetition, she thought as she retied his laces. Did other mothers grind their teeth? She wished she had some good mam friends to ask, but she didn't. Just friendly acquaintances from the daycare.

Aiden flew down the seawall ahead of her, as sure-footed and energetic as a young colt, and Anne found herself humming the inane nursery rhyme. She recalled a day at the Pediatric Clinical Research Center and the child singing down the corridor while she waited for Aiden.

Mary had a little lamb,
Little lamb, little lamb.
Mary had a little lamb
Whose fleece was white as snow.

The voice came through the open door of a room just down the corridor from the waiting area where Anne sat. It was a mournful wee voice—a girl or boy, she couldn't say.

Mary had a little lamb,
Little lamb, little lamb.
Mary had a little lamb
Whose fleece was white as snow.

The wain sang the opening lines over and over and over, failing to move the song forward. Now the child began to cry, and someone closed the door. Anne turned back to her book and tried to concentrate.

A woman came down the hallway toward her pushing a little girl in a wheelchair. The child had dark hair plaited into thick braids and tied with pink ribbons, which matched her sweatshirt and sweatpants. Even her stocking feet were pink. The little girl's shoulders were hunched, and her hands balled into fists, which she waved around. Her face was contorted in a grimace, and she was drooling. The woman stopped and wiped the girl's chin and Anne could see from the resemblance that this must be her daughter. The child moaned and waved one fist and the woman caught it in her hand and kissed it.

Gran's voice echoed in her ear.

"Its own child is bright to the carrion crow."

She immediately felt ashamed thinking that. The woman noticed her looking and smiled. Someone might have thought it was a simple, genuine smile. But most women didn't smile like that, not mothers, and especially not mothers of children who were different, not quite right, strange. Smiles were armor.

Anne smiled back and turned away. She walked to the end of the corridor and bought herself a Diet Coke and a packet of crisps from the vending machine. She was so tired of this waiting area where she'd spent hours that summer.

Hearing tests, vision tests, image recognition tests, the alphabet, color matching, shapes, and numbers. Dr. Shelley and her research assistants had walked Aiden through those as well as dexterity tests and tests that measured his sensitivity to color, light, and sound. Most of this was accomplished through games, and Aiden didn't like to play with others really, so Anne was skeptical about what they might elucidate about her son.

Dr. Shelley had asked Anne to call her Amy, which she'd tried and failed to do, Amy seeming far too informal an address for a doctor. To her credit, Dr. Shelley had listened to Anne's doubts, though she had an air about her as if she'd heard it all. *Parents*, she seemed to be thinking.

"You've got to trust me, Anne, and let me finish the process," she said.

Anne could tell that Dr. Shelley believed wholeheartedly in this "process." So did Tim's parents, who had suggested it in the first place.

"They're the best in the field," her father-in-law said. "Experts in pediatrics. They'll tell you what the boy needs."

It made her want to scream when Tim Senior said things like that. This from a man who had never changed a diaper in his life or toilet trained a wee child or walked the boards in the small hours with a teething baby. Yet he thought he had all the answers.

She watched Aiden climb the steep trail and leap in and out of the little red trolley. He danced toward the door of the cottage and stopped himself, glanced back at Anne, and dutifully rapped on the door. When Anne reached him, Aiden knocked again. It was quiet but for the sound of birds in the trees, the waves splashing below. Her disappointment rose and she realized how much she'd been looking forward to seeing Frankie.

"Looks like Miss Frankie is not home, love. We'll have to say hello another time."

She set the bread on the windowsill where Frankie would see it. Aiden stood in front of the door a moment longer, as if unwilling to accept Frankie's absence. He swung around and skipped past her down the path. She followed him, with love and sorrow tearing at her heart.

Back at the beach, Aiden dutifully zipped on his life preserver, and they wandered down the dock toward the boats. Aiden lay on his belly and peered between the slats of the dock. She sat next to him and leaned her back against the wall of the little building that was the store during the summer. She listened to Aiden humming and the plonking of the boats in the water.

She thought of her mother's letter and the mention of the All

Souls' Day Mass in honor of everyone lost during the long decades
of The Troubles. Of course, she knew about the Mass already because Mrs. O'Faolain had written to her after Easter, right before the
spring concert. She'd asked Anne to please be there if possible. Even
before the invitation, with the Good Friday peace agreement all over
the news, Anne felt herself closing down, moving into a bubble of
silence that grew and grew. She couldn't talk about it. How could she
find words for the inky blackness that bloomed around her? She
woke to it, fell asleep to it, and swam around it all day; like some dark
sea creature, it threatened to pull her under and hold her down. And
then came the night of the spring concert, when she went under.

The college campus had been decorated by students from the the-
ater department to reflect the varied heritages of the graduating se-
niors. Luminarias lined the walkways, their flickering votive candles
turning the brown paper bags into magical way markers. The large
cottonwood tree had been adorned with traditional German *Kerzen*
that flamed in the twilight. Giant papier-mâché puppets from a recent production of *A Midsummer Night's Dream* embraced the lampposts around the courtyard, their large, whimsical faces laughing
and crying. Bright multicolored flags of various countries adorned
the white chairs facing the stage. The evening performance would
highlight the graduating class of 1998, Cornish College of the Arts.

Anne had considered skipping it but couldn't lie to Patrice, who
was her friend as well as the department chair. Trying to explain
seemed harder than simply showing up, keeping to herself, and leaving early. She only had to introduce one student, Melissa Baine.
Lovely Melissa from Vermont had been bright, so hardworking, and
had a natural ear for music and the Irish language. That evening
she'd be singing "Spancil Hill"—an old song by Michael Considine
about an immigrant longing for home. Anne gave a brief introduction and retreated backstage as Melissa stepped into the spotlight.
She looked so young and lovely in her white dress with a eucalyptus
wreath in her dark hair. Every bit the May Day maiden. Her diction

was perfect, her timing, her phrasing, and her interpretation. She brought such life to the old song; it was just brilliant to hear. And in that moment Anne realized with a shock how much Melissa reminded her of her friend Katherine O'Faolain. Katherine who was now lost to her.

Katherine had been invited to Cornish first. But her mam was sick and her father needed her, so Katherine had stayed and Anne had gone in her place. Because she stayed, Katherine was in the north last year to perform on Easter weekend. Katherine was at the outdoor market when a car crashed into the crowd—no accident at all. And Katherine—sweet and funny and loyal and talented, who should have been in Seattle—was dead. Dead a year when that Good Friday peace deal was struck.

Anne had felt that feeling for the first time then, ice water in her veins, the feeling that she was there and not there. The audience applauded and tossed flowers onto the stage at Melissa's feet. The world tipped and a high pitch whined in her left ear. Then Melissa was pulling Anne onstage for an encore, wanting to share the moment with her favorite teacher. It was so generous of her, so kind. She whispered and started to sing. Anne heard the first rising notes of the tune and the beat of the bodhrán drum behind her. She looked out into the twilit audience, their faces distorted by the shadows, and heard Melissa finish the first line in Irish. She turned to Anne, her young face shining, and waited for Anne to take up the verse in English.

> *I am stretched out on your grave*
> *And will lie here forever.*
> *If your hand were in mine,*
> *I'd be sure we could not sever.*
> *My apple tree, my brightness,*
> *It's time we were together.*
> *For I smell of the Earth*
> *And I'm worn by the weather.*

Anne opened her mouth to sing, and it was impossible. The drum kept beating. She saw Melissa's face fall. Melissa turned back to the audience and tried to carry the song. But Anne couldn't hear Melissa over the guttural sound she realized was coming from her own mouth.

Time had bent and folded. She didn't remember anything after that until she was backstage with Patrice. She couldn't have said how much time had passed before Tim arrived, his face creased with worry and Aiden in his pajamas. As Patrice walked them to the car, Anne noticed that the courtyard was dark. The *Kerzen* had been extinguished, the giant puppets lying prone on carts, and the luminarias flickering out.

After that, all the feelings Anne had worked so hard to bury came roaring back. The previous year was a blur of grief, but she'd slogged through the months and clawed her way back to some kind of normal. She truly had been feeling better, until the anniversary of Kat's death, until the letter from Mrs. O'Faolain, until the international news of the peace accord, made her grief erupt all over again. And guilt too, for if Kat had been in Seattle instead of Anne, she'd be alive, wouldn't she?

Following the spring concert, she knew she'd tried everyone's patience to the limit. No surprise Patrice had put her on leave, though she'd been so kind about it.

"It's okay, Anne. I think you just need some time," she'd said.

And then her in-laws had pressed the assessment. Could she blame Tim for going along, with how absent she'd been the year before? She longed to talk to him about it all, but she couldn't. That was a terrible truth; she didn't trust him.

A light rain began to fall, and she pulled her hood over her head. She coaxed Aiden to his feet, and they walked back down the dock as the rain began to fall harder, darkening the air and turning the sand gray. She could see the lights on in the big house at the far end.

Aiden ran ahead of her toward Tim, who was standing on the patio with beach towels.

Tim draped a towel around Aiden's shoulders but did not try to hug him or pick him up. They'd both surrendered that sweet closeness after Christi's birthday. That bloody awful party. A knot rose in her throat.

Family, like composition, was a layering of parts. It had so many planes in its anatomy: responsibility, obligation, love, longing, fear, hope. But what was the fascia that pulled it all together? That knowledge was illusive, immaterial, and yet so imperative. The emotional interpretation was up to the family itself. Yet there was no guidance in this, no helpful notes in the staff. Nobody could tell you how to fix the errors in the composition of your singular family, your partnership, your marriage. Anne and Tim were the composers, performers, and conductors all in one. Their success or failure was in their own hands. He turned to her, expectant, and she searched his face for some sign of assurance, some indication that he was worried too about how to move forward. That whatever happened next, they would be in it together.

Tim held out a towel, and she accepted it, though she was hardly wet at all, because it was what he had to offer.

15

IMMATURE ALERT

Mimicry is well documented in captive birds. However, many wild songbirds also employ imitation in composing songs and calls.

—*G. Gordon's Field Guide to the Birds of the Pacific Northwest*

*Why, Mary loves the lamb, you know. The lamb, you know, the
    lamb, you know.*
Why, Mary loves the lamb, you know the teacher did reply.
Mary loves the lamb, you know.
Mary loves the baby crow.
Once upon a time there was a baby crow. The baby crow
    had a mama and a daddy.
The mama loved the little crow so much so much. The
    daddy loved the little crow so much so much.
Daddy loves you so much. Daddy loves you.
No, thank you, Mama! No, thank you! Too much too much
    too much!
Daddy loves you, little crow.

16

THE MURDER

How unrecognizable our forests, fields, wetlands, and coastlines would be without the feathered creatures that inhabit them and have become so dear to us.

—*G. Gordon's Field Guide to the Birds of the Pacific Northwest*

The crows were gathering up in the woods. Frankie could hear them calling to each other in the waning dark. As the shoulder of dawn pulled away from the fingers of night and moved upward over the hillside, she rolled over to listen. Their voices drifted down through the woods on a breeze that skimmed her bare legs.

Frankie had turned seven that spring, and for as long as she could remember, she'd loved the birds that lived in the forest above the lake. Crows were among those she heard most often, and their yawping was especially noticeable this time of year, this liminal in-between season of not summer and not quite fall. But this morning their chatter was different from the usual raucous calling. There was an urgency in it. Something was the matter, something important had happened, and everybody needed to pay attention. That's what the crows were exclaiming to each other through the trees.

She sat up, shivering in the morning chill, and climbed out of bed. She pulled on her sweatshirt and looked over at the sleeping form of her big brother, then slipped out the screen door. She walked quickly into the trees, her bare feet finding the trail in the near dark. The troubled voices of the crows increased as she neared the meadow, and she climbed quietly into the bird blind. If she'd been a grown-up or a child less at ease in the woods, what she saw next might have frightened her. But what Frankie saw felt like a wild, beautiful secret the woods offered up for her keeping.

More than one hundred crows perched on the low branches of blushing vine maples and feathery tamaracks, their ebony heads poking out as they called to each other. A dozen or more flew across the expanse of the clearing and back. They alighted on the ground in pairs and stalked in a close circle.

Frankie peered into the center of the meadow for a rabbit or deer carcass. But these crows were not quarreling over any prize. Instead, she saw the body of a single crow lying prone with its twiggy feet poking in the air. The crows took turns descending from the trees, pacing the grass near the fallen crow, and flying back up to roost in the branches. The black, jostling bodies crowded the trees ringing the meadow. Their voices rose and fell together in a sad and worrying way. Their cawing overlapped in a loop of call and response, the sound surging to a high point and then dropping as the birds landed and left in a regular rhythm. It was like they were paying their respects or saying goodbye. That's what it looked like to her child's eye. The crows were having a funeral.

Frankie didn't know how long she knelt in the bird blind watching, but eventually something shifted. A message circulated, a change of mood. The crows began to rise into the sky over the meadow. The clamoring and calling increased as the birds gathered in a swirling, dark cloud of purposeful motion. They spun in a wide, bawdy circle and then disappeared over the pines into the high dark forest, leaving a silence in their wake.

Frankie climbed down out of the blind and crossed to the body of the dead crow. She bent down and stroked the glossy wing with one finger. A single feather came free of the bent wing, and she tucked it in her sweatshirt pocket. She wondered if she should bury the bird and decided to let the woods reclaim it. It wasn't her place to interfere. She straightened up and looked at it one last time before turning to walk back to the cottage.

She never told anyone about what happened next. It seemed like a secret gift, the first important thing that had ever happened to her. When everything else unraveled, it was there. She kept it tucked away in her heart, like that feather in her pocket, along with the morning sunlight streaming through the understory, the wind in the trees, and the stillness in the meadow.

As she began to walk back down the hill toward the cottage, she heard the whistle of wind in feathers. She glanced behind her and saw a black shape winging toward her. It was a large crow, the largest she'd ever seen, but that might have been because it was the closest she'd ever been to a crow. The bird seemed to slow its flight. It hovered above her, and its bright black eye bore down into Frankie's blue one.

"*I see you there*," the crow seemed to say. "*Now you belong to us.*"

And that changed everything forever.

Frankie poured a second cup of coffee, willing the caffeine to quiet the banging in her head. She'd awoken with a sour mouth, dry eyes, and pounding temples. Then the shame descended—just one drink had become the rest of the bottle, a mess in the kitchen, shattered glass on the hearth. As she'd cleaned up, the voice in her head clucked its tongue and scolded her for such weakness—that she couldn't have just one. That other people could handle their alcohol. By midmorning the voice had quieted and retreated to the dark corners of her mind. She felt well enough to work. Work, as always, was a helpful distraction, if not a solution.

Charlie Crow was muttering in a contented tone, having just eaten. From her seat at the table Frankie could see him in the bathtub preening himself, running his shiny beak through the feathers of his back and tail and fluffing his still-downy breast. She listened a while longer, then scratched a description in her notebook under the column she'd begun marked "Vocalizations."

She'd kept taking notes over the course of his convalescence out of habit. Physical appearance, water intake, calories consumed, sleep, and overall demeanor. And, as she was wont to do, she found herself cataloging the sounds. Several were easily discernible, like the begging and hunger calls. Those were recognizable by their cessation when she fed him. Occasionally he honked out what she figured was a contact call, trying to connect with his crow family. He did that less often now, and she was anxious to get him back to the woods before he stopped calling for them altogether. There were the whispering noises he made in his sleep, and her favorite, the contented churring he made whenever she held him or smoothed his feathers. She did that when she picked him up to examine his healing leg, knowing she shouldn't handle him any more than absolutely necessary.

Her interest in crow vocalizations had begun the summer before when she'd worked briefly with Dr. John Marzluff. Her Mount Rainier trip had been delayed while the undergrads on her field team assembled their paperwork, so Dr. Grant had loaned her out to Marzluff for a week. She was happy for the distraction because she never knew what to do with herself when she wasn't working. That would have been the time to hang out with friends, she thought wryly, if she had any.

Marzluff's research was focused on corvids and their ability to identify human faces. The experiments had transpired like this: Marzluff and his students donned caveman masks and captured and banded several crows near the UW arboretum. They released them and then returned to the scene of the crime later to see if any crows remembered them. His research showed that the crows remembered the caveman masks and raised an alarm whenever they appeared. Moreover, Marzluff had shown that crows could teach other crows to

beware of certain people. For though no additional crows were captured or banded by mask-wearing researchers, the arboretum crows
continued to voice alarm whenever the mask-wearing researchers
appeared—weeks, months, or even years later. The story was passed
from crow to crow until their numbers had far surpassed the original
crows that had been caught and banded. And word spread. By the
time Frankie helped Dr. Marzluff that past summer, alarm calls had
been documented all over the campus.

Frankie had only been obligated to help for a week, but she'd
become fascinated by the ideas at play, especially after witnessing the
crows furiously dive-bomb the mask-wearing researchers. After a
couple of weeks reviewing Marzluff's data, Frankie developed her
own question: What if the crows weren't just voicing a general alarm
call? What if they had developed a specific caveman alarm? Marzluff
had encouraged her to pursue the idea.

"Just don't tell Dr. Grant until you've got something solid," he
said with a wink.

Marzluff was a generous scientist. He gave Frankie copies of recordings from his studies and a stack of research papers on corvids.
Frankie hadn't looked at any of it since last year, but after Charlie
arrived, she pulled it all out and waded back into the world of crows.

Now she flipped through an article by Dwight Chamberlain, who'd
first investigated the communication among *Corvus brachyrhynchos* in
his seminal paper in the 1970s. A young researcher at the time,
Chamberlain recounted how he'd tested the calls with speakers
mounted on the ski rack of a car. In his first study, he'd identified more
than twenty-three distinct calls: assembly, scolding, alert, dispersal,
squalling, moribund, threat, immature hunger, contact, announcement, duet, courtship, juvenile, contentment, rattling, wow-wow,
carr-carr, whisper, coo, wah-hoo, screams, mimicry, and interspecific
response to distress calls.

Frankie thought of the churring sound Charlie made and wondered if that was a contentment call. Of course, it could be something

else, something Chamberlain hadn't documented. As he'd written in that study, "These vocalizations are not all the sounds of the common crow known to the authors or other workers. The vocal repertoire of the common crow shows considerable diversification and specialization in relation to behavior patterns concerned with flocks and with predators."

The Popsicle stick clicked against the tub as Charlie Crow puttered back and forth. He flapped his wings mightily and his head rose above the edge of the tub. Frankie knew it was time to release him back into the woods to reunite with his parents. It had been a welcome distraction, tending to the little bird, but a distraction no less. A distraction. She sighed, propped her elbows on the table, and folded her hands under her chin. That's what Dr. Grant had said in January.

"It's a distraction, O'Neill," he'd said, drawing a line through a page of her thesis, and then another. "Just take out this little section about communication and use the data from our 1994 study, okay?"

The problem was that the "little section" was the heart of her work, her own research. What he called a distraction was the only part that was not a rehashing of her advisor's well-worn research on northern spotted owls. The look on his face when she resisted, that she dared to challenge him! Faithful Frankie, Reliable O'Neill, "the darling of Davis Grant's lab," they'd called her. She winced remembering that.

A sudden banging made her jump. The back door rattled on its hinges under a barrage of knocking, and Charlie Crow squawked in alarm. Frankie saw the top of Aiden's curly head through the window and rose, laughing, to open the door. He stood on the step looking like a miniature pirate in his black-and-white striped shirt, cargo shorts, and red curls standing up at a rakish angle.

"Hey, Aiden," she said.

He waited, his gaze trained on the interior of the cottage. She looked past him for Anne but didn't see her.

"Would you like to—"

Before she could finish, the boy had bolted into the house, tucked his little shoes inside the door, and sailed across the room. His small hand grazed the bottom of the barometer as he passed, then he touched the cushions of each armchair as he arrived at the couch. He paused there, hunching his shoulders as he paged through the dog-eared bird book. He came back around the couch then and stood uncertainly, shifting his weight from side to side and looking toward the bathroom, where Frankie could hear Charlie chuckling in the tub.

"Charlie Crow has just eaten. Want to say hello?" she asked.

Aiden glanced toward her, his gaze hitting her knees, and moved toward the bathroom. Frankie joined him and knelt next to the bathtub.

"Be very quiet and watch, okay? I'm going to check his leg now."

The little bird hobble-hopped away and back, giving a pert *"Wook!"* Charlie Crow looked at Aiden, who curled his hands over the side of the tub and watched. Frankie, talking softly, cupped the crow's soft body in both hands, lifted it, and held it in the crook of her arm, smoothing feathers into place. She turned it carefully and examined the splinted leg. She'd noticed the crow tugging at the tape the day before and saw it was nearly worn through. She gently pulled it free, discarded the splint, and set the fledgling in the bottom of the tub. The little bird cawed brazenly, flapped, and strutted about. Aiden watched closely.

"*Eeeeh. Eeeeh. Eeeeh,*" the bird muttered.

"Looks like it's time to let this little guy go find his folks. Want to help me?"

She swaddled the bird in a towel and waited for Aiden to pull his shoes on and open the door for her. In the sunlit clearing behind the house, she set the little bird down in the shelter of the ferns where she'd first seen it.

"You go find your folks, now, Charlie bird," she said, stepping back.

The little crow fluffed its feathers vigorously and paced back and forth. It looked at Frankie and then opened its beak and vocalized up at her. It was a funny, almost plaintive sound.

"*Coo-coo-wook!*"

"Go call your family, little fella," she said.

Gazing at her, the bird repeated the cry and then hopped deeper into the woods. Frankie soon lost sight of it.

"Now we just hope he finds his folks," she said to Aiden, and glanced toward the top of the trail. There was still no sign of Anne.

"Speaking of which, I think I'd better walk you home, you little vagabond."

The boy tapped the trolley with one small hand as he passed it and skipped down the trail. Frankie felt cheered at the thought of seeing Anne. She'd been hoping for another interruption from the neighbors, she realized. So much for privacy and guarding my territory, she thought.

Her heart sank when she saw Tim Magnusen standing on the seawall. Aiden ran toward his father and stopped just short of him. Tim crouched low, and Frankie couldn't hear what he said, but he wasn't smiling. Tim stood and held out a small life jacket with Snoopy dancing across the back. The boy slipped it on and ran down the beach without a backward glance. Tim leaned over and picked up a cordless drill before he noticed Frankie. His smile was polite but mechanical. She cringed, remembering their encounter on the dock, and raised a hand in greeting as she walked toward him. Her headache returned and her temples began to throb.

"Hey, Frankie," he said as she reached the seawall.

"Hi, Tim," she said. "Thanks for helping me land the other night. It was stupid of me to be out on the water in that weather. I should have—"

Tim waved a hand magnanimously, interrupting her.

"Don't worry about it. We've all done it—gunning down the lake from the marina. Crystal and her sorority sisters nearly ran the boat aground more than once when we were in college."

Frankie bristled. She wanted to be grateful, but he sounded so pompous, and she didn't like being compared to his irresponsible sister and her spoiled friends.

"Sure," she said shortly.

"So, how have you been? How's UW?" Tim asked, turning the drill in his hands and looking at the bottom.

Frankie never knew how to answer questions like that. People weren't really asking what they were asking. They were just—what? Just making some sound to fill the space. Some sort of contact call? What would he say if she told him the truth? That it was a big fucking mess? She realized Tim was staring at her, waiting for her to respond. She shifted her weight and crossed her arms.

"Good, yeah. Just fine, thanks. I thought I should make sure you knew where Aiden was."

She should have asked him the same meaningless questions, she knew. But she couldn't make herself do it, and now she'd accelerated the conversation, which made things more uncomfortable. A look crossed his face—embarrassment, she decided.

"He was up at your place again? Thanks for the other day, by the way. We appreciate it."

But he didn't sound appreciative. He sounded irritated. She looked at the drill.

"Boat chores?" she asked.

His smile was strained.

"Endless, right? I'm installing a new set of nav lights Dad ordered, but I think this drill is dead. I'll have to get a new one when I run into town."

He clicked the switch on and off as if to convince her that it was broken. Frankie could see that the battery was not in place. She held out her hand and he passed it to her, watched her open it up, reverse the battery position, and snap it back together. She turned it on, and the motor whirred.

"All the money in the world can't buy common sense," her father would say.

Tim flushed as she handed it back and gave a forced laugh but did not thank her.

"Well, that's one thing off the list! Things are sort of a mess at the house too. Crystal was up here last with her boyfriend. She promised to take care of all the seasonal chores. But I think she figured she'd just pawn it all off on your dad."

Frankie blinked and felt ice water flooding her veins. Tim flushed, looked up at the cottage and then back to her.

"Sorry, I didn't . . ." He trailed off. "I'm really sorry about your dad, Frankie. Jerry just told me the other day."

He reached toward her then. To what? Put a hand on her forearm or grasp her shoulder? She didn't wait to find out. She simply wheeled around and walked away from him and whatever he was saying— some apology or trite condolence or who knew what. She knew it was rude or weird, but she didn't care.

She climbed the hill swiftly and passed the house. Her feet pushed against the damp earth of the path and the growing sense of helplessness that threatened to swallow her. She kept climbing and the cool air raised gooseflesh on her arms. She passed the bird blind and the sunny meadow with its tangle of wildflowers and grasses going to seed. She remembered that long-ago day with the crows and their funeral. That morning she was excited to tell her dad, but she hadn't told him. There were so many things she hadn't told him. And now it was too late to tell him anything. Her heart ached and all she could think was that he wasn't there. Never would be there again.

She kept climbing and lost track of time, hearing her pulse in her ears. She looked up and saw the top of the Lightning Tree, that huge cedar that towered above the rest of the shaggy woods. She kept climbing, and when she reached the top of the hill, she walked toward it, taking in the scorched scar where lightning had struck the tree, splitting it from the ground upward. She leaned her head against the red trunk and breathed in the smell of warm cedar, sweet pine needles, and the petrichor of an approaching storm.

The air grew cold and humid, but she didn't feel it. She was cracked wide open like the tree. She only felt her grief colliding with the dam of her heart. It was unwieldy and untrustworthy, a wild and raging thing inside her. She didn't know how to manage it or how to bear it.

Her anguish washed over her in great waves, and she stepped inside the hollowed-out core of the tree. She sat down and leaned against the trunk, breathing in the pungent cedar, the scent of rain and damp earth. She recalled one rainy summer evening years ago sitting around the stove with her parents and Patrick. Jack told them about a huge storm over the lake when he was a little boy and seeing lightning flash high on the hill. Afterward he and his sister climbed up to the big tree and found it still smoking from the lightning strike. It had become his special place then, though his sister thought it was too far to climb.

In the dim light, she reached up and found the niche Jack had hollowed in the tree's interior. As a boy he'd kept a collection of special things there—army men, arrowheads, bright blue robins' eggshells. Frankie had struggled to imagine her father as a child, but she could see him now, a small boy tucking his treasures away for safekeeping. She pulled out a snail shell. Then her fingers found a marble. She held it up and recognized the cloudy blue glass bead that had been her father's favorite as a boy. He'd thought of it as a tiny version of the earth, he'd said.

"The world in my pocket and me in charge of keeping it safe."

She loved that idea of her impish boy father. And for a minute it felt like he was there with her, sitting shoulder to shoulder in the great old tree, still standing despite the hit it had taken. She closed her eyes and listened to her own breath and felt her heart slow.

She thought of Jack's funeral then. Judith standing next to her in the dim light of the cold church as Father Brash blessed the coffin. Patrick's eulogy. Dean Anderson driving them to the cemetery behind the hearse. The bright April sunshine, which seemed incongruous with the fact that they were burying her father. Judith was so stoic through it all, with Patrick holding her arm. Father Brash said the prayer of interment and a brisk wind stirred the daffodils someone had planted on an adjacent grave. Then, after they had lowered the coffin, that awful coffin Frankie was sure Jack wouldn't have wanted, Judith and Patrick had left without her. Their neighbors, the Nilssens, had driven them home. Later Patrick explained that they thought she had a ride with Dean, but Dean had taken Father Brash back to the rectory. Frankie had wanted a moment alone by the grave to say goodbye, and when she reached the parking lot, everyone had gone.

She stood alone watching a flock of migrating cedar waxwings flutter about the small pond. After a while, she noticed Hank standing next to her. Big, quiet, gentle Hank.

Hank Hansen had worked for her grandfather, Ray, when he was a young man and Jack was a boy. Hank had emigrated from Denmark after World War II and worked his way west with the railroad. How he landed in Hood River was one of many mysteries about the big quiet man. Hank didn't talk about himself much. But he was a fixture in their lives—kind and comforting. Some of Frankie's first memories were of perching on his lap, leaning against his thick cotton work shirt, which smelled pleasantly of pipe tobacco and soap. At Sunday dinners and holidays throughout her childhood, Hank played endless hands of Go Fish and Crazy Eights with her and Patrick. And in the drowsy hour after dinner when they all sat around the TV, Frankie would crawl up next to him, poke her thumb in her mouth, and rub his shirt cuff between her small fingers. By the time she was in school, Judith had a part-time job at the credit union, so Frankie would do her homework at the tavern before it got busy.

Hank would sit next to her doing a crossword puzzle. As she'd grown older, Hank always wanted to hear about what she was learning in her science classes, especially biology. Unlike the rest of The Irregulars, he never teased her about boyfriends. He was her pal, her ally, her big bear of a friend.

And there he was, reliable as ever when everyone else had forgotten about her. Hank drove her home and hummed along to the radio, not expecting her to talk. When he pulled up at the house, she saw people milling around in the small yard: Deacon Cobb, crabby Mrs. Safer, her mother's real estate colleagues, and nosy Nancy Gates. She couldn't get out of the car.

"Can I go with you? Please, Hank."

He glanced toward the house and back at Frankie.

"Sure, kid," he said, and they drove downtown.

As soon as they walked through the door of the River City Saloon, she felt better. There they were—Clarence, Maxine, Old Joe, Billy, and Nils. The regulars who liked to call themselves The Irregulars. Most of them had been at the funeral, but they'd never have felt welcome at Judith's house. They'd have their own wake. They had loved her father so much, and she felt seen by them. She sat in the familiar room while a group of musicians played the music Jack had loved—old Irish ballads, bluegrass songs, fiddle tunes. The windows steamed up and ran with condensation as everyone told stories, toasted Jack O'Neill, and wept openly at his loss.

Frankie had grown up with these people. Those school-day afternoons she sat at the bar listening to them talk and on weekends watched college basketball with them. As she grew older, she shared their pitchers of beer and memorized their stories, their jokes, their tall tales. They'd cheered her on when she left for UW and were all proud of her. And now they wanted to comfort her, wanted to help her bear this terrible loss. She knew they were trying to be kind, buying her round after round. It wasn't their fault, or Hank's fault, or anyone's fault but her own that she kept picking up the glass that someone put in front of her. She didn't remember Patrick coming to get her, or Hank helping him get her in the car. She did remember waking up on the bathroom floor of her childhood home and her mother standing in the doorway in her robe. Judith hadn't said a word, but Frankie knew what she was thinking.

"Just like your father."

Frankie had wanted to apologize, to try to explain. *"It's not like that, Mom,"* she wanted to say. *"I don't let it get away from me."* But Judith was gone when Frankie awoke late the next day, queasy, head pounding, and burning with shame. She'd left for Seattle and hadn't been back since. She'd called once or twice, but Judith hadn't been home, and she hadn't left a message. She didn't know what to say.

Thick thunderheads passed overhead and moved east toward the Yakama Nation. Frankie stood and stepped out of the Lightning Tree and rested a hand on the scorched trunk. As she walked down the hill, fingers of sunlight broke through the understory. She paused by the woodshed and peered into the ferns, but there was no sign of Charlie Crow. On the windowsill, she found a loaf of bread, still warm, and knew Anne must have come by.

She took the bread inside and stood in the kitchen looking around the familiar room and felt a terrible sense of absence. She missed her father and her grandparents. She missed her mother, who seemed lost to her. She missed Hank, whom she hadn't seen since that awful night. She missed the little fledgling who'd been such a comfort. The feeling threatened to overwhelm her, but then she remembered the one thing that she could count on—work. She was an O'Neill, and O'Neills knew how to work.

She spent the next two days splitting, limbing, and cutting up the dozen or so big trees she'd cleared off the trail. Once they were manageable in size, she'd rolled them down to the platform in front of the woodpile, split them, and stacked them. The rhythm of the work soothed her and blocked out other thoughts. At the end of the second day, she was exhausted but calmer. Her hands and arms ached from the effort and her clothes were covered in pitch and dirt.

Dusk had fallen by the time she put her tools away. She heard the keen of the osprey and the far-off call of the crows. She was almost expecting them when they arrived—three dark shapes fluttering down out of the trees in the fading light. Charlie Crow and his crow parents landed in the clearing and gazed up at her. One of the parents cawed three contact calls, and the other answered.

"*Karr! Karr! Karr!*"

Charlie looked back at them and then hopped toward her, stopped, and made that little plaintive cry from before.

"*Coo-coo-wook*," he called.

"Hey there, little guy," Frankie said softly.

She sat on the bench outside the back door and watched them. Charlie looked good and he had a fine-looking family too. She pulled a bag of peanuts down from the windowsill and tossed a handful toward the birds. None of them seemed interested.

Charlie Crow hopped close to the smaller adult with a lowered head, which Frankie knew was a request for allopreening. The adult complied, running its beak down the back of Charlie's head, smoothing feathers. The larger adult strode back and forth in front of them, chuckling and murmuring, eyeing Frankie and occasionally giving a loud "*Karr!*" They carried on like that for several minutes. And then the larger crow seemed to decide the show was over. It sounded an alert and flapped away. The smaller adult followed. Charlie Crow looked back at Frankie and then followed them into the thick, dark woods.

Frankie was entranced. It was almost as if the adult birds were presenting the young crow to her. The idea rang a bell, and she went inside to the stack of studies Marzluff had given her. She found the reference—an abstract from a researcher at the University of Alaska about an encounter with an injured raven.

"After tagging and releasing the young raven and confirming that it had rejoined its parents, we noted that the family returned to the release site daily for the next three weeks. They expressed no interest in the food we offered but continued to return to the viewing platform day after day. They showed no fear of the graduate students who'd rescued the little bird. Our best guess is that the parents wanted us to know the young raven had survived. If we didn't know better, we'd say they were trying to thank us."

Frankie reread the study as night fell across the woods and blackened the lake below. She heard a chorus of crickets rise and the voice of a lone tree frog. A pair of owls called back and forth to each other, and coyotes sang on the ridgeline. Frankie sat up late into the night listening to the music of the nocturnal creatures, feeling very human and very alone but not unhappy and no longer quite so lonely.

17

THREAT CALL

Birds are ruled by a handful of basic instincts—hunger,
socialization, and reproduction, but also important is the
impulse to attack or flee.

—G. Gordon's Field Guide to the Birds of the Pacific Northwest

The card from Christi was a thick, expensive paper stock—an elegant ivory etched with scarlet, ochre, and golden leaves of fall. Within the border of leaves was Yeats's poem "The Wild Swans at Coole," which began, "The trees are in their autumn beauty / The woodland paths are dry / Under the October twilight the water / Mirrors a still sky."

Everything about the card was perfect—a lovely message from a thoughtful mother-in-law that was not only seasonally appropriate but also offered a nod to Anne's home country by choice of poet. It was as if Christi had tried to think of every possible way to be considerate, attentive to detail, and conscientious. It made Anne want to scream.

Inside the card was a message in Christi's flawless cursive inquiring after Anne's health and her daily activities. She didn't mention Tim, and Anne knew she wrote to him separately and frequently. There was something about that that bothered her. But why should it? She didn't show Tim letters from home, did she? Margaret's pages of newsy gossip about the island and Gran's short, concise notes. Or maybe she'd shown him, but he hadn't seemed interested?

Anne trained her eyes back to the card. Christi quickly got to the point of her missive. There was ever a point with Christi.

"We're planning the annual fall gala to coincide with Halloween this year in the great Italian tradition of the masquerade ball. We think the power brokers of Seattle deserve this kind of cultural showcase."

Anne read the rest and snorted.

"Your mother really is one of a kind," she said.

Tim looked up from the instruction manual he said was for a bilge pump.

"Let me guess. The gala? What—you don't relish the idea of 'celebrating the royalty of the New World with the spirit of the Old'?"

They laughed and it felt like old times. Once more, they were coconspirators against Christi's elaborate plans, almost like disobedient children. She tapped the card on the counter.

"Ever gracious, your mother wants to represent my home country. She asked me to let her know who the most famous king and queen of Ireland are so she can get appropriate costumes for us."

"Oh no," Tim said, and put his hands over his face.

"Yes, she really did."

It was no surprise that Christi failed to understand that there had been no royalty in Ireland since Anne's country had freed itself from the yoke of British monarchy less than one hundred years ago.

"Well," Tim said. "She did always say she went to college to get an MRS degree."

Christi did not mention Aiden, which should have made Anne happy, but it made her anxious instead. She pushed the thought away.

"I'll tell her Queen Medb and High King Brian Boru. Let her figure that one out."

During her years of acquaintance with Christi Magnusen, Anne had acquired considerable armor. It had surprised her at first, the need for defense. In her own small family, people spoke their minds and weren't afraid to disagree. It had taken her some time to under-stand that what the Ryan family viewed as honest and direct, the Magnusens considered coarse.

Anne recalled her lunch with Christi in June, during which she had, admittedly, behaved coarsely. She hadn't wanted to go, but Christi wouldn't take no for an answer, insisting on a ladies' lunch. When Anne arrived at Anthony's on Lake Union, Tim's sister, Crys-tal, was nowhere in sight.

"Just the two of us," Christi said, smiling and patting the chair next to her.

Christi looked effortlessly elegant in a sky-blue linen tunic over black capri pants and white slingback heels. Anne had never seen her without full makeup. Even at the lake, Christi rose hours before ev-eryone else to do a workout video, shower, and "put on her face," as she said. Her timelessly blond hair conveyed a dedication to a salon schedule that never varied, and her skin was luminous despite years on the tennis court and boating with her husband. Anne sat down feeling frumpy in her jeans and striped T-shirt.

Christi had ordered a bottle of chardonnay, and Anne accepted a glass to be polite. Wine didn't agree with her during the day, but with Christi, she often found herself saying yes to things she didn't want to do because it was easier than arguing every point.

She listened as Christi chronicled her detailed plans for remodel-ing the guest wing. The carpet would just have to go, obviously. And she was tearing out the tile in the shower and installing a new glass door. The light fixtures would be updated, and the towel bars would need to be replaced to match. She was looking at heated towel bars, which cost a fortune, but what could you do, she asked, turning her palms up as if she were at the mercy of contractors and not her own whims.

Anne loathed this kind of small talk and had no experience to of-fer in return. She and Tim lived in a perfectly satisfactory two-bedroom apartment in Fremont and had changed nothing since they moved in. Her parents lived in the house her father had been born in, which hadn't been so much as repainted in the nearly thirty years since Anne herself had been alive. The interior had suffered considerably over the years, but no one paid any mind. A gouge in the plaster could be covered with a picture, and a scratch on the wooden floor disappeared under a well-placed rug. If Christi could see the state of it! The idea made Anne want to laugh.

She was so tense that it was almost a relief when Christi turned the subject to Aiden, which Anne suspected was the real reason for the lunch. She began by asking about his daycare and if they were thinking about kindergarten programs yet.

Anne shook her head.

"We're going to wait at least another year on kinder. He'll be going back to Sunflower this fall and then . . . we'll see. He's comfortable there," she said.

Christi frowned.

"Are you sure you want to do that? I mean, we all know you've had a hard time this past year, Anne. Losing your friend. But I think your family needs you to focus now."

Anne flushed and tried to keep the anger out of her voice.

"Thank you for your concern, but we're doing just fine, Christi."

Christi looked thoughtful and leaned toward her.

"You're such a devoted mother and he's a darling, Anne. But if I may offer a bit of advice, mom to mom?"

She didn't wait for any sign of acquiescence but carried on saying that it was clear that Aiden was a headstrong and willful boy. She should know! Tim and Mark had been the same. But Anne just needed to take him in hand.

"You're his mom, Anne. Not his friend," Christi said, gesturing with her glass. "That's the problem with your generation, you know. You want your kids to like you. In my time discipline was a cornerstone."

Anne nodded noncommittally. She didn't agree but she didn't want to argue. She just wanted to get through lunch.

"What that boy needs is a firm spanking every once in a while. That would straighten him out. Now, I probably should have told you this when it happened," Christi said, pouring herself more wine. "Last time you were at the house, I caught him looking through my records without asking and I spanked his little bottom."

Anne flushed and her breath caught in her throat.

"Christi, Aiden knows he needs to ask permission first, but it's not okay—"

"I know, I know. I told him that's why I was spanking him," Christi interrupted. "Grandma's house and Grandma's rules. That's what I'm saying, you need to be firmer with him. Take charge!"

Anne shook her head and her voice quavered.

"No, Christi. Tim and I have been very clear with you that we do not believe in physical punishment. It's not for you to decide that."

Christi laughed and waved a hand at her.

"Oh, Anne! I think I know a bit about parenting! I've raised three of my own. And look at them—all successful young people."

"And they're all terrified of you," Anne wanted to say. *"They just want you to love them."*

"You'll thank me someday. I'm sure your mother would do the same."

Her mother would do no such thing, Anne knew. And Margaret Ryan would eat this woman's head off for laying a finger on her grandson. Heat rose in her chest and neck.

"Christi. With respect, you have no right—" Anne started.

"Please," Christi interrupted. "I mean, if you can't handle just one, how do you think you'll be able to manage when you have one or two more?"

Anne told Christi that was between Tim and her and nobody else's business, thank you very much.

"Of course it's our business, dear," Christi scoffed. "Tim works for us, and we support you. Magnusen Media is a family company and how your family grows is absolutely our business. Though I do have to thank you for being thoughtful with your family planning. When Tim first met you, I said to his father, 'Look out! She's Irish and they breed like rabbits!'"

Anne jerked to her feet and her wineglass toppled. She leaned over Christi and told her in no uncertain terms that what she didn't know about the Irish could fill the bloody halls of Parliament. Furthermore, the activity of her uterus was nobody's damn business but her own. And lastly, that if she knew what was good for her, she would keep her bloody hands off her grandson.

She stormed across the patio banging into chairs as she went and aware that she was being stared at. She was also aware by the time she reached the sidewalk that she'd made a terrible mistake. Christi had pushed all the right buttons, hadn't she? Anne felt like she'd played into some kind of trap. Soon thereafter, Christi and Tim Senior had brought up the idea of the assessment at UW.

"The boy is a challenge," her father-in-law had said. "Seems like you kids could use a little help, especially with both of you working."

It was no secret that Tim Senior disapproved of Anne's career. Children needed their mothers, he was certain. Why was it always the men who were experts on mothering? she wondered.

Tim had risen briefly to her defense.

"Anne's career is as important to her as mine is to me, Dad," he'd said.

Anne squeezed his hand under the table. Then her father-in-law, chuckling, said surely it wasn't as financially important, and Tim hadn't said anything.

Now Anne pushed the card aside, resolving to answer it later.

Tim stood at the door zipping up Aiden's sweatshirt.

"We're going to finish some boat chores. See you in a bit."

She wanted to go with them, but Tim's face reminded her that she'd agreed not to hover.

"Crack on, then. Good man helping your daddy," Anne said, and blew a kiss.

They walked away together, Aiden trying to match his father's stride. Frankie appeared at the head of the dock and stopped to talk with Tim. Anne had been hoping to see their intriguing neighbor again and was pleased to see her continue toward the house. At the door, she looked shy and held up two small jars.

"I wanted to thank you for the bread. These are huckleberry and gooseberry jam," Frankie said.

"Thank you so much," Anne said, taking the jars. "How lovely. Huckleberry and gooseberry! And I must tell you I have no idea what you've just given me."

Frankie laughed and explained that the huckleberry was a kind of wild blueberry that grew in the West. The gooseberry was a domestic fruit from the old days.

"My grandmother kept a patch going up here behind the cottage."

She shifted from one foot to the other and glanced at Anne and away.

"Anyway. I hope you like them," she said, and stepped back toward the patio.

"These look wonderful, and I just made some scones," Anne said. "Do you have time for a cup of tea?" Frankie looked startled, as if such an invitation had not occurred to her. There was an awkward pause.

"But I won't keep you if it's not a good time," Anne said.

She could hear the disappointment in her own voice.

Frankie flushed.

"No. I have time. Thank you. Tea would be great."

"Tim told me Aiden was up at your place again," Anne said as she filled the kettle. Maddening, how Tim had let Aiden wander while working on the boat. Worse still his failure to mention until hours after the fact that Frankie had brought Aiden back.

"I'm so sorry and I told him it's not okay."

As she said it, she wasn't sure if she meant Tim or Aiden. Frankie shrugged.

"It's no trouble. Aiden's easy," she said simply.

Anne wanted to laugh and turned away to put the kettle on. Who ever said that about Aiden?

Frankie scanned the ceiling above the great windows facing the lake.

"I installed that light for Christi," she said, pointing to a fixture Anne had never noticed before. Frankie reached under the counter and flipped a switch. Anne exclaimed as the light illuminated a painting of a mermaid that hung in the center of the wall.

"Bloody hell! Nobody has ever turned that light on before! Swear on my life."

Frankie laughed.

"My dad told Christi she'd forget to use it if he put the switch under here. But she didn't listen to him. She told him the light was an essential piece of the design."

"That sounds just like Christi," Anne said, laughing.

She set the tea to steep and put a plate of scones on the counter. She opened the jars of jam and spooned a bit into little bowls. She pulled out small plates and saw Frankie's gaze sweep the counter from the scones to the sourdough bread, the cookies, and the lemon cake. Her face flushed and she forced a laugh as she pushed the scones toward Frankie.

"I've been in a bit of a baking fit," she said. "Had some time on my hands."

Frankie wore that blank look Anne had seen when they first met. Impossible to read.

"It must seem a bit mental," she said with a laugh. But she did feel a bit of a loon.

Frankie shook her head.

"No, it's just I can't think how you did all that," she said. "My grammy was a great baker, but I was hopeless. She stopped trying to teach me after I nearly set the kitchen on fire."

"But you made this jam," Anne protested, waving a piece of scone. "It's gorgeous, by the way."

Frankie shook her head.

"Patrick made this. My brother. He takes after Grammy and my mom, I guess. Dad and I are maintenance crew."

Her voice caught and she looked down at her hands.

After a moment Anne said, "Tim told me your dad died this spring. I'm really sorry, Frankie. You must miss him terribly."

Frankie looked up, and her eyes were wet.

"Thank you," she said quietly and shook her head. "Everyone else says 'passed,' or 'gone to the other side.'"

She sighed.

"He died. I wish people would just say that. Doesn't make it easier to use fluffy words."

Anne swallowed against the knot in her throat.

"I know just what you mean. They tell you he's resting in the bosom of our Lord, and it makes you want to punch someone in their stupid face, doesn't it?"

Frankie wiped her wrist across her eyes and smiled.

"Exactly," she said.

"What was your father's name?" Anne asked.

"It was Jack," Frankie said.

"Jack O'Neill," Anne said, leaning her elbows on the counter. "That's a nice name. What was he like, Jack O'Neill?"

Frankie said he was dependable and always ready to lend a hand. He'd give you the shirt off his back. He was handy and a great worker but often forgot to send a bill. He always had time for a story. He was funny and kind.

Her voice grew easy, and then Frankie asked about Anne's parents. She told Frankie about her father's fishing boat, her mother working at the fishermen's co-op. Gran living just over the wall. Frankie had loved her grandmother too, and they talked about what a gift that was to grow up with them.

By the time Tim and Aiden came back from the boat, the afternoon sun was slanting low across the yard. Aiden sidled up to his mother's chair. He glanced at the tall neighbor and looked away with his secret wee smile. He climbed into the window seat and twirled the feather he'd tucked into his storybook.

Tim and Frankie were talking about the boat, and she offered to look at the bilge pump, which didn't appear to be working properly.

"Thank you for the tea, Anne," she said.

She glanced toward the window seat and said, "Bye, Aiden."

The boy's eyes flicked toward her and away as Frankie and Tim left.

Anne cut a piece of scone for Aiden. The boy climbed up on a stool with his book. He had it opened to "Briar Rose." The illustration showed a lovely maiden standing in the woods surrounded by small creatures and birds. Anne recalled the old lullaby she used to sing to him when he was a baby. Gran had sung it to her when she was little.

"*Éiní, éiní, codalaígí, codalaígí,*" she sang.

Little birds, little birds, go to sleep.

Aiden traced the figure of a bird with a finger. Blackbird, raven, crow, robin, lark, wren, and thrush.

> *An londubh is an fiach dubh,*
> *An chéirseach is an préachán,*
> *An spideog is an fhuiseog,*
> *An dreoilín is an smóilín.*
> *Téigí a chodhladh, téigí a chodhladh.*

Préachán ach amháin. Only a crow.

She glanced up at the light fixture over the garish mermaid. Christi liked bright, bold things. In Seattle, she'd begun collecting glass sculptures by an artist called Chihuly. His pieces were gorgeous lights, whimsical baskets, cylinders, and ikebana. And Tim Senior had chosen the signature piece of her collection for her sixtieth birthday party—a tall, ornate cylinder that Anne knew had cost over $10,000. Actually, Christi had picked it out and insisted that her husband "give" it to her at the party at the club. Anne felt her stomach drop remembering the evening, which had been the start of so many things going wrong—with the Magnusen family but also between her and Tim.

When Tim's parents had announced the party, which would take place the first weekend in August—Anne had dismissed the idea of bringing Aiden, although his name was on the invitation. It wasn't simply that he'd be the only child there, as Tim's siblings had no children. There was also the fact that larger gatherings were hard for him. Too much noise, too many people. Harder for her too, she admitted, especially after the spring concert four months earlier. Since then she'd felt broken open again in a way that made it difficult to manage the superficial social niceties required by such functions. She'd suggested she stay home with Aiden, but Tim wouldn't hear of it. He wanted her there with him.

"Tell your mam we'll get a sitter, then. It will be too much for Aiden, and he'd be better off at home, don't you think, Tim?"

Tim had agreed, but then Christi left a voicemail about Aiden's tuxedo-fitting appointment.

"Did you not tell her he wasn't coming?" she asked Tim over dinner that night. He widened his eyes and shook his head.

"Oh, Aiden's coming," Tim said. "My suggestion that he skip it went over like a lead balloon. Unless you want me to be cut out of the family and set adrift on an iceberg, I think it's best we bite the bullet on this one."

Anne swallowed her anger and did not ask for details. There was something between Tim and his parents, especially his mother. She cowed him. When push came to shove, he would fold to whatever

Christi demanded. Anne didn't understand it, as vocal disagreement was a regular part of life in the Ryan household. Then again, she didn't know what it was like to have family and work all mixed together.

The fitting had been a disaster. It was a lot to ask of any little child—standing still, being measured, trousers and cuffs pinned in place. But Aiden also hated tight clothes and seemed sensitive to rough textures like polyester. Anne asked the tailor to size up the tiny tuxedo so it might be a little roomy on him, which could help. The evening of the party, she knew the best solution would be for the two of them to stay out of the fray. She reckoned it might be boring for them both, and she brought his storybook and the Irish memory card game to help pass the time. The party, however, turned out to be anything but boring.

The Columbia Tower Club was located on the seventy-fifth floor and offered stunning views of the city, the Olympic Mountains, and the Puget Sound. When she, Tim, and Aiden stepped out of the elevator, they were some of the last to arrive. What her in-laws called a "small gathering" numbered about fifty people—the newspaper board, a few key advertisers, top staff, and family. Tim strode into the dining room to find his parents, leaving Anne alone in the foyer. Tim Senior had hired a Beatles cover band, and the musicians had dressed the part. Anne saw them through the doorway to the large dining room before turning to follow Aiden, who'd circled back to the elevator. They weren't terrible, but the sound system was out of balance—the guitars too loud and heavy bass.

Back in the elevator, Aiden shed his jacket and shoes, as she expected he would. As they descended, the bellhop told them that they would fall nine hundred feet in a matter of seconds. There was a sense of vertigo as she felt their bodies drop down the steel chute. He let them out in the lobby and did not comment when they reappeared ten minutes later for a trip up and then back down again, on repeat. Each time they reached the lobby, Aiden would circumnavigate in a counterclockwise motion. Anne followed him, pausing to look at the art on display.

"Hopi Crow Mother," the card read in front of one piece. Draped in a red-and-white gown, the doll had a black face and bright yellow eyes that matched its pointed beak. A pair of black wings sprouted from the shoulders, and it had human arms and legs. The arms were extended as if to accept a baby or some other precious burden.

Someone had made this little doll with their hands, cradling it gently while sewing the garments, stitching beads on and gluing feathers. It had to have been a woman, she thought, someone like her own gran, though the card did not include the artist's name. A telling oversight since the installment purported to "celebrate Native artists." The little Crow Mother had such a plaintive face, like she well knew what a raw deal motherhood was. Being a mam felt like you were two halves of different people stitched together. Or three-thirds, or some days, seven-eighths, because none of it added up to a whole person, just one slightly crazed twenty-eight-year-old coming apart at the seams.

Riding back up the elevator, Aiden pressed his face against the narrow window. Anne leaned into the wood-paneled wall, grateful to the bellhop, who pretended it was completely normal for guests to ride up and down, disappear for a lap of the lobby, and then repeat the process. He only said, "Good evening," when they reappeared. And "Club floor?"

As the car slowed at the top of its rise, Anne gazed out the window. A pair of gulls surfed past and peeled off on the updraft. She looked at her son and felt a rush of love.

The doors dinged open and revealed Tim looking so handsome in his tuxedo. He also looked impatient. Anne took Aiden by the hand. She turned and thanked the silent bellhop and saw amusement flit across his face as the doors slid shut.

". . . everyone is waiting," Tim was saying. "We can't do the toast with my family absent from the table."

The band sounded louder now.

"Dinner started half an hour ago," Tim said, looking down at Aiden.

"Jesus, Anne. Where is his jacket? And his shoes?"

That Aiden was wearing most of his clothes was a miracle—the trousers, shirt, and waistcoat. She held up the shoes hooked on her fingers and the jacket over her arm, and Tim took them from her. The band began playing The Beatles' "Birthday" and Anne heard people clapping along out of synch.

"Anne, this is a really important night for Mom. Aiden, stand still, buddy."

He pulled the boy's arms through the jacket and buttoned the middle button. He bent down and Anne watched him struggle to push the shoes on Aiden's feet. The music grew louder, and the speaker whined with feedback. Their son squirmed away and kicked the shoes off. It would have been funny, if not for the panic on his little face.

"Tim, just leave them off. For goodness sake! No one will notice."

Tim shook his head, and his face reddened as he forced Aiden's feet into the shoes.

"It's a special occasion, Anne. I don't think it's asking too much—"

Aiden kicked his shoes off once more and struggled to get away. His breathing grew labored, and Anne felt a bite of fear at what was unfolding.

"Tim, just hang on a minute," she said, but he didn't listen.

He forced the shoes on, scooped Aiden up, and carried him toward the dining room. Anne hurried after them.

"Tim! Wait!" she called.

Aiden's body had gone rigid in his father's arms.

"Tim!" Anne called.

Tim Senior, standing at the head of the room, was telling a story about Christi, which earned a ripple of laughter. Tim paused by the dessert and gift table, where presents were piled high around the centerpiece gift—the beautiful new Chihuly.

Tim Senior raised his glass.

"To my darling, Christi," he said. "The light of my life and the mother of my children."

He signaled to the servers, who began to light the candles on the cake. The guests started singing "Happy Birthday," slightly out of tune and tempo dragging.

Aiden was pressing his father's chest with his small hands, trying to make some space between their bodies. His face had gone white. He was making a small noise that grew louder over the sound of the singing.

"I'd leg it out of here, you eejit."

It was as if Katherine were right at her shoulder.

But Katherine wasn't there and wouldn't ever be there. Katherine wasn't anywhere.

Anne tried to reach them but couldn't move. Like the night of the spring concert, she felt like she was underwater. She heard Tim's reprimand, knew that Aiden could not because his fear had taken him elsewhere. She watched them in slow motion. Aiden's face went from white to red in his panic. A stranger might have read it as rage, but it was fear, she knew, that propelled him to twist out of his father's grasp. He pushed himself free and stood, fists clenched and eyes closed tight, his panicked breathing competing with his grandmother's voice as Christi began a speech of thanks.

"Aiden," Anne said, but he could not hear her.

Tim reached toward Aiden to contain him, and the boy erupted. His small mouth opened in a roar of anguish. Anne wanted to reach him, to catch his wee hands and stop him from hitting and slapping himself on his beautiful head and face as he screamed and screamed. But she couldn't move.

She watched Tim as if from far away as he grabbed Aiden's shoulders and tried to hold him. Aiden wrenched himself away and anchored himself with the tablecloth. His eyes were shut tight, and he screamed as if to put it all at bay—the hot room, the tight clothing, the out-of-tune music, the crowd of strangers, and the adults who simply wouldn't leave him be.

Tim stepped back and raised his hands in a surrender that was almost comical. Anne felt a serenity descend over her then as she watched Aiden clutch the tablecloth and pull with all his might. Her boy brought it all down. The cake, candles, china plates, and Grandma Christi's birthday Chihuly, all of it smashing into a thousand pieces.

18

MORIBUND CALL

Bird populations may be reduced by various human actions that cause death, egg destruction, and direct or indirect environmental devastation.

—*G. Gordon's Field Guide to the Birds of the Pacific Northwest*

Once upon a time there was a baby crow.

They said he needed a good spanking.

The baby crow said he did not want to wear that jacket because it was much too tight and too scratchy and the music was much too loud.

No, thank you, Mama, he said. No, thank you! No, Mama, thank you! Feels like too much. Too much too much! No, please, thank you!

They said he was very naughty, very naughty.

Once upon a time there was a baby crow.

He felt very sad, and he wanted to fly away.

19

INTERSPECIFIC CALLS

Successful feeding of young birds is key in the rearing of healthy populations.

—*G. Gordon's Field Guide to the Birds of the Pacific Northwest*

⤜⤛

In 1987, the summer that Frankie O'Neill was fifteen years old, Cherry 7Up landed on store shelves and caused an uproar with purists. *The Witches of Eastwick* was a blockbuster hit at the Hood River Drive-In. The Whitney Houston song "I Wanna Dance with Somebody" topped the billboard charts, and Pac-Mania was the most popular arcade game in the US. Frankie was vaguely aware of these cultural milestones through other kids at the lake. They shared snippets of news and celebrity gossip as they came and went from the store and sunbathed on the beach. But that summer, she was mostly uncomfortably aware of the fact that her mother was forming a separate life.

That summer was the first Judith didn't spend the entire season at the lake with the rest of the family. She was studying for her real estate license and began spending periods of time in town. Frankie felt her absence like a wound. Couldn't she study at the cottage? she asked. Judith told her there were too many distractions, which hurt Frankie's feelings. Was she a distraction?

The rest of them carried on with the season—Frankie, Patrick,

Jack, and Genevieve. Ray had died the previous year and Patrick helped his grandmother more now in his mother's absence, but that was the only material change. Frankie missed Judith so much, and yet the days she was there, she was less and less present. Judith seemed distant, disappearing into her notebooks and going to bed early instead of playing cards with the rest of them. Frankie remembered trying to cajole Judith into joining them one night.

"I'm not feeling so lucky," her mother had said.

Everyone laughed like Judith meant it as a joke, but Frankie felt stung. The next day Judith left for town early, and Frankie felt heartsore that she hadn't said goodbye. Her grandmother noticed her moping and whipped up a Dutch baby for breakfast. She sprinkled it with powdered sugar and dropped a kiss on Frankie's head as she sat down to eat.

"Don't be too hard on your mother," Genevieve said. "She does her best. Judith has just had . . ." Her voice trailed off. "Some disappointments," she finished and wouldn't say more.

Frankie understood that Judith had had a hard childhood, though she didn't say much about it. She was the oldest girl in a big family that didn't have much money. Her mother died when she was little, and the woman her father married after that was unkind. Frankie had absorbed this general understanding over the years without the specifics.

Once she complained about the cold at the cottage, and Judith mentioned how she used to sit around the gas stove for warmth with her little brothers.

"We'd do that whenever the electricity got shut off," she said.

Who shut it off and why? Frankie asked. And she was puzzled when Judith said her folks didn't pay the bill sometimes. Why not? Frankie wanted to know. Judith looked like a stranger for a moment and told Frankie she was too young to understand and never talked about it again.

Now Frankie recalled that had been Grammy Genevieve's last summer at the lake. She died on a snowy, sunny day the following

February. From her spot at the kitchen table, Frankie glanced at
Grammy's overflowing spice rack, the weathered cast-iron pans, the
bread mold with the cornucopia pattern for her signature sponge
cake. The beloved Wedgewood stove Grandpa Ray and Hank had
lugged up the trail in 1947 to delight Genevieve crouched in the center of the kitchen like a dormant creature. Frankie looked at the coffee cake and scones Anne had sent home with her. She and Grammy
would have gotten on like a house on fire.

She turned back to her notes and Dr. Wood-Smith's editorial letter. She'd finally returned to the revision of her manuscript after days
of procrastination. She knew Dr. Wood-Smith's suggestions would
be harder to work through than Dr. Andreas's. One of the only women
with tenure in the avian biology program, she was kind, if a bit reserved, and demanded the best of her students. Frankie had read
through Wood-Smith's letter several times and understood the broad
suggestions of her review. But scanning the manuscript, she found
detailed notes far beyond those in the editorial letter. On every page
it seemed there was a question or suggestion for further inquiry. With
growing alarm, she flipped through the manuscript and found the
pattern continued throughout. Frankie felt dismayed at the scope of
changes Wood-Smith had outlined. But then, on the very last page,
she found a handwritten note from the professor.

Dear Ms. O'Neill,

If you've reached this page in your revision process, you've no doubt
noticed the depth and range of my comments exceeded the changes I outlined
in the editorial letter. I apologize if this is confusing. I believe that the minor
changes I suggested in the letter are sufficient for submission of your thesis
and completion of your master's program. The editorial letter is part of the
formal record that Dr. Grant has from me as a committee member. These
further suggestions are meant for you personally to consider how you might
deepen your own independent inquiry when you continue with your doctoral
studies elsewhere. You are a bright and talented researcher with interesting

and unique ideas. The strongest inquiries come from the questions we just can't seem to shake. It is my hope you will pursue your own questions as you continue to develop as a scientist. I wish you great success. Please consider me available to assist in any way.

Regards,
Jacqueline Wood-Smith

Frankie flipped back through the manuscript.

"It seems as if your earlier draft contained more regarding parent-brood communication and audio detail," Wood-Smith had written on one page. "A great idea for continued study. See also pages 25, 37, and 48," on another. Then, "Consider how the concept of vocal variations could be used to further investigate territorial boundaries." The comments went on like that throughout. Dr. Wood-Smith noticed that she had removed much of her own original research from the manuscript, though she probably didn't know why.

"The editorial letter is part of the formal record that Dr. Grant has from me as a committee member," she read again. And, "You are a bright and talented researcher with interesting and unique ideas."

Dr. Grant had not found her ideas unique or interesting. He called them a distraction to her thesis. And when she'd objected—in a rare show of standing up for herself—he got angry.

"O'Neill, I've been the head of this department since you were in diapers," he'd said, glaring. "I think I know what's best. Just get it done."

He was cool toward her after that, and then everything fell apart at the spring symposium.

That day Dr. Steven Lench had given the keynote about his discovery that certain species, including crows, exercised theory of mind similar to humans. Being able to imagine what another animal was thinking, they could predict the behavior of prey and use this knowledge to hunt more successfully. His work had won him significant recognition in animal behavioral studies and an award from the tristate consortium of Washington, Oregon, and Idaho universities. Davis had dismissed him with derision.

"He's a storyteller—all anecdotes. That's not science."

But Frankie had listened, rapt, as Lench recounted corvids' use of planning to access food. He told about groups of crows chasing ground squirrels into traffic to make a meal of them. Crows who learned that if they rang the doorbell of a particular house, the occupant would come out and feed them. Crows worked in pairs to steal food from dogs—one pulling the unfortunate canine's tail and the other swooping down for kibble. Crows in teams stole fish from the very claws of other birds and swiped cups of coffee, sandwiches, apples, and even cigarettes. One enterprising crow stole a pie from a pair of Idaho campers and returned the pan the next day, dropping it on their tent.

"People deride crows as pests, carrion lovers, and trash birds," Lench said. "And yet, a family of crows will consume up to forty thousand caterpillars and crop pests in one nesting season, which is a clear boon to farmers. This intelligent, invigorated Species of Least Concern has so much to teach us about bird behavior, human behavior, and the spaces where our worlds intersect."

At the reception, Frankie tried to work up the courage to introduce herself. She bought a beer and downed half of it quickly. The group of people around Lench thinned and Dr. Marzluff approached and shook his hand. He waved her over and introduced her to Lench as a student of Davis Grant's.

"She also gave me a hand with some data collection last summer," he said.

Marzluff excused himself to talk to someone and left her standing there with Dr. Lench. She tried to think of something to say, and Dr. Lench looked her up and down.

"Wonderful to meet one of Davis's prodigies," he said, leaning close enough that she could smell whiskey on his breath. "How's his little owl project going? *Nature* is publishing his latest, hmm?"

Frankie knew that Grant's "little owl project," which had received enormous funding for years, was the envy of other researchers. But she also knew that recent studies were failing to produce the results he'd hoped.

"Oh, actually, *Nature* rejected the last paper," she said without thinking, and immediately regretted it as she saw a satisfied smile bloom on Dr. Lench's face.

"But, I mean, we're reworking it, for, for reconsideration," Frankie stammered. "There was just a question about the data set by the, by the third reviewer who—"

"Oh, certainly, certainly," Dr. Lench interrupted. "Sounds like a minor hiccup to me. Easily ironed out."

Dr. Lench appraised her tall figure, sipping his drink.

"And what are you working on? Any special projects?"

"Well, my dissertation is on owl pair bonding. But like Dr. Marzluff said, I'm interested in corvids too. Last summer when I helped Dr. Marzluff—"

She was excited to talk about her idea, which was coming into clear focus. It burned in her throat, this secret magical question she'd stumbled upon, this inquiry into the corvid world. But then Dr. Grant was at her shoulder.

"Hello, Steven," he said. "Wonderful talk. I enjoyed your stories. I see you've met Miss O'Neill."

He clapped a hand on Frankie's shoulder, and it felt possessive.

"Indeed. She was telling me about your faulty data set. Too bad about the *Nature* rejection," Dr. Lench said, frowning with false sympathy.

The air grew taut, and Frankie wished she was somewhere else.

"Just a minor problem that the review committee asked us to clarify," Dr. Grant replied frostily.

"Yes, yes, you keep at it. Persistence pays off."

Dr. Lench turned to leave and waved his drink at Frankie.

"Keep in touch about your little crow project, my dear," he said. "WSU might be interested."

Frankie had been waiting for the right moment to tell Dr. Grant about her crow theory. And this was not that moment. But in the silence that ballooned after Dr. Lench sauntered away, it came tumbling out.

"It's nothing really. It's just something I noticed when I was helping Dr. Marzluff with the caveman recognition study. Some of the audio data we captured in the arboretum—"

"You're developing a project with Marzluff?" he interrupted.

Her scalp prickled with heat.

"Nnn-oo," she stammered. "You asked me to help him last summer, remember? Ben and I worked on the facial recognition project when you—"

"Yeah, I remember. I owed him a favor. I didn't expect you or Ben to actually be interested in Marzluff's ridiculous corvids."

Her face grow hot.

"Davis, you're not listening. When we were recording the audio data—"

"It's a violation of your contract, O'Neill," he said, talking over her. "It's illegal for you to use my lab to pursue competing research. Not to mention a betrayal of my trust. And after all I've done for you."

He walked away and left her standing there. She felt everyone staring, and that was the beginning of the end.

Frankie had seen Dr. Grant lose his temper before and hoped he might cool down like he sometimes did. Later that week when she went to work, her key card wouldn't let her into the lab. She took it to the department secretary, apologetic.

"Sorry, Angela. This one is bad. Could you give me a new key card?"

Angela replied primly that she'd need to talk to Dr. Grant about that. Frankie turned, red-faced, and walked to his office. Dr. Grant was chatting with a trio of new graduate students. She leaned on the door jamb and waited for a break in the conversation. The students laughed at something Dr. Grant said, and he looked up at Frankie with a false smile.

"Sorry to interrupt, Davis. Angela said I needed to talk to you about my key card?"

"Oh yes, Ms. O'Neill. Ms. O'Neill worked in my lab previously," he told the graduate students.

Frankie stared at him, and the world tipped.

"Since you've moved on to other things, you won't be needing access to the lab any longer. So no need for a key card. But always here to help if you have questions. Good luck to you, Ms. O'Neill," he said.

And overnight her friend and mentor Davis became Dr. Grant. Frankie, his protégé, became Ms. O'Neill, his former student. That was the unraveling of everything: her job at the lab, her place on the owl study. Even her thesis committee, which Dr. Grant had hand-picked. When she emailed them that summer about her defense, they'd directed her back to Dr. Grant. He continued to avoid her and did not return her emails. She was required to finish her thesis to receive her master's but had no idea how to move forward. The deadline passed for her May defense date. She'd sold back her books to cover groceries and rent and spent the summer trying to figure out what to do. She filled the long days walking—through the arboretum, around Lake Union, and south to Seward Park on Lake Washington.

She leaned back in her chair and looked out at the pump house through the window. If she was being honest, she'd also spent the summer drinking. Just once in a while, she'd said then, and after a particularly bad day. But there were many bad days. She hadn't told anyone about any of it. Who would she tell? Somehow, she'd spent seven years at UW without making any lasting friendships. Her friends from home were busy with work and babies. Patrick had his hands full working for the judge. It had been years since she'd confided anything to Judith. Dad would have helped her sort it all out, she thought.

Frankie glanced down at Dr. Wood-Smith's note and sighed. The way to her once-promising career felt fatally blocked. She thought of the empty Bushmills bottle. Her mind began manufacturing a reason to run down to Mill Three and stop in at the little store. It didn't have to be a big deal. Just a six-pack. Just some beer. Frankie pushed herself away from the table and left the house to get away from the voice in her head.

As she climbed the hill a crow called, and another answered. The day was warming, and the sun felt hot between her shoulder blades. She stepped into the bird blind and looked down at the lake through her binoculars. The mist was breaking up over the water and moving into the trees like a dream retreating from wakefulness. A varied thrush trilled over the burble of a robin. They flashed across the meadow, similar medium-sized birds but so different in their songs. Using a Sharpie, she added them to the list she'd begun her first day back at the cabin. The list was long and growing longer—nearly fifty species in less than two weeks. It was anchoring to catalog the birds here. A round of robins. A hermitage of thrushes. A charm of goldfinches.

A group of crows passed overhead—a cabal, a congress, a murder. Something about the way they flew pleased her, their wingtips spread like fingers, their squared-off tails. She couldn't say why. She marveled that people dismissed crows out of hand. It was almost as if the health of their numbers, especially in urban areas, made people uncomfortable. But humans were the ones who'd drawn crows into cities over the past two decades. They came for the open trash pits of the dumps and the parks and leafy streets with fewer predators.

She decided to check Grammy Genevieve's secret chanterelle spot. It was early for the earthy golden mushrooms to sprout, but it had been so rainy, they could be out. Anne might know how to cook them. Oh, how she missed her little grandmother just then.

"Don't be too hard on your mother. She's had some disappointments."

Flashes of memory then. Judith rocking her to sleep in the rocking chair. Judith sitting with her on the dock for the Fourth of July. Judith pulling a blanket close around their shoulders the night of a big storm. When had her mother become so distant? Why was she different with Patrick?

Frankie climbed through the woods and let her mind go blank. By the time she'd reached the top of the hill, the sun had moved high in the sky. She breathed in the scent of sun-warmed pine needles, the green smell of rain, and late summer yarrow and aster. She listened to the drilling of a woodpecker and the drowsy drone of nuthatches high above. She put her palm on the rough bark of a fir and a quiet settled in her as she pondered the conversation of the wind, the woods, and its creatures.

A terrible crack ricocheted through the woods behind her. Crows exploded out of a large hemlock clamoring with alarm. A man stood under the tree with a rifle still pointed high. She recognized him from the day of the storm when he'd slunk off into the woods.

"Hey!" she yelled, striding forward without stopping to think.

He turned and lowered his gun, then sauntered toward her. When he was close enough, she could see there was something slightly off in his gaze. His hair was a lank dirty blond, and his skinny wrists poked out of his too-small jacket. His chin was covered in red stubble.

She wanted to back away, but her protectiveness for the woods overrode her aversion and she held her ground. The man, taking note of her height, slowed his pace.

"Mornin'," he said, holding the gun across his body. His knees poked through holes in his pants and his tennis shoes were soggy with mud. "Didn't expect to see nobody else."

Something in his smile made her shudder, and Frankie struggled to control her voice.

"How did you get up here?" she asked.

The man scoffed and spat.

"What's it to you?" he asked.

"Well, you're on private property. And I saw you up here before, didn't I?" Frankie said.

He stared and didn't respond.

"Where'd you come from?"

"Over there," he said, waving vaguely behind him.

Frankie crossed her arms.

"Well, that way," she said, pointing over his shoulder, "belongs to the Yakama Nation. And behind me Beauty Bay Resort. So I guess you must have come from Yakama land."

"Guess so," he said flatly.

"Well, we don't allow hunting on our land," she said. "So, you need to leave."

That wasn't entirely true. The Yakama Nation had hunting rights on Beauty Bay property. But Frankie doubted this man was a member of the Yakama Nation.

"Who said I'm huntin'?" the man asked. He hitched the gun up over his shoulder. "Just target practice. You know."

"Target practice," Frankie repeated.

He jutted his chin.

"Yeah—jays, crows. Whatever. Don't matter."

Frankie flushed with anger.

"Actually, it does matter. There's an international treaty protecting most North American bird species. It's a felony to shoot them."

He grimaced and spat. Frankie willed herself not to flinch.

"That so?"

"Yes, that's so. And we don't allow shooting in these woods. At all," she said firmly. "If you follow that stream behind you uphill, you'll find your way back to the Yakama land. The agency office should have a map for you too."

"What do I need a map for?" he asked.

"So you don't get lost again," Frankie said.

He narrowed his eyes and wiped his mouth with the back of his wrist.

"Sure," he said. "You have a nice day."

Frankie waited until he was out of sight and strode over to the hemlock. She found the bodies of four crows at the foot of the tree. The shot had mutilated their small torsos. From their size she guessed they were mature adults. The blue-black feathers were beautiful even in death.

Sick with fury, she turned and hurried down the trail. While it was true what she said about international law protecting bird species, it was also true that the Washington Department of Fish and Wildlife issued permits to hunt crows and other birds. She thought about what Dr. Tandy had said about another humble bird, the passenger pigeon. So robust in numbers that they blocked out the sun when they flew across the plains of the Midwest. And hunted to extinction by 1914—an entire species a casualty of human amusement. But she knew that guy didn't have a permit from the state or the Yakama Nation. She'd have to call the sheriff and the agency office, which meant a boat ride to town.

In the boat, she pulled on her dad's old jacket and turned up the collar against the breeze. She drove down the lake as fast as she could and reached the marina in late afternoon. The hot, dry air of the post office lobby struck her in the face when she opened the door. Donna rose and turned down the radio when she saw Frankie.

"Hello there, Frankie O'Neill," she said. "You sure are a popular gal."

She pulled out a large pile of mail and pushed it across the counter.

"If you don't mind, there are a few things for the neighbors too. You'll save Jerry a trip up if you can carry them for me."

"Sure, Donna. No problem."

Frankie changed some dollars for the pay phone and dialed the sheriff's office first.

Miranda, the dispatcher, had worked at the sheriff's office for as long as Frankie could remember and seemed ageless. She asked for the man's physical description, the location, their conversation, and the number of dead birds.

"And you saw him discharge his firearm?" Miranda asked.

"Well, I heard it and when I turned around, he was standing over a dead bird and holding his gun. Is that good enough?"

"Yes, that'll do. I'll let Sheriff know," she said. "You be careful up there, Miss O'Neill. People can be unpredictable. You should call the Nation too."

Frankie thanked her and called the Yakama Nation agency office. A woman answered and told her to wait. Frankie heard her set down the receiver and walk away. She waited, listening to the sound of children playing, the slam of a door, the bark of a dog. After a few long minutes, someone picked up the receiver.

"Councilman Miller," the voice said.

"Hi, um, this is Frankie O'Neill. We have a place— My family . . . we're the caretakers up at Beauty Bay," she stammered.

She told him about the hunter and that she'd seen him before.

"He was on our side of the boundary, but I imagine he came from your side because it's all boat access from the west."

"He was a white guy?" Councilman Miller asked.

She flushed.

"I mean—I think so," she stammered.

"Skinny guy? With a red beard?"

"Yes," Frankie said.

Councilman Miller exhaled.

"Yeah, I know who that is," he said. "Anything else?"

She recognized the name then.

"Um, are you related to Jim Miller?" she asked. "He was a friend of my grandfather's, Ray O'Neill. They used to fish together?"

There was a pause, then the man said, "Yes, James Miller was my father. He died three years ago. Anything else?"

Frankie felt stung and embarrassed.

"No, nothing else. I just thought you all would want to know. Anyway—thanks," she stammered. "I'll call if I, if anything else comes up."

She hung up and leaned against the glass wall of the booth. What was she expecting? Did she want to be thanked for letting the Nation know someone was trespassing on Beauty Bay land, which had once belonged to the Yakama people? And that business about her grandfather. "Indian Jim" is what her grandfather had called his fishing buddy. She wouldn't have said that to Councilman Miller. It seemed impolite, so why hadn't she ever said so to her grandfather?

Her mind was roiling with feeling, and she felt dizzy. She closed her eyes and saw Dr. Grant storming away from her at the symposium. Then the man in the woods spitting on the ground, and the bodies of the dead crows. Judith looking at her watch, impatient to get away from the courthouse.

Frankie pushed open the phone booth door and moved toward the store. The shadow of a bird fell across her path, and a pair of crows flapped across the park. One barrel-rolled over the top of the other, yawping playfully. You couldn't miss that it was play.

Frankie halted and looked at the little store and its cheerful red and white sign. "C'mon in! We're open!" it read. Then she returned to the boat, cast off, and headed north. She wanted to get back to the woods and the birds and the cottage. After her conversations with Miranda and Councilman Miller she felt an urgency to be there. She thought of the meadow, the bird blind, and the majestic Lightning Tree high on the hill. She thought about Charlie Crow and his parents, their brief and wonderful visit to her, and so many other birds in the forest around the house. And in that moment, the place trumped everything else—her loneliness, her grief, even the idea that relief might come in a bottle. Nothing mattered so much as getting back, as quickly as possible, to her territory, that sanctuary, her home ground.

20

PARENTAL INVESTMENT

Nest building is a task that falls oftentimes to the female.
—*G. Gordon's Field Guide to the Birds of the Pacific Northwest*

Aiden pulled his Snoopy life preserver on over his sweatshirt, a reminder that Anne had promised to take him out in the rowboat. After breakfast, she told him. He picked at his Cheerios like a little bird while she tried to finish a letter to her mother. In her last letter Margaret had asked breezily about Christi's birthday do and if they'd taken any photos of Aiden in his little tuxedo. She longed to tell her mother about that terrible evening, to unburden herself, but she couldn't. It was too much. Still—if she could put it into words, perhaps she could put it behind her, behind them. Anne could still feel the aftershocks in her body—Aiden's distress, her failure to help him, and the awful way Tim had behaved.

It had taken Aiden hours to calm down that evening. He'd continued to scream after everything came crashing down. He was so deep in his private misery that he didn't seem to register the breaking glass, the shattering sculpture, or his grandfather standing over him shouting. His anguished cry persisted as Tim scooped him up and strode from the room holding his rigid little body. Anne followed, silent and furious.

In a small anteroom near the elevators, Aiden threw himself against the floor, beating his fists against the carpet and screaming like his skin was on fire. Tim swore and stepped back. He turned to Anne, and under his anger she saw a look of fear that almost made her forgive him.

"Go," she said. "I'll sit with him."

Tim's face folded down and he leaned over the small form on the floor.

"Aiden Matthew Ryan Magnusen! You stop it right now or you'll get the spanking of your life!" Tim yelled.

Anne grabbed his arm.

"Tim. Get out right now, or you'll be very sorry you did not."

Her voice was flat with fury, and he didn't argue.

She shut the door and sat down next to Aiden and waited. His little voice grew hoarse, and he continued to wail. She coaxed him out of the hateful jacket, and that helped. He'd flung off his shoes in the dining room, and she pulled off his socks, knowing he preferred to be barefoot. When his crying softened into hiccupping sobs, she tried to take his hand and he snatched it away, arched his back, and erupted all over. His anguish tore at her heart.

After a time, he curled up in a little ball and quieted. The moon sailed past the window on a skiff of clouds. The faint sound of the band bled through the wall, and she lost track of time. Later, the elevator dinged repeatedly as the guests left. Later still Anne heard the band talking and laughing as they loaded their equipment in the service elevator. Then Tim returned. He stood in the doorway looking chastened, but he did not apologize for any of it.

"Are you ready to go? I called us a cab," he said.

He held out his hand, and Anne let him help her up. Aiden stood on his own and led the way to the elevator. Anne followed and didn't try to touch him. He pressed his face against the window as the car descended.

In the days that followed, Aiden had remained guarded, especially around Tim. He wouldn't let either of his parents hold his hand or hug him or pick him up. If they tried, he'd pull away, strike them, or worse, slap his own wee face and head. It broke her heart.

Anne called his pediatrician, kind Dr. Anaya, who'd told her to give it time.

"He's an independent little guy," Dr. Anaya said. "You've said he makes his own rules. So let him take the lead on this."

That's what she'd done. She missed the feel of his little hand. She had to stop herself over and over from wrapping her arms around him. She let him decide what kind of contact he wanted. Sometimes he'd lean against her or hug her briefly. But if she tried to touch him first, he'd retreat for days, and her heart broke anew. Anne wished he could tell them what he'd been feeling that awful night. And what he was feeling now.

Tim's refusal to apologize was a wall between them. It was an important occasion for his parents, he kept saying. He'd lost his temper, but he still didn't think he was wrong. It wasn't asking too much for Aiden to manage such an evening, he'd said more than once. Anne disagreed completely. And even if she had agreed, physical punishment, the very threat of it, was nonnegotiable. He had crossed a line. But his refusal to explain himself was most unforgivable.

Anne put Aiden's cereal bowl in the sink and zipped up the life preserver.

"You go wait by the rowboat. I'll be down in a few minutes, and we'll go on an adventure," she said.

His face lit up, and he scampered out the sliding door. Anne watched him make his way along the seawall, stopping from time to time to gaze up at the sky, pointing at something, and cupping his hand over his mouth.

She glanced down at the letter to Margaret. She'd manufactured a cheerful version of the last couple of months—the lazy days of summer, her sabbatical, as she was calling her leave, a trip to the lake before Aiden returned to daycare at Sunflower. Anne didn't want her to worry. She could almost hear her mother's voice.

"But it's my job to worry about you, dearie. I'm your mammy."

There are things a mother forgets and blessedly so. In the fog of postpartum, a mother forgets the inhuman pain of labor, which no woman is ever adequately advised of or prepared for. That pain was a place, a different planet to which she'd been removed while everyone else carried on. While Tim held her hand and the nurses moved blithely around the room like everything was perfectly normal, Anne was in another solar system of agony. But then came the relief of the epidural and the memory of pain had softened.

A mother can also forget the first weeks of infantile tyranny when a baby won't sleep, wants to eat when you're knackered, and seems so often in need of a nappy change that you want to throw up your hands and let it loll around naked for a year or two. Sore nipples, a ravaged undercarriage, and, as the final insult, a belly that refuses to disappear for months.

A mother can forget those things in the rush of mad joy that one is also unprepared for. When the baby's smile cuts through the fatigue of an early morning. His look of delight at tasting a strawberry for the first time. Or his gasp of wonder at some otherworldly beauty, like the neighbor's cat. For months the sight of the ragged old tabby next door would send Aiden into paroxysms of shrieking joy. There were his first wobbling attempts to stand, as heroic as an Olympian doing a dead lift as he pulled himself up on the coffee table. Who could forget her child's first laugh, delivered with unfettered delight when he saw her come into the room in the morning to free him from his crib?

And most unforgettable, his first words.

Aiden's first words had been "So much!" He would hold out his little arms and say, "So much, so much, so much!" when he wanted to be picked up. Anne reckoned he was imitating the way she said "I love my boy so much! So much!"

Aiden spoke early and picked up many words and phrases in his first year. "Kitty" was an early one, and "Mama" slightly before that.

"At least I rank higher than the cat," Anne had joked to Tim.

"Dada" came later after "more," "mine," "night-night," and "no."

Most boys speak an average of thirty words by the time they're eighteen months old, Anne had read. But Aiden was speaking in full sentences by then. He was small for his age, which, combined with his loquaciousness, made him seem like a little professor. He'd greet the neighbors in the apartment elevator and lobby, wishing them a good day, saying thank you to anyone who paused to hold the door. The Halloween he was three, he'd dressed as a sailor and hollered "Ahoy, maties!" at everyone. That December, he'd wished a very Merry Christmas and Happy New Year to strangers when he and Anne walked the neighborhood. He liked to sing as well. At Christmas, he'd perched next to Anne on the piano bench as she played carols after dinner. Aiden sang along with her to "Silent Night" and "Lo, How a Rose E'er Blooming." He didn't really know the lyrics, but he followed the melody with little sounds and made-up words. He leaned his head against her arm as she played and fell asleep there. Such a wonderful night. At the time she hadn't appreciated it. Now the memory flooded her with grief.

Everything changed last spring, eighteen months ago. She'd gone over it so many times in her mind searching for some understanding of what had transpired. Aiden had had a cold and then she did. They were both sick for about a week. Tim, who'd been at a conference in San Francisco, dodged it. By the time he returned, they were both fine. Later Anne recalled that Aiden had cried easily and seemed tired. But she didn't think much of it.

Then came the news of Kat's death. Margaret's voice broke as she said Anne's name and then passed the phone to Matthew, who told her the school had been trying reach her with this unspeakable news.

Lovely, beautiful Katherine was gone. Her parents had the funeral right away and Anne, on the other side of the world, grieved by herself. Maybe if she'd been able to attend the funeral it would have helped somehow. But nothing could change this shocking and terrible truth: Her beautiful friend Katherine O'Faolain was gone forever.

It was in that first dull blur of grief that Aiden had changed. Anne barely remembered the first two months after Kat died. Spring semester had finished during that period, but she never could recall any specifics. She'd missed many classes and the other teachers had stepped in to help out. Patrice told her to take all the time she needed and Anne had somehow managed to get her grades in by the end of the academic year. She was home more then, but left Aiden at Sunflower during the day anyway. She told herself it was better for him, but the honest truth was she wanted to be alone. At least once a week, she'd forget to pick him up and the staff would have to call to remind her. The ringing phone would jolt her out of her reverie, and she'd find herself standing at the kitchen sink or in the middle of the living room with no idea what she'd been doing.

Tim was exceedingly patient those first couple of months. When he'd come home to find her asleep on the couch or sitting at the table surrounded by piles of old sheet music, he'd kiss her and go into the kitchen to start dinner without comment. Over time, however, she sensed his patience wearing thin. When she promised and failed to get to the grocery to get Aiden's preferred snacks, when she missed Aiden's doctor's appointments, when she canceled his fourth birthday party at the last minute because she couldn't bear her in-laws just then. Was it any wonder she hadn't noticed Aiden's gradual disappearance? She missed so much that spring and early summer.

Now Anne flushed with shame recalling that Tim had noticed the change in Aiden first. One day he'd come home from work and Aiden did not run to the front door to greet him. No small figure barreled down the hallway and into his father's legs. No little voice demanded to be lifted onto shoulders. No screaming laughter. It was oddly quiet. Anne was at the kitchen table trying and failing to read the paper. She stared at the words, but they would not form sentences in her head.

"Where's Aiden?" Tim asked.

"He's in his room, I think?" she said.

She followed Tim down the hallway to where Aiden was playing quietly with his Legos. He didn't look up when Tim called his name and remained focused on his toys until Tim picked him up and tickled him. Then Aiden giggled and let himself be carried into the living room. But things were different after that. Their boy grew quieter and more reserved until one day it seemed like he had disappeared into himself.

Dr. Anaya had checked his hearing, which seemed fine. She did blood work and allergy tests and quizzed Anne about his diet and sleeping patterns. She advised them to be patient.

"He's growing so much right now. Try not to worry and give him some time."

Time had yielded only more and more quiet. By Fourth of July at the lake with the family, everyone noticed: Aiden had simply stopped talking.

Anne looked at her boy now sitting in the stern of the rowboat waiting for her, his hands tucked into his life preserver. They'd been living with his silence for a year and a half now. These were the moments that gutted her, the times she let herself remember the way things had been before—that little Halloween pirate, the Christmas greeter, all sunshine and smiles. Her beautiful child. Her perfect boy who would not speak.

She remembered Dr. Anaya's asking, so kindly, if there'd been any big life changes. Anne had said no. She wasn't lying. She just didn't see it then. Eventually she could pin the beginning of Aiden's withdrawal to those first weeks after Kat died, those months she was lost in her grief.

Out on the lake, the wind was pushing whitecaps toward the

shore. She set the letter to Margaret aside and scribbled a note to Tim, who'd driven down the lake to call his father from the marina.

Went to see Frankie O'Neill. Back soon. XO, A.

She rose and gathered a loaf of bread and several scones into a tea towel and wrapped a scarf around her neck. She walked down the beach to the rowboat, where Aiden sat waiting.

"It's too windy to row, love. Let's go say hello to Miss Frankie."

At the mention of Frankie, Aiden scampered down the seawall and shed his life preserver at the bottom of the trail. By the time she reached the back door, Aiden was already inside. From the doorway, Anne could see him flipping through the pages of a book on the coffee table. Frankie stood in the kitchen and raised her mug in greeting. She was in sweatpants and a T-shirt. Her face was pale, and her hair stood on end. She laughed as Anne scanned the room.

"Come on in if you dare," she said.

The kitchen table was piled high with books and notebooks. They cascaded onto the chairs and floor. Loose leaves of paper spilled across the kitchen counter. A large computer monitor hummed in the corner, and a small end table held a tape recorder and stacks of cassettes. A corkboard propped up against the wall was covered in photos and notes.

"Crikey," Anne said. "You sure we aren't interrupting?"

Frankie waved a hand.

"I'm taking a break," she said. "I was on a bit of a tear last night."

Anne held out the bread and scones.

"Me too, apparently," she said and accepted the offer of coffee.

Anne crossed over to Aiden standing in front of the couch.

"Be gentle with Miss Frankie's book, please, love," she said quietly.

She knew he heard her though he didn't look up. She studied the photos on the corkboard—all crows, she realized. Crows in flight, crows sitting on a power line, baby crows in a nest, hundreds of crows perched in a large oak tree. She took the cup from Frankie and gestured at the photos.

"I thought you said you were studying owls?" Anne said. "I must have misunderstood."

Frankie pushed a hand through her short hair and looked shy.

"No, you heard me right. This is a bit of a . . . side project. It's something I've been thinking about for a while and last night I was sort of inspired . . ." She trailed off. "In the clear light of day it all seems like a big mess."

"Oh, I know that feeling. I get the best ideas late at night. Next morning, they're often absolute tripe! But occasionally, something magic happens, right?"

Frankie nodded.

"It's like I don't have a choice. It's like it chose me—the questions, the research. It's just something I have to do."

Anne turned back toward the bulletin board.

"What's this?" she asked pointing to a long list of words under the heading "Vocalizations."

"Those are the most common sounds crows make and an approximate meaning. As far as we can figure anyway," Frankie said.

"Vocalizations," Anne read. "I didn't know they sang."

Franked cocked her head.

"It's not really singing. Though they are technically part of the passerine order, which is, broadly speaking, songbirds. But they don't really sing. The vocalizations are more about what they're saying to each other, to other birds. And what they might be saying to people."

"So, you're studying crow talk?" Anne said. "Why does that interest you?"

Frankie frowned.

"Why does it interest me?"

She sounded almost defensive.

"No, I mean, what about it interests you?"

Frankie's face relaxed.

"Oh. Well. Crows are smart, curious, and long-lived. I figure they must have a reason for what they choose to say. I find birds more interesting than most people, actually."

She looked shy again.

"I must sound sort of wacko."

Anne shook her head.

"No, I think it's lovely. I've got absolutely zero scientific inclination myself. But I love the idea that you can just pick something like this and follow your nose. Oh, the little crow!" she said, remembering, and looked toward the kitchen.

"He's gone," Frankie said. "I let him go the other day—when Aiden came up here. He helped me send Charlie Crow back to his folks. Right, Aiden?"

The boy glanced toward her, and his face bloomed open.

"Did he now?" Anne asked. "Wee sly fox."

She felt so many things. Pride in his independence, sorrow that he could not tell her about the experience, anger still at Tim for letting him wander. She did not see any judgment on Frankie's face and decided to let it be.

"Why did you decide to study birds?" Anne asked.

"Growing up here," Frankie said, gesturing around. "They were part of everything, and I just, I just loved them, I guess. When I found out you could do something like get paid to study birds, it sounded too good to be true."

"And when did you become interested in their vocalizations?" Anne asked.

Frankie opened her mouth to reply, and a terrible screech ripped through the room.

"Sweet Mother of Christ!" Anne yelled, clutching the back of the chair.

Aiden stood in front of the tape recorder looking startled. Her heart was hammering in her chest, and she felt a layer of sweat spring up on her palms. For a split second she'd thought it was Aiden screaming and felt herself go cold and then hot and then cold. Aiden put his hands behind his back and stared warily at the bulky tape player.

"Aiden! You'll be the bloody death of me!" Anne yelled.

Frankie was doubled over with her hands on her knees, helpless with laughter.

"Sssssorry! It's not funny! You should just—just see your face!" she stammered. "Both of you!"

Tears rolled down her cheeks as she laughed. Anne crouched down next to Aiden, fighting for her breath. She could almost hear his little heart banging away too.

"Gave yourself a fright didn't you, you wee trickster?"

He smiled and looked down.

Frankie, chuckling and wiping her eyes, showed Aiden how to plug in the headphones.

"You can listen like this. Let's start with the volume a little lower. Now, put these on—"

Anne flinched as Frankie stepped toward him with the headphones, but Aiden helped her slip them over his seashell ears. She showed him how to turn the tape recorder back on. Aiden pressed the earphones to his head and squeezed his eyes shut.

"If you want it louder, just turn this dial here, okay?"

He opened his eyes and touched the dial with one small finger.

"Yep, that's the one."

Aiden sat down on the floor and leaned against the couch.

Frankie, chuckling, dabbed at her eyes and gestured to the back door.

They sat in the sunshine on the bench at the back of the house. Birds flitted through the branches of the trees. The air was full of twittering and chirping, clacking and crying. Frankie identified them for her. The black-capped chickadee called "*chicka-dee-dee-dee-dee*" and hopped about near the white-throated sparrow crying "*Old Sam Peabody!*" It was the northern flicker that shouted "*Cheer!*" as it flashed through the trees. And the melodious song of the Swainson's thrush spiraled up into the shadows. A high zinging noise was the territorial hummingbird that had spotted them as soon as they came outside.

North America had about two thousand distinct species of birds, Frankie explained. Many around the cottage were remarkably long migrators and probably getting ready to head south to warmer climates for the winter. Those little sparrows, for example, raised their babies in the Northwest Territories and the Yukon but might winter in Florida. The osprey chirping over the water would fly as far as Arizona for the winter, while that little hummingbird buzzing past could end up in Mexico, more than three thousand miles away. Whether or not they made it depended on so many factors, including parental investment in feeding, protecting, and teaching them how to survive.

"It feels like we're in the middle of nowhere up here, but June Lake is located along the Pacific Flyway. It's quite important to migratory species this time of year."

Anne shook her head in wonder as the hummingbird hovered near late-blooming foxglove.

"I never thought of it before, their migration, I mean," she said, breaking off a piece of scone. "I wouldn't have a clue about how the birds in Seattle are different from the island."

Frankie brushed the crumbs off her fingers.

"How did you end up in Seattle?"

It was such a simple question; you'd think it would have a simple answer. In the past Anne would have said she'd been invited to be a visiting artist at Cornish and life had happened—Tim, Aiden, and the rest was history. It was an easy answer if not the full story. But with Katherine so much on her mind, the easy version felt impossible.

The silence lengthened, but Frankie didn't press her. Anne dropped her hands into her lap.

"I was invited to Cornish as a visiting artist. I was runner-up, really. The other girl couldn't come."

She looked at Frankie and saw the question in her eyes.

"She was my best friend. Her name was Katherine."

Her voice broke as she said the name, and the rest of it tumbled out. Kat's father needed her to stay. Kat had insisted Anne go for both their sakes. How she was going to come visit, but then Anne got pregnant and got married and had Aiden and it never seemed like the right time.

Tears dripped off her chin. She removed her glasses and wiped her face but managed to say the rest. Last year, during Holy Week, Katherine was in Northern Ireland when a car crashed into an outdoor market. Six people died, and her beautiful, talented friend was one.

Frankie squeezed her arm once but didn't say anything, and Anne let herself cry. She couldn't remember the last time she'd cried and realized how very tiring it was, going around not crying all the time, holding everything in, pretending you were fine. And they sat there like that for some time as a breeze stirred the branches of the tamarack and the maple trees wept some of their golden leaves.

After a while, Anne wiped her eyes again. She cleaned her glasses on the hem of her shirt and put them back on.

"Thank you for listening," she said.

"Of course," Frankie said.

Anne was grateful. No embarrassment, or worse—cloying platitudes.

The faint sound of a boat motor rose in the distance. They walked to the lookout and saw the *Peace-o-Heaven* coming around the point.

"I should head down and catch him," Anne said.

Back in the cottage, it was so quiet, she thought Aiden must have fallen asleep. He was sitting on the floor with his back against the couch, headphones firmly pressed to his ears with both hands. Anne called his name, and he opened his eyes and looked right at her. A joyful smile flashed across his face, and she felt a small explosion in her heart. Through the earphones she could hear the low sound of chattering crows.

"Time to go now, love. Let's say goodbye and thank you," she said, trying not to betray her emotion.

The boy was reluctant to go. Frankie showed him how to turn the machine off, and he stood holding the headphones against his chest. He glanced at the photos of the crows on the bulletin board and at the door to the bathroom.

"Come listen another day, Aiden," Frankie said.

Back at the house, Aiden climbed into the window seat with his storybook. Tim was full of news about his call with his father and excited like Anne hadn't seen him in ages. Things were changing quickly at the company, he said. They sat in front of the fire and watched a squall blow down the lake, and Tim told her about his father's new plans. All editors in chief would be promoted to assistant publishers—at the newly acquired papers in Spokane, Portland, and Ashland as well as Tim in Seattle.

"Wow, assistant publisher," she said. "Won't you miss being editor?"

Tim shook his head.

"I'll still be editing. I told Dad I'm not ready to the leave the newsroom altogether. Eric will manage more of the day-to-day details, but I'll lead editorial meetings. This way I can stay close to the reporters but have more free time to think about the big picture. Since we've acquired the new papers in Washington and Oregon, Dad wants me to help create the vision for the next phase of growth."

He frowned and tossed a log into the fireplace, sending up sparks.

"What will that entail?" Anne asked.

"Long term, I know the plan is for me to be publisher of the Seattle paper, but that's a ways down the road. Right now, we need to work out how to fold the new markets into our existing corporate structure—Portland, Ashland, and Spokane."

Dr. Anaya had said something about Spokane. A pediatric speech therapist there, Anne recalled.

"But, of course, Seattle remains the center of everything," Tim was saying. "Anyway. Enough work talk. How about I make dinner tonight and give you a break?"

"Go on, then!" Anne said, kicking off her shoes and pulling her legs up on the couch. "I'll take a glass of wine while you're at it, please."

Tim turned on the radio to listen to the news. President Clinton was under continued scrutiny for his affair with a White House intern. A peace and reconciliation process was being planned for Rwanda. Russia was fighting economic collapse.

Anne finished her letter to her mother. She wrote about how Aiden had befriended the neighbor, who was an ornithologist and oddly at ease with him. She wrote about the birds in the woods and how the color of the lake reminded her of the sea around the island. She wrote about the bird lullaby and asked if Margaret remembered it. She didn't say anything about Christi's birthday or answer her mother's questions about her return home. She knew that her mother would not push. Privacy was highly valued by her family. She sent her love to Gran and Da and put the letter in a blue airmail envelope. Aiden walked with her down the seawall and opened the letterbox for her. She told him to raise the flag and explained that Mr. Jerry would see it on his next trip up the lake and take the letter on its way to Granny in Ireland.

As they walked back to the house, Aiden reached up and grabbed her wrist, and she tried not to react. He held on to her briefly, then released her and skipped ahead of her down the seawall.

The moon was rising over the mountain now, luminous and perfectly halved. Anne looked at the invisible dark half, the half that you couldn't see but knew was there. It was the absent portion that made the illuminated quarter moon so lovely and bright.

She thought of what Dr. Anaya had said about trauma.

"Trauma is broader than you think, Anne. So many things can shake their worlds when they're small. Accident or illness. The absence of a parent. Or a death in the family."

But Anne wasn't surprised at all. She understood perfectly well now. Because she'd gone over it so many times in her mind, every detail, every nuance, searching to understand what had happened and how her son had changed so dramatically. She knew it was on her.

She'd lived in a fog those first months after Kat died, muddling her way through the semester and zombielike at home. She forgot Tim's birthday and their anniversary. But that was nothing compared with how she'd failed Aiden. Not just forgetting to pick him up from school, or making him the wrong snack, or missing doctor's appointments. Or all the times she'd started a game with him only to have him wander off because she'd stopped paying attention.

She remembered one afternoon the first summer of his silence when they'd been sitting in the living room together, Aiden with his records and Anne leafing through old notebooks. Tim was in the basement doing laundry and Anne had fallen into a light doze. She awoke to the sound of the door banging open. Aiden stood in the doorway, eyes wide. Someone yelled down the hall behind him. He ran past Anne to his room and Mrs. Silva appeared in the open doorway clad in a bathrobe with dripping hair.

"You need to teach that kid some manners, Mrs. Magnusen!" she shouted. "He can't just wander into other people's apartments without knocking! I should call CPS!"

Anne had apologized, but the neighbor was not appeased and stormed back down the hall. Anne went to Aiden's room and asked him what had happened. Why had he wandered off without her? Why had he gone into Mrs. Silva's apartment without knocking? Was he okay? He looked up at her with those big, scared eyes and said nothing. He wouldn't tell her or couldn't tell her. The next week was the Fourth of July with Tim's family. When Tim Senior had asked Aiden to pass the butter, the boy refused to look up from the napkin he was flipping back and forth in front of his eyes.

"Dammit, Tim!" he thundered. "When are you going to decide to do something about this child's manners!"

But Tim couldn't make him do anything. None of them could. Aiden could hear them, and he was shutting them out.

Anne registered then that he'd been slowly slipping away all spring. She remembered times he'd come to her with a question or a request and she'd been unable to respond or follow through. Gradually he stopped trying and soon it was typical for the two of them to be silent in the room together, the quiet broken only when Tim came home from work and forced them both to engage. He grew ever more silent until he stopped speaking altogether.

It was perfectly clear to her now, and she wished she could tell Dr. Anaya, tell someone, but she didn't have the courage.

She knew the truth and everyone else would know it eventually. Her beautiful, perfect boy had disappeared into silence because she was a terrible, absent mother.

21

DUET CALL

Many species with limited vocal ranges demonstrate the capacity for what some might call instrumental composition.

—*G. Gordon's Field Guide to the Birds of the Pacific Northwest*

Once there was a crow.

He was a very handsome crow. He had a little cane for a leg. And when he walked, the cane would go *tap tap tap*.

Once there was a crow. He was a handsome young crow. The handsome young crow met a boy.

The crow said, "Hello there, young man! My name is Charlie Crow. What is your name?!"

And the young man, the young man. And the young man said.

Well, he didn't know what to say.

22

MOBBING

Territorialism is pronounced in some species and in others absent altogether.

—*G. Gordon's Field Guide to the Birds of the Pacific Northwest*

The Halloween Frankie was four and Patrick was five, Grammy Genevieve had made them Paul Bunyan and Babe the Blue Ox costumes for Halloween. Frankie watched her carefully cut the tissue paper patterns and affix them to the fabric with neat lines of straight pins—a fuzzy blue polyester suit and ears for Babe and red-and-white checked cotton for Paul Bunyan's lumberjack shirt. Patrick wore his blue jeans and a stocking cap and bearded his face with a burnt cork. Frankie wore her patent leather church shoes to look like hooves. As they posed for a photo, Frankie thought she looked more like a blue dog than an ox and would have preferred to be a lumberjack too. But she didn't want to hurt Grammy's feelings, so she hadn't said anything.

Judith drove them to the tavern for Downtown Trick or Treat, a Hood River tradition. Frankie was thrilled to be outside at night for the first time. When Patrick announced he wanted to hand out candy at the tavern instead of trick or treating, it didn't occur to her not to go. She simply headed out the door with her laughing mother on her heels. Frankie insisted they stop at every single doorway on Oak Street, including the library, which was at the top of a steep set of stairs, and Sheppard's Farm and Tractor, which was far enough between lights that most kids wouldn't make the effort. Back at the tavern she divided her spoils equally, giving half to Patrick. It was only fair, she said, as she'd told people she was collecting for her brother too.

"That's my girl! Oxlike persistence!" Her father had laughed, pushing a cup of cocoa across the bar. At the time Frankie hadn't known what it meant, but she liked the sound of the word. Persistent. Later her professors called her that too, Dr. Grant included. Maybe she did have an oxlike propensity to just keep going. Persistent. The word ever after evoked for her the color of Babe the Blue Ox, the memory of fuzzy fleece, the sound of her black patent leather shoes tapping the sidewalk as she hurried between the lampposts of Oak Street with a chill October wind blowing the leaves off the trees.

She remembered that now, reading the letter from Oregon State University that Jerry brought with the mail. She stood on the dock and scanned the page, holding her breath and feeling a spark of hope.

> Dear Ms. O'Neill,
>   We are pleased to offer you a position in the 1999
> doctoral program at our Corvallis campus. Your
> persistence and dedication to your research is what we look
> for in our graduate students . . .

It was everything she'd hoped for—a chance to study with some of the region's best avian biologists, a tuition waiver, and a teaching position to support herself. There was even something about graduate student housing. And at the bottom:

We look forward to welcoming you into our community
in the winter quarter of 1999.

Sincerely,
Dr. John Twyhee

She tucked the letter in her pocket and walked back up to the
house, where she plugged in the coffee pot and paced the kitchen.
The OSU offer was perfect, but she knew they couldn't hire her without the official completion of her master's. She looked at her piles of
notebooks on the kitchen table and her revision that she'd been ignoring for days now as she'd distracted herself with Charlie Crow
and her notes from Marzluff's study. There was only one way forward. She'd submit her manuscript, write her formal letter of completion to her committee, and request a date for her defense. It was
all she could do, and the next move would be theirs. Dr. Grant might
want to ignore her, but surely her other committee members would
help move things along?

She fired up the computer and opened the latest draft of her thesis, "Family Ties: The Role of Pair Bonding in Habitat Rejuvenation
for the Spotted Owl." She checked her revision outline to gauge what
she'd completed. Tending to Charlie Crow and rereading Marzluff's
research had felt like playing hooky, but the time away from her
manuscript had sharpened her focus. As she settled into the work,
she found the flow she needed. Methodically, she completed Dr.
Wood-Smith's edits, double-checked Dr. Andreas's suggestions and
Dr. Grant's notes—which were mostly about excising her original
research. She worked long hours for two days, stopping only to make
a sandwich or heat up a can of soup. Time disappeared and she lost
herself in the process. She went to bed the second night knowing it
was the best she could do and hoping it was enough.

The next morning dawned cool and cloudy. After breakfast, she
headed down the lake with fresh copies of her thesis, letters to her

individual committee members and the department, and a response to Dr. Twyhee at OSU accepting the offer. At the post office, she handed everything across the counter to Donna. It felt ceremonial, but of course Donna couldn't know that.

Frankie puttered back up the lake slowly, feeling at loose ends now that this monumental task was complete. The lake water was quiet and the mountain heavier with snow. She considered going fishing at the mouth of the Windy River and tried to remember where she'd seen the rods and tackle. By the time she landed the boat and located the fishing gear in the back of the pump house, it had begun to rain. She decided to wait until it lightened. She lay on the couch and stared out at the lake as it dimpled with raindrops. She tried to rest in the feeling of accomplishment or at least relief, but a familiar anxiety crept over her. Frankie never knew what do with time on her hands. She spent the afternoon cleaning the cottage. She put all her owl research and notebooks in boxes and tucked them in her grandparents' old room. She swept the floor and did the dishes, which had piled up considerably. She washed her clothes in the ancient washing machine and hung them to dry when the rain quit. She split more wood, and when she couldn't think of any other chores, she went inside and tried to read one of Patrick's dog-eared novels. But she couldn't settle.

Her eyes strayed to the corkboard covered in crow photos that she'd left propped up against the wall. She recalled her first day helping Marzluff last summer, the feeling of sun hot on her back as she'd crouched behind a laurel bush holding the boom of a microphone. A group of sorority girls walked by and, startled by the sight of Frankie crouched there, had shrieked and clutched each other. They laughed as they hurried away, and Frankie knew they were laughing at her, but she didn't care. She was exactly where she wanted to be.

Marzluff's research began with crows' acuity with facial recognition. But beyond that he'd shown that the crows on the UW campus also taught other crows to recognize certain faces as dangerous. They were communicating something specific to each other. But how?

Frankie had studied the crow vocalizations for hours that summer. She'd listened to recordings of threat calls collected from various crows around the Pacific Northwest as well as the crows in Marzluff's study. After some time, she became convinced she could discern a distinct pitch, tone, and duration to the call of Marzluff's caveman-mobbing crows. She developed a simple theory: The UW crows didn't just recognize the caveman mask wearers; they had developed a unique threat call for them too.

She worried Marzluff might not welcome her idea. After all, she wasn't connected to his lab. Just a grad student on loan, an extra pair of hands. But she worked up the courage to tell him, and he congratulated her and told her to keep working on it. He invited her to come talk it over any time before revealing it to Dr. Grant.

She'd certainly bungled that, hadn't she?

At the kitchen table, she flipped open the notebook with her notes on Charlie Crow. She'd documented his behavior out of habit, and her curiosity about crows had been renewed. She chuckled, remembering Aiden's fascination with the crow recordings. That curious boy had tucked himself against the couch, pressing the headphones to his ears. What was he hearing? she wondered. What was he thinking? You could feel the bright spark of his mind within his silence. She pulled the headphones on and as the afternoon shadows lengthened over the lake, she immersed herself in the world of crows talking.

The next morning, the barometer pointed to "Fair," which boded well for the berry-picking excursion she'd suggested to Anne. The berry pails were not in the root cellar, so Patrick must have left them in the store. Frankie climbed down the trail to the dock and stood at the door to the little building. She pulled her key ring out of her pocket.

"The keys to the kingdom!" her father had said, handing her this same key ring on her sixteenth birthday. She could still read his quirky left-handed printing on each key: "Root Cellar," "Pump

House," "Cottage," "The Peggotty," "Store," "Outboard." There were unmarked duplicates and keys to various padlocks that had gone missing. But Frankie knew each key intimately and could have found the store key with her fingers without looking. She unlocked the door and pushed it open with her shoulder.

The old wooden door sighed into the low-ceilinged room, and Frankie flipped on the lights. A fine layer of dust covered the wooden counter, and the sunlight caught a tangle of spiderwebs in the far window. The refrigerator door yawned wide and empty. She knew the store hadn't opened that summer. Patrick had been busy with his clerkship. And Jack—a knot rose in her throat, and she made herself finish the thought. Jack hadn't been there either.

She found the berry pails in the storage cupboard where she thought they'd be. She pulled them down and shut the cupboard and looked around the small room. She could almost see her grand-mother at the counter selling pints of fresh huckleberries, wild spring morels, or early fall chanterelles. Grammy Genevieve in her signa-ture overalls and flowered chambray shirts charmed her customers— the Beauty Bay neighbors as well as day-trippers who came up to fish and swim on the north end of the lake. Later it was Patrick sitting on the stool there, usually with a paperback open on the counter. Like Genevieve he was friendly and a good listener.

She recalled the summer Patrick had taken over the store ten years ago. It was the summer after Genevieve died—right before Frankie's junior year in high school. Judith had her real estate license by then and announced she'd be staying in town the entire season.

"Frankie can run the store, and Patrick can help you with the maintenance," she'd said to Jack.

Jack objected, which was rare. The discontents of their marriage were more commonly about Judith insisting Jack do or stop doing something and Jack breezily ignoring her. But this was different— Judith opting out of established routine completely. He and Judith had such a fight about it that they didn't speak for three days. Things eventually blew over. Jack, pretending there had been no slamming of doors and throwing of tools in the garage, sidled up to Judith one night as she washed the dishes and put his arms around her.

"Look out, Hood River," he said. "Judith O'Neill is an absolute shark!"

She leaned back into his chest. A truce. She still did that then, Frankie remembered with a pang of sorrow.

Jack might have felt his wife's abandonment keenly, but for Patrick and Frankie, those summers had been good ones. Patrick knew Frankie hated the store, with its requisite chitchat. Frankie knew she was just as good if not better at helping their father with caretaking duties. So they swapped jobs. Jack didn't comment and nobody mentioned it to Judith. The summer residents grew accustomed to the sight of Jack O'Neill and his gangly daughter showing up with a toolbox and ladder to work on their houses. And on the weekends, when Jack was at the tavern, Frankie worked by herself. Patrick ran the store just as well as their grandmother had, if not better. He brought in more fishing gear and things he knew kids would like— ice cream bars, soda, and chips. Like Grammy, he sold fresh berries and wild mushrooms and could offer advice on which flies to use for fishing and what spots on the lake the fish might be biting.

Now Frankie set the berry pails on the counter and opened the fly-fishing cabinet to see what flies Patrick had left. Unsurprisingly, the sparse inventory was full of summer flies. She shut the cabinet and leaned against it, looking out the dirty window at the water.

She had loved those long summer days at the lake with her dad and brother. The sun rose early and set so late the sky would still be greeny-yellow at 9 p.m. In a flash of memory, she recalled sitting on the dock outside the store with Jack and Patrick at the end of a hot July day. She was tired after a long afternoon helping Jack hang gutters on the Condons' house. Jack was telling some joke to a fisherman who'd stopped to buy ice and the guy was laughing. Everyone loved his jokes. Jack cracked open a cold Rainier. Talking to the guide, he set the beer down and carried on with his story.

Later, after he'd gone up to the cottage, Frankie noticed the can of beer sweating in the sunshine. She rolled it between her palms and raised it to her mouth. The first cool, bitter gulp foamed out her nose. She hated the taste but drank it anyway. After that, she would sneak a beer from time to time, and Jack hadn't seemed to notice. Patrick was the one who brought it up. One Saturday morning as Frankie restocked the beer cooler, she made a joke about setting aside a sixer for herself. Patrick looked up from the inventory list.

"You should be careful with that, Frank," he said.

Her body flushed with embarrassment.

"You're just jealous," she said.

Patrick shook his head and returned to the inventory list.

"Nah," he said. "But we're Irish, you know. I'm pretty sure Grandpa Ray was an alcoholic. And it runs in families. Just something I think about."

Frankie scoffed, annoyed that her big brother had ideas that never occurred to her. It was years before she understood what he meant. Now that she understood so clearly, she wondered why it had taken so long to grasp the truth about it all.

Unwillingly her thoughts turned to last Thanksgiving, that terrible day her family had unraveled. It had begun as a nice afternoon. Judith had made an amazing meal with Patrick's help, and her parents seemed to be getting along. Frankie wasn't saying much but she always felt quiet around her mother. She listened to Judith talk about work and Jack describe the lineup for the annual post-Thanksgiving poker tournament at Hank's. Judith was bragging about Patrick's raise at work, and Patrick downplayed it with his typical modesty. Then Jack jokingly asked for a loan to set up a second tavern in the Hood River Heights.

"Make an easier commute for your old man," he'd said.

He was joking, but something about the way he said it made Frankie look closely at him. Four years older than her mother, Jack O'Neill was only fifty-two. But while Judith had the energy of someone half her age, Jack sounded tired, and his eyes were puffy and red.

Judith stood up with the gravy tureen and marched into the kitchen.

"I'm kidding, my darling!" her husband called after her. "I want to retire and take you to Aruba!"

He hummed the Beach Boys song and waved his napkin in the air over his plate, waggling his eyebrows at Patrick and Frankie. Judith returned and thumped the tureen down.

"You know I don't want to go to Aruba, Jack O'Neill," she said, her voice low and tense.

Frankie looked at Patrick, who rolled his eyes. This was not a new argument. Judith had long been after Jack to sell the tavern and invest in something else. Jack put her off, laughing and noncommittal. But now he looked angry too, which was unlike him. He took a pull on his beer and set the bottle down hard.

"It's difficult to track just what you want, my dear," he said.

Frankie rose with the water pitcher. Anything to get out of the room.

"Mary Frances O'Neill, sit down," Judith commanded.

Frankie sat. Patrick stared at the ceiling. Judith crossed her arms and glared at her husband.

"You know what I want," Judith said. "I want you to sell that god-forsaken building."

Jack tried to laugh her off, but she persisted.

"I want us to build something new at the waterfront. It's a chance for you to rise above where you came from."

"Where I came from?" Jack sputtered. "What's wrong with where I came from?"

Judith gestured around her.

"Look around you, Jack! You can do better than this. You should do better than this!"

Grandpa Ray had built the little house in the 1940s. He and Genevieve had given it to Jack and Judith after Frankie was born, and the joke had long been that it was their starter home. Judith had lost her sense of humor about that joke years ago, as the little house had not aged well.

Jack's face flushed red.

"My father built this place with his own two hands!" he said, his voice rising. "He wasn't ashamed of honest work, and neither am I!"

Judith planted her palms on the table and leaned forward, her voice low and furious.

"Your father was a lazy, unambitious dreamer who disappointed everyone around him."

"My father—" Jack roared.

"Your father drank away the best years of his life!" Judith shouted.

Frankie looked at Patrick. His face betrayed nothing. How long had they been fighting like this?

"He did not—" Jack began.

"Oh, come on, Jack!" Judith interrupted. "Your father was an alcoholic and probably his father before him!"

And then she said the thing they never said.

"It's part of your family history, and it's part of you! You need to face it, Jack. You're an alcoholic, just like your father!"

Jack looked like he'd been slapped, and Frankie could barely look at him.

"Don't let it ruin everything for us. Pull yourself together," Judith said. "And just sell the damn building!"

Jack sat back and gave a short laugh. He wiped his mouth with his napkin, folded it, and lay it on the table. His anger had left him as quickly as it had come.

"Well, Judith, that isn't going to happen," he said in his normal voice.

He looked at Judith with such love. Couldn't she see that? That pained Frankie as much as how sad and old he sounded. He ran a hand through his hair.

"Oh, Judith, surely you know," he said. "Are you going to make me say it out loud, then?"

Judith stiffened and her face creased with anger.

Jack clasped his hands and leaned toward his wife.

"I will not be selling the River City Saloon, my dear," he said. "Because the River City Saloon is not mine to sell."

He paused.

"Judith, Dad left the building to Hank."

The silence that followed was deafening. The drip of the faucet echoed off the walls and the clock ticked furiously. Judith stood up with the turkey platter, stalked to the kitchen, and slammed it down on the counter. Shards of china and turkey skittered across the floor as Judith walked out the back door.

Frankie never knew where her mother went that night, but she was not home in the morning when Frankie got up. She called Patrick's and Judith wasn't there either. Though her parents had argued in the past, this was different. Neither one of them had ever spent the night elsewhere. Everything felt blown apart, shattered like the Thanksgiving platter.

Judith had not returned by the time Frankie left for Seattle that afternoon, two days early. Jack drove her to the bus stop, and they didn't talk about any of it. He didn't try to cajole her into staying any longer, like he usually did. Something had gone terribly wrong in the family, and Frankie felt lost.

"I'm so proud of you, Frances," he'd said, holding her by the shoulders and looking her in the eye. "You've no idea."

When he hugged her, he felt somehow fragile, her once larger-than-life father, and it made her feel worse. She climbed on the bus, and he raised a hand in farewell as she found her seat. She remembered the sorrow in his face as he turned away, put his hands in his pockets, and walked down the empty sidewalk. She remembered it all, the last time she'd ever seen him alive.

Her heart felt heavy now with the memory of that day, of all the things she hadn't said and wished she had. The time she'd lost by staying in Seattle for Christmas and Presidents' Day weekend and Saint Patrick's Day. Afraid of Judith's anger, her parents' fighting, avoiding the heartache. Until that terrible day Patrick had called to tell her their father was dead.

She turned away from the window and looked around the dusty store, once bright and happy and now so small and sad. Frankie shut the door and walked up the dock with the empty berry pails and felt the rush of grief.

Oh, Dad, she thought. Why'd you have to leave? Why now and why like this?

23

THE TUNE

Songbirds are born with the ability to create melodies but
also learn by listening to other birds—even those of different species.

—*G. Gordon's Field Guide to the Birds of the Pacific Northwest*

Frankie had told Anne that the best berry spot was quite a far bit
into the woods. She'd cautioned Anne about the distance, the need
for water and snacks, and the slight possibility of rain. She'd advised
jackets and sturdy shoes and suggested Anne bring berry pails if she
could find any at the house. She'd recommended hats in the unlikely
but possible chance there were ticks in the woods. But she'd not said
a bloody thing about bloody snakes.

The quick brown thing slithered across the trail nearly under the
toe of her trainer as Anne walked past the outbuildings.

"Holy sweet Mother of Jesus!" she yelled, dropping the berry pails
and sweeping Aiden up in her arms. "Bloody hell! Holy fecking shite!"

Frankie betrayed no concern about the snake but was, instead,
doubled over laughing, which didn't seem very polite, Anne thought.

"I'm sss-orry," Frankie stuttered. "I think you jumped about a foot
in the air. I mean, you really cleared some distance!"

Aiden wriggled free and Anne backed up, sweeping the ground
with her eyes.

"Where'd the bastard go? Did you see it?! Where's he gone to?!"

"It's okay, Anne," Frankie gasped, laughing. "It's just a little garter snake. He's more afraid of you, I sss-wear."

She reached down and lifted the wriggling thing out of the grass. It twined around her wrist, flicking its tongue and gazing around with beady eyes. Anne shuddered and sucked in her breath.

"Look—this little guy is just trying to find a safe place to hide. He wouldn't hurt a fly. Well, maybe he would eat a fly. But he wouldn't hurt a person."

Aiden wandered closer and looked up at the creature on Frankie's arm. She crouched down and motioned for Aiden to remove the headphones he'd commandeered at the cottage. When he'd seemed reluctant to take them off that morning, Frankie said he could wear them on the hike, assuring Anne she didn't mind. Aiden pushed the foam discs off his ears and leaned toward the little snake as Frankie explained that it liked to eat slugs, frogs, and worms.

"He'll hibernate up here this winter," she said. "He'll have a nice sleep until things warm up in spring. In reptiles it's called 'brumation.'"

Anne declined Frankie's invitation to come closer, but Aiden reached out and touched the snake. His face bloomed with wonder. Her heart swelled and she had to turn away. Retrieving the buckets she'd flung into the underbrush, she composed herself.

"You okay over there?" Frankie called.

"We don't have snakes in Ireland," Anne said lightly to mask her emotion. "Surely you've heard of Saint Patrick?"

"Of course. The patron saint of beer and fun runs."

"Exactly right."

They resumed hiking and crossed a small meadow of tangled grass and daisies. Anne noticed a circular structure at the far side of the clearing. A bird blind, Frankie explained. It had never been used much for hunting, though. She seemed to hesitate and then led the way up into the blind.

"This is where I first started watching birds as a kid," she said.

Anne looked at the weathered wood and saw lists of birds scrawled there year by year.

"What a marvelous record," she said.

Aiden pressed his forehead against the slats and peered out into the meadow. A pair of crows flapped down to the ground followed by two more. They paced in a broad circle gossiping to each other.

"Karr! Karr! Karr!"

Two of the birds were smaller than the others. One of them hopped close to the largest bird and bent its head forward. The bigger bird began to groom it.

"Is that part of mating?" Anne asked.

Frankie shook her head.

"No, that's just some sociable grooming. The little one is too young to mate. Baby crows live with their parents for several years before starting their own families," she said. "The bigger one is probably a parent or an older sibling. They spend the winter in big groups—hundreds or thousands of them. And then they split off into their territories for the spring. I've never been up here so late in the year. I'd love to find out where this bunch roosts."

Anne remembered the story about the zoo murder Tim had mentioned.

"There was some story about a big flock in Seattle near the zoo this summer. Did you know about that?"

Frankie frowned.

"Yes. The neighborhood wanted the city to remove them. One of my professors testified about it at city council."

She shook her head.

"People don't seem to understand you can't just move animals around like furniture."

"What would you tell the folk who are bothered by them?"

"Get rid of open pit dumps for one thing," Frankie said. "And start composting. We leave so much trash lying around. How can we blame them? Other than that?"

She watched the quartet of birds lift off and fly into the trees.

"Appreciate the fact that they clean up roadkill and control the rodent population. Nobody likes rats," she said. "Not even me."

They climbed down out of the blind and carried on up the hill. The crows cawed up ahead of them. Anne told Frankie the story of Saint Kevin, the Irish patron saint of crows. A hermit, Saint Kevin lived in a cave near the lake valley of Glendalough. It was said that the crows trusted him so that one laid an egg in his hand as he stood with his arms outstretched in prayer.

"And he stood like that until it hatched."

Frankie laughed.

"Well, that is a miracle, given that a crow's egg gestates for sixteen to eighteen days. I bet his arms were tired. Way to go, Saint Kevin!"

Anne told Frankie another old story about the Corvus constellation, named for Brân the Blessed, killed in a battle between the Britons and Irish in defense of his sister. His soul became a raven.

"It's somehow connected to the ravens in the Tower of London. They've been there for ages."

"Since the late nineteenth century," Frankie said over her shoulder. "I learned that in Bird Bingo."

The sun warmed her neck as they climbed. Aiden had no trouble keeping up. He walked between the two women, holding the headphones clamped over his ears.

Anne did not move effortlessly. She could feel a rivulet of sweat dripping down her back. Exercise had never brought her joy, she thought wryly as she struggled to control her labored breathing. Frankie kept talking about crows and did not seem to need any response. Anne listened to her voice, let her mind drift, thinking about the big crow grooming the little crow. Allopreening, Frankie had

called it. She thought about Saint Kevin standing with his arms out
in prayer, Brân defending Brânwen. There was another Irish story
just on the edge of her memory. Another story about crows and a
woman. What was it?

By the time they reached the huckleberry fields at the top of the
mountain that Frankie kept insisting was just a hill, Anne had almost forgotten about the snake. And there Frankie's earlier failure
to mention the possibility of small snakes was eclipsed completely by
the appearance of a very large bear.

Anne pulled Aiden back and swore in a long, furious whisper.
Frankie grabbed her arm.

"Don't run," she said quietly. "Don't move."

The animal looked like a giant teddy bear sitting in the middle of
the sunny berry patch. The sun streamed through its fur and turned
it reddish at the ends. It grunted happily as it raked enormous paws
through the bushes and scooped berries into its mouth. Terrified as
she was, Anne saw it was beautiful. They watched it for what seemed
like ages. Then the bear pointed its snout, rolled to its feet, and lum-
bered away into the shelter of the woods.

Frankie bent over and put her hands on her knees, laughing glee-
fully.

"You sounded just like my father then," she said, wiping her eyes.
"I thought I was going to wet my pants."

She looked down at Aiden, who was looking to where the bear
had disappeared. She tapped his headphones and pulled them off his
ears.

"Your mother swears like a sailor, but you are one cool cucumber.
That's just the right thing to do. Never run from a bear. Just be very
quiet and back slowly away, giving it lots of space."

She straightened up and looked at Anne.

"That's a black bear and they are usually scared of people. The
mamas are dangerous if they've got babies with them. That looked
like a young male. But truly. Good job, Aiden."

Anne, collecting herself, wiped her glasses on the edge of her shirt and put them back on her face.

"Yes, well done, sweetie. Nerves of steel like your mammy," she said dryly.

They waded into the berry patch in a companionable silence. There was something meditative about pulling the purple berries free of the bushes. The fruit smelled smoky and sweet and plunked into the bottom of the pails. Aiden put the berries directly into his mouth, and his fingers and lips were soon stained purple. The wind picked up and blew through the trees around them. Anne watched their slender trunks bending and swaying, and a flurry of golden maple leaves blew down as the wind gusted. She hummed a little tune.

The sun moved skyward and cast a shade across the berry patch. Their pails were full by then, and they moved to a sunny spot to eat lunch. In the middle of the clearing was a strange pine tree. It had grown around a boulder; its roots were thick and gnarled and the trunk had taken a sharp turn skyward. Yet it looked strong and healthy. Anne sat with her back against a sun-warmed log and closed her eyes. The whispering breeze sounded like the ocean at home.

Frankie watched the sky as they ate. Occasionally she'd point and name a bird flashing above. Eagles and osprey. Sassy spotted towhees and pert little wrens. Brash Canada geese and wood ducks. Anne asked about the drowsy tonal call they kept hearing.

"That's a nuthatch," Frankie said, smiling. "You have a good ear. That's one of my favorites. They're tiny little things to make so much noise. They're high in the trees so we won't see them up close."

There was a zinging noise and Anne followed Frankie's gaze. The sound doubled and she raised her binoculars to look.

"Oh, wow. Would you look at that?" she murmured.

She dropped the binoculars and looked at Anne, her face lit with joy.

"Hummingbird nest!" she whispered. "So late in the season too!"

She motioned for Anne to come to her and showed her how to

focus the glasses and where to point them. A blur of green and brown, then it came into focus: a tiny perfect nest of golden moss and two impossibly minute baby birds with featherless heads and gaping beaks. Then a flash of red and gold as the mother and father darted in to feed them.

"Hummingbird babies are the size of bumblebees. They need to be fed every few minutes," Frankie murmured. "It's an absolute marathon."

Anne passed the glasses back, and Frankie raised them to her eyes.

"A glittering of hummingbirds. That's what you call a group of them. Or a tune. A tune of hummingbirds. Isn't that perfect? I think they sound just like Tinker Bell."

Aiden stood and Anne watched in astonishment as he pushed his way into Frankie's lap. Aiden, who didn't like to be touched. Aiden, who didn't respond to strangers. Aiden, who wouldn't let his own parents hold him. Her quiet boy plopped himself down on Frankie O'Neill's legs and reached for the binoculars with both wee hands.

Frankie lowered the glasses to his eye level and explained how to see through them. She held them and Aiden curled his hands around hers and leaned back against her chest.

"Can you see them there, Aiden? The little baby hummingbirds?"

Anne could hear his soft breathing, a pause, and then a delighted tinkle of laughter.

"Isn't that something?" Frankie said. "Aren't we so lucky?"

Anne turned away to hide her tears and could not speak. But speechlessness seemed appropriate to the rare moment.

After a while Aiden walked back to sit near his mother. Anne looked at him, her little changeling, her heart full and turbulent. She wanted to squeeze him tight and congratulate him. She wanted to grab him and kiss him. She wanted to celebrate his connecting with another person. And she was terrified it would make him retreat once more.

His wellness check that past spring had marked a year since

Aiden began to withdraw into silence. And Anne admitted that his behavior alarmed her sometimes. His meltdowns, while rare, had seemed to increase in intensity. She felt his frustration came from his inability to communicate. This time Dr. Anaya had recommended speech therapy and a new treatment based on play—music, drawing, and games.

Anne thought those options sounded worth exploring, but Tim was unsatisfied.

"How do we fix it?" he'd asked, his voice rising. "He was talking and now he's not. What's the solution?"

Dr. Anaya waited a beat before she spoke. Her voice was characteristically kind, but Anne heard the firmness in it.

"In cases like these I find it's best to proceed slowly, Tim. These things can take some time and you must be patient."

Tim stood up and left the office. Anne apologized for him, but Dr. Anaya shook her head.

"I understand his frustration. It can be harder for dads," she said. "Let's try these therapies and we'll go from there."

But Tim hadn't been willing to do that, and he'd found allies in his parents. It was Tim Senior's friend who pulled some strings to get Aiden tested at the University of Washington Pediatric Clinical Research Center.

"Advice from the experts. That's what you need in a situation like this," Tim Senior had pontificated at a Sunday dinner soon thereafter. Anne was speechless with anger, which her father-in-law mistook for gratitude.

"Just get my grandson well. That will be thanks enough," he'd said.

Anne wanted to throw her plate down the table at him. Everyone seemed to think her boy needed fixing. Could they not just give him time?

She shook off the memory now and braided a crown of daisies for her son's head.

"Oh, my one and only, you've gone across the sea. I stand in the wind and watch the sun set low. When will you come back to me?" she sang.

Aiden patted his knees and bobbed his head to the rhythm of the song.

"I know that song! My grammy used to sing that to me," Frankie said.

"It's an old one. I teach children's songs in my introductory classes," Anne said. "English and Irish. It's an easy way to introduce students to the new language."

Frankie asked her to sing it in Irish and she did.

"It's beautiful," Frankie said when she'd finished. "My dad really wanted to go someday to Ireland. The other day I was trying to remember what village Grandpa Ray was born in so I could tell you, and I thought, Oh, I'll just call Dad and ask."

Her voice caught and she looked away. Anne's heart clenched watching her.

After a minute, Anne said, "It's so hard when people are just—gone, isn't it?"

Frankie wiped an arm across her eyes and looked up.

"They say it gets easier?"

Her voice was plaintive. She looked at Anne and Anne knew she was asking about Katherine. Easier wasn't the right way to explain it. Anne's heart felt heavy with the finality of Kat's death, the impossibility of seeing her face or hearing her voice ever again. And then, almost imperceptibly, she felt a shifting of that weight as if Frankie's very question had changed the shape of her own grief ever so slightly.

"Not easier exactly. It just becomes . . . a part of you."

She looked at the tree growing around the boulder, its sinewy roots wrapped up and over the granite obstacle and still thriving somehow.

"Maybe like that," she said.

She didn't know if it made any sense, but Frankie nodded, and they didn't speak for a few minutes. They both seemed to be listening to the wind, the tinkling hummingbird parents, the inevitable passage of time.

Frankie stood and brushed off the seat of her trousers.

"Are you two game for a slight detour on the way down?"

They called it the Lightning Tree, she said once they were standing at the foot of the grand old cedar, its enormous branches reaching above them. She told them about the hundred-year storm and the thunder that had shaken the cottage. How her father and his little sister waited until the rain had stopped and climbed the hill and found the giant tree blackened and smoking. And how the hollowed-out bottom had become a special place for her boy father and later for Frankie and her brother.

Anne leaned down and peered inside the hollowed-out tree. She breathed in the smell of cedar and moss. Sunlight winked through the cracks in the weathered wood.

"It's gorgeous," she said, "like a little sanctuary."

Aiden slipped past her and stepped inside the tree. The interior was more than tall enough for him to stand upright. He reached up and pulled down a large blue-and-green cat's-eye marble. Frankie laughed and explained how her father had kept his treasures there as a boy.

"Patrick and I did too. There's all kinds of stuff stashed in there."

Aiden rolled the marble across his small palms.

"Put it back now, love," Anne said.

"It's okay," Frankie said. "You can keep that if you want, Aiden. Put one of your own treasures in there next time."

The child stilled the marble and kept his eyes on his hands.

"That's lovely, isn't it? You can take that with you. Isn't that nice of Miss Frankie?"

They walked the rest of the way down the hill in near silence. Anne watched her son tripping down the hill behind Frankie. Aiden was going to be Aiden, she thought. What Tim's parents thought about him was not her concern. She would let him be who he was going to be. And Tim? She wanted to trust that he would too, but she really didn't know. She just didn't know.

When they reached Frankie's cottage, Aiden leapt onto the little trolley and Frankie offered to ferry him down to the beach. Anne descended the trail alone. She looked out over the green face of the lake, which shimmered to corduroy in a light breeze. She could see the lights on in the big house at the end of the seawall where Tim waited. She felt a surge of love for him and wanted to tell him about all of it—the snake, the bear, and Aiden with Frankie and the hummingbirds. There had been a time she'd told him everything, hadn't there? But not anymore, and not about Aiden. Not since this bloody assessment. Not after he'd been talking with his parents about things Anne felt were private.

She swallowed around the knot in her throat and felt the tangle of grief in her heart. It was all knotted up with Katherine's death and Aiden's silence, but also, she knew, her loss of trust in Tim. The report from UW would change things, and she didn't know how to prepare.

She reached the bottom of the trail and heard Aiden's tinkling laugh. Frankie was helping him down from the trolley with one hand and saying something. He turned back and laughed up at her. Then he scampered off the trolley and down the seawall toward the house, his face lit with delight. Frankie waved as the little cart climbed back up the hill, and Anne walked toward the house.

In the kitchen, Tim leaned across the counter and kissed her.

"I just made myself a sandwich and I'm going to keep working."

Anne was grateful when he returned to the sunroom and left her alone in the kitchen to wash the huckleberries. Her heart was so full that she didn't trust herself to speak to him. She went to bed and felt her sorrow trailing behind her like a quilt. She didn't try to fight it or explain it away. She let the weight of it fall across her body. Tim did not speak to her when he came to bed, perhaps thinking her asleep.

As she lay in the dark, she thought about Frankie and Aiden laughing together at the bottom of the trolley tracks. Frankie, who'd become such an unexpected ally. Her sadness began to shift and transform, breaking up like mist over the water. She thought about Kat and the joy of making music with her. She peeled back that layer and tried to recall where her own music began. Before she met Kat, before they'd discovered such harmony in their collaboration, her music had come from elsewhere. She recalled the feeling if she couldn't quite name the source. A mysterious well she'd found in silence, in deep listening, in that voice that came from within her but that was not her. That voice that offered up old stories and bright images so generously, as if to say, *"Use this if you can. If not, perhaps someone else will."*

In a half sleep her thoughts drifted—the wriggling snake, the fat black bear, the exquisite hummingbird babies, Aiden's delighted face, and the burn scar on the cedar tree. Crows flying above the meadow and the tree growing around the boulder. Images flashed across her mind as she listened to Tim's deep breathing.

In her mind she heard the wee trill of the hummingbird, the drowsy call of the nuthatch, the saucy yawp of the crows. She remembered then the old myth she wanted to tell Frankie, the story about the woman and the crows. Morrigan. Then she felt it—the old feeling, so long lost. The voice rose to the front of her sleepy mind. *"I have a story for you,"* it said. *"Are you ready?"*

She slipped out of bed and went into the kitchen. The lake was dark and quiet, and the wind murmured as it rushed over the roof. She found her notebook, sat down, and began to write.

24

CONTENTMENT CALLS

Some longer journeys are not migratory at all but under-
taken to satisfy various impulses.

—*G. Gordon's Field Guide to the Birds of the Pacific Northwest*

❧

A mama crow lays between three and seven eggs in a summer.

Baby crows live with their parents for years before starting their own families.

Brother and sister crows will stick around to help feed the new baby crows.

A baby hummingbird is the size of a bumblebee.

A baby hummingbird must be fed every few minutes. It's a marathon.

An adult hummingbird weighs about four grams. That's less than a teaspoon of sugar!

Hummingbirds fly south for the winter, some as far as Mexico. That is called migrating.

The American crow does not migrate.

25

SQUALLING CALLS

The nesting site is most naturally abandoned by young
birds after they learn to fly.

—*G. Gordon's Field Guide to the Birds of the Pacific Northwest*

⁓

Crow's-feet, as the crow flies, eating crow. Something to crow about.
Up with the crows. A crow to pull. Crow bait. These were just some
of the many idioms Frankie had learned from Dr. Tandy in Bird
Bingo as an undergrad. It amused her then and since whenever she
heard people use the phrases—one more way the clever birds had
infiltrated the human world.

Jerry Sewell had terrific crow's-feet, Frankie thought as she
watched them crinkle when he laughed. Jerry leaned against the side
of the store with his hands in the pockets of his old windbreaker offering gossip about the lumber camp; a disagreement between the
foreman and the Forest Service supervisor about the boundary line
was really about an old feud over a woman they'd both loved in high
school. The cook was up in arms about someone pilfering the cooking sherry and the sawyers were grumbling about overtime pay.
Jerry always had time to stop and shoot the breeze. Frankie listened
and wondered idly how old he was. Older than her parents, but Jerry
seemed timeless.

". . . they're starting to wrap up," Jerry was saying. "Foreman said they'll end this week. I'll help run gear and crews down and then pull the boat."

He glanced up at the snowy face of the mountain looming over the lake.

"They're pushing it this late in the month. The snowline is really coming down. We could get a big dump anytime, I told him."

"You don't sound too worried," Frankie said.

His face was boyish and he held his palms up.

"What can I say? It's all hardship pay! And I don't mind a good storm," he said. "Drives Marilyn to distraction."

He turned the conversation to gossip about Conner's barn, where the locals all stored their boats for the winter. Jerry reported that Conner's son was managing now and wanted customers to make reservations so he could plan the arrangement of boats. The old-timers thought that was uproariously funny, given the chaotic state of Conner's barn.

"Dale asked him if there'd be valet parking," Jerry said, slapping his leg.

He reached into the boat and handed her a stack of mail, and Frankie watched him load the Magnusens' mail into their box.

"Have you seen much of young Tim and his family?" Jerry asked. "They'll be heading down next week from what he told me."

Frankie felt a pang of disappointment. Of course they'd be leaving, though. She'd grown to like Anne and her quiet, curious boy so. When might she see them again? What came next in a new friendship? She didn't know.

She untied Jerry's bowline and watched the old Hewescraft head west across the lake toward the logging camp. Back up at the house, she plugged in the coffee pot and sifted through her mail while the percolator wheezed and chugged away. Her stomach flipped over when she saw a thin envelope from the University of Washington. She'd waited so long and here it was.

"Eating crow" was the phrase that leapt to mind as she scanned the page.

> To Whom It May Concern,
>   This letter serves as notification that you have failed to provide the appropriate documentation from you and your committee members as required by the University of Washington College of Arts and Sciences to graduate fall quarter, 1998. As such, your program completion date will be postponed for the 1998 calendar year. You may reapply after January 11, 1999, at the onset of winter quarter. If you care to appeal this decision, please contact the chair of your department directly to ask for assistance . . .

She stared at the page for a long minute, not wanting to believe it. She'd sent the copies of her manuscript, and Dr. Grant and the others hadn't even bothered to reply themselves? The letter was from the dean's office. Her mind felt blank. After months of guessing and imagining various outcomes, it really was just over like this. Her ears rang and the walls of the little house seemed to bulge toward her and away. She went outside and sat on the bench.

Without her thesis defense, there would be no job at OSU. Could she contest it? The letter said to contact the chair of her department, and that was Dr. Grant. She remembered the only communication she'd received from him since the symposium—a short, angry email reminding her that it was illegal for her to use his lab to pursue competing research and he could sue her. Did her life as a scientist just stop here? Where could she work? All the seasonal winter positions with the Forest Service or field teams would be filled by now.

Frankie looked up into the dark forest behind the house. She heard them before she saw them—Charlie Crow first and then his parents swooped down and landed in front of her. The parents muttered and chatted to each other. One of them fed the young nestling and returned to the air as Charlie Crow gulped down the food and hopped toward Frankie.

"Hi, little buddy," she said. "Look at you getting around."

The fledgling cocked his head. He trained his beady little eye on hers and made that funny little cry he'd made before.

"*Coo-coo-wook!*"

With a flash of wings both parents flew down and flanked him. Frankie didn't move and held her breath, looking at the three beautiful birds. To behold a wild creature up close was a gift, a rare brush with something bigger and more important than petty human concerns. She admired them—Charlie's blue eyes turning dark, his parents' glossy black feathers and strong, dark beaks and legs.

The fledgling cocked its head at her and repeated that plaintive sound.

"*Coo-coo-wook!*"

It wasn't a begging call. It wasn't an alarm call. It wasn't a scolding call. She didn't know what it was. She waited, not moving, and the little bird repeated the sound. She closed her eyes and listened. It was a three-toned ascension with a punctuation at the end. Maybe a juvenile alert call?

Then, a wonder, one of the parent birds repeated it—a short, three-note pattern with a rising pitch.

"*Coo-coo-wook!*"

Frankie listened and felt the sound resonate in her chest. What were they saying? She was enthralled by them, these wild creatures and their magical language.

Charlie and the smaller adult repeated the call and then the largest of the crows echoed them. Then it sounded an alert, and they all flew off into the shadowy understory.

Frankie watched them depart and a tiny spark bloomed in her chest. The woods, the birds, the snug little cottage, and the mutable lake at the foot of the mountain. No matter how uncertain her future, she knew she belonged here. Her eye traveled to the tower of firewood she'd split and stacked and the pile of windfall still waiting to be cut. She could stay here for the winter, she thought. There was no hard-and-fast rule that they had to close the cottage. As long as she provisioned well and kept the pipes from freezing, there was no reason she couldn't. She'd winter here and apply for spring field teams. Just thinking about it eased her mind, and she began to formulate a list of food and supplies she'd need. She sighed, thinking of her bank balance. She'd need to talk to Patrick about money, and that was a conversation she had to have in person. If he could lend her some money today, she could provision while she was in town.

In the house, she closed the flue on the stove and pulled on her father's wool coat. As she cast off from the dock, she looked up toward the Magnusens' house and saw Anne and Aiden standing on the patio. The sight of them together made her feel happy and lonely. She tooted the horn and Anne waved. On the way down the lake, she thought of the baby hummingbirds. Would those little bumblebee-sized babies be ready for the long journey to Mexico?

The old truck was cold, and she sat in the cab letting the engine warm up before heading down the Old BZ Highway. It had rained in the night and the scent of damp earth and wet evergreen trees pervaded. The White Salmon River flashed by, running high and fast with the autumn rain. The falls were a white flurry tumbling and dropping into the steep slot canyon. A man stood on one of the Nation's fishing platforms over the river. He scooped a dip net in and pulled a wriggling fish free of the rushing water. The river, the rapids, the fisherman—it was like a song she'd always heard playing in her head.

When she arrived downtown, Frankie stood on the sidewalk outside Patrick's office and looked down the hill toward the Columbia River. A skein of geese glided above the whitecaps and landed smoothly in the cove of the Nichols Boat Basin. She could smell coffee roasting at Dog River and watched the plate glass door at Bette's Place swing open. A little girl ran out and halted on the sidewalk at an admonishment from her parents. Frankie spotted the roofline of the tavern and decided to go see Hank before she left town.

Nancy Gates was at the reception desk at the law office and waved her inside. She was on the phone and wiggled her fingers at Frankie. Nancy had been a cheerleader in high school and was so nosy. Frankie was grateful to dodge small talk with her old classmate. She made her way to Patrick's office. He got up to hug her and she looked at him and laughed.

"I just can't get used to you dressed like this. You look like a banker. Or an undertaker."

Patrick smoothed his tie and posed.

"Coming from you, that's a real compliment, Frank."

She looked down at her Carhartts and their father's wool jacket.

"So I've gone a bit feral," she said.

Patrick sat and leaned his elbows on the desk.

"How's it going up there? You getting ready to head back to Seattle? I can bring the trailer up and help you shut down before we pull the boat."

Frankie looked out the window, stalling. She thought of the many closing weekends with her family over the years—pulling all the perishables off the shelves, draining the water system, installing the storm shutters, and cleaning out the gutters. They'd have a quick lunch huddled around the stove and then leave the little house to weather the winter storms.

". . . already paid Conner for storage," Patrick was saying.

"Thanks for doing that," Frankie said. "I'll pay you back for my part."

"Whenever," he said. "It's not a problem."

"I need to talk to you about money, actually," she said. "And I think I'll be staying for a bit longer."

"With Mom?" he asked, looking surprised.

She shook her head. She would never ask, and Judith would never offer.

"No. Up at the lake."

"For how long?" Patrick asked.

"Through the new year, I think," Frankie said.

Patrick frowned.

"We've never kept the place open in the winter," he said, looking uneasy.

"Yeah, but there's no reason we can't," Frankie said, trying to sound more certain than she felt. "I've got plenty of wood. I cut up tons of the windfall I cleared off the trail. And Grandpa used to open up in the winter for Christmas-tree cutting, remember?"

"But what about Seattle?" Patrick asked. "Don't you need to get back to the lab?"

Frankie propped her chin on her fist and told him everything then—about the spring symposium, losing her job, Dr. Grant's threats, the denial of her defense—all of it. Patrick listened, not speaking, just letting her talk. She told him about selling her books back to pay rent and losing her deposit when she broke her lease.

"I'm so sorry, Frank," he said when she'd finished. "Can he do that? Won't your other committee members help you?"

Frankie pushed her hair out of her face and slumped in the chair.

"I haven't been able to reach anyone all summer. And Dr. Grant is vindictive as hell, Patrick. It's always the other guy who's wrong."

"But you must have some recourse," Patrick said. "Can't you talk to your committee or the dean?"

"Yeah, there's a process to challenge the decision. But it's too late to sort out this year. I'll have to wait for winter quarter to start."

She didn't tell him that the letter had directed her to contact her department chair, which was Dr. Grant, and that the entire prospect seemed doomed.

"So it's three months at the lake. Not a big deal," she said. "I need some money, though. Not much—just enough for food and gas. I'm sorry to ask, but I wondered about the money from Dad that Peter mentioned."

It embarrassed her to have to ask. O'Neills took pride in their self-sufficiency. And her brother was avoiding her eyes.

"Sorry. Is it a problem? I thought that maybe the estate thing would be settled soon," she said.

Patrick rubbed his hands across his face and tugged on his tie.

"There's been a delay," he said. "Because of things with the tavern."

"The tavern? What are you talking about? It's not part of the estate. The tavern belongs to Hank, right?"

Patrick groaned and tipped back in his chair, and the springs complained.

"Officially, yes. Grandpa Ray left the building to Hank. Apparently, it was some agreement they had from way back when Grandpa first hired him. Sweat equity at first and later Grandpa borrowed money that he never repaid. They drew up an agreement with Weatherby so it's all documented. Dad said he always knew about it, and he didn't begrudge Hank that."

Frankie nodded, unsurprised. Their lovable grandfather was notoriously bad with money.

"As for how the business was organized, Dad never explained it to me, but Mom—" He stopped and met her eye. "You won't like this, Frankie. Mom filed suit against Hank over the tavern."

Her body flushed with heat.

"Patrick, what the hell?"

He looked pained as he relayed the details. Judith's lawsuit maintained that the River City Saloon had been in the O'Neill family since the 1930s. Ray had left the building to Hank, but the business itself had never been deeded. Judith argued that the name and the physical contents of the tavern belonged to the surviving members of the O'Neill family. She had requested compensation and had filed a cease and desist order. Hank was legally required to close the tavern until the suit was settled. In the meantime, Jack's estate was tied up in the inquiry.

Hank, who'd been her father's best friend. Hank, who'd been like a grandfather to Frankie and Patrick. Hank, who would do anything for them.

Frankie gripped the edge of the desk and her ears rang.

"The tavern is closed? So, Hank can't work," she said, her voice choked.

"Yeah."

"And everybody knows? Everybody— What did Hank say?"

Patrick looked ashamed and stared down at his hands.

"You haven't talked to Hank?!" Her voice rose with indignation. "Jesus, Patrick!"

"It's complicated, Frankie. Mom said—"

"Oh, Mom said!" she interrupted. "Mom said let's betray one of the kindest men on earth. Is that what Mom said?"

"Frankie, you don't understand what it's been like for her—"

Frankie pushed her chair back and stood.

"I understand completely, Patrick. Poor Judith. She worked so hard and never got what she wanted. I grew up listening to what it's been like for Mom. And now she thinks she deserves the tavern. She doesn't surprise me one bit. But how could you, Patrick? To Hank?"

She turned to leave and nearly collided with Nancy, standing at the door, mouth agape. She laughed her tinkly cheerleader laugh.

"Whoops! Didn't mean to interrupt any family chitchat. Your appointment is here, Patrick."

Frankie turned back to her brother. The sorrow on his face broke her heart, but she was so angry she couldn't say anything more.

"I'll call you later," she said, and left.

She drove down Cascade and slowed as she passed the River City Saloon. The blinds were drawn and the "Shut!" sign hung in the window. Her heart ached thinking of Hank and the little gang who gathered at the tavern every day. What did they all think of the O'Neills now?

She drove west toward Hank's place. She slowed as she turned down Wasco Court, which served as the driveway to the cluster of trailers and manufactured homes there. A dog bounded the length of the fence line, following the truck with silent menace, and then erupted in mad barking at the end of its yard. She looked through the rain-spattered windshield at Hank's trailer, realizing she'd never been there without her father. Now she felt like an intruder, but she continued down to the end of the road and pulled up at his door.

She couldn't remember a time when she hadn't known Hank. In fact, there was a picture in the family album of Hank holding her the day she'd come home from the hospital. Her small, swaddled body looked tiny in his big hands. He was looking down at her sleeping face, his own solemn with worry.

"When we asked him to be your godfather, you'd think he was taking an oath of office." Her father would laugh, telling the story.

She recalled Hank helping her with her math after school at the tavern and teaching her to play chess after Sunday dinners at the house. He always looked up and smiled when she walked through the door of the River City Saloon. How many times had he slid a Coke down the bar at her with a wink? Unlike the rest of The Irregulars, Hank never drank with her. Why had she never realized that before? She remembered how he'd waited for her in the parking lot after the funeral and took her to the tavern when she couldn't bear to be at the house.

Now she stopped in front of his trailer and climbed out of the truck. The screen door creaked open, and Hank stepped out on the small porch. As she climbed out of the truck and crossed the driveway, the sight of his open, familiar face overwhelmed her.

"Well, hello there, kid!" he said raising a hand. "Ain't I the luckiest guy in town today?"

She opened her mouth to speak and found she couldn't. She couldn't see Hank and not see her dad. Jack and Hank were a mismatched set—one tall and lean, the other tall and broad. Twenty years apart in age and somehow a perfect pair. Hank alone looked all wrong.

Her grief rose in a great wave. She struggled to compose herself, tried to apologize, and couldn't speak. Hank crossed the driveway to her but didn't say anything. He just squeezed her shoulder once and waited. Frankie stared down at the gravel in the driveway and tried to steady herself. She listened to the dog barking. The wind rushed over the pines, and a crow croaked.

"Woke, woke, woke."

"Sorry," she said after a while.

Hank wagged his head.

"Nothing to be sorry for."

He handed her his freshly pressed handkerchief, an old-fashioned idiosyncrasy she loved about him. She pressed it to her eyes and breathed in the scent of summer.

"Lavender," she said.

"Mrs. Mancini does my laundry," he said and shrugged.

They sat in a pair of old canvas camp chairs on the porch. He'd been whittling, and Frankie saw the shape of a dog appearing in the small piece of wood there next to his penknife. He called them his little critters. Kept his worries away, he said.

He braced his hands on his knees, clad in the thick green work pants he wore, though long retired from the railroad.

"So then," he said. "You heading back to the city? Back to school?"

She shook her head and pointed her chin north.

"I'm staying up at the lake for a bit," she said.

Hank gazed north too and looked thoughtful.

"Well, it must be just lovely up there right now, if a bit chilly. I told Patrick to let me know if he needed any help getting *The Peggotty* stored for the winter. Or anything else."

Her heart clenched. Of course he'd still be willing to help.

Hank cleared his throat.

"Solid old gal, except for that choke," he said. "Naggin' old thing, ain't it?"

Frankie looked at the ground, gathering herself, and then agreed that it was. They talked about the best ways to prime the carburetor—a little splash of gas and a tincture of time before firing up the engine. The conversation lagged and Frankie struggled to find the words she needed to say.

"Hank, listen. I just talked to Patrick about this thing with Mom. I don't want you to think that I, that we—"

He patted her shoulder with his big hand.

"Don't worry about all that, Frankie," he said. "It will all work itself out."

"But I just—"

"It's going to be fine," he said, and the only kindness she could offer was pretending to believe him.

"If you say so, Hank."

He rubbed his hands together and stood.

"I'm glad you came by. I have something for you."

He went in the trailer and came back holding a small black calendar, which he held out to her. She recognized it as her father's. It was a cheap freebie they gave out at Franz Hardware. Every year Jack swore he'd get organized. New Year's Day he'd map out all his grand schemes for the year—maintenance at the tavern, the house, and the cottage. Letters to the editor and new business ideas. By March the little book would be so jammed with wrinkled receipts and scribbled notes he'd rubber band it together. He never did get organized, but he tried every year, all the way through December, when the process would start all over. Pictures, stickers, inspirational quotes. "The Grand Plan," he called the messy little book.

"Your dad left it in the office. I thought you all would want to have it."

Frankie let the book fall open. Taped to the inside cover was a picture of her and Patrick, aged seven and eight, sitting together in *The Peggotty*. She shut her eyes against hot tears. She tried to thank him but couldn't speak and knew Hank understood. The morning wind picked up and tossed the branches of the willow in the field next door.

"I should get going," she said when she could speak.

Hank walked her to the truck.

"You stay warm up there," he said, rocking lightly on his heels. "Let me know how the fish are biting next time you come through town."

She wanted to hug him. She wanted to put her head down on his big shoulder and cry, to feel like a little kid. She wanted to tell him how much she missed her dad. How she needed Jack's advice about her trouble with Dr. Grant. But she wasn't a kid anymore. She held out her hand and he shook it. She drove away looking in the rearview mirror at Hank standing in the wind. He raised a hand and turned slowly to walk back to his trailer.

The rain renewed, and the glistening streets were quiet as she drove through town and crossed the bridge over the river. Apple harvest was in and the fall logging mostly done for the season. A cluster of boats was anchored at the mouth of the White Salmon River, a sure sign of the steelhead run.

She thought of the tavern, dark and quiet, blinds drawn over the windows like the whole building was in mourning. She recalled countless afternoons she'd spent listening to the banter of Jack and the others. Hank looking up from his crossword with a smile. A college ball game on the TV, old jazz and fifties pop on the radio, and Irish ballads on Saint Patrick's Day. The laughter of men and the crack of peanut shells. Her first legal beer, which her father slid across the bar with great ceremony. Before that the occasional beer he split with her on Saint Patrick's Day and other holidays when she was in high school. It made her feel special, drinking with her dad, until it didn't. The night of her twenty-first birthday, she and Jack got home around 2 a.m. and she heard her parents arguing after she'd gone upstairs. The next morning, Judith had sat across from her at the breakfast table talking about healthy choices, responsible behavior. Frankie had a headache and didn't want to listen.

The memory came then—the night before last Thanksgiving. She hadn't wanted to think about it. She'd shoved it away in the back of her mind because things were already too painful. But now it all came roaring back.

That Wednesday night before Thanksgiving, she'd been the only passenger to get off when the bus pulled into downtown Hood River. Her father had said he'd meet her, but the snow-dusted sidewalk was empty. She shouldered her backpack and headed toward the River City Saloon.

All down Oak Street, the buildings were dark—the library, the John Deere store, Bette's Place, and the courthouse. The Hood River Soroptimist club had adorned the lampposts with twinkling white lights and fat red ribbons as they did every year. It started to snow, and Frankie felt her heart clench with longing. It was so beautiful, so familiar, and yet somehow, she never belonged here.

The River City Saloon was the only lit storefront. Frankie could see inside the large plate glass window from half a block away. A single voice rose in song above the murmur of men's conversation. She stood for a moment looking in at the familiar faces, some so dear to her. Clarence, Old Joe, and Maxine—often the only woman in this friendly band of misfits. There was Hank on his stool behind the bar, arms crossed and eyes on the game. And there was her dad standing behind the bar talking to a couple of men sitting across from him. Frankie moved toward the door and then stopped.

Jack was in the middle of a story. Through the transom she could hear the rhythm of his voice but not the words. Watching him, Frankie felt a growing unease. His voice was just a little too loud and his face flushed red. Then he swept his hands apart as he reached the punch line and knocked over the glasses of the two men seated at the bar. Everyone roared, and Frankie knew they were not laughing at the joke. She watched her father stagger as he cast about for a towel, and Hank rose to retrieve the mop. The sound of laughter carried through the transom, and she heard her father shout that there would be no charge for the joke.

She stood for a moment watching Jack wipe up the bar and laugh at himself along with the rest of them. Then she turned around and walked to the pay phone outside Grace Su's China Gorge. Patrick was there in ten minutes with no questions about why she'd called him instead of meeting their father as planned. Patrick knew without having to ask, and his not asking was meant as a kindness.

She went to bed that night, heartsore, and heard Jack banging into the house around 2 a.m. The next morning, there he was standing over the stove flipping pancakes, smiling and laughing as he hugged her. Calling her Lanky Frankie, fussing over her and feeding her. Never asking how she'd gotten home or why she hadn't come to him.

Of course he knew, she thought now, driving into the shadow of the trees along the Old BZ Highway and north toward the lake. Even before everything broke open on Thanksgiving Day, they'd all understood. Patrick had warned Frankie about it when they were teenagers, and Judith had finally said it out loud. *You're an alcoholic, just like your father! Don't let it ruin everything.*" Because it had ruined so much already. This was the thing they never talked about, the unspoken heartbreak of the family, the secret they guarded in their hearts and never said aloud.

But what could she say? What does a daughter say to her father, who lets her down over and over? How often had he forgotten to meet her at the bus, or call on her birthday, or pick her up from school? How often had he embarrassed her in public by talking a bit too loud and by being noticeably altered when he was working at the tavern? She remembered a testy exchange with Mr. Condon at the lake when he'd smelled alcohol on Jack's breath.

And yet, amid the worst times, there was always love. Tremendous love. Frankie knew her father loved her. He loved her the best he could and the only way he knew how. That Thanksgiving morning, her funny dad, waltzing around the kitchen with the plate of pancakes held aloft, singing "Mack the Knife."

All the while his eyes held that plea, unspoken yet understood. Forgive me for my weaknesses, my darling, darling girl.

Frankie drove north, and the rain came down. She felt alone in the world, stranded, and without allies.

26

DISPERSAL CALLS

At the end of summer in the northern hemisphere inhospitable weather systems force many birds to seek gentler climes.

—*G. Gordon's Field Guide to the Birds of the Pacific Northwest*

⁓

Anne sat in the dawn light of the kitchen listening to the quiet, which was not the same thing as silence at all. She heard the mechanical whine of the ice-cube maker in the refrigerator, the click and tap of the preheating oven, the hum of the teakettle warming on the burner. A small branch tapped the window in a slight breeze outside the patio door. She heard the waves hitting the sand and the rising complaint of gulls.

This was an exercise one of her favorite professors had taught the composition students at Trinity College—this close listening. It was a practice of gathering the ambient noise of a physical space and considering the layers of sound. Professor Mara encouraged the same exercise when they were learning a choral piece. Listen for the melody line, the higher and lower harmonies, the dissonance, and the overtone—that mysterious resonance created by all the other voices vibrating against each other. When the harmony was most true, it twined together to create the fundamental first harmonic. The ninth voice, as Anne thought of it.

Having a good ear, Anne had warmed to this exercise naturally. It was something she was born with, the ability to listen deeply for layers of sound and meaning. Ambient layers and harmony came easily to her, and so did overtones and undertones. If Irish was in her blood, music was nearly as close.

"Music is your third language and hardest won," Professor Mara had written in Anne's graduation card. "Always remain faithful to your art, Anne."

Of course she would, she thought, reading that. Who was she without music? She felt most herself when writing, performing, and teaching. Music was with her at the lowest points, like that first dark winter in Seattle when she was so lonely in the strange city. The voice in her head accompanied her, whispering suggestions as she walked the wet sidewalks of Capitol Hill or sat in Bauhaus Coffee & Books watching the rain lash the windows. After she'd met Tim, and when she was pregnant, she wrote songs. The voice woke her up early, almost shouting her out of her dreams, and she'd scramble to capture the narrative before she was fully awake. After Aiden was born, she wrote about the heart-altering experience of becoming a mother, like she'd moved to a new planet. Or become a new planet.

But for a year and a half she hadn't written a word. With Kat's death, the voice had gone quiet, and she'd felt like some essential part of her was missing. Like a hand or an elbow. She never felt the glimmer or heard the voices through her dreams. There was no pressure to harness an idea because there were no wild flights of imagination. Occasionally she'd sit down and try to force herself to write, but it made her feel ill. Of course, her music was ever tied to Katherine. For the past eighteen months, it had seemed like her creativity had died along with her friend.

But something had happened in the woods with Frankie earlier that week. Anne had heard the voice then, quiet at first, murmuring in the back of her mind as they walked down the hill in silence. Later, when she was alone in the dark, quiet house, the story came rushing to the forefront of her mind. It was like the old days, when it all seemed to come from some mysterious elsewhere and she was racing to keep up. She had three stanzas down but resisted looking them over. She wanted to keep her mind blind to the idea and just follow the story. It was a small beginning, but she felt so much like herself, more than she had since Kat died.

The bud of joy she'd felt after that had been squashed by the arrival of the mail the next day. Tim had driven down the lake to have a call with his father and brought a pile back from the post office. There was a postcard from Tim's brother, Mark, on vacation in Hawaii, the Cornish College newsletter, and a stack of correspondence from the newspaper staff. And at the bottom of the pile, a bulky manila envelope from the University of Washington Department of Pediatrics. Long-awaited and dreaded, the nine-by-twelve paper envelope somehow took up all available space in the room. As far as she could tell, Tim had not opened it.

Dinner felt strained. Tim said he had a lot on his mind.

"A big conversation with Dad. He's considering some changes beyond what we discussed the other day. I need to think things through."

He said he didn't want to talk about it just then. After they put Aiden to bed, Tim suggested they read the UW assessment together, but she couldn't.

"You go first. Then I'll have a look and we'll talk tomorrow."

He'd agreed and stayed up long after she'd gone to bed. She lay in the dark unable to sleep, wondering what he was learning and what he was thinking. She fell asleep before Tim came into the room.

Now Anne put her notebook aside and poured water over her tea. Her heart felt heavy and resistant, but she knew she couldn't put it off any longer. She flipped open the thick folder and leafed through the pages. There were the results of Aiden's vision, hearing, and dexterity tests and reports on his physical exam and blood work. It all drew a picture of a healthy, active kid. Anne paged to the section on home life, socialization, and behavior.

The following is a summary of the child's behavior taken
from parental questionnaires. This information may be used
in combination with the child's formal assessment to develop
a clear picture of his/her needs. The goal is to identify the
child's most disruptive behaviors in order to determine the
most effective treatment.

She scanned the page.

Behavior: Withdrawn, won't make eye contact or interact
with others.
How often: Daily.

She bristled at that. Certainly she'd written "occasionally" not
"daily." That must be from Tim's questionnaire.

Possible causes: Don't know.
Effective strategies: Singing.

Now, that answer was hers, and it lifted her spirits. She could draw
him out with music. She felt such joy seeing his eyes light up when
she sang to him, clapping his wee hands. For those few moments he
was there with her. Right there. She was seeing the real Aiden then.
And lately she was seeing him with Frankie. Unaccountably and yet
without a doubt, he was engaging with their tall new friend who
dressed like a lumberjack and talked endlessly of birds.

Behavior: Screaming.
How often: Varies.
Possible causes: Not sure.
Effective coping strategies: NA
Duration: Minutes to hours.

Yes, the screaming was disruptive, but disruption wasn't the half of it. What do you call it when the person you love most is in agony over something you can't understand? How does it feel to be a mother who cannot comfort her child, when that is the very least a mother should be able to do? Her breath caught as she read the next section.

> Behavior: Self-harm.
> How often: Varies.
> Possible causes: Don't know.
> Effective coping strategies: NA
> Duration: Intermittently for hours.

When Aiden hit himself and bit his hands, he barely seemed to register the pain, but she felt every blow like it was her own body. She would take his poor wee hands in her own and try to shelter him from himself. Sometimes he bit her by accident. But it was the wildness in his eyes that hurt her. *"Aiden, love, come back to me,"* she wanted to say.

She flipped through the reports of the graduate students' sessions with Aiden, and a section about communication and relationships. It was too much to take in and she found herself skimming. She flipped to the summary letter in the back of the report.

> Dear Mr. and Mrs. Magnusen,
> We appreciated the chance to observe and assess your son, Aiden, aged 5 years, during August 1998. We thank you for your patience in waiting for our final report on Aiden's abilities and deficits. We found him to be a bright and healthy child, though notably withdrawn and showing severe disabilities in socialization and engagement for his age.

She didn't really read the rest. Her eye fell to the bottom of the page.

Diagnosis: Autism Spectrum Disorder (ASD) and/or
Childhood Disintegrative Disorder (CDD), also evidence of
Pervasive Developmental Disorder (PDD).

As defined in the *Journal of Pediatric Neurosciences,*
"CDD is a rare condition characterized by late onset
(greater than 3 years of age) of developmental delays in
language, social function, and motor skills. It is grouped
with the pervasive developmental disorders (PDDs) and is
related to the better known and more common disorder of
autism."

Pervasive Developmental Disorders are characterized by
qualitative impairment in the development of reciprocal
social interaction, verbal and nonverbal communication
skills, imaginative activity, and a restricted repertoire of
activities and interest. Within PDD, the DSM-IV
recognizes severe autistic disorder with onset in infancy or
childhood and the residual Pervasive Developmental
Disorder Not Otherwise Specified.

Recommended Treatments: Applied behavioral analysis,
sensory integration therapy, antipsychotic medications.

ASD, CDD, and PDD have no known cause or cure. We
urge you to place your faith in occupational therapies and
education, which are improving all the time. There are
many excellent programs that can help Aiden thrive. I look
forward to discussing this assessment with you in greater
detail.

Respectfully,
Dr. Amy Shelley

She let the folder fall closed and stared out at the lake. It was there
in black and white now, but none of it was new information. There

was just a label now, a long, complicated label. What good would it do their boy? Their family?

Aiden pattered down the hall behind her in his yellow-and-purple Aladdin pajamas. He paused at her side and stood there for a moment. Anne tried to remember what his voice had sounded like when he greeted her in the morning. It had been so long, she couldn't remember, which made her heart ache. She touched his curls lightly with her fingertips.

"How about pancakes for breakfast, young man? If you want to go outside for a bit, I'll call you when they're done."

He smiled and glanced away from her. Then he was out the door and down on the sand, pulling his Snoopy life preserver on as he went. She pushed the folder away and pulled out mixing bowls and ingredients for pancakes.

When Tim came down for breakfast, he didn't say anything about the report and neither did she. They didn't talk about it later when the three of them went for a boat ride and Tim showed them a hidden waterfall on the far side of the lake. They didn't talk about it while Anne made dinner or when they watched *Dumbo* for what seemed like the hundredth time with their small son rocking from foot to foot as he stood next to the coffee table. But Anne felt the weight of it between them. As the hours wore on, it took up more and more space in the room.

Anne tucked Aiden into bed and read him a story while Tim did the dishes.

When she came out, Tim had opened a bottle of wine and poured two glasses.

"What did you read? Wait. Let me guess. 'The Crow and the Pitcher'?"

"Gold star for you!" Anne said. "I about have it memorized. I'm looking forward to the next obsession, really, although it is a sweet story."

Tim handed her a glass of wine and pulled her over to the couch. They sat looking out at the lake, which was almost invisible in the dusk. The green-yellow light of the western sky curved over the black tree line on the far side of the water. The lonely cry of a loon echoed across the bay.

"Do you want to go first, then?" she asked.

He turned sideways to look at her. His face was neutral, and she could hear him try to keep his voice measured and careful.

"Well, I think it was a thoughtful and complete assessment. I think it's helpful to have it all in one place and to get the input of experts. We're just so close to him, you know."

"Okay," she said. "Fair point."

"I think the idea of medication is a bit much, frankly," he said.

Anne nodded, wondering if her relief was visible on her face.

"I appreciated Dr. Shelley's diagnosis and recommended therapy, which will be helpful when he starts school, to figure out what program to put him in."

She didn't say anything but kept her face open. Her pulse quickened and she tried to stay calm, tried not to think about what she knew he would say next.

"This is the key thing—that he has an official diagnosis—"

She bridled then and her voice rose in frustration.

"Why is an official diagnosis so important, Tim? Aiden is Aiden! Why does it help to have a label?"

Tim sighed.

"Anne, it's not an insult. It's how the education system works here. Having a diagnosis will open doors for him. It will get him the support he needs and help us decide—"

"Open doors?" she said. "How will it open doors for him to be pigeonholed by the public education system before he starts kindergarten?"

She could hear her voice rising and tried to return to a reasonable tone.

"Look. We're keeping him at Sunflower this year. Why don't we just see how things go? He loves Elena and the other staff. He's doing just fine there, and it's easy for me to drop in from Cornish at lunch. It's working for him, and it's working for me."

Tim looked irritated and scrubbed at his eye with the heel of his hand. They'd gone round and round about this for months already. It was the same old argument, and she knew he was as frustrated with her as she was with him. Tim had wanted him to start kindergarten that fall—even if it meant starting late after their return from the lake—and Anne wanted to wait a year. But what he said next took her completely by surprise.

"What if you aren't at Cornish next term?" he asked. "That would change things, wouldn't it?"

She sat back with a laugh.

"And why wouldn't I be at Cornish next term? Patrice gave me leave for summer and fall. I can't just disappear for winter quarter and remain employed."

His face was somber.

"What if you stopped working? What if you didn't have to work?"

She threw up her hands in frustration and stood.

"Oh, for the love of Mike, Tim! I'm not in the mood for one of your creative visualization strategies right now. I can't manifest some bloody magical reality."

Tim took her hand and pulled her back down.

"No. Not that," he said. "I mean it for real. What if you really didn't have to work?"

"Tim, what in the name of Jesus are you talking about?"

"I told you I had a big conversation with Dad yesterday, right?"

Anne fought to keep the exasperation out of her voice.

"Yes, you did. And you didn't want to talk about it until you'd thought it through. So, what did your father have to say, then?"

What Tim said then was not what she expected at all. Or, more accurately, something she expected to hear years from now: Tim

Senior was stepping down as president of the company. Effective November first, Tim would be at the helm of Magnusen Media. His face was lit with excitement. With the company growing so fast, Tim Senior thought it was time. He would remain on the board, but it was time for Tim to become president.

Anne stared at him, speechless.

"I told him I needed talk to you about it, and I didn't want to tell you until I'd sat with it for a bit. It's going to be a huge change for me, and I need your support, Anne."

She nodded, wanting to understand, wanting to be happy for him. He said he would be busy and that would mean more time away from her and Aiden. Late nights, trips, and meetings. And then he was talking about her role as his wife and how he would need to lean on her. He was talking about quarterly advertising dinners and monthly social events with board members, the Christmas gala, and the spring golf tournament.

Anne remembered too keenly last year's Christmas extravaganza, at which her mother-in-law—dressed in a red velvet dress and Santa hat—had regaled the room with a version of "Santa Baby." A triumph, Tim Senior had called it.

Anne pulled away, shaking her head.

"Tim, you can't possibly think I'd be interested in any of that," she said. "That's your world, not mine."

"It's our world, Anne. I'm going to need your help," he said.

"And you'll have it, but not like that. I've got to go back to work."

"But with this salary, we can get by without you working!"

"You don't understand, Tim. I want to go back to work. I love my job."

Tim slumped against the couch.

"I thought . . . I thought you'd be excited for me. This is a really big deal. I mean—president!"

He looked like a disappointed child, and she wanted to laugh, but she knew she shouldn't. She took his hands.

"Of course it is, and I'm so pleased for you, Tim. Really, well done! I know your dad's faith in your abilities means loads to you. It's going to be grand. Now, tell me when he's going to announce it."

He brightened and told her they would announce it to the board in mid-October, so they'd get the transition organized before the holidays. The public announcement would be at the fall gala— Christi's Halloween ball. He pulled out a piece of paper and sketched a diagram of the company's new structure with the Seattle headquarters and flagship paper at the top. Spokane, Portland, and Ashland were second-tier newspaper markets recently acquired, and Magnusen Media had decided to purchase radio and TV companies in those markets as well. Tim's brother, Mark, would become publisher of the Seattle paper. They'd need to consider new management for the other papers and radio and TV companies, and Tim would oversee that too. They also wanted to digitize the printing process to consolidate all production in one location.

He stopped and looked expectant, and Anne didn't know what to say.

"Wow—that sounds like . . . a lot," she said.

"It's huge growth for Magnusen Media. Dad thinks the Internet is going to change everything and this is our chance to grow into other regional markets."

"So, you'll be doing what, then? Day to day, I mean," Anne asked.

Tim ran his hands through his hair. It had begun thinning at the temples like his father's.

"Meeting with advertisers and the advertising reps. Face time with city council and the chamber of commerce and the downtown business association—in Seattle and all the other markets. One-on-one with the mayor when I can and getting to know the leaders of these new tech firms—like Adobe and Amazon. The Microsoft folks, of course."

"What about editorial, the newsroom?"

Tim shook his head.

"I'll write something occasionally for the editorial page. But, no, I'll be out of the granular editorial details. This is a leadership position."

She knew he only wanted to hear positive things, but she couldn't help herself.

"But, Tim," she said, and he already looked defensive. "You hate meetings. You love the newsroom. Are you sure this is the right move?"

"Of course it is," he snapped. "This has been the plan all along. It's just sooner than I expected. And bigger."

She heard the anxiety in his voice and tried to keep hers calm.

"I know the plan has been for you to take over for your dad. But, what I mean is, is this what you want?"

"Is it what I want? It's what Dad wants," he said, his voice rising. He threw up his hands.

"It's what the board wants. It's the way forward."

Anne rose, moving away from him.

"Well, don't eat my head off for asking a simple question, thank you very much," she said. "I'm happy to revisit this topic when you're in a more sanguine mood."

He grabbed her wrist.

"I'm sorry. Please sit and talk with me about it. I want to tell you the rest. It's all a bit overwhelming and I need your help to sort it out."

She sat, willing herself to be patient.

"I'm listening," she said.

He took her hand in both of his.

"It's just . . . a lot," he said. "Like I was saying, lots of travel and meetings. I'll be gone a lot more than I ever have been. It will have a big impact on us."

"It will be fine, Tim," she said. "We've always managed a busy schedule."

He looked at her and seemed to hesitate.

"I'll be on the road at least a week a month at the beginning to make sure I'm familiar with the different papers. And getting to know TV and radio will be totally new."

"I understand, Tim. I know it's a great opportunity for you. And if it's what you want, then I'm all for it."

There was something pleading in his look.

"Thank you. I really appreciate that. That's why I'm asking you, please, just extend your leave through spring quarter and we'll see how it goes."

She pulled her hand away and shook her head. If it wasn't so annoying, she'd have laughed.

"Tim. I've got to go back to work. I love teaching and I want to get back to performing. My sabbatical—"

"It's not a sabbatical, Anne," he interrupted. "Patrice put you on administrative leave because she was trying to keep you from getting fired for your behavior last—"

She jerked away.

"Behavior!" she spat. "One silly mistake at the graduation concert and you'd think I was on trial for murder."

Tim was shaking his head.

"It wasn't just the one thing, Anne, and you know it. You told me yourself. You'd been forgetful, late for class, missing meetings, short with your students. Everyone knows last year was hard for you—"

"I don't need you to remind me of my professional failings, thank you very much," she interrupted. "All the more reason for me to get back to work. I'm trying for tenure eventually, you may recall."

"I know, I know. But that can wait, Anne. We've got to—"

"Why should it wait, Tim? I don't understand what you're on about. Tenure is important to me. My work is important to me. And don't forget that Aiden needs me too."

Tim's face darkened.

"Other people can help with Aiden, Anne."

"Yes, yes, they can, and they do. He'll be ready for kindergarten next year, and in the meantime, he's doing just great at Sunflower with Elena and her staff."

"No, no, Anne. I'm not talking about Sunflower and public kindergarten," he said.

His voice was level as he said the next thing, the impossible thing, as if it made all the sense in the world.

"I think Aiden needs to go to a residential school. A private facility with professional staff who can support him."

She stared at him, uncomprehending.

"Anne, listen. Aiden needs specialists who can help him reach his potential. You're such a good mom and you've done what you can. But this is better for him, for us—for everyone."

Anne laughed in astonishment, and Tim kept talking.

"Dad's friend recommended a great place. Mt. Holy Oak is just an hour from Seattle. I had a conference call with the place with Mom and Dad yesterday. They both think it's a terrific school. You can visit him anytime, and he'll come home for holidays. He'll do great there."

She felt ice water dripping through her veins. Tim was talking about how beautiful the school's buildings were and the park surrounding it, and she cut him off.

"Tim, Mt. Holy Oak is an institution. You want to make it sound like a boarding school, but that's so off the mark. We heard about those places—"

"Anne, they're experts. They're the best in the field. Everyone says so," Tim interrupted.

"Everyone who?" she said, her voice rising. "Your parents and their rich friends?"

"Listen, Anne. They'll keep him safe and help control his behavior," Tim said.

"He doesn't need controlling, Tim!"

She was shouting now.

"He just needs a little compassion from his own family, who—"

"He'll be well looked after," Tim said talking over her. "He'll be with other kids like him."

She stared at him, speechless. Other kids like him?

His gaze softened as he looked at her and he took her hand.

"It's not just the new job. I want us to have another baby, and soon. Our family can't be all about Aiden."

The distance between them then was immeasurable. She couldn't speak.

Tim dropped her hand and looked angry.

"What do you expect, Anne? After Mom's party?"

"Yes, exactly. You're surprised he didn't behave himself at the Columbia Tower Club with the power brokers of Seattle? He's five years old, Tim! Perhaps your expectations are the problem. And your parents' expectations."

"My parents are trying to build a competitive business—"

"Fine! But why does their grandchild have to be any part of that?!"

"Because I'm part of it, and you and Aiden are too. It's a family business. There are expectations."

"Well, maybe that's the problem, then. My family's only expectation would be that Aiden be happy," she said with barely controlled fury.

"Easy for you to say when they are thousands of miles away. My family is part of our day-to-day and my parents are just trying to be practical. It's like my mother said. If we can't expect Aiden to be normal—"

She stood up abruptly, her body hot with anger.

"Normal?" she hissed. "Normal? I expect Aiden to be himself."

"Anne—" he said, reaching for her.

"Leave me alone, Tim. I cannot talk to you right now."

She pulled on her jacket and went outside. As she walked along the seawall, the air cooled her face and she caught her breath. The sky was inky black and moonless, and the stars were brilliant. She tipped her head back and scanned the hazy Milky Way. She knew the Corvus constellation was not visible this time of year but looked for it anyway. Back home, you could see it from January to May on a clear night. She felt a deep yearning to see the familiar night sky over the island.

Home, she thought. *Baile.*

She was filled with such longing that she nearly wept. She missed her family so much. She wanted her parents and Gran to see Aiden, to know him. She knew they'd love him for who he was. They would not label him or expect him to be anyone but himself. She closed her eyes and shivered. She thought of what Tim had suggested. Besides the horrific idea of the school for Aiden, how could he not understand what he was asking of her, to leave her work, abandon her music?

Standing with her feet in the cold sand, she felt like several people trying to fit into one body and failing. Anne the artist. Anne the mother and wife. Anne the teacher. And Anne of the island who was someone's daughter, someone's granddaughter, and Katherine O'Faolain's best friend.

"You silly bitch," Kat said in her head. *"If you give up music, well then, you really will be stark raving."*

Something gave way in her heart then. She cracked open and felt the grief pour out—grief for her friend, for her son, and for her marriage. But also for herself. For the thousand ways she'd failed to be the woman she'd hoped to be, the artist she'd hoped to be. It was all too much to hold in anymore, and in that moment she let it all go.

She thought of Kat's laughing face. Kat sitting on the kitchen counter at Gran's. Kat waving madly as Anne entered the boarding bridge to the plane. Kat onstage beaming at her before they began to perform. Katherine would forever be a part of her, a root wrapped around the boulder that was her heart, a root feeding the rest of her life as it branched out and grew skyward.

In the morning, she watched Tim pour his coffee and listened to him talk about how he'd need to spend the weekend in Seattle with his father and would be leaving at noon and of course he didn't expect her to come. She and Aiden walked him to the boat, and she kissed him goodbye. They both pretended that everything was fine. But nothing was fine. Everything had changed and would never be the same again.

27

RATTLING CALLS

Young birds raised in captivity will nonetheless create songs and calls characteristic of their species though they lack the opportunity to hear them performed by adults of their kind.

—*G. Gordon's Field Guide to the Birds of the Pacific Northwest*

<hr />

Once there was a little crow and he was a naughty crow.

They wanted to send him away up the Holy Oak Mountain.

Up the mountain they would make him a good little crow, a normal little crow.

But the American crow does not migrate, he told them.

28

THE CAULDRON

No one will dispute birds' usefulness for hunting, forestry, and even cultivation. Moreover, they increase our connection to Nature and delight us with their beautiful songs, feats of flight, and ingenious behaviors.

—*G. Gordon's Field Guide to the Birds of the Pacific Northwest*

Frankie flipped off the light in the pump house and watched the glimmer of dawn blossoming above the forested hillside behind the cottage. A mist hovered over the lake, and a loon called on the far side of the bay. Where the mist had cleared, she could see the flat, dark water laid out like a green mirror. She shivered and pulled her collar up around her neck. When she'd turned on the tap that morning, the old pipes hummed the song of their emptiness, and she realized she was out of water. The pump had to be primed and babysat before it began to draw water from the spring into the reservoir. The pipes repressurized with a familiar and comforting dirge and the old pump chugged along in a soothing rhythm. Somewhere in the back of the dark little outbuilding, a chorus frog bleated out a late-season call but got no answer.

Frankie felt depleted by the events of the previous day. She'd lain awake half the night imagining furious conversations with her mother. How could she do this to Hank? Yes, Judith hated the tavern, but could she really live with this, taking away his livelihood? Her father's best friend? What did Judith stand to gain anyway?

In the root cellar she surveyed her dwindling provisions. She could still ask Patrick to lend her enough money to get through the next three months, and she should catch and freeze fish while the salmon were running. But those were short-term solutions to the larger problems at hand. It was too much to think about.

Frankie went inside and sat on the couch in front of the cold hearth, pulling a blanket around her shoulders. She reached for *G. Gordon's Field Guide to the Birds of the Pacific Northwest.* Aiden had left it on the table in the usual spot. He did that with her headphones too, setting them back next to the recorder where he'd found them without being asked. And his shoes—tucked inside the front door before he scampered to touch the barometer and the two armchairs. Then he'd land at the table and riffle through the book before retrieving the headphones. Funny kid.

She turned the book over in her hands. The front cover bore a close shot of a fat American robin perched on the branch of a blooming apple tree. She remembered the anticipation on her dad's face as she'd torn open the wrapping paper. Jack loved giving gifts. He could never afford expensive things, but he paid attention to people's small joys.

She flipped to the back pages of the book and saw the list she'd started there with such determination in the summer of 1979. In her childish scrawl she'd written "1) Cliff swallows 2) Northern flicker 3) Sandpipers 4) Pileated woodpecker." Her p's were written backward, a habit that had taken some years to outgrow.

She remembered the early days of tuning her ear to the wind in the trees and the voices of small birds. Up in the swaying treetops she heard the peeping of goldfinches and yellow-rumped warblers. She heard the zing of a hummingbird. And a voice saying, *"Pay attention, Mary Frances. What do you hear?"* It was an adult voice, it was a woman's voice, and it was, she now realized with a jolt, Judith's voice.

She remembered then sitting next to her mother in the bird blind with their backs against the sun-warmed cedar slats, listening. Judith in shorts and a T-shirt, her dark hair pulled back into a low ponytail, arms clasped around her knees and face tilted skyward. She was still so young then—not even thirty. Her beautiful mother who held her hand when they walked together and loved the woods so. How could she have forgotten? It was Judith who'd taught her to listen to the woods. Judith who'd shown her how to sit cross-legged and quiet. Judith who'd named those first birds and showed her how to write her p's properly and wanted to know what birds she'd seen every morning at breakfast.

When had Judith changed? By the time she was in junior high, Frankie remembered coming home after school to an empty house and her mother's absence from the lake. Her parents' bickering had started then, first over Judith's license but increasingly over other things. Now Frankie recalled that her father was drinking more those years. Or maybe it just seemed like he was drinking more because she was old enough to notice such things. But in every memory, he seemed to have a glass in his hand—at family reunions, weddings, and Saint Patrick's Day parties. She'd notice that his voice was slightly louder than everyone else's, his jokes a bit off. Everyone loved him, but Frankie noticed people laughing at him, which embarrassed her. She'd look around for Judith and realize she wasn't there. Gone home without saying goodbye to anyone.

Frankie thought of Judith at the funeral. Every hair in place, a sensible dress, and practical heels. The perfect widow. Chin up, shoulders back, she kept her eyes on Father Brash through the service. She'd responded to every condolence card and flower arrangement with a handwritten note in her perfect script. Her determination to do the right thing carried the fervor of a political campaign. That entire terrible week before the funeral, Frankie had waited for her mother to drop her guard. She waited for a moment to give or receive comfort. She wanted to sit with Patrick and their mother and mourn their collective loss as a now smaller family. But the moment never came. The day after the funeral, she'd gone down to the kitchen and found a note from her mother saying she'd gone to the office and hoped Frankie had a safe trip back to Seattle. It was a dismissal. After the way she'd behaved the night before, could she blame her? Frankie had packed her things and called Patrick for a ride to the bus stop. She'd returned to Seattle and tried to bury herself in her work. Her longing for her family haunted her then and haunted her still.

She heard the rumble of a boat engine and recognized the sound of the big Sea Ray. From the lookout she watched Anne and Tim loading boxes into the boat. They must be leaving, she thought, and without saying goodbye. Her heart was leaden. She wanted to go down to them and could not.

She walked back to the pump house as the sound of the boat engine receded. They were gone and now she had the place to herself like she'd wanted from the start. She'd never felt so lonely in her life. Lanky Frankie, loner, weirdo, party of one. She hadn't minded before. Why should she mind now? She turned off the pump. In the quiet, the little chorus frog bleated once more in the dark. She felt her aloneness like a weight around her neck.

They came down then, Charlie Crow and his parents, calling to each other as they flew through the woods, landing in the clearing behind the house. Charlie Crow settled near her feet, tipping his pert head to regard her. His feathers had darkened and taken on a glossy sheen, and he was lovely and plump. She could hardly detect his limp at all as he strutted back and forth.

Frankie sat on the bench by the back door and pulled the bag of peanuts off the window ledge. She tossed him one and watched him crack it open and gobble it down. The adults landed behind him. They paced and chuckled to each other, glancing at her from time to time. Charlie Crow hopped closer and offered that strange cry from before.

"Coo-coo-wook!"

The smaller adult mimicked the sound, ignoring the peanuts.

"*Coo-coo-wook!*"

Frankie felt her heart in her throat. They'd come to find her for some reason. They recognized her, and they had even named her. They'd created a name for her in their crow language, she was certain of it. Amid the turbulence of her human life, when nothing else was certain at all, this naming was a tremendous gift.

A flash of red off to her left, and there was Aiden with his Superman sweatshirt and crazy curls. He came slowly toward Frankie, his eyes on the birds. The crows watched him but didn't startle. The boy slipped up onto the bench next to Frankie and looked at the birds.

"Hi, Aiden," she said quietly. "That's Charlie Crow and his folks."

Charlie Crow bowed his head to one of the adults and the larger bird preened him. He churred with contentment as the parent ran a beak over his head and neck. The other adult gave a sudden, sharp alarm call and the three birds disappeared into the woods as Anne emerged at the top of the trail slightly out of breath.

"There's my young man! Hiya, Frankie!"

Frankie felt a catch in her throat.

"I thought you'd all left just now. I didn't . . ." She trailed off.

"Just Tim. Crikey that's steep!" Anne said, bending over to catch her breath. "He had to go to Seattle for the weekend."

Aiden kicked the ground in front of the bench and stared out into the woods.

"You think we'd leave without saying goodbye? Our favorite new ornithologist?" Anne said.

Frankie was embarrassed by how pleased she felt to hear that and invited them in.

Aiden tucked his shoes inside the back door and lined up his mother's next to them. He tapped the barometer lightly as he passed it and then each of the armchairs as he circled around to the couch. Anne sat at the kitchen table and Frankie pulled her grandmother's hot chocolate pot off the wall.

"How is your work going? Are you nearly finished?" Anne asked.

Frankie didn't know what to say. She reached into the refrigerator for the milk.

"Sort of. I've reached a stopping point and I'm waiting for, for input, I guess."

Well, that wasn't exactly untrue. But stuck was a better way to describe it. Could she explain it to Anne? Her derailed thesis defense and, consequently, her job offer at OSU. Her financial straits, her anger at her mother. Was this mess of her life appropriate for conversation between new friends? She didn't know.

There was a sound then, a sharp smack. Aiden stood over the table clapping his hands together. Anne moved swiftly toward him. The clapping grew more forceful as he banged his small hands together. Before Frankie heard his low growl, she knew this was not happy clapping. As Anne reached him, his small body erupted. He slapped his face and his head and stomped his feet against the floor. His voice rose to a hoarse wail of absolute anguish.

Anne was speaking to him, but Frankie couldn't hear what she was saying over the sound of Aiden's crying. His face went white and then red as he screamed and screamed. He threw himself against the wall next to the couch, slamming his small elbow into the wainscoting over and over. He bit his small hands with a terrible fury.

Anne stood near but did not try to contain him. Her face broke open with helplessness. Aiden banged his head against the wall, and his mother reached for him, pulled him away from the wall. His eyes flew open and swept the table, then shut again and his wailing grew louder. Frankie understood then—shoes, barometer, chairs, book, headphones. His circuit had been interrupted. Aiden was looking for her bird book. She scanned the room. Where had she left it? There it was on the windowsill next to the back door. She retrieved the book and moved quickly to where Anne stood pleading with Aiden.

"Try to tell mammy. Please, Aiden, what is it, love? Let me help you."

Frankie crouched low and put the book in his hands. Like water from a closed faucet, the screaming just stopped. Aiden blinked, huge tears rolling out of his green eyes, and hiccupped a sob. He flipped through the book, placed it on the table, and pushed past her. He slipped on the headphones and clicked on the crow tape. He sat on the floor and leaned against the couch cupping his hands over his ears.

Anne put her face in her hands and sat on the couch, shoulders shaking as she wept. Frankie sat next to her and waited. The muted sound of crows' voices from the headphones was a low undertone in the room. Outside a squall blew down the lake and the surface of the water dimpled with rain and the wind chimes tinkled.

"Well, that's the last time I'll move that book. I won't be messing with Aiden's agenda," Frankie said after a while.

Anne looked at her with brimming eyes.

"It seems like he's very clear about how he wants things," Frankie said, uncertain now. Was it okay to joke about?

"Oh yes—he is. He most definitely is! Sorry," Anne said.

She leaned forward and touched Frankie's wrist. "You don't understand—"

Her voice caught and she sat back and wiped her eyes.

"Let me try to explain," Anne said.

Yes, Aiden did want things a certain way, and he did communicate his ideas, but most people didn't understand like Frankie did. Most people expected him to talk. And in fact, he had once. This curious, silent boy not only spoke, but had spoken early and in full sentences, paragraphs! And then, a year and a half ago, he'd grown quieter and quieter until he stopped speaking altogether. He'd stopped looking at people too. He'd stared at his little book of fairy tales and barely acknowledged anyone. He fell to pieces like this when he couldn't communicate.

"This kind of thing you just saw—that meltdown. He gets like this, and I know it's because he can't say what he needs."

Frankie considered Aiden. Despite the headphones, she could tell he was listening. They sat in the silence for a few minutes.

"Well, that makes sense to me. It would be hard not to be able to explain yourself," Frankie said.

"I think so too. Everybody else thinks he's just being an awful brat."

There was such sorrow in her voice, and Frankie wondered who "everybody else" was. She wanted to ask, but it seemed so private. She was afraid she might say the wrong thing and not know it.

"As far as not speaking, he must have a good reason," Frankie said. "He's such a little thinker. I mean, you can almost hear the gears turning in there."

Anne chuckled and wiped her eyes.

"Yes, he is. He's a clever wee fox, aren't you, Aiden?"

The boy didn't acknowledge her.

"Tim's parents—" she started and stopped. "I just wish we lived closer to my mam and da."

Frankie moved over to the stove and rekindled the ashes of the fire. She asked Anne to tell her more about the island, which she seemed to enjoy talking about. Anne curled her feet under her and told Frankie about a little house perched on a knoll above the sea, the sound of the wind singing down the power lines, the small village that had been home to her family for generations. She told of her grandmother next door and her bossy mother and her gentle da, who was a fisherman. The gulls in the harbor and the red-billed choughs nesting on the cliff.

Outside, the sunlight winked and sputtered. Rain pattered on the roof and Anne told Frankie that the water around the island she grew up on had the same dark green color as the lake. She told how her father went out to fish when it was dark, and she'd run down to meet his boat in the early afternoon when she got out of school. She described the fog in the harbor on fall mornings like this one and the storms that blew up along the coast in winter. Frankie heard the longing in her voice. She kept asking questions until Anne closed her eyes and dozed.

Aiden had turned off the recorder and slipped up next to Frankie still wearing the headphones. He looked so calm now, though one cheek still flamed red from where he'd hit himself. She felt terrible for him. What did it feel like to not be able to say what you wanted, to not be understood?

Aiden picked up a deck of cards on the table—a memory game of bird species—and shuffled through it, then put it down. He opened the bird book and shifted it into her lap. Frankie glanced at the open page and read aloud.

"The American crow is listed as a Species of Least Concern by the National Audubon Society. Can you hear me with those things on?"

She tapped the headphones with a finger, and he pulled her hand down to the page. She chuckled and kept reading.

"Crow eggs range in color from blue-green to olive green, and the mother lays three to seven eggs per brood. Eggs take eighteen days to incubate, and nestlings remain in the nest for four to five weeks."

She read a bit more about the life of the American crow and then Aiden pulled the book away.

"Okay." Frankie laughed. "Done with me, then?"

The rain had stopped, and the muted light silvered the air above the lake. A trio of ospreys whistled and chattered as they flew low over the lookout. A duet, they were called in a group, Frankie remembered. She took her binoculars outside and peered down at the birds gliding over the lake below. A fish flashed as it cleared the water. Aiden appeared next to her.

"Want a look?" she asked.

He clambered up on the stump next to her and took the binoculars from her. She told him the ospreys were after those fish jumping for midges. They were probably rainbow trout, which were not too hard to catch and tasted good. Another jumped and then another. She pointed to the flashing fish and saw the boy find them with the binoculars. One of the birds flew low, dipped its toes, and came up with a silver body.

"Bingo!" Frankie said.

Aiden followed the bird's flight with the glasses as it flapped away with its prize. Then a dark shape dropped out of the sky and bumped the osprey. A crow. The osprey fumbled the fish, and as it fell through the air, the crow snatched it up and flew off cawing.

Aiden looked up at Frankie, his eyes round with understanding. He threw back his little head and laughed and laughed. It was that belly laugh Frankie had heard the first day when Aiden was on the dock with Anne. He understood this joke—to have won one moment and lost the next. That impish trickster crow who reminded you not to hold on to anything too tightly.

Later that evening as she warmed a can of soup, she thought it might be fun to take Aiden and Anne fishing. She could almost taste Grammy Genevieve's trout chowder. Patrick would know the recipe. Her heart heaved at the thought of her brother. The look on his face as she left his office. His trembling hands as he'd delivered the eulogy at the funeral. The sound of his voice when he called her to tell her their father was dead. There was so much they hadn't talked about. What had it been like for him to take that phone call from Judith? Did he have questions like she did? Questions about the day their father died?

Questions weighed on her. What if Jack had accepted help instead of trying, as usual, to do things his own way? Her lovable, irascible, and impossible dad, who'd stayed late that night at the tavern. Why had he chosen that night, a random Monday in April, to stop off at the dump on his way home to drop off the load of cardboard that had piled up in the tavern basement all winter? Hank had offered to help and so had Patrick, but he'd put them off, saying he would get around to it. But he'd waited until that rainy Monday evening, when everyone else had gone home, including Chubby Harden and the rest of the staff at the Hood River County Transfer Station. The recycling center was never locked, and people often went after hours. So, there was no one there to see Jack pull in and climb out of the truck. No one for him to holler hello to and engage in small talk. No one to watch him unload and notice when the brake slipped and the truck rolled and knocked him down. Nobody around to push it off him as his rib cage punctured his lung. Nobody to hold his hand and tell him it was okay, the ambulance would be there soon, as he slowly suffocated. He was not missed until the morning by Judith, who'd gone to bed early as she often did. It was Chubby who'd found him and called the sheriff. He had died alone like that—lying on the pavement in the cold spring night.

And what about Judith? By the time Frankie made it home, Judith was a picture of poise—chiding her daughter to pull herself together. Frankie knew Judith thought Jack had no one to blame but himself. Nobody said it, but they all assumed he was drunk. *"Poor Judith,"* you could almost hear the town whisper. *"What a shame."*

Frankie ate her soup and sifted idly through the piles on the table. There it was—the calendar Hank had given her. Flipping through it, she saw Jack's notes and scribbles decreased as the year went on, but he had planned major events through the end of the year. Her birthday was marked, and Patrick's, Judith's, and Hank's. He'd written in the dates for March Madness. Saint Patrick's Day, of course. She flipped to early September. He'd planned to pull the boat on Labor Day weekend, she read. Frankie located the present date: September 25, 1998. He'd written: "Clean keg lines 4 homecoming wknd." Of course. Jack's passion for college basketball was only eclipsed by his devotion to high school football. And what did he have planned for the rest of 1998, the final quarter yet to unfold? She paged through to her parents' anniversary.

"Oktoberfest in Leavenworth with J!" he'd written.

Her heart flipped over. She wondered if Judith knew that.

Loose notes and receipts fell out of the back of the book and a white envelope. "Judith" was written on the front in her father's distinctive left-hand printing. Her breath caught and the hair on her neck stood up. The envelope was unopened. A message for Judith. She tucked it back in the calendar.

She rose and stoked the fire. She lay down on the couch and pulled a quilt over herself. For the first time in her life, it felt too cold to sleep on the sleeping porch. Her mind whirred with memories of Jack's funeral and those of her grandparents. She saw Judith in front of the courthouse, Patrick behind his desk, Hank in the back of the church. She ached for all those people missing from her life. And right before she tumbled into sleep, she thought of Anne and Aiden and Charlie Crow. She heard Charlie's strange cry. She heard the little boy laugh as he threw his hands up in the air. He laughed and laughed, and his voice was like a golden bell and the sound made her heart rise and carried her off to sleep.

29
ANNOUNCEMENT CALLS

Migratory birds do not fly unceasingly but instead take days or weeks to reach their chosen overwintering grounds.

—*G. Gordon's Field Guide to the Birds of the Pacific Northwest*

Aiden marched back and forth brandishing a piece of driftwood like a sword. He set it on a growing pile of weathered planks and plunked himself down in the sand still clad in his Aladdin pajamas. He cupped his hands over his ears and looked down the beach. At what? Anne wondered. He rose, collected two more sticks of driftwood, and stacked them in the pile. After some time, he chose one stick and stood it on end in the sand. He twisted and shoved, trying to bury it, but it wouldn't hold. He surrendered it to the pile again and stood with his hands on his narrow hips.

Anne watched from the patio table, thinking about what had happened at Frankie's house. Aiden had fallen apart over the misplaced bird book and screamed himself hoarse. She'd stood there feeling helpless, powerless to do anything for him. This feeling was familiar but still agonizing—being unable to comfort the person she loved most in the world. Somehow Frankie had understood what he needed and simply delivered the book into his hands. The relief on his little face broke her heart.

Later, when they were all sitting on the couch, Anne watched as Aiden inched ever closer to Frankie as she read to him. He didn't look at her, but he was listening. You could almost see his wee ears perking up, taking in every word their new friend was saying.

"My little fox," Anne remembered thinking to herself as she dozed listening to the fire crackle.

She'd started awake not sure where she was. In her dream her mother-in-law had shown up, surprising them all, and taken Anne to task for not dressing the salad properly.

"I think I know a thing or two about salad, Anne!" Christi had said in the dream, and Anne felt cowed and ashamed. The feeling hung over her as she came awake and looked out through the screened-in porch toward the lookout.

She could see Frankie and Aiden outside with their backs to her. Aiden took Frankie's hand and climbed up on the stump next to her. Anne marveled. When was the last time he'd reached out to someone else like that voluntarily? To Tim? Frankie passed the binoculars to Aiden, and the two of them leaned their heads together looking at something. Anne recognized the distance between father and son now. Here at the lake, Tim had taken Aiden with him to do chores, but with a sense of duty, it seemed. When was the last time he'd tried to play with Aiden?

Frankie and Aiden turned away from the water, and Frankie raised her palms as she explained something. Aiden listened, threw his hands over his head, and laughed and laughed like the perfect little boy that he was. Perfect just as he was. Surely Tim would see that.

That night, after she'd tucked Aiden in, and with Tim away in Seattle, she sat down with her notebook and drafted another song. This one was inspired by the images of crows in Frankie's meadow. The kernel of it was an old myth she'd been trying to remember. Morrigan—a magical woman who lived in the shadow of the trees and was always accompanied by crows. She sat by the fire capturing the story as it raced through her mind. It was the third song she'd written since her music had returned to her. It was exhilarating to become lost in the flow of writing again. But just as wonderful was knowing that source was there even when she wasn't writing. That well, that reservoir, it was deep within her and had not deserted her after all. She was still herself. When the weekend was over and Tim had come back from Seattle, that feeling of groundedness remained.

Now, down on the beach, Aiden had resumed his marching. Anne sat up and pulled a pink binder toward her on the table. "Magnusen Lake House!" was written across the front in Christi's florid script. Tim had pulled it out that morning. They'd be leaving in a couple of days and he had asked her to begin the necessary chores for tidying the house. Of course she would, Anne said, but raised an eyebrow when Tim produced the binder with his mother's checklists. He shrugged.

"You know how Mom is," he said.

"Empty refrigerator completely and wipe shelves down. DO NOT neglect vegetable drawers!" Anne read.

The list went on: "Run dishwasher and put dishes away. Remove all perishables and leave canned goods in root cellar. Leave refrigerator door cracked. Sweep, mop, vacuum. Shake out rugs. Wash and dry all bedding. REMOVE ALL TRASH."

Anne would have done these things anyway and found it irksome that Christi spelled everything out like they were children. Another time she would have tried to joke about it with Tim, but not now. Now she would tidy the house while he worked on a report for his father. After their brutal row, she was looking for some neutral ground. She could do this small series of tasks and get them packed to go. Then they'd get home and back into their routine. And as Tim started his new position as president, he'd see that it was better for all of them if Anne went back to work and Aiden stayed at Sunflower. He'd see. The preposterous idea of residential school would blow over and they would let Aiden become Aiden.

She recalled what Frankie had said about his silence.

"He must have a good reason," she'd said, and she sounded so sure that Aiden's not talking was a choice. As soon as she said it, Anne knew it was true. She wouldn't have been able to articulate that before, but now that Frankie had, it was clear as day. He was choosing to be quiet for some reason.

"We'll love him just as he is," her mother had written in her last letter. "Just as he is and as well as we can."

Anne felt such a longing then to be with her mother and Gran. Oh, to be sitting in the kitchen with the two of them now! Tea and village gossip.

The lake was calm and quiet. Morning light angled across the green water and the gulls perched on the log boom laughing. She saw the island in her mind, the wind blowing across the water, the fishing boats at the wharf, the smoke curling out of the stone chimney. It had been four years since she'd been home, the only time her family had seen Aiden. She could almost feel the wind on her face as she sat on the ferry crossing the short stretch of the Atlantic Ocean from the mainland. She imagined her parents standing at the wharf waving madly. Her body warmed with a rush of joy just imagining it.

"*Baile*," she said to herself. Home.

Out on the seawall Aiden stood with his hands cupped over his ears. He'd be old enough to remember a trip at this age. They could fly into Dublin and then on to Shannon. She felt a stab of grief as she thought of that. Dublin was Trinity and Trinity was Kat, and Kat was gone. She recalled Mrs. O'Faolain's letter from last spring, asking Anne to please come back for the memorial in November for All Souls' Day in honor of the Good Friday peace accord.

It will not be a funeral but a celebration. We want to remember the joy that Katherine brought us all. I know it is far to come, dear Anne. But we'd be so grateful if you could be here.

The letter had burned in her hand then and the very thought of it was too much. But now something slid sideways in her heart and clicked into place. Of course she would go and be with Katherine's parents and the others. She felt a rush of longing to see her classmates and her teachers. They'd all lost Katherine and now Anne understood how lonely she'd been in her grief, how sharing it might help. And Aiden could see his grandparents and her gran.

The patio door slid open, and Tim sat down next to her. He hadn't shaved and his stubble gave him a messy look that suited him. His eyes were red, and she wondered if he was sleeping as badly as she was. He squeezed her hand and for a moment everything was okay. She wanted to reach out and touch his cheek. She wanted to tell him that she loved him and that he was going to be brilliant at his new job. She wanted to ask for his assurance that everything would be okay with their little family. But she couldn't find the words. Tim glanced down the seawall at Aiden, his expression unreadable. Was he cross that Aiden was still in his pajamas? Tim pulled the binder toward him, and a look of amusement crossed his face. Maybe they'd have a laugh after all? But when he spoke, his voice was somber.

"Thanks for taking care of this stuff. Dad hired Jerry to drain the water system and put the storm shutters on after we go. But the rest of this—thanks, I appreciate it."

Small talk, then.

"Not a problem," Anne said. "What day do you want to shove off, then? I can get through this list in two shakes."

In a couple of days, he said. He wanted to be home by week's end. There would be lots of work to do before his father announced his retirement and Tim's promotion.

Anne listened and reflected that most of fall semester yawned before her. She had more than three months of leave before she started teaching in January. All the more reason to take a trip home with Aiden. The thought cheered her.

"This fall will busy for you," she said.

Tim frowned and she found his hand.

"You're going to do a fierce job of it. I know you will, Tim."

His face softened and he thanked her, leaning in to kiss her. She breathed in his smell—coffee, toothpaste, something woodsy, so familiar and comforting. Now she did reach up and touch his face and he took her hand and kissed it.

"So, I was thinking this might be a good time for a trip. For me and Aiden, I mean. I want to take him home to see my folks and Gran. And there's a memorial Mass—"

Tim dropped her hand and was shaking his head.

"Look," she said, trying to carry on. "It will only be a couple of weeks and we'll be back for the holidays. I'll miss the fall gala thing, but you know I hate that kind of do anyway. And since I'm on leave I have the time, so—"

"No, Anne," Tim interrupted. "No, this is *not* a good time for you and Aiden to take a trip. This fall it's important for you to be home with me."

"I disagree," she said firmly. "You'll be busy with work, and I want my parents to see him. It's been years since I've been back. And there's also a special Mass—"

"Did you not understand what I was saying?" he interrupted again. "This job, it changes everything for all of us. I expect you to be focusing on what's best for our family."

Stung, she sat back and gave a short laugh.

"What's best for our family," she repeated. "And what might that be?"

Tim pressed his lips together and she noticed how much he looked like his father.

"For starters, I'd like us to move out of Fremont, so you could find us a house. Mom said she's got a good Realtor. And moving and getting settled in will take a while. As for you returning to work in January, I just don't think that's best for us."

"Oh, I'm sorry!" she said. "I didn't realize I worked for you now. I had the misapprehension that I was employed by Cornish College of the Arts, not Magnusen Media!"

"Your employment seems a bit tenuous, doesn't it?" he shot back. "Patrice put you on administrative leave because you were doing a crappy job—"

Anne pushed her chair back and stood. Her fury made her voice squeak, which made her angrier.

"You don't know the first thing about my work, thank you very much, Timothy Magnusen. So you can keep your opinions to yourself—"

"And you were doing a crappy job at home too!" Tim said, talking over her and rising too. "Which is another reason that Aiden needs to go to a residential school. You can't give him what he needs!"

Anne stared. His anger made him unrecognizable to her and the hurt she felt drained all her fury away.

"You think I can't give him what he needs?"

It was a simple question. He looked away from her, his jaw clenched, and she followed his gaze to where Aiden was sitting on the beach. And when he turned back his eyes brimmed with tears. She saw the old Tim, the one she knew and loved. But then he blinked, and his face grew stern.

"The staff at Mt. Holy Oak will give him what he needs," he said. "That's what I've decided. And my parents agree."

He went into the house without another word. Anne felt like she'd been slapped. Her heart hammered in her chest and her pulse thrummed in her ears. Was he serious about this, then? Mt. Holy Oak. That place? Impossible.

One of Dr. Shelley's graduate students, Michelle, had first mentioned the school to her. Michelle had done a rotation there.

Michelle had explained to Anne, "They call themselves schools, but they're just old-style institutions. I saw the worst of it— overmedicating kids so they're practically zombies. They use restraints all the time when they don't need to. I didn't see much in the way of OT or speech therapy. I'm just saying, they can call it a school, but it's not."

Anne, horrified, asked Michelle how it was legal.

"Well, if their parent or guardian places them there, they do agree to let the facility decide on treatment. But those places aren't the norm," she said, registering the alarm on Anne's face. "I shouldn't even be talking about that! You'll find a great program for Aiden. We'll help you. There are integrative models all over Seattle. When he's ready for that stage, Dr. Shelley will help you decide."

"That's what I've decided," Tim had said.

Since when were they not deciding things together? Anne felt a deep and terrible loneliness. The distance between them now felt immeasurable, unbridgeable.

She left the patio and crossed the sand to where Aiden sat and knelt next to him. He'd organized the pile of driftwood by size and was stacking the pieces into a round. She was struck by the beauty of it.

"That's just lovely, sweetie," she said, wiping her eyes. "Do you want to go for a rowboat ride with Mammy?"

She pushed the boat through the damp sand and held it steady as he clambered over the side and into the bow. She shoved off and rowed them out into the flat green water of the bay. Aiden leaned over the side, trailing one hand in the water and watching the pattern his fingers made. After a while he glanced up and past her. She gazed at his beautiful, open face.

How could Tim think of sending him away? The very idea of Aiden's physical removal felt painful. Was it different for a father? Anne had been altered forever by becoming a mother. Aiden had been a literal part of her. Those months he'd lived inside her body, the way he did somersaults when she sang to him. The press of his little feet against her spine. The minute he was born, when the midwife lay him on her belly and he stared up at her, there was a moment of recognition. There you are, she'd thought. He belonged to her and she to him. She would never leave him in the care of strangers.

She knew she was not a perfect mother. She'd failed him this last year and a half lost in her grief. But she would not fail her boy now.

She pulled the oars and the boat cut through the water. The sun blinked in and out of the clouds and lit up Aiden's auburn curls. He lay his cheek on the gunnel and looked up at Frankie's cottage. Anne could hear him humming to himself. She recognized the melody of the little bird lullaby and sang it softly to him.

Éiníní, éiníní, codalaígí, codalaígí.

Little birds, little birds, go to sleep. Then the roll call—blackbird, raven, crow, robin, lark, wren, and thrush.

An londubh is an fiach dubh,
An chéirseach is an préachán,
An spideog is an fhuiseog,
An dreoilín is an smóilín.
Téigí a chodhladh, téigí a chodhladh.

He patted his hand in time to the song. They rowed along the shore until the wind picked up and she headed back to the house. Tim stayed in the sunroom for most of the day and they were frostily polite to each other at meals. She pretended to be asleep when he came to bed. He stood over her, looking down.

"Anne," he whispered, but she didn't respond. He sighed and walked around to his side and climbed in. Soon he was asleep with that maddening ease she once teased him about. Now it felt like an insult. How could he sleep when they were falling apart?

She couldn't still her whirring mind and slipped out to the kitchen. She sat by the light of the dying fire and looked out at the water glinting under the waxing moon, a silver sliver in the inky sky. They had reached an impasse and she knew it. Tim was doing what his parents wanted him to do, like a good son. He was choosing them over her and Aiden. She felt her heart in her throat. Could she blame him? Their marriage had been off-balance from the start.

They'd barely known each other, and they came from such different places.

People got divorced all the time, she told herself. So why did this feel like such a tragedy? She felt gutted remembering Tim at the silent auction, the way he'd made her laugh that first night at Serafina. She remembered rushing home from work to check her answering machine and thrilling to the sound of his voice. The day she told him she was pregnant. Their rushed wedding at the courthouse. Those first months in the little apartment. What a first-rate father he'd been when Aiden was a baby.

But she knew it in her heart, and she felt the dark weight of it: This was the end of something. They didn't have a future together, not like this. She had to leave. As soon as she completed the thought, she felt a flood of relief, even as her heart broke with it. Tim had chosen his family over her and Aiden. But she would choose Aiden. Always.

She thought about the island, her parents and Gran. And she knew home was the answer. She could stay with her parents for as long as she needed to get herself sorted with work and a good school for Aiden. That probably meant living on the mainland. But she'd be home.

"We'll love him just as he is," her mother had written. She knew they would. She would call her mam, as quick as she could, and explain everything. Mam, Gran, and Da—they would welcome her and Aiden. Margaret would help her figure out her plan for getting home. Frankie would help her too. Frankie would get her down the lake to the phone to call home. Her mind, released from the tether of uncertainty, began to formulate her migration.

30

MIMICRY

Distinct from other creatures in their ability to fly, birds also offer astounding vocal capacities and fascinating habits that teach us much about the natural world.

—*G. Gordon's Field Guide to the Birds of the Pacific Northwest*

The American crow is listed as a Species of Least Concern by the National Audubon Society.

Crow eggs range in color from blue-green to olive green, and the mother lays three to seven eggs per brood. Eggs take eighteen days to incubate, and nestlings remain in the nest for four to five weeks.

Older siblings help care for new hatchlings and will live in their parents' territory for up to five years before starting their own families.

Cooperative breeding, which is uncommon among animals and birds, is central to the life of the crow.

Crows spend the winter congregated in large numbers with many family units sharing territory.

The American crow does not migrate.

31

MIGRATIONS

It is the alteration of daylight hours that often triggers the migratory urge in many birds, including those that migrate the farthest.

—*G. Gordon's Field Guide to the Birds of the Pacific Northwest*

A wind had arisen in the night and whistled around the corners of the little house. High in the treetops it lowed in a sustained murmur like an invisible train passing endlessly behind the house, car after car rolling along. The wind so dampened the sounds rising off the lake that Frankie didn't hear Jerry's boat approaching. Once he landed, the sputtering sound of his motor carried up the hillside. Frankie saw the flash of his yellow float coat from the lookout and went down to the dock. Jerry had only tied up the bow and kept the engine running.

"Hey there, kid! I'm glad you caught me. I'm headed over to the lumber camp to overnight and help them pack everything up. I'll leave for Mill Three in the morning. I might run back up here tomor-row afternoon with some sheeting for the Condons' project if the weather holds. If I don't see you, have a great winter, my dear."

That was it, then. If Jerry was done, the season really was over. Anne and her family were headed down in a couple of days too, and Frankie would be alone at the lake. That was sobering.

"You too, Jerry. I'll try to stop by and say hello on my way through town."

"Getting ready to shove off yourself, then?" he asked her.

He climbed back into the Hewescraft and dug around on the dashboard.

"Oh heck, Frankie. I forgot your mail! I had this box for Tim and walked out without getting yours. There was a pile too. Sorry about that, kid. I'm going in all directions at once today."

He set a file box on the dock and climbed out.

"I left my lunch at the house too. One of those days. I swear if my head wasn't screwed on!"

"It's no problem, Jerry. I was going to run down today anyway."

She needed to call Patrick—about the money but also because she felt terrible about how they'd left things.

"Do you want me to take that box up to Tim and Anne?"

He shook his head.

"No, thanks. I need to speak to young Tim about closing, so I'll hop up there myself. Anyway, if you're headed down today you should go before that weather comes in."

Frankie glanced up at the mountain and saw the blue glacier had disappeared under snow. Clouds gathered to the north.

"Okay, well, good luck tomorrow. Tell Marilyn I said hello. And tell her—"

She paused when her voice caught.

"Tell her I said thank you for the brownies and the card. Thank you both. It means a lot."

Jerry's eyes grew wet, and he looked away and cleared his throat. The silence was uncomfortable but necessary because it was part of the grief. There was her own sorrow and the sadness of others that rose to meet it. Jerry passed a big hand over his eyes and gave a short laugh.

"Well, Jack O'Neill was one of a kind and we miss the old son of a gun, all of us. If you ever need anything, you just ask. You know that, right, Frankie?"

"I do. Thank you, Jerry."

He hugged her hard and turned away, walking up the dock with the box under one arm.

Frankie ran up to the cottage to get her wallet, then climbed in the boat and cast off. As she motored away, she saw Anne walking down the seawall with Jerry. Anne looked so small, and Aiden was not with her. Frankie realized she hadn't ever seen Anne without Aiden. Her friend raised a hand, and Frankie waved back and turned the boat south down the lake.

The water was placid and beautiful, so she motored close to the basalt cliffs along the eastern edge of the lake where the Yakama land began. Cottonwood trees grew down close to the water there and were all golden now. She knew that just beyond that line of trees, the Wishram River rushed over the falls where the Yakama Nation members gathered in spring for the salmon feast. Jim Miller had invited Grandpa Ray once and he had taken her with him. She'd spent the afternoon quietly watching the ceremony from her grandfather's side, feeling shy and fascinated by speeches and songs in a language she didn't understand. He told her it was important to be quiet and respectful. She thought of her phone call to the agency office and her conversation with Councilman Miller. He wasn't being unfriendly, she thought. His father probably had lots of fishing buddies on the lake.

At the marina dock, Frankie tied up and pulled her fenders out. She walked across the empty parking lot and felt a cool breeze on the back of her neck. The post office lobby was hot, and she shrugged off her jacket. Donna appeared and pulled a stack of mail out from under the counter and pushed it across to her.

"I tried to catch Jerry, but he was hustling this morning. This is everything I have for you," she said.

Frankie made change for the pay phone and thanked her. Sifting through the mail, she found a bulky package from OSU, which made her stomach flip over. Probably orientation information. She knew she'd hear from them soon about needing proof of her master's. Well, she didn't have it, did she?

She found a letter from Weatherby's office and a note from Patrick. She opened the note, which said something about their mother wanting to come up for closing. Her anger at Judith about the lawsuit lifted slightly at that. Judith wanted to come up to the cottage? Maybe it was a peace offering.

Crossing the parking lot, she pushed into the phone booth and dialed the law firm, praying Patrick was in. Happily, it was too early for Nancy Gates to be answering the phone, so the call rang straight through to Patrick's office.

"It's me," she said when he answered, and Patrick sighed.

"Nice to know you're still alive up there, little sister," he said. "Thought you might have absconded to the wilderness."

She could hear the tentativeness in his teasing.

"Absconded, hey?" she said. "Learning big words there at the firm, I see."

"Just trying to keep up with my baby sister the academic."

Frankie gave a short laugh.

"Well, former academic, is what it looks like."

Patrick sighed.

"Sorry, Frank. That's just—I mean, there must be some way to appeal it, right? Some formal process? Otherwise they leave themselves open to legal action."

"You sound like a lawyer already, Patrick."

She wanted it to sound like a joke, but she thought she might cry.

"Yes, I think there is a process. But the letter they sent directed me to start my appeal with the chair of my department, and that's Dr. Grant. Believe me, I've seen this before. I won't get anywhere with it."

"Well, hell. I'm sorry, Frank," Patrick said. "So . . . what's your plan?"

"Well, I might see if OSU would take me in some sort of adjunct position."

She knew that was unlikely, but she didn't want him to worry.

"But for the time being, I guess I'll stay up here for the winter. I know you don't like the idea, but I don't have much of a choice."

The silence hung heavy between them, and Patrick sighed again.

"Frankie, did you pick up your mail?" he asked.

"Yes, I've got it here. I got your note. Mom wants to come up to help close? That's weird, isn't it? But it would be nice. I mean, if I stay, you two could come up for the day. We could go chanterelle picking! I was thinking about Grammy's soup. It could be fun."

Patrick didn't say anything, and she felt embarrassed.

"Or not. I mean, it's no big deal."

Her brother sighed down the phone.

"Frankie, you should have a letter from Weatherby's office," Patrick said.

"Yeah, I saw that, but I didn't understand it. It's about the estate?"

Patrick groaned and she imagined him leaning his face on his hand in a gesture that mirrored their father.

"Mom is getting a survey, Frankie. That's why she wants to come up. She hired Karl Okari to do the survey. You got a letter from Peter because any major change with the O'Neill Family LLC must be formally registered with Weatherby's office."

"A survey? Why does Mom want a survey? What are you talking about, Patrick?" Frankie asked.

He hesitated and then said the most impossible thing.

"Mom's putting the cottage on the market, Frankie. She wants to sell."

She heard his words, but what Patrick said didn't make sense. The world tilted and she grasped the edge of the phone booth.

"But—she wouldn't . . . She can't! We, we, we own it. All three of us!" Frankie stammered.

"Yes, but Dad made her executor of his estate and directing member of the LLC. The way it's structured, it gives her a majority share and decision-making power. It's . . . I'm sorry, Frankie. The decision is hers to make. Legally, she can do this and doesn't need our permission."

"But, but . . . I just. I don't get it. Why would she . . . It's . . . It's all I have left!"

She would not let herself cry. She couldn't.

"Look, you're already at the marina. Just come down and we'll talk about it. I'm meeting her for lunch. Maybe we can reason with her."

"Okay. Yeah, I can do that."

"Good. Try not to worry. We'll figure something out."

She hung up and looked up at the mountain heavy with snow. She wished she could pray but didn't know how.

The image of Judith came to her then. Her young mother, up at the lake. Judith with her dark hair pulled back into plaits, looking so happy. Judith sitting next to her in the bird blind with her arms around her knees and her face tipped to the sky. Judith laughing at something Jack said. The sound of her laughter carrying through to the sleeping porch, where Frankie lay in the dark listening to her young parents.

Her heart ached remembering those days, and she longed for her mother. All the way to town, the memories came flashing. Mile after mile she was inundated with one after the other—images of the way it had been before, when the four of them felt like a family.

When she pushed through the door at Bette's Place, she saw Judith before Judith saw her. She was sitting across from Patrick and looking up at a tall man standing next to the table. Frankie's heart lifted at the sight of her mother, yearning toward her. She crossed the room and stood awkwardly waiting for the man to move, but he didn't notice her. Her mother did not acknowledge her, and her hope withered under Judith's familiar disregard.

Patrick stood, and the man shifted over. Frankie recognized him as Greg Robusto, a Realtor from Judith's office. He said hello to

Frankie and that he hoped to see them all that evening at homecoming. As he left, Judith looked her up and down and Frankie realized her clothes were rumpled and spotted with pine pitch from splitting wood. She sat down next to Patrick feeling self-conscious.

"Hello, Mary Frances. We ordered for you because I'm on a tight schedule," Judith said and tore open a packet of Sweet'n Low and stirred it into her tea. "We have homecoming tonight. We have to be there before the parade starts, and it is a workday. For some of us anyway."

Frankie's body flushed with heat, and she glanced at her brother. She knew she was not part of Judith's "we."

"Patrick and I were just going over the plan for the survey up at the cottage," Judith said without preamble. "Karl and I will be coming up Monday to take care of the preliminaries and you'll need to pick us up from the marina. I told him nine a.m., so please be prompt."

Bette arrived with their food and Judith was talking, stirring her tea, gesturing to Bette to put the plates down. Frankie felt like she was watching a movie. Judith was talking about the survey, which was scheduled for Wednesday, weather dependent. They couldn't show the cottage until spring, of course, but it would be good to get it all in order. She had a few leads she could pursue over the winter in Portland and Seattle. Judith kept talking, explaining market fluctuations and interest rates and demographic changes to the second-home market. Patrick listened attentively, though Frankie was sure he'd heard it all before. She watched Judith's mouth moving, Patrick agreeably nodding his head, and the pressure she'd felt growing and growing had no more room to grow. She brought her hand down hard on the table, rattling the silverware.

"Mom, please. For God's sake, just stop talking."

Her voice was loud enough to momentarily silence other conversations in the diner. Judith looked startled and set her glass down carefully.

"Really, Mary Frances. There's no need to cause a—"

"Mom. Please," she said. "You need to listen to me right now."

Miraculously, Judith remained silent. Frankie gathered herself and told her mother everything. About being fired from the lab and spending the summer jobless in Seattle. About her defense denial, which would now cost her the job offer at OSU. And what a great offer that had been. And in summary, that she had nowhere to go and no idea what to do next.

Judith didn't speak. Emboldened, Frankie told her how the cottage was a refuge, a haven. The beloved place was so important to her.

"I miss Dad so much. And Grammy and Grandpa Ray. I miss our family. I just want to feel . . ."

She felt overwhelmed and trailed off. Patrick squeezed her arm.

"It's okay, Frank," he murmured.

She felt Judith watching her, and for a moment, Frankie saw her young mother there, the laughing, green-eyed beauty who let herself be waltzed around the kitchen standing on her husband's feet. The woman she'd called Mama, who'd taught her to swim, who'd waded in the cool water of the lake hunting for fool's gold, who picked berries with her on lazy summer afternoons.

"Well, congratulations, Mary Frances," Judith said finally.

"For what? They aren't going to give me my diploma. All that effort was for nothing," Frankie said, and her voice broke.

"Exactly," Judith said. "All talk and no follow-through. Just like your father."

Frankie bolted to her feet, knocking her water glass to the floor. She grasped the edge of the table until her knuckles turned white.

"Well, at least I know Dad loved me," she choked out. She leaned toward her mother, and Judith shrank back.

"Your lack of regard for other people's feelings is just stunning, Mother."

She turned to her brother.

"And you, Patrick. Would it kill you to stick up for me for once?

You talk a good game when it's just the two of us, but then Mom shows up, and you're doormat of the year. Thanks for nothing."

What else could she say? She'd said it all, she'd offered her very heart in her hands, and it had been summarily declined. Frankie pushed her hair out of her face and looked around. The room was silent, everyone staring, and all the anger drained out of her then. Bette brought out a broom and began to sweep up the broken glass.

"Sorry, Bette," she said.

"Don't worry about it, sweetheart," Bette said quietly.

Her kindness made Frankie want to weep. She looked at Patrick and Judith, and then she left. Outside, the west wind cut against her back, and she hurried to the truck. Heading toward the bridge, she drove past the tavern. The blinds were drawn, and the old building looked as lonely as Frankie felt. Alone, but at least she knew the score now. She passed the fairgrounds and saw the floats assembling for the afternoon—Toastmasters, Hood River Rotary Club, 4-H, and Hood River County Fruit Growers. Blackstone Realty would be among them preparing a throne for her mother.

Following the parade, everyone would gather at the football field under umbrellas and raincoats for the homecoming game. And after, in the high school gym where the big potluck took place, Judith would bask in the gentle compassion of her neighbors. It would be her official coming-out day as a new widow, her first formal event since Jack's death nearly six months earlier. She'd insist Patrick accompany her, and no wonder Judith didn't want Frankie there. People might ask about school or offer condolences about her father. Either would steal the limelight from her mother. Judith needn't worry. She was leaving and wouldn't be back.

The wind was wild at the marina and the trees in the little park swayed grandly. Frankie cast off and sped up the main channel. At the halfway mark near Arrow Point, she threw the boat into neutral. She stood at the wheel and her sorrow flooded her. It was all too much to hold in—Jack's death, Judith's coldness, Dr. Grant's be-

CROW TALK   293

trayal. Even Patrick's passivity. And now the end of the cottage, her safe haven about to disappear forever. There was no island, no place to regain her footing. Her breath was ragged, and she cried until her throat was raw. The grief came in wave after crashing wave.

She was so lost and so alone. But then she felt a sharp heat in her belly that grew and expanded out to the tips of her fingers. It took her a moment to understand what she was feeling: Fury. How dare he, Davis Grant, dismiss her after all she'd done for him? And Judith, refusing to show any compassion at all. But she was also furious with Jack—her beloved, irresponsible father. How could he go like this and leave the family in such a mess? Everything she'd stifled for these past months, that she'd tried to bury with work, boiled up and poured over. Pain, loss, and heartbreak.

She felt so alone standing there in the boat in the middle of the lake high up in the Washington woods. Everything she loved most had been taken away—her father, her work, and now her beloved place at June Lake. What did she have left? For a moment it seemed easy to believe that her small, inconsequential life did not matter. That nothing mattered.

The air around her blurred with white, and she understood it was snowing. She shivered, realizing she'd left her dad's jacket at the post office. The snow fell cold on her bare arms, drifting silently across the quiet lake. The world was transformed by the muting snowfall, and the simple beauty of it shocked her out of her grief. Large, perfect flakes hung suspended in the air and then landed on the surface of the water and melted away into the dark green depths. There was no wind, no birdsong. Just the silent beauty of the falling snow.

Frankie wiped her arm across her eyes and felt the tremendous privilege of witnessing this simple splendor. She found her breath and returned to the helm. The water was a sheet of glass as she headed back up the lake. She coasted into the dock as the snow drifted around her.

Up in the house she built a fire, and it quickly warmed the room.

The wind whistled over the roof and blustered up into the woods. Frankie changed into dry clothes and bundled up to sit on the bench behind the house with a cup of hot chocolate. She looked up at the trees surrounding the cottage, the golden tamarack and flaming red vine maple dusted with melting snow. Hemlocks and noble fir were scattering their cones on the forest floor and the old ponderosa pines leaned out over the cliff as they had for more than four hundred years. She loved this place with all her heart.

As the wind dropped, bird sounds trickled down out of the forest. She heard the crows yawping at each other. Frankie wished she could see Charlie Crow once more before she left. She wished him a long and healthy life here in the woods above June Lake. Within her sadness, she remained curious about that little crow and what he'd been trying to say to her. What was that strange cry she'd heard from him and from his parents? She thought of what Dr. Wood-Smith had written in her manuscript.

"The strongest inquiries come from the questions we just can't seem to shake."

It rang so true to her then, that idea. It didn't seem to matter that her academic career was over and that her thesis would never see the light of day. She remained interested and curious, with questions to ask. She would entertain this inquiry that had started with Dr. Marzluff and continued with Charlie Crow. Did crows have a specific threat call—in this case a caveman threat call? Could crows have a specific ally call as she imagined she'd heard from Charlie Crow and his parents? She would try to answer those questions. She would write up her research about crows talking. Why not? She had nothing left to lose. It would be her last academic offering and her farewell to this beloved place, the lake and the woods, before she left forever.

Back in the house, she sat down and began. The process of organizing her notes and her data calmed her. The outline seemed to write itself, and she realized that she'd been building toward this idea all along. Dusk dropped, and the sky grew dark. She worked all night without tiring.

When she finished, Frankie pushed herself up from the table and walked to the couch. She sat down, exhausted, but lighter and freer than she'd felt all year. She lay down and closed her eyes. She drifted off and as she did so, she was aware of someone else sitting there with her. And as she fell asleep, she realized who it was. It was seven-year-old Mary Frances O'Neill, lover of birds, ears tuned to the woods, taking notes on the wild world around her.

She was always there. She always had been, and she always would be. Wherever life took her.

32

THE MUSTER

Birds demonstrate uncommon agility and quick reactions
in varied circumstances.

—*G. Gordon's Field Guide to the Birds of the Pacific Northwest*

≫— —≪

It's long been suspected that birds can predict a storm. Researchers
in Tennessee were the first to prove the behavior when golden-winged
warblers fled in advance of a series of tornados. Some theories have
postulated that low-flying birds signal falling air pressure, and many
have noted birds grow quiet just before a storm hits. But even the most
casual observer will notice a change in their behavior in advance of
a significant shift in the weather. While a gentle rain shower might
draw birds out of the woods to bathe and drink, hopping through
puddles and twittering away, a big storm will have them tucked out
of sight and silent, bracing for the force of whatever is coming.

It was not the absence of birds or the storm itself that woke
Frankie, but the sound of a boat engine. She jolted awake and found
herself lying on the couch in her clothes from the previous day. Her
thoughts were jumbled—Judith, Dr. Grant, and the caveman masks.
She pushed herself up and struggled to pull her boots on. Jerry had
said he might stop by that afternoon but hadn't said anything about
morning. By the time she reached the lookout, the Hewescraft had

pulled away from the dock and was headed out into the main channel. She wondered what had brought him back to Beauty Bay on his
way down to Mill Three.

The ground around the lookout was dusted with snow. It lingered
on tree branches and the roofline of the house and the outbuildings.
As she came fully awake the snow cheered her, the simple beauty of
it, even though the rest of her world was falling apart. Frankie went
back inside and surveyed the piles of books and notes on the table
and the flickering screen of the computer. It had seemed like a dream,
but there it was, a complete manuscript. "Crow Talk: What Common
Corvids Have to Say about Enemies and Allies." It was her first paper that was totally independent of Dr. Grant and his data and felt
like the best thing she'd ever written. How strange to think that she'd
been gathering all the pieces for the last year, saving studies and
references and tucking them away in her mind and her notebooks.
Storing the shiny bits for later, just like the crows themselves.

She'd submit it for publication to *The Auk* or *The Journal of Avian
Biology*, she decided. The idea was interesting enough, and she didn't
need Dr. Grant's help. Dr. Marzluff would agree to be second author,
certainly. Dr. Wood-Smith might still be willing to assist her too,
despite her failure to complete her thesis. It felt like a good way to
close the door on UW and move on. Maybe it would convince the OSU
folks to take her on as an adjunct. At the very least it might increase
her chances of landing a better Forest Service position. Maybe something permanent. She wouldn't mind that, she told herself. Maybe the
world of academics was out of reach, but at least she would be sup-
porting herself. And she liked working on field crews. Maybe she'd
go to the Oregon Coast for another plover season or work the sage
grouse study at the Malheur National Wildlife Refuge. For now,
she'd head to the Bend Bureau of Land Management field house,
where she could stay for a couple of weeks. They always needed vol-
unteers in the fall.

She spent the morning organizing her books and notes, burning what she didn't need in the stove. After lunch, she went out to the woodpile to resupply and noticed how quiet the woods were. The typical chatter was absent from the trees around the cottage. She heard the whistle of wings and looked up to see a solitary crow heading up into the woods.

"Expect fine weather if the crows fly together. A crow flying alone is a sign to get home." Another gem from Bird Bingo.

The sunlight flickered in and out of the muted clouds and the air felt cold and humid. Back in the cottage she looked at the barometer and saw that it had crashed. It had fallen from "Change" past "Storm" to "Gale." That hadn't happened in all her years at the lake. Then again, she'd never been up so late in the season. Winter was unknown territory and just around the corner. Well, she wouldn't be leaving today anyway. She stoked the fire and looked out the window. Gathering clouds obscured the face of the mountain, and the lake reflected a dark and moody sky.

Her stomach dropped as she thought of Jerry. She hoped he'd abandoned the idea of a return trip with supplies for the Condons' house, as he'd suggested. She grabbed her binoculars and strode to the lookout. The clouds were rolling quickly down toward the water as she scanned the horizon. There was no sign of the old red boat, and the lake was a sheet of glass. Then the air grew dark around her like it was twilight instead of midday. Something passed through her line of vision, and as she turned, a little brown wren tumbled by as a massive wind bore down on the lake. A wind line sprang up and huge whitecaps unfurled across the black water, which had been a green mirror an instant before.

Frankie ran to the mudroom and grabbed her raincoat. Outside, the pelting rain blinded her as she picked her way down the trail, which was already slick with rain. She loped down the dock to *The Peggotty* and pulled out the old canvas cover, which flapped and snapped about. The wind nearly tore it out of her hands, and then it pulled taut. She saw Tim Magnusen then, holding it down on the other side of the boat. Together they snapped the cover in place and zipped it shut. He nodded to her and they hurried over to the Magnusens' boat and did the same, and then they both checked their boat lines and fenders to make sure they were secure. The boats bucked in the stormy waters as the wind tore across the bay.

Frankie ran under the cover of the store roof and pulled her hood up around her face. Tim ducked under the eaves next to her, and the two of them stood in the shelter of the little building watching the drama unfold across the water. Lightning flashed over the lake and thunder roared close on its heels. It was terrifying and thrilling at once. Tim's laughter rang over the receding thunder.

"Wow!" he yelled. "That came up fast as hell!"

"I know!" Frankie yelled back. "I'm so glad you were here to help me!"

Tim said something she didn't catch, and she leaned toward him. "What?"

"I said did Anne not want to get wet?"

He looked up toward the cottage. She tried to understand what he meant, and a sharp crack made them both look up the hillside. Behind the Condons' house the trees were swaying wildly, the tamaracks bending nearly in half. The wind gusted hugely, and the tops began to snap. They cracked and toppled like broken pencils. A big ponderosa went over, its root ball popping clear out of the muddy soil. A stand of trees arrested its fall as it careened toward the Condons' house. There was a loud crash as something hit the ground out of sight.

"Holy hell!" she yelled, but she could barely hear herself.

She thought of Jerry and hoped he'd made it to Arrow Point to wait out the storm, or maybe he'd decided not to leave Mill Three when he saw the weather change. The wind gusted, and thunder rolled over the lake and the woods. She turned back to Tim and lightning flashed above them.

"What about Anne?" she yelled.

"I asked why she didn't come down to help you!"

Frankie looked at him, confused, and shook her head.

"She probably didn't want to leave Aiden?"

He frowned.

"But she left Aiden with me. She said you two were going . . ."

Thunder crashed, and the wind tore his words away. Frankie kept shaking her head.

"Tim, I haven't seen Anne today."

He looked at her like she was speaking a foreign language.

"She's not at your house?"

"No," Frankie said. And then her heart dropped. Anne had said Aiden was afraid of thunder.

"Tim, where's Aiden?"

They ran through the rain to the Magnusens' house and searched the rooms. But the boy was nowhere.

Tim stood in the kitchen with the rain streaming off his jacket. His face was white.

"I thought he'd be okay on his own for a few minutes while I . . . I shouldn't have left him."

Frankie remembered the afternoon Aiden had first crept into her house.

"I'll go look at my place," she said. "Check your outbuildings, okay?"

She ran down the seawall and climbed the slick trail to the cottage. The back door was ajar, but when she checked the rooms, there was no sign of the quiet, impish five-year-old boy.

Tim shoved through the door to the mudroom.

"I can't find him anywhere! I don't know what to do! And I have no idea where Anne is."

His voice rose in panic.

"Tim, start at the beginning. Anne said she was coming here? When?"

He rubbed a hand across his face.

"Hours ago! First thing this morning. I wasn't totally awake. She said the two of you were hiking up to some big tree at the top of the hill and wouldn't be back until late afternoon."

"And she left Aiden with you?"

"Yeah," he said, his face creased with worry.

Frankie's mind raced. When had she seen Anne last? What had they talked about? She couldn't remember. And then she recalled Anne, her slim frame and red braid, standing on the dock next to Jerry and waving at her as she left the dock yesterday. And the sound of the boat that morning.

"Tim, did you see Jerry today?"

He shook his head, and she could see he was only half listening to her.

"She said she was going to your place and she didn't want to bring Aiden because the hike was too far . . ."

"Tim," Frankie said. "Take a breath, okay?"

He nodded, jaw clenched.

"Okay, listen, I saw Jerry swing by the dock this morning. Is there any reason Anne might have gone down the lake with Jerry? Did she have an errand or maybe some calls to make?"

His shoulders slumped and his hands fell to his sides.

"We had a fight. I said some things—" He looked up at the ceiling. "Jesus! I'm a fucking idiot. I just didn't listen . . ."

Frankie turned away and scanned the living room.

"I think I know where Aiden is," she said.

She grabbed a pair of headlamps from the mudroom and gave one to Tim. Leaving the the door slightly ajar in case the boy returned, she led Tim up the trail into the woods. The wind blew the rain in her face as she pushed up the hill. From time to time, she looked back to make sure Tim was behind her. The wind made it too difficult to talk, and she was breathing hard. She'd never hiked the trail so fast, and Tim struggled to keep up. Once she stopped and asked if he wanted to slow down, but he just grimaced and shook his head.

They pushed on, both slipping in the mud. Frankie lost track of time and couldn't see her watch in the stormy light. As they neared the top of the hill, she scanned the ridge for the Lightning Tree but couldn't locate it in the gloom. Everything looked different with big trees down everywhere. She clambered over a fallen hemlock and heard Tim slip and swear.

"I'm fine!" he called. "Keep going!"

The rain came down in sheets and Frankie pushed on, willing her feet to find the once-familiar way in the darkness of the storm. They passed the huckleberry meadow and she thought of the currant bush with the tiny nestlings. She hoped the little birds were safe. Then the Lightning Tree sprang into view—whole and standing. The wonderful giant of the woods had once again bested the storm. Frankie felt a jolt of joy and quickened her pace.

As she reached the big tree and peered inside the little cavern, the beam from her headlamp touched the face of the little boy with the auburn curls and green eyes. He was wearing Frankie's headphones and pressing them to his ears with his hands. His face was streaked with tears, and he hiccupped a sob.

Frankie turned off her headlamp and crouched low.

"Oh, Aiden," she said. "How did you get up here all by yourself?"

The little boy looked up, then stood and walked to her. He grabbed her hand in his two small ones. And then she heard a high, clear voice.

"Where is my mama?" Aiden demanded.

Then Tim was there. He squatted down and held out his arms and Aiden walked into them. Aiden let himself be carried down the hill. He lay his head on Tim's shoulder, twined his arms around his father's neck. Frankie could hear Tim murmuring to the boy all the way out of the woods.

The rain began to lighten, and the clouds grew opaque; the black thunderheads gave way to a lumpy gray sky. Around her, Frankie could hear the birds begin to burble and chirp at each other. A roll call, sounding all clear, checking to see who was missing and who had found safe passage. Among the twitter and chirp, a crow called that distinct *"ha ha ha ha ha!"* Overhead a pair of crows winged by, diving and chasing each other blithely as if the whole forest hadn't just cheated death. Or perhaps because it had.

She walked back with Tim and Aiden to the Magnusens', hoping to be helpful. While Tim ran a bath for Aiden, she searched the kitchen for something to make for dinner. The cupboards were full of ingredients that defeated her. Of course, Anne would not be one to buy canned soup. She located a box of macaroni and cheese and rummaged around for a pot. Then she heard the distinct sound of a boat engine. She called out to Tim and ran outside and down the seawall. Jerry had made it! And Anne would be with him. Surely, she would be! When the boat was close enough to see clearly, her heart plummeted. It was not the red Hewescraft but the black hull of the Bureau of Indian Affairs boat bouncing across the water toward the dock.

She didn't recognize the driver, but the man who threw her the stern line was a wildland firefighter and medic she'd seen before. Both men looked grave. And as Frankie cleated the line and turned back to the boat, she saw the body stretched out on the bottom. One of them had lain a towel over his face. Big, kind Jerry, with one foot bare, the other still booted, and his hands crossed over his belly like he was napping. His fingers were blue.

She turned away, her mind spinning. She saw her dad in the open casket at church. Father Brash on the altar, and Dean Anderson with the coffin brochures. Anne's laughing face. Her ears rang and the world tipped. She put her hand on a piling to steady herself.

". . . found him with the boat just off of Arrow Point," the medic was saying.

Frankie turned to look at him and struggled to speak.

"This was the closest dock, so we came here to regroup and radio for the medical examiner. You know him?"

"Yes," she said. "It's Jerry Sewell."

Her voice broke and the world surged toward her and away. She struggled to find the words to ask about Anne.

"Did you check the boat?" she asked.

The radio crackled and the driver picked up the headset.

"Copy that, Miranda. We have confirmation that it's Jerry Sewell."

He was quiet, listening.

"Damn shame. Yeah, I know. Okay. We'll sit tight up at Beauty Bay. Over."

He paused again.

"That's an affirmative. We're at the dock now," he said into the mic and then to Frankie, "Are you Frankie O'Neill?"

"Yes. But Jerry . . . his passenger—" she said, stunned to slowness.

"Copy that, Miranda. Over," he said and pulled the headphones off.

"The sheriff will be here in an hour or two," he said. "A Mayday report got as far as Mill Three, but the connection was so bad they didn't know who it was."

Frankie fought to find her voice and the man stepped out of the boat.

"I'm Jim Miller. Councilman Miller. You called the tribal offices about that poacher, right?" he said.

Frankie heard a high-pitched whine in her ears as she tried to form a sentence.

". . . been squatting up there for some time," Miller was saying. "A nuisance, but mostly harmless. He was trying to get 'back to the land,' he told us. Meant to get you a message and . . ."

Frankie nodded, registering his words as she struggled to speak.

". . . one hell of a storm," the medic was saying to Miller. "He shouldn't have been out on the water."

"Did you check it—the boat?" Frankie said again.

The medic shook his head.

"No, we just pulled him in. We'll need a tug to flip it. Why?"

"He had a passenger," she said.

Someone was yelling. Dazed, she turned and saw Tim running down the dock. He had Aiden wrapped in a blanket and his face was full of emotion—fear, hope, longing, and love.

"Did they find her!?"

It didn't take long to explain. Miller radioed Miranda and told her they were heading back down to Arrow Point to look for Jerry's passenger. Tim thrust Aiden into Frankie's arms and ran back to the house for his raincoat. Miller and the medic had a quiet conversation and then lifted Jerry's body swiftly out of the boat and laid him gently on the dock. They drew a tarp over the body, tucking it in around his head, shoulders, and feet.

Aiden leaned his head on Frankie's shoulder watching them. She felt like she should say something to explain to the boy why Jerry was lying on the dock not moving. But she had no idea what to say.

Tim ran back down the dock and hugged his son.

"We're going to look for Mama," he said to Aiden. "I'll be back soon."

As the boat pulled away, Tim's eyes met Frankie's and she read the fear and despair there.

Oh, Anne, Frankie thought.

The boat kicked up a white rooster tail of water as they sped away. Aiden watched the boat until it disappeared around the headland.

"Don't worry. He'll be back soon. I promise," Frankie said.

She didn't make any promises about them finding his mother, and she waited for Aiden to say something. He only hiccupped a sob.

"Do you want me to carry you, or do you want to walk?" she asked.

He wriggled in her arms, and she set him down. They stood together looking at Jerry Sewell stretched out under the roof eaves of the store. Just yesterday he was alive and full of plans. They had stood right there talking and he'd hugged her goodbye. It didn't seem possible that he was just gone. She thought of Marilyn and felt heartsick.

"Mr. Jerry will be okay down here now, Aiden. Some people are going to come get him in a little while."

Aiden took her by the hand and led her up to the cottage.

She made hot chocolate, and they sat in front of the fire. Aiden flipped the bird book open, then shut it and pulled the bird memory game toward himself, examining the cards one by one. She regarded him, so curious about what was going on in his mind and what he chose to reveal. Hearing his voice had surprised her because of its perfect clarity. But it didn't really surprise her that he could speak. The first day she'd met him, when he'd snuck into her house, it had been clear that there was a full sense of Aiden-ness. She wondered if Anne knew he was talking again. Tim had just looked at her like she was out of her mind when she told him, in a low voice, that his son had spoken to her. And Aiden had fallen silent again. Was she out of her mind? Had she imagined the whole thing?

She added a log to the fire. Aiden set the cards aside and pulled the bird book into his lap. She slumped against the back of the couch and willed herself to stay awake. She closed her eyes and listened to Aiden turning pages. Then it fell quiet. She could feel him looking at her and she opened her eyes. He was holding the book open on his lap. He turned to Frankie and his little face was grave as an old man's.

"The American crow does not migrate," he said firmly. And she laughed and fought the urge to cry.

Time crept by as they waited. Dusk had fallen by the time she heard the boat and went to the lookout. In the near dark she made out the shape of the woman's body and the man's tall frame and her heart leapt. But it was not Anne and Tim. It was Patrick who raised a hand and Judith next to him heading toward the trail.

Her heart dropped and she walked around the side of the cottage to meet them. As she reached the back of the house, a wave of sound rippled through the woods around her. She looked up into the clearing over the trees and saw the twilit sky alive with crows. They swirled about overhead, hundreds of them. Their voices rose in a song of gathering, naming, and calling to each other. "*I see you, I am here, we are together.*" They circled and circled over the house and above the meadow and then with some unknowable signal, they banked east and disappeared high up into the woods.

Patrick and Judith appeared at the top of the trail and her mother paused and grasped the railing of the trolley, catching her breath. Judith's words rang in Frankie's head.

"All talk and no follow-through. Just like your father."

She braced for another altercation and stood her ground. Judith seemed to hesitate and then moved quickly up the path. To Frankie's utter surprise, Judith embraced her. She leaned in and pressed her head into Frankie's shoulder and Frankie noticed how small her mother was. Frankie looked at Patrick and was at a complete loss. When was the last time Judith had hugged her? She stood very still and breathed in the scent of her mother's perfume. Lilacs, she remembered, and felt like a child again. Then Judith stepped back, and Patrick took her arm. Patrick's gaze told her nothing. He had their father's jacket in one hand.

"You left it at the post office. Donna gave it to me when she saw us in the parking lot."

Judith wiped her eyes and composed herself.

"Always so conscientious, Donna," she said, almost conversationally.

Frankie looked from Patrick to Judith.

"What are you doing here? It's been a terrible day and I can't take any more surprises. Jerry Sewell—" she started and stopped.

Patrick looked somber.

"We know, Frank. The sheriff ran us up from the marina. He's down on the dock with the medical examiner now."

"Why were you at the marina? Is this about the survey? Because I just can't . . ." She trailed off.

Judith looked stricken and sat on the bench.

"We got a call from county dispatch that there was an accident on the lake," Patrick said. "The message was pretty garbled."

He hesitated and swallowed.

"They said a boat capsized, a man drowned, and a young woman was missing. When we heard it was Jerry, we figured the passenger was you."

"Oh," Frankie said. "I see."

Patrick's eyes filled and he hugged her hard. She looked at her mother, who met her gaze and looked away but reached out and grabbed her hand.

The door creaked and Aiden stood just inside and looked out into the woods.

"Mom and Patrick, this is Aiden Magnusen, Tim and Anne's son. Aiden, this is my mom and brother—Judith and Patrick."

The boy looked past them toward the trail.

"Aiden is waiting here with me until his folks get back. Tim is with the BIA boat. We think his mom was with Jerry."

"Oh dear," Judith said quietly.

Frankie turned back to the boy.

"Let's go check the lookout, Aiden."

They walked to the lookout, and Aiden peered down the length of the lake with Frankie's binoculars. Patrick and Judith watched him, and Patrick raised his eyebrows in a question. Frankie shrugged. After a while Frankie coaxed Aiden back inside the house after assuring him they'd check again soon.

Patrick started dinner, haranguing his little sister about the lack of what he called "real food." She knew he was trying to lighten the mood, but she could barely muster a smile. She thought about Anne, wished she would just walk in the door. The moment with her mother had passed and she didn't know what to say to her. Watching Judith move about the room made her feel awkward, like she suddenly didn't belong there. She sat on the couch with Aiden.

Judith turned on the record player and put on one of Ray's albums— Ella Fitzgerald and Louis Armstrong. Frankie hadn't touched them all month, preferring the silence. But now the music reminded her of her girlhood and those early years. The warmth and comfort of the cottage crowded with her family—grandparents, cousins, her aunt and uncle, Patrick and Jack. Her mother had been there too. And Judith, impossibly, was here now. The scent of her mother's perfume lingered on Frankie's clothes, and she could almost feel her mother's small weight against her body. A spark bloomed in her heart as she watched Judith begin to set the table for dinner.

Frankie remembered their early years. Judith laughing as she and Jack danced to this same record. Judith making the most beautiful birthday cakes for Genevieve's and Ray's birthdays, which were both in August, and decorating them with huckleberries she and Frankie had picked. Her mother had been there those years, and she'd been happy then before she'd withdrawn. It occurred to Frankie for the first time that her incorrigible father might have been hard to be married to. Her mother noticed her watching and her eyes were full of questions.

"Forks on the left and knives turned in, Judith. We aren't savages, now, my dear," Frankie said, imitating her mother, and Judith laughed.

Later, while Judith did the dishes, Frankie remembered the little calendar. She picked it up and held it for a moment, this relic, this touchstone of her father's life.

"Mom," she said and held it up.

"There's something from Dad. A letter."

Judith took the little book from her and opened it. She glanced down at the envelope and, without a word, went into the room that had belonged to her and Jack and closed the door.

"Hank gave it to me," Frankie said to Patrick. "Dad left it at the tavern."

Aiden refused to eat anything. He left the table and began pacing in front of the stove. Frankie could see he was growing increasingly anxious. She went to him and gathered the cards of the bird game, shuffled them, and handed them to him.

"How about a game of cards, Aiden?"

He took them from her in both hands and threw them on the floor. He stamped his feet and resumed pacing, pulling on his fingers and emitting a low growl.

"Patrick, could you turn down the stereo?" Frankie asked and Patrick lowered the volume.

Frankie picked up her headphones, which she had set near the stove to dry.

"Want to give these a try again, Aiden?"

He grabbed them from her and pressed them over his ears. She watched his body relax and he quieted.

"They seem to help him tune things out," she explained to Patrick, who watched the boy rocking from foot to foot by the stove.

After a few minutes she tried the cards again.

"I know you know how to play this one," she said. "Your mom said you're a crackerjack memory-game player."

This time Aiden took the cards from her, shuffled carefully, and dealt in perfect columns, straightening their edges with great concentration. The action seemed to calm him. She remembered Anne laughing about how Aiden usually won when they played.

"Watch out. This boy is a right card shark!" she'd exclaimed. *"He lets you believe you're neck and neck and then goes in for the kill, like. Don't you, my little fox?"*

Her laugh was a golden bell, just like her son's.

Frankie wanted nothing more just then than to hear that laugh, to see her friend's face, her new friend who'd come so unexpectedly into her life. Her lovely friend Anne Ryan. Frankie understood friendship now. There was nothing complicated about it at all. You listened, you talked. You remembered the other's important stories, private joys and wounds, and shared yours. You tended these small things.

She had so many questions for Anne, and so much to tell her about her curious little boy and the sound of his voice that afternoon. About how he seemed to have a lot on his mind.

She thought of Jerry's still form, his blue fingers. She knew how cold the September waters of June Lake were. She knew Anne was not a strong swimmer. She looked at Aiden's bowed head and fought the tightness in her throat.

Aiden leaned across the table and turned over two cards—California quail and American robin. Frankie struggled to control herself. Falling apart now would not help anyone, especially not this sweet kid who'd agreed to let her distract him with this game.

She turned over a varied thrush and a black-capped chickadee and then put them face down again. Aiden kept his eyes on the cards. She could hear him humming that tune. It was that song she'd heard Anne singing to him the first night they'd shown up and Anne had waited for Aiden to emerge from the boat. The one Grammy Genevieve had sung to Frankie as a girl.

"Oh, my one and only, you've gone across the sea. I stand in the wind and watch the sun set low. When will you come back to me?"

It had only been a few weeks, but it felt like she'd known Anne and Aiden for years.

Aiden flipped over a snow goose and a wood duck. What would his life be like without his mother? It wasn't fair. It just wasn't right. Aiden needed his mom; he deserved to grow up with her, though of course Frankie knew the world didn't work like that. The world was not about fairness.

She tried to keep her hand from shaking as she flipped over the Pacific wren and the American robin, then turned them face down again.

Aiden glanced at her, a look of triumph in his bright green eyes, and turned over the pair of robins. He held them up and flapped them next to his face, smiling right at her.

The wind gusted over the roof and through the dark woods like an aftershock from the storm. The lights flickered and the record player slowed for a warbled verse then resumed. Rain swept over the house and down across the lake. The faint rumble of a boat engine below, the staccato beat of footsteps on the trail. The back door banged open, and Jim Miller stood in the doorway, rain streaming from his jacket. His face was formidable, and Frankie couldn't read it.

"You should come down to the dock," he said.

33

PARTIAL MIGRATIONS

Many birds arrive at those winter quarters after slow and methodical and almost meandering itineraries, often-times stopping for irresistible seasonal caches of food.

—*G. Gordon's Field Guide to the Birds of the Pacific Northwest*

Anne was wearing a brand-new pair of plimsolls—navy blue with white polka dots and white laces—which she thought were very posh. They'd been a gift from her parents and Gran for Easter. She liked how the blue toes flashed as she hurried toward the quay to meet her da's boat. Clutching her stuffed red kitten in the crook of her elbow, she hummed as she tripped along toward the docks. It was a new song and now her favorite song, the one that Gran had taught her that very morning, a song about all the birds—blackbird, raven, crow, robin, lark, wren, and thrush.

Across the pasture, over the stile, and along the cliff line she went. As she descended the rocky path, the sound of the crashing sea increased. She paced along the worn wooden planks of the wharf, counting the cracks as she went, keeping time and singing the song.

Éiníní, éiníní, codalaígí, codalaígí.

Glancing up, she saw her father's berth was empty and caught sight of his boat, *The Kestrel*, just passing the jetty into the small harbor. Chuffed to get there before he landed, she picked up her pace, looked down at her pretty new shoes, and ran straight off the worn old wharf into the cold, silent sea.

The dark water held her tightly in its icy grip. It boiled up and filled her eyes. Her hair streamed around and when she looked upward for sunlight, there was nothing. She scanned the black water for the mermaids. She felt herself sinking down, down, down. A face then, a man's face above her and a large hand that reached down and pulled her up to the surface. Robert Cleary, she thought, disturbing her tea party with the pretty ladies. But as she broke free of the water, it was Jerry Sewell there leaning over the side of the red boat. He staggered as a set of waves pummeled the prow.

"Grab my hand!" he shouted. And something else, but the wind snatched his words away. Anne reached for him but couldn't see Jerry or the boat or anything but towering dark water all around her. She began to swim in what she hoped was the direction of the cove they'd been aiming for. She lifted her arm from the water, and it felt impossibly heavy. The bulky float coat impeded her movement, and she heard the swimming instructor from uni.

"You've no more than fifteen minutes to exit the water."

Her clothes dragged and her breath choked. She tried to kick off her shoes, but her legs were leaden. She thought she heard a voice and looked back for Jerry but saw only waves and dark sky. She felt less cold then and so tired. The faces of her parents swam before her, Tim and Aiden, Katherine and Frankie. Gran singing the bird lullaby.

Aiden, she thought.

Then she didn't think anything.

When she opened her eyes, she couldn't say how much time had passed. The water was gone, the darkness was gone. Her bare hands were dry, as were the cuffs of her jumper. There was the tangerine duvet cover, weak sunlight streaming through the curtains. She heard the murmur of voices—Tim talking to someone. Another man, a woman. And then she heard high, tinkling laughter and the unmistakable voice of her son.

Anne bolted out of bed and down the hall. In the kitchen Tim was pouring coffee for a tall man and a petite woman. Frankie sat by the fire with Aiden. And Aiden, her one and only, was perched next to Frankie on a stool with his storybook. In a bright, clear voice, he was reading aloud. When he noticed her, Aiden jumped down and marched toward her, his book tucked under his arm like a tiny librarian.

"Good morning, Mama," he said, taking her hand. "Come sit and listen. I'm reading a lovely story. It's 'The Crow and the Pitcher.'"

Anne laughed in astonishment, fell to her knees, and pulled him close. Aiden leaned into her and pressed his wee face against her neck and let her hold him. Tim crossed the room and enfolded them both in his arms and Anne had no words for all she felt.

Later, after the O'Neills had gone, Tim told her how he and Frankie found Aiden tucked inside the great tree high up on the hill. Frankie had said he'd spoken to her, but Tim had been so crazed with worry he hadn't listened. He told her about going in the BIA boat and spotting her yellow float coat on an old log boom at Arrow Point. How they'd pulled her in and how they thought at first— He'd stopped then. It would be days before he could describe that moment to her, an eternal moment he thought she was gone.

She leaned against him and apologized for leaving without explanation and for causing so much worry.

"It's not your fault, Anne. I said some really stupid things. I was angry. I didn't mean it . . ." He trailed off and looked away.

But there was something there, some gap between them. Because he did mean some of it.

"And Aiden?" she asked and laughed, astonished. She looked at their boy, who was sifting through the CD collection.

Tears brightened Tim's eyes, and he looked bewildered.

"We brought you into the house to get you warm, and he marches over and orders me to make you a nice cup of tea. Tuck you in by the fire and you'll be sorted in two shakes. Those were his exact words."

Tim drew a hand across his eyes.

"He sat with you reading stories from his little book until I made him go to bed."

Aiden was sitting cross-legged in front of the CD player rocking back and forth listening to "Mary Had a Little Lamb." As the song ended, he reached up and started it over and Anne didn't even think to stop him.

The day passed, night fell, and the morning bore them away down the lake in a light snowfall. Anne looked back at the house through the receding wake of the boat, dark and quiet, and the woods whitening around it. Midway down the lake at Arrow Point, Tim did not slow the boat, but Anne looked toward shore and her eyes found the old log boom and the spot where she'd last seen kind Jerry Sewell. After he'd strapped her into that float coat and got her as close to the log boom as he could. Before the boat capsized and they'd both ended up in the water. Jerry hadn't been wearing his float coat when they found his body, Tim said. And Anne had to add that to a list of unanswerable questions: Would Jerry have survived if he'd had time to put his float coat on? Would he have even attempted the return trip if he hadn't taken her to Mill Three in the first place? What if she'd waited and asked Frankie for a ride, as she'd initially planned? She'd never know.

In the weeks that followed, Jerry's death weighed on them both. They went to see his wife and tried to find adequate words for apology, for condolence, for gratitude all at once as they sat in the living room of the small house just outside Mill Three.

Anne wept and it was Jerry's wife, Marilyn, consoling her. Tall, broad-shouldered Marilyn was dry-eyed, keeping her sorrow to herself.

"I've been expecting this for years, my dear," Marilyn said. "Jerry made his own choices."

Her steely gray eyes made Anne think of her mother.

Anne was grateful, so grateful, and not simply to be alive. If not for Jerry she'd have missed the astounding reemergence of her son.

They took him to see Dr. Shelley at UW, and Aiden had a nice long gossip with her about all he had learned about crows during his trip up to the lake. The doctor was fascinated and asked Anne and Tim for permission to document his progress. Anne wasn't sure about that and said she'd give it a think. Dr. Anaya, for her part, seemed a tiny bit smug at Aiden's checkup.

"Looks like you just needed a little time, hey, Aiden?" she'd said.

Her boy pursed his lips like a little professor.

"I was thinking about things," he said, and didn't elaborate.

The question of residential school never resurfaced. And when Anne, Tim, and Aiden went to her in-laws' house, they fawned over their grandson, asking him questions and demanding to be kissed. They hugged him without asking if it was okay with him. Aiden preferred to initiate contact, Tim said, but they didn't listen. Tim Senior had talked too loudly, and Christi pulled off his headphones, though Anne had explained Aiden wore them when he needed a little extra quiet. It was all lost on her in-laws, who simply wanted to celebrate that their grandson was acting "normal" again. They didn't understand. Aiden whispered for permission to leave the table to read his book, and she gave it, wishing she could go with him.

As for Tim, Anne wanted to talk about what had happened, but the breach was so large it swallowed her words. She knew he was sorry about the things he'd said, or at least the way he'd said them. She could forgive all that. But what she couldn't forgive was the way he'd let his parents steer things. Decisions the two of them should have been making privately. Tim didn't seem to realize that was the worst blow of all.

Anne booked tickets home to Ireland for her and Aiden. They'd arrive on the bank holiday and stay for three weeks. Tim voiced no further objections, but she didn't know how he felt about it. They were all busy the month of October—Anne preparing for the trip home, Aiden back at Sunflower, and Tim busy with the newspaper's merger. So busy that Anne could avoid the questions that hung over her, her marriage, her husband, their failures, their wounds.

Were they meant to be a family together, the three of them? This was one question that she couldn't answer. She ached to talk to Tim about it and didn't know how. At night she lay awake and knew Tim was awake next to her instead of sleeping with his characteristic ease. Neither one of them seemed to know how to break the silence.

The Saturday before Anne and Aiden were to fly to Dublin, Aiden was invited on a playdate with a friend from Sunflower. A friend! It was lovely to see him head down the sidewalk with Mannie and his mam, the two boys chattering nonstop. But the apartment was uncomfortably quiet. Anne couldn't recall the last time she and Tim had been alone together. He seemed as awkward as she felt. She busied herself folding laundry, and Tim wandered from room to room. He leaned in the doorway and watched her, and she remembered that long-ago day they'd had their spat about the laundry and created the joke about lovely Suzy. She wished he would say something to resurrect the joke, the warmth between them that had been there. But he just looked as sad as she felt. The moment passed.

"I guess I'll go to the gym," he said.

He packed his gym bag and kissed her on the cheek. As he opened the apartment door to leave, Anne heard Christi's voice and sighed. Another drop-in visit, though they'd asked Christi repeatedly to please call first.

In the living room, Christi, in a white leather trench coat, was attempting to hang an enormous garment bag on the flimsy coat rack and complaining to Tim about traffic on the bridge.

"Goodness! I forget how far in the hinterlands Fremont is. It will be so much more convenient when you move out closer to us. I forgot to tell you! I think Ron has found the perfect place for you."

Convenient for you, Anne thought. Ron the Realtor was doing his level best to find them a house within spitting distance of her in-laws, and she was the only one who seemed to have any reservations about this idea.

"Oh hello, Anne dear," Christi said. "I've brought your costumes over to try on. You're going to look just stunning, I know it. And we can do some alterations if need be."

Christi shed her trench coat and unzipped the garment bag. She revealed a voluminous saffron-colored gown with puffy sleeves and a high lace collar.

"What do you think? It's Elizabeth I. And this," she said, pulling out green velvet breeches and a waistcoat, "is Henry the Eighth!"

Christi threw herself down in the armchair and looked from Anne to Tim, triumphant.

"I couldn't find the ones you asked for, Anne. But these—just gorgeous, don't you think?"

Anne surveyed the costumes, speechless. Christi had managed to land on possibly the most insulting monarch in the history of the British Empire, the sixteenth-century queen who'd stolen the ancient homelands of the Irish clans for British settlers. And Henry, who'd established the Kingdom of Ireland in a brutal power move.

Christi looked past Anne down the hall.

"Now, where is my grandson? Aiden, come give Nanny a kiss!" she called. "I brought you some candy!"

Anne felt a flash of anger at this performance of the doting grandmother.

"Aiden is at a playdate, Mother," Tim said.

"Oh well. That's a shame. I have a hair appointment downtown in thirty minutes. I'll just leave these chocolates for him."

Anne didn't say anything, though she had explained multiple times that they did not allow Aiden to have sweets except on special occasions.

"Now, go try these on, you two. I want to see how they look. Anne, then we can talk about how to do your hair. It's the very color of Queen Elizabeth's, I think! And, Tim, we'll have to get you some kind of beard."

Anne wasn't angry that Christi somehow thought she'd be going to the ridiculous gala. She'd told her about the trip to Ireland. She couldn't think of anything to say and wasn't troubled about it because Christi didn't listen to her anyway.

"You'll have to excuse me. I'm on my way to pick Aiden up from his friend's house."

"Well, Anne, I came all this way. You've got to at least try it on!"

It was Tim who replied and in a voice Anne had never heard him use with Christi before.

"No, she doesn't, Mother," he said. "She doesn't have to do anything."

"Well, it's a bit inconsiderate—" Christi said.

"You're the one being inconsiderate, Mother," Tim interrupted. "We didn't know you'd be dropping by, and we're both quite busy this weekend. We've asked you to call first."

Christi raised an eyebrow and crossed her arms.

"I don't care for your tone, Timothy," she said.

"And I don't care for your presumption," he said, his voice rising. "Nobody asked you to bring these costumes and Anne already told you that she won't be here. She's going to be visiting her parents that weekend with Aiden."

He glanced at Anne.

"And she's got a very important All Souls' Day Mass—"

"Oh, you can just change the ticket," Christi interrupted, waving a hand and leaning back in the chair. "I'll pay for it. It's no problem. Whatever it takes to have the king and queen at my gala."

The silence boomed.

Christi tipped her head and looked up at her son. How alike they looked when angry, Anne thought.

"We are planning to announce your new position that evening, Timothy. How will it look if your wife is not there representing the family? A king all alone?"

Tim crossed his arms and looked at Anne. She knew the easy way lay in saying yes of course I can be there. In saying thank you so much for paying to change our tickets. She also knew she could no longer take the easy way and that there was, in fact, no easy way out of this thicket that was the Magnusen family.

"I'm afraid I'm not available, Christi," she said, keeping her voice light. "I hope it's a lovely evening. Now, you'll have to excuse me."

She walked along Lake Union past Gas Works Park, listening to the gulls complain. The maple trees were in full color of scarlet, ochre, and gold. The wind picked up and a confetti of leaves whirled through the air around her. She thought of being in Ireland with her family and what it might feel like to stay there. The idea fell around her like a warm cloak. What would it be like for Aiden to grow up as she had—with her mam and da, and Gran just over the wall? But of course she wouldn't be able to find work on the island. So it would be Cork or Dublin, then. Still, that much closer to home, how would it feel? What might it be like if Aiden spent summers with Tim in Seattle and the school year with her in Ireland? People got divorced all the time, she told herself. She'd been telling herself that. Patrice would understand and would give her a good reference. They'd had lunch that week to talk about her coming back in January and what classes she'd teach winter term. She told Patrice that things with Tim were not great, she might stay in the apartment, and he was buying a house near his parents.

"We might be separating," she said.

She'd tried to sound matter of fact, but Patrice had leaned over and hugged her.

"I'm so sorry, Anne. This is not a choice anyone wants to make," she said.

And it wasn't. It tore at her. But she knew things would only get worse when Tim started his new job. Less time for her and Aiden, more pressure on her to quit her job. And living in the same neighborhood as Tim Senior and Christi. Be a helpmate. A cheerleader, Christi kept saying. It made her want to scream.

"Cheerleader?" she could almost hear Kat say. *"Valkyrie is more like it with that hair helmet."*

On the way home from Mannie's, Aiden asked if they could stop at the park. He sat on the swing and pulled his storybook out of his little rucksack. He twirled the feather that he kept there as a bookmark. Anne heard the croak of a crow. A solitary bird floated across the park above them murmuring to itself. Aiden tracked its flight with an imaginary telescope.

"Mama," he said. "Do you think Charlie Crow is cold up there in the woods in all the snow?"

"I don't think so, love," Anne said. "I think he's snug up under the branches of a big tree with his mates having a grand time."

Aiden was quiet, kicking his heels against the ground.

"Do you think I'll see him next summer?"

"I don't know, sweetie. He'll be a grown-up bird then. Do you reckon you'll be able to single him out of all the others?"

He thought about that for a time and then shook his head.

"I don't think so. They do look alike. But Frankie could help me."

Anne agreed that yes, Frankie could help him.

"She's very clever," Aiden said. "She knows so many things about birds, and fishing, and the woods, and bears, and snakes."

Anne felt a stab of envy—the simplicity of Frankie's life. What might Frankie do in her shoes? Was Frankie back at the university starting some new project? The day they'd parted at the lake, there was so much Anne had wanted to say. Frankie had found Aiden in the storm and kept him safe while Tim was looking for her. Frankie had become a friend and a rare ally to her, to Aiden. But in the brief time they'd seen each other at the house, Anne was still in a bit of shock, and she'd only been able to say thank you. Frankie had looked shy and shrugged. The O'Neills left to give the Magnusen family space and Anne hadn't had the chance to say a proper goodbye. She had Frankie's mother's phone number and yearned to call her tall, quiet friend.

She recalled what Frankie had said about her work one day at the cottage.

"It's like I don't have a choice. It's like it chose me—the questions, the research. It's just something I have to do."

A child shouted and a group of youngsters ran for the playground, two mothers trailing behind them chatting. They said hello, and Aiden watched the littlest ones clamber onto the swings near him. After a while, he went to his mother and tugged her toward home.

They walked along, not speaking, and she felt the thread that joined their hearts, an electric thing that connected her to this boy, her child.

The day Aiden was born, Anne looked into his little face and was struck by the most uncanny idea; Aiden had come from someplace else specifically to find her. He'd come to her because she belonged to him and he to her. Aiden had chosen her, she knew that. And what else? Music. Music had chosen her. She was a composer and a performer and a teacher. She simply was those things. The idea of giving any of it up was nonsensical. But was she meant to be Tim's partner? Their connection had been so accidental, if well intended. No surprise that their paths could diverge. It didn't have to be a heartbreak. They could remain close and be good parents but not together. She thought of how she would bring it up with him. She should say something before she left because she'd need to make arrangements while she was in Ireland. Prepare for the future and what it would hold for her—a mother, a musician, but no longer a wife. They could be friends. Eventually. Couldn't they? She tried to make herself believe that even as her heart broke with the thought.

At the end of their street, they stopped at the little market and Anne bought a pair of pie pumpkins.

"We can carve one to leave with Daddy so he's not lonely on Halloween," Anne said. "And I'll make us a nice soup with the other."

Tim's gym bag was in the hallway, but the apartment was empty. Aiden took off his little shoes and tucked them just inside the door and waited for Anne to kick off her clogs. Then he lined them up next to his shoes and ran off to his room.

In the kitchen, Anne halved one of the pumpkins and scooped out the seeds and membrane. She cut it into large pieces, set it on a baking tray, and slid it into the oven. She pulled out her suitcase and began packing. Warm clothes for the island. Something nice for Dublin when her parents came to meet her and Aiden. Something special for the All Souls' Day Mass. She found her silver and green dress and realized the last time she'd worn it was the night of the spring concert. It would be chillier in Ireland. What could she wear with it? She pulled out the gauzy shawl Tim had given her the previous Christmas—loosely knitted green cashmere that matched her eyes. It was fine but not fussy and she loved it. She held it to her face and her heart ached at the thought of telling him she was leaving and would not be coming back.

The apartment door opened and closed. Tim called hello to Aiden. He came down the hall and stood in the doorway. Something in his look made her blush. She turned away to hide her face.

"You didn't go to the gym, then?" she asked. "I saw your bag in the hall."

Tim sat on the bed and began refolding the clothes she'd already put in the suitcase. She looked up at him and his face was unreadable. He looked at her straight on like he had something on his mind.

"I hope you remembered to pack a sufficient number of bloomers," he said, deadpan.

Her laughter burst out and she thought she might cry.

"What's it to you?" she asked. "Are you some kind of travel expert now?"

"Magnusen Media has decided to expand into the travel business," he said, nodding. "We have opinions about these things. Many important opinions."

Then his face grew somber.

"I skipped the gym to go talk with Dad about the gala."

Her heart dropped and she felt a flash of anger and she turned away. Surely he wasn't going to try to get her to change her mind about that bloody gala.

"I explained it wasn't going to work out because you're going to see your folks and you have a really special event at home. And I told him I wouldn't be able to go either because we all need to be together. As a family."

Dumbstruck, she turned back to him.

"If you want me to go, that is," he said, looking shy. "Maybe I should have asked you first."

She put down the shawl and went to him and took his hands. She looked into his face and remembered the first time she'd seen his tall frame from across the room, the first time she'd heard his laugh. She saw his lovely dear face, older, changed, forever changing. Family, like composition, was a layering of parts and always shifting, never static. But what was the fascia that held it together? She knew the answer now; it was a song of love, forgiveness, and love again. She leaned in and kissed him. Anne Ryan, Tim Magnusen, and Aiden Matthew Ryan Magnusen. Together.

34

BROODING

When fed conscientiously and with care, how rapidly the young grow!

—*G. Gordon's Field Guide to the Birds of the Pacific Northwest*

Once.

There was.

A boy.

Once there was a boy.

Once upon a time there was a boy.

35

STOPOVER SITES

Birds appear to find their way by means of an inborn compass. A complete understanding of their migratory abilities and compunctions will likely always remain a partial mystery to us.

—*G. Gordon's Field Guide to the Birds of the Pacific Northwest*

Frankie leaned the ladder against the roofline and climbed up to the gutter. Using a gloved hand, she scooped out acorns and dried leaves, which rained down into the gravel drive with a satisfying patter. The gutters were so chocked with debris that she soon accumulated a substantial pile. She'd rake it all into the old garden patch and let the squirrels ransack the acorns before burning the leaves.

Earlier, she'd found Judith's note on the kitchen counter, characteristically terse: "Showings at 10 and 2. Back by 4. Mom."

Frankie knew she'd be done long before 4 p.m. and could have the yard cleaned up by then as well. Though the gutters hadn't been cleaned in ages, it was easy work and she didn't mind it. In the weeks since she'd come down from the lake, she'd had far too much time on her hands, which made her restless.

They'd closed up the cottage the day after the accident. The storm had crushed her confidence about staying up at the lake over the winter alone. And Jerry's death had just knocked her sideways. Ageless, kind, and capable Jerry. She thought about how he must have felt when he realized he shouldn't be out on the water—and with a passenger who depended on him. Frankie knew he must have done all he could to get Anne to safety. When the BIA boat brought her back to the dock, she looked so small. Her skin was bluish, and Tim picked her up like she weighed nothing and carried her down the seawall to the big house. What a day it had been. But Anne was alright, and Aiden was safe.

Frankie reached the end of the west gutter and climbed down to move the ladder to the south side of the house. She worked her way along the roof, sweeping out leaves and acorns. When she reached the end, she pulled herself up on the roof and leaned back against the wall of the house in a weak October sunbeam. The huge oak spread its branches over the yard, and a breeze from the west sent a handful of leaves fluttering over the garage. A Steller's jay swooped down and stood in a puddle, looking around with authority. The garage could use a fresh coat of paint, Frankie thought. That would have to wait until spring—power washing, scraping, caulking, priming, and painting. Four days' work, she estimated. The idea of the chore cheered her, and yet she remained surprised to find herself at her mother's house, a guest, and an invited guest no less.

The morning after the storm, as she and Patrick discussed closing tasks over coffee, Judith joined them at the kitchen table.

"I'll put things away in here and I can pack up your books, Frankie," she said.

Frankie stared. Which was odder? Her mother calling her Frankie or offering to help with closing chores? She couldn't recall the last time either had happened.

". . . wait to drain the water last so I can do these dishes," Judith was saying. "And we should be able to get home by dark if we stay focused."

Home? Frankie thought, looking at her mother.

"Of course, it makes the most sense for you to come stay with me until you get things sorted out," Judith said matter-of-factly.

Frankie didn't know what to say. Since she'd left for college, Judith had never encouraged her to come home for any length of time. On holidays she'd felt like a tolerated guest. And she hadn't been back to the house since last Thanksgiving other than for the funeral.

Judith regarded the bottom of her coffee cup.

"That is, if you'd like to come," she said. "I'd like you to come."

She rose and began washing dishes. Patrick pantomimed a silent scream and Frankie had to stifle her laughter. But she went. Where else could she go?

The first few days were awkward. After that initial burst of emotion when Judith had hugged her, she'd retreated again. She wasn't unfriendly, just reserved. It made Frankie afraid she'd say the wrong thing, so she tried to stay out of the way. She banged around in the tiny attic room of her childhood, having forgotten how to navigate the space. One day she returned from Franz Hardware with supplies to fix the dripping kitchen faucet and noticed her mother making up the bed in the guest room.

"I was thinking you might be more comfortable down here," Judith said.

She folded the quilt over the foot of the bed and gestured to the closet.

"I left a few of Dad's things in there for you. Some of his sweaters and long-sleeve shirts. You're about the same size, and you share his . . ." Judith trailed off and looked away.

"Sartorial slobbishness?" Frankie said, looking down at her Carhartts, work boots, and the old plaid jacket.

What a beautiful laugh Judith had, Frankie thought then. How lovely to be the cause of it.

Frankie climbed down the ladder and carried it to the garage. The wind stirred the branches on the big oak tree. Leaves blew down Hatch Street and whirled around the jack-o'-lanterns on people's porches and stirred the homemade ghosts and witches that hung from tree branches along the sidewalk.

In the house, Frankie tidied the kitchen, which was something she did now. Judith cooked, Frankie washed the dishes, and they took turns going to Little Bit Grocery and Ranch Supply. As the days passed, they'd fallen into a routine and Frankie sensed the gradual change in her mother like a shift in the weather. Or maybe it was a change in her own perception. Judith's prickliness, which Frankie remembered since high school, had softened. She understood that Judith was a private person, but very much a feeling person. She understood that her mother loved her, though she might not say so aloud. There was much about her that Frankie didn't and couldn't know.

One afternoon, Frankie returned from the library and found Judith sitting on the front porch in one of the peeling Adirondack chairs. It was strange to see her mother at rest. Judith was usually going somewhere—the realty office, a showing, a meeting at the port, city council. But now she sat, hands resting in her lap like she was waiting for the bus. It was unnerving.

Frankie sat down next to her and followed her gaze across the yard.

"We really should sell that old beast," Judith said, looking at the truck Frankie had parked next to the garage. "If you'll be driving back and forth to the lake next summer, we should buy a new one."

Since they'd come back to town, Judith hadn't mentioned the land survey or putting the cottage on the market.

"Your dad would have wanted you to be driving something safer," Judith continued. "Especially after that damn thing ran him over."

They hadn't spoken of Jack's death either, and Frankie didn't know what to say.

"The parking brake had been broken for ages, and he said it wasn't a problem. Well, I call it a problem."

Her voice was weighted with sorrow, not anger, and Frankie understood Judith was blaming the truck and not Jack for the accident that caused his death. Frankie stayed quiet and watched her mother's face. Judith leaned back and looked up at the big oak tree.

"Your dad and I were so young when we met, Mary Frances. I was still in high school."

Frankie knew her mother had grown up in the small town of Maupin and had met Jack at a homecoming game. Judith looked at Frankie and her dark eyes twinkled.

"Did you know for our first date he took me to the senior center to play bingo?" she said. "All the other kids were going to the drive-in, but Jack O'Neill takes me to meet all his octogenarian friends. Said it was important to know the elders in your community."

Frankie smiled hearing that. Yes, she could imagine her father saying that, even as a teenage boy.

"Your dad was so funny and kind. I'd never met anyone like him. He was so different from the people I grew up with. You know my mother died when I was little," she said.

Frankie listened, rapt. Judith never talked about her family. Judith looked away and out over the yard.

"Mom left me a little money when she died. I'd planned to go to business school after I graduated. I went to the bank with my passbook—so excited and proud. I needed to pay for the first semester. But the money was gone. My father had emptied the account over the years little by little. He was cosigner and there was nothing I could do about it."

Frankie could imagine her young mother standing at the bank counter realizing that betrayal, that humiliation. Judith's face darkened.

"You kids never met my father, and I never wanted you to. He was a drinker and he got mean when he drank. My stepmother, well, she didn't ever try to stop him from—from . . ."

She trailed off and went quiet for a while.

"Anyway. I went back to visit once after your dad and I got married. That was enough."

She paused and regarded her left hand, twisting her wedding ring.

"I thought things would be different for us. Of course, he was already working at the tavern when we met, but he never drank much. Not then."

She sighed.

"He changed after Ray died. I don't know why. Things got pretty bad when you were in high school, and he wouldn't talk to me about what was going on."

Frankie nodded.

"I remember. The summer you got your real estate license."

She recalled coming down from the lake one afternoon to pick up supplies for a window repair at one of the lake houses. She hadn't told her parents she'd be staying the night and came home to find them in the middle of a full-blown argument—the first she'd ever seen. Jack was yelling loud enough for Frankie to hear him from the street as she pulled up. He quieted down when Frankie came in the house, but it scared and embarrassed her.

"He took it personally that I wanted a career. But I'd always wanted to do something like that. Once you kids were in high school, it felt like the right time," Judith said. "He thought I was saying he couldn't provide for us. You thought I was being awful. Oh, how you defended him! It seemed you were always taking his side."

Judith laughed but there were tears in her voice.

"When I joined Blackstone Realty, you accused me of carpetbagging, if I remember correctly. 'A Portland company, Mother!' you said. 'How could you?'"

Frankie remembered that fight—one of the few times she'd ever yelled at her mother. Judith grew somber again.

"When you got older and started drinking with your dad, well, I tried to talk to you about it. You needed to make your own choices, I guess. I backed away then. I just didn't know how to . . . I should have tried harder, Mary Frances. I'm sorry."

Frankie remembered the morning after her twenty-first birthday—aching head and sour mouth—when Judith had tried to talk to her about the dangers of alcohol. And countless times after that when she'd had just one more with her father when she knew she shouldn't. But Frankie thought it was just a little fun, and it was okay because Jack was doing it too. Even when something about it felt wrong. She burned with shame now and shook her head.

"Don't be sorry, Mom. I made my own mess."

"No, honey! Look at all you've accomplished!" Judith said and squeezed her knee. "Straight As all through school, good at math and science. I was envious! I was never smart like that. And then college and graduate school."

Judith envious of her? Petite, beautiful, confident Judith? Frankie didn't know what to say.

"Your dad was so proud of you, always. So proud."

Her voice caught.

"And he was trying to change. I didn't see it. I was so busy being mad and wanting to be right. I just didn't see it, even those last few months. I noticed he wasn't drinking around the house, but I didn't comment. I assumed he was drinking at the tavern and trying to hide it from me."

Her eyes brimmed with tears.

"That letter you gave me, Mary Frances, in the calendar. He'd written it at the end of March to tell me he was three months sober."

The letter said he'd quit drinking after Thanksgiving, that he was sorry for letting her down, and he was going to try his best to be the husband she deserved and that he loved her so much. He asked her to please forgive him and try to see the best in him. And he died before he gave it to her, died thinking she thought the worst of him.

"I have to live with that, Mary Frances."

Frankie heard the anguish in her voice, and her heart broke open for her mother. She leaned toward Judith and put her arm around her mother's slender shoulders. Judith leaned lightly against her. Frankie didn't say anything because she didn't know what to say. They sat like that for a while, and then Judith went inside to start dinner. Frankie sat alone on the porch feeling a recalibration, the strange shift of

becoming an adult child. Judith could not mitigate the wounds life
dealt her daughter. Frankie had to heal on her own, just as Judith did.
Yet they could bear witness for each other in their healing.

Part of that healing was having Hank back in their lives. Judith's
anger about the tavern seemed to evaporate after reading Jack's letter. She dropped the lawsuit and when she went to Hank to apologize, he said there was no need. It had all been a misunderstanding,
he said. He offered her half ownership in the building too, and she
accepted, but insisted on getting an appraisal and paying for half. He
protested, saying he was going to leave it to her children anyway, but
she was unmoved. Capital improvements, she said. So now the River
City Saloon was owned jointly by Judith and Hank, who were planning a fine update of the interior.

Then Patrick surprised them all when he confessed that he
wanted to work at the saloon. He'd didn't want to be a lawyer, he told
them, and wasn't applying to law school. He'd been devastated to see
the tavern close and now he wanted to be part of it.

"Sorry, Mom," he said. "I guess only one of your children is going
to be a young upwardly mobile person."

That made everyone laugh. Frankie the yuppie!

Patrick was content at the saloon, as comfortable as his grandfather had been and his father after that. What a revelation that big,
quiet Patrick was a born barkeep. He was a great listener, and people
loved him. He insisted customers behave themselves and had no
qualms about cutting someone off or escorting them out if they became unpleasant. That was usually a tourist, and The Irregulars
would applaud.

When she dropped by, Frankie could feel her dad's presence. She
could almost see him there behind the bar, towel over his shoulder,
hands spread as he told a joke. She remembered that night before
Thanksgiving. She forgave him that, but she didn't want to forget it.
It served to remind her of the choice she was making—to leave alcohol out of her life. Especially after talking with Judith about her

unknown grandfather, it seemed like the right choice. Whatever relief alcohol had briefly given her wasn't worth the risk, she decided.

Now Frankie dried her hands on a tea towel and sat down at the kitchen table to review the contract from her old boss at the Forest Service. Samuel Ortiz had been thrilled when she called to say she was looking for work.

"I thought we'd lost you to the ivory tower," he'd said.

Frankie didn't try to explain. She just said she was looking to get back to work in the woods.

"Well, that's great news. We're so busy these days, Frankie," he'd said. "Not just timber either. There's more trail building for recreation. Portland hikers have discovered the Columbia River Gorge. And we have a new agreement with the Yakama Nation to work out."

Sam invited her to an intergovernmental meeting, which had been held the day before.

"Just to give you a sense of who you'd be working with," he said.

When she walked in the door of the conference room at the Forest Service building, Councilman Miller was standing with Sam at the front of the room. Her body went hot and then cold as images flashed through her mind. Tim lifting Anne out of the BIA boat in the rain. Aiden running down the dock toward them. The sight of Jerry Sewell's blue hands. It took a moment to catch her breath.

Councilman Miller crossed the room and said hello. His face was somber, and he asked after Anne. Frankie said she was back in Seattle.

"She was lucky. Maybe someone watching over her," Miller said. Frankie nodded.

"Too bad about Jerry Sewell, though. He will be missed. You probably knew him a long time?"

Frankie nodded, unable to find any words to describe the loss of kind Jerry Sewell.

Miller stood back and regarded Frankie, his face stern.

"You know that guy you called about, the poacher?"

"What about him? Has he been back?"

Miller gave a low chuckle. He didn't seem as formidable then.

"No, I do not think he will be back. We made it quite clear that there would be consequences if he did return. He was harmless, but like you said, he was sort of target practicing indiscriminately. The incident revived an old conversation on the tribal council. We want to survey our resident bird populations and keystone migrators. That's what I came to talk with Sam about."

That bird survey was part of the contract Sam had offered her. She'd spend the coming spring and summer completing the survey as the first step in a years-long census of the bird population of the twenty-two hundred square miles of the Yakama Nation. Fall and winter she'd mostly be in the office, but spring and summer she'd be leading field teams. It was appealing, the idea of spending weeks high up in the woods. She'd be putting her education to use too, she told herself. And the pay was decent. She could afford to rent her own place or maybe split a house with Patrick. The contract started November second, which was Monday, just three days away.

She paged through the contract again. There was no reason not to sign it. Her thesis process was dead, and the OSU job was no longer viable, though she had yet to write and decline the offer. Maybe after she submitted the paper on Charlie Crow she would feel the closure she needed. She would submit it and leave her academic life behind.

She'd polished the draft since she'd returned from the lake, and felt excited about it. What if the UW crows had a specific caveman threat call? What if crows also had the ability to create a distinct ally call—as she thought Charlie Crow had done? She was confident Dr. Marzluff would support the submission of the paper, but it was Dr. Wood-Smith she decided to call first. She'd done such a careful review of Frankie's thesis and made suggestions about how Frankie could continue her research. "Please consider me available to assist in any way," she'd written.

Frankie pulled the phone toward her and dialed the campus directory. When Dr. Wood-Smith answered, Frankie steeled herself for
the feelings of shame and failure. After all, her committee had decided not to let her defend her thesis. She'd have to convince Dr.
Wood-Smith that there was merit in helping her, a failed graduate
student. She braced herself for that line of questioning.

"Ms. O'Neill! I'm so glad to hear from you. I was wondering what
happened to you. You seem to have vanished from campus. Have you
been out in the field all this time? Davis kept you out late this season."

Out in the field? Frankie thought.

". . . I imagine that's why we haven't heard from you," Wood-
Smith was saying. "I assumed you'd planned to defend your thesis in
December. But when I asked Dr. Andreas the other day, he said he
hadn't heard. Have you decided to postpone until spring, then?"

Frankie's mind was whirling. She didn't know. Andreas didn't
know. Why didn't they know?

"Nnn-oo," stammered Frankie. "I, I—I had planned to defend in
December. But the department denied my application. I got a letter.
They said I'd failed to meet my deadlines with required paperwork
from my committee."

"But what did Dr. Grant say?" Dr. Wood-Smith asked, sounding
puzzled. "Did you turn in your manuscript by the deadline? I'm sure
he didn't mention anything about it," she said.

Frankie let that sink in. Her humiliation was not widely known,
then. For some reason, Dr. Grant had kept it to himself. Then she
told Dr. Wood-Smith the entire awful story: the spring symposium,
getting fired from the lab, Dr. Grant avoiding her last spring, her
emails unanswered. How she'd sent copies of her final draft, all revisions complete, by the deadline. How she'd addressed copies for Dr.
Wood-Smith and Dr. Andreas, as well as Dr. Grant.

There was a long silence on the other end of the phone, and when
she spoke, Dr. Wood-Smith's voice was ice.

"You're telling me you met your obligations and deadlines and you've heard nothing from Dr. Grant in response."

It was not a question, but Frankie answered in the affirmative.

"Hang on one second, Ms. O'Neill."

Frankie heard the squeak of her chair and the sound of a door closing, the scrape of the handset as Dr. Wood-Smith picked it up. With an edge in her voice, she explained that since Dr. Grant was her advisor all paperwork went through him. Department policy required that he approve Frankie's revisions before passing them along to his junior colleagues. In this way, as a senior faculty member, he wielded great control over the process.

"However," Dr. Wood-Smith said, her voice growing steelier with each word. "It is strictly against our bylaws for him to fail to notify other committee members of the status of a graduate student's application for defense. So if what you are saying is true, and I don't doubt that it is, Ms. O'Neill, Dr. Grant is in violation of established rules of the department and the university."

As her words sunk in, Frankie felt a spark of hope.

"Does that mean there's a way for me to reapply or something? I mean, I wasn't going to bother because I figured he would just keep ignoring me."

"Oh, he won't do that, I promise you," Dr. Wood-Smith said. "You will not be ignored. It is my top priority to get this sorted out as quickly as possible. Now, what's the best way to reach you?"

Frankie hung up and sat in the quiet kitchen letting Dr. Wood-Smith's words sink in. She didn't know what to expect. But she felt better, undeniably lighter. Somehow the events surrounding her rift with Davis Grant had become entangled with her grief over her father. Her life, often solitary, for the past several months had grown ever narrower. Now she felt things opening up. More uncertainties, yes, but possibilities too. So many questions lay open-ended. The thing about questions, though, as she'd been reminded by her conversation with Dr. Wood-Smith, was that the strongest inquiries come from the questions we just can't seem to shake.

Frankie glanced at the clock and saw it was nearly time for her mother's return. She took a quick shower and changed her clothes, then went to the garage to retrieve the small altar she'd built and placed it on the table by the front door of the house. She arranged the framed photos that Judith had left out—Grandpa Ray and Grammy Genevieve on their wedding day, a photo of Jack behind the bar at the tavern, and a young Jerry Sewell standing on the dock next to the mail boat, mugging for the camera. Judith, she knew, would bring home candles and flowers to adorn the All Souls' Day altar.

Tomorrow they'd gather at the River City Saloon to watch troupes of costumed children swarm the sidewalks. Fairies and witches and Supermen and ghosts and princesses. They'd hand out candy to the little kids and drink apple cider and visit with the parents—all her old friends from childhood now out with their own children. They'd come back to the house to have a late dinner with Hank and Patrick. They'd light candles on the altar to honor all the loved ones who had left them. They'd take turns telling stories about them, happy ones and sad ones too. Frankie had learned this now from the people she loved: By sharing our sorrow, we can give it wings, lighten its weight, and let it fly.

36

ROOSTING

Large gatherings have been noted in various species. However, these annual congregations are not generally classified as migratory in nature but something altogether unique and not well understood.

—*G. Gordon's Field Guide to the Birds of the Pacific Northwest*

Mary Frances O'Neill was a young woman of many firsts. She was the first person in her family to complete a master of science. She was the first graduate student in her program to publish in a national journal before receiving her degree. She was also the first academic scheduled to speak at the University of Washington Spring Symposium in the School of Environmental and Forest Sciences on Good Friday morning in 1999.

Sunlight slanted through the windowpane, and a lone crow fluttered to the ground outside the window. Its glossy black feathers marked the bird as a mature adult, Frankie noted as she watched it strut across the red bricks of the quad. Setting one foot in front of the other, the bird fairly swaggered with authority. Like the brave corvid sheriff of the University of Washington. Well, one of many, as the first crow was joined by three more. They fluttered down to the bricks and stood together regarding the people streaming past, hurrying by with their petty human concerns, unaware that they were deep in crow territory.

Frankie resumed her seat in the empty classroom in Hitchcock Hall and looked over her notes for the last time, though she knew she had her talk memorized. It was called "Enemies and Allies: Corvids Connecting with Humans." She wasn't nervous, just excited. With her newly minted master's degree and fresh into her job at Oregon State University, she was relatively inexperienced to be giving a keynote. However, there had been strong interest in her research following the acceptance of her paper by *The Auk* last fall. It didn't hurt to have Dr. Marzluff as second author on the paper. He'd offered great suggestions on her draft and helped craft her submission letter. It was unusual for *The Auk* to publish a paper by a graduate student who'd yet to defend her thesis, but her research had stood out, the editors said.

"We are impressed by Ms. O'Neill's analysis of existing data as well as the development of her own unique ideas. This young academic shows great promise, and we look forward to her next submission with great anticipation," they'd written.

Of course, Frankie was fully matriculated now. She'd received her diploma in the mail just before Christmas break, another sign that the department was eager to dot i's and cross t's after her defense.

What a day that had been! Dr. Tandy, bright-eyed and spry as ever, brought her entire Ornithology 101 class to observe. Judith, Patrick, and Hank were there to cheer her on as well. She wished Anne could have been there, but of course she couldn't have come so far.

She'd stood in front of her committee that day—Dr. Wood-Smith, Dr. Andreas, and Dr. Grant—feeling nervous but confident as she defended her thesis. Her committee's questions had been thorough, but she handled them. Dr. Grant was so terribly civil she could hardly keep from laughing and had to avoid looking at her brother. Dr. Louis, dean of the college of sciences, sat just behind her committee along with the provost, Dr. Rowan. It was unusual for the dean and provost to attend a master's defense, and Frankie knew they were there to keep Dr. Grant in line. He had glanced back at them looking annoyed.

Dr. Louis had shaken her hand and congratulated her, sounding quite sincere.

"You are a credit to our college, Ms. O'Neill. Congratulations."

Dr. Grant left without speaking to her, which was just fine. As a tenured faculty member, he hadn't suffered any real consequences for his behavior, but she knew he was embarrassed to have been caught out. It was Dr. Wood-Smith who brought it all to light—Dr. Grant's failure to distribute Frankie's thesis to committee members, or to offer a plausible reason to deny her defense, or to make an official record of any of it. He had violated a host of department bylaws and had jeopardized the academic career of one of the department's most accomplished students. That was all official record, which pleased her.

She didn't think about it much these days, content with her work at Oregon State University. She loved teaching undergraduate classes in ornithology, where she'd introduced her own version of Bird Bingo to her students. And she was happily immersed in her new area of focus: avian communication.

Now she folded her notes and glanced at the clock. She wished her dad could have been there for her defense and today at the symposium. Though he would have pretended to be confused by her research.

"It's all over my head, child," he'd say, whistling and chopping the air with his palm.

But that would just be an excuse to let her talk about her work, which was his way of showing he loved her.

She knew she would never stop missing him, but now she understood that missing him didn't have to be sorrowful. Missing him reminded her of how much she loved him and had been loved. She could imagine what he'd say if he were there right then. He'd be wearing his ratty buffalo plaid jacket, despite Judith's objections. He'd put his hands on her shoulders and give her a little pinch.

"You got this, Frankie. Make your old man proud."

They talked about Jack often now—the good times, his jokes, his quirks. They were absorbing his absence into their lives. Her family was re-forming, taking on a new shape around their grief, collective and private.

Judith was different these days. Looser, lighter, inclined to call Frankie for no reason at all and chat about work or Rotary. She went to the River City Saloon occasionally too. Not if there was a game on, but on Monday nights, Patrick ran an open mic for local musicians. Judith would go early to help him set up and sit at the bar with a single glass of wine.

And Hank—Frankie had seen more of him in the past six months than she had in years. It was lovely to have Hank back in their lives. Frankie knew he would be at the table for Easter dinner, big hands braced against his knees as he considered the chessboard between himself and Frankie while Patrick and Judith stormed around the kitchen. It made her heart fill just to think of it. Her family.

She wondered about Anne and Aiden. In her last letter she'd asked how they were getting settled in their new home, if they missed Seattle with its soft gray skies, the hum of traffic, the Olympic Mountains rising above Puget Sound. She asked if Aiden thought about Charlie Crow and the day he'd helped Frankie return him to the woods.

She could hear the growing sound of voices as the auditorium began to fill. She stood and walked toward the door. Out the window, the clouds of the Good Friday morning parted, and the quartet of crows squawked and jostled each other. They stalked about briefly, then rose in the air one by one and headed off into the wooded canopy of the arboretum. She wondered if they were siblings, or parents and young. She wondered if they knew the story of the cavemen who haunted the crowds of humans that streamed along the sidewalks of the UW campus. She wondered if Charlie Crow was busy helping his parents defend their territory and prepare for a new spring brood in the woods above June Lake.

The event tech poked his head in the door and said her introduction was starting. Frankie thanked him and tucked her notes in her back pocket and walked toward the auditorium.

She thought of the cottage high on the cliff with windows shuttered like sleeping eyes, and the woods emerging from the melting snow as the sun warmed the mountain and the birds returned. It was all there, waiting for her to come back in summer. She'd go to the lake to work on her new research and take her students up to help with the Yakama Nation's survey of bird populations. The lake and the woods called her back, reminded her who she was and where she started. A child of the woods, a wanderer, and a bird listener. The one chosen so long ago by a single crow flying over the meadow. The crow who seemed to say, *"I see you there. Now you belong to us."*

And that had changed everything forever.

37

NESTING

How and why a bird constructs her nest can only be said
to be heritable.

—*G. Gordon's Field Guide to the Birds of the Pacific Northwest*

Anne sat at the piano with the choir just to her left. They'd finished
their vocal warm-up and had run through the song cycle once. Anne
had given them some notes on phrasing and was letting them take a
break and chat before running the series again. The singers had
handled the score brilliantly. She'd walked them through the Irish
pronunciation, especially the bit on the recurring phrase that anchored the first song.

"The woman who walks over field and stone. The woman who
follows the crows alone."

All the members of the Trinity College Chorale were Irish, but
only a couple spoke the language with any fluency. They had helped
the other singers learn the inflection and phrasing of the lyrics.
Hearing their growing ease with Irish made Anne remember that
composition was a growing, living thing, a collaboration between
composer, director, and performers. It was thrilling to see the choir
making it their own. The song cycle told the stories of five mythical
Irish women: Morrigan, the woman who follows the crows; Macha,

Áine, and Brigid, who were the goddesses of war, summer, and healing, respectively; and the banshee, the wandering woman who
grieves for lost love.

Hearing the songs performed by a choir as she'd heard them in
her head was slightly surreal. The first time the students sang the
series, she was overcome. It moved her so that the songs sounded as
she'd imagined them. The songs were the first she'd written without
Kat, which seemed a fitting tribute to her friend's memory. Still, she
wished Kat could be there to hear the performance at the Good Friday Agreement celebration, which was to be held at the National
Concert Hall in Dublin that evening.

Anne had learned about the Good Friday celebration when she'd
returned for the All Souls' Day Mass the previous fall. She hadn't told
any of her old friends she was coming then because she wasn't sure
she'd be able to keep her nerve. But then Tim decided to join her and
Aiden. The three of them and her parents walked into Trinity Chapel
together. Kat's parents saw her come in and rose to embrace her.

"It's like having a bit of her with us here, love," John O'Faolain
said, weeping openly. They insisted Anne's family sit in the front
with them.

The reception after was crowded with former classmates and
teachers, and Anne felt a golden glow kindle inside her. She'd only
thought how hard it would be to be back in Dublin with Kat gone.
She hadn't considered how good it might feel to be among old friends,
to grieve, to celebrate, to sing. For you can't have a room full of musicians and not expect an impromptu concert to break out. Anne had
stayed late, singing and talking with her friends while her parents
and Aiden went back to the hotel to play cards and watch telly. Tim
stayed by her side all evening.

It was so dear to see Aiden with his granny and granda. The following day, while Anne and Tim went to the pub with Katherine's
parents and siblings, Margaret and Matthew had taken Aiden to
visit the Rogerstown Estuary to see the fall migration of whimbrels.

They'd gone on the bus, which Aiden was nearly as excited about as the birds. After, he told Anne he'd hadn't needed to wear his headphones, which he brought with him in case it was all too much.

"It's true," Margaret said. "Didn't pull them out once. But your man was well prepared."

Now Anne shifted on the piano bench and looked at the clock. They should get started. They had time for one more run-through and then she'd let everyone break for lunch. She could see singers coming back in and getting ready to start. She put her hand in her pocket and felt the feather Aiden had insisted she take with her, his special feather from the woods at June Lake.

"This is a magic feather, so if you get lost in Ireland you can use it to fly home, Mama," he'd said.

Aiden. The fact that her son could speak to her about everyday things felt like nothing short of a miracle. Aiden had disappeared inside himself, and Aiden had come back. His speech had returned, not in fits and starts, but in full sentences and paragraphs. He sounded just as Anne expected him to, the boy she'd known was there all along. He insisted he was talking all the time, it was just that he couldn't hear his own voice through all the noise around him. It was Frankie's headphones that settled everything down enough for him to come back to them.

There was one other child in Aiden's new class whose language had returned seemingly overnight as his had. Angela was a little older than he, aged eight, and diagnosed much earlier—at two and a half. Some of the children in his class had no trouble with language and some did not speak aloud at all and never had. They found different ways to communicate. This is what Dr. Shelley meant when she said every child's autism was different.

Dr. Shelley and her students were tracking Aiden's progress, and her clever son was keen to help, curious about their questions. She was so proud of him, and so was his father.

Tim had called late the night before, forgetting the time difference, when he got home from the office.

"It's so quiet here without you," he said. "We miss you."

"If you're a smart man, you'll enjoy it while you can," Anne teased.

She thought of Tim and Aiden at home in their little house across
the street from Cannon Hill Park in Spokane. It was close to her job
at Gonzaga University and near Aiden's school. The little house felt
like home to her, though they'd only been there since January. Moving day had been cold and snowy, and just before she'd flown to
Ireland last week, spring had begun in full force—an explosion of
daffodils and tulips, lilacs, and lilies of the valley. Ducks and geese
congregated on Cannon Hill pond. One morning she saw a heron
high-stepping through the reeds on long legs. It made her think of
June Lake and her tall, quiet friend Frankie O'Neill, whom she owed
a letter to.

They would see her this summer, as Tim would have a decent
vacation this year. A less hectic schedule was one of the benefits of
declining his father's offer to become president of the company and
instead becoming publisher of the Spokane paper. A smaller market
than Seattle, it was still an important news source for the region.
Tim was happiest in the newsroom, and his younger brother, Mark,
was more suited to the boardroom. Tim's parents didn't understand
his lack of ambition, as they called it, but seemed satisfied that Mark
had taken the helm of the family company as president. Anne could
see that Tim was truly content and that was what mattered. After all
that had happened last fall, she was so grateful for that.

It gutted her to realize how close she'd come to leaving, taking
Aiden to Ireland, and giving up on Tim and their marriage. They'd
come back together just before they'd come apart. She loved him
even more after all they'd weathered together.

Everything fell into place in Spokane. The newspaper, the opening at Gonzaga, the speech therapist recommended by Dr. Anaya,

and, best of all, the special class Dr. Shelley told them about. Part of the public school system, it was a classroom for neurodiverse students with a remarkably talented teacher. The kids ranged in age from six to twelve and each had an individualized education plan. Aiden spent part of each day in Mrs. Proffet's classroom and part of the day in a traditional kindergarten class. He was reading far above his grade level and skilled at math, so academics were in hand. His main challenges were dealing with his auditory processing and managing his response to noise. He was doing a fabulous job of it. More than anything, Anne loved to see him among friends. When she walked him to school, he'd drop her hand and run to the playground to play with the other kids before school started, laughing and chasing his mates. Just like any other child. Her perfect boy.

Anne stood and called the choir together. They dropped the loose ends of conversations, put down water bottles, and rose out of their chairs. They held their music in front of them and looked at her expectantly. And she experienced in that moment the sensation that she so loved as a musician and a composer—that coming together in song with others. Instead of twenty-two separate people, they were one instrument—soprano, alto, tenor, and baritone voices, and the pianist, and Anne conducting. It was human life translated, briefly, impossibly, into something bigger and more enduring. It was a gift and an offering. Every time they began a song, it was the chance for a new beginning—for everyone.

38

FLEDGING

Fledglings develop differently depending on resources, climate, and many other factors.

—*G. Gordon's Field Guide to the Birds of the Pacific Northwest*

⁓

Aiden stood at the front of his class with his drawing tacked to the board behind him. It was the image of a boy and a crow. He had his story memorized, but he'd written himself some notes just in case. He held them in his hands now to reassure himself. Then he fixed his eyes on the wall in the back of the classroom and began.

"You don't have to look at people," Mrs. Proffet had reminded him. "Just look like you are looking at them. Look over their heads if their faces are too distracting."

"Hi my name is Aiden Magnusen today I'm going to tell you a story I wrote called 'Crow Boy,'" he said all in one go.

He stopped and looked at his teacher.

"I forgot the periods," he said.

She told him it was okay, and he could start over.

"Do you want me to clap the periods for you?" she asked.

"No, thank you. I can do it in my head."

He took a deep breath and began again.

"Hi. My name is Aiden Magnusen. Today I'm going to tell you a story that I wrote called 'Crow Boy.'"

He paused and saw the whole story in his mind.

"Once upon a time there was a boy."

This part was about letting people know the story was starting and in a familiar way they could understand.

"The boy lived with his mother and his father in a house on a lake in the woods and the woods were full of crows."

"Caw!" someone yelled from the back of the room. "Caw! Caw!"

It was Danny Keller, his best friend, standing on his chair and flapping pretend wings. Mrs. Proffet reminded Danny that this was practice for everyone. The part he was practicing was being a good and respectful listener. Danny cawed once more and sat down. Angela, sitting on the other side of him, growled and slapped her hands together. Mrs. Proffet told her it was okay; they would keep going.

"Go ahead, Aiden."

"One day the boy was walking in the woods, and he found a tree that was also a house. Inside the treehouse lived a talking crow."

And then he was off to the races. The talking crow, its friendship with the boy, how the crow hurt his leg and had to be helped by the boy, the big storm, and the thunder that crashed and banged down from the sky. And how the crow helped the boy not be scared.

His classmates were squirming in their seats and Danny resumed cawing, especially once Aiden talked about the different sounds crows made, but it was okay. He was focused on what he was saying and by the time he got to the end of his story, none of the rest of that mattered.

"And then the crow said to the boy thank you for saving me. And the boy said thank you for helping me too. We will be friends forever. The crow flew away into the woods and the boy had tea and scones. The end. Thank you and goodbye."

Mrs. Proffet had told him it was not appropriate to say goodbye at the end of a presentation, but he couldn't shake the feeling that he needed to say something formal like that.

"Great job, Aiden!" Mrs. Proffet said, clapping. "This is when we clap, everyone."

His friends clapped and Aiden bowed, though his teacher had said that wasn't necessary either. He took his drawing down from the board behind him and went back to his desk.

Of the twelve students in the class, only Aiden, Angela, and Sarah were giving talks that day. The rest of the kids had different kinds of language. They weren't talking outside yet, was how Aiden explained it to his parents.

Aiden sat next to Danny and watched Angela tack a series of maps to the board. He tried to pay attention as she began her talk on the deserts of the world. He thought about his own presentation and realized he'd liked telling his story to the class, though he couldn't look at their faces because faces were too distracting. He liked it almost as much as he'd liked writing the story. He would tell Mama when they picked her up from the airport. Or maybe he would wait and tell her and Daddy when they were sitting down at the new table in the new house having dinner. Or perhaps he would tell Daddy when they went for a walk at the park after dinner that very night. They could go down to the pond and sit at the water's edge, though that might scare the ducks and the geese away a little bit.

Aiden would lean against the tree trunk and explain how it felt to tell his story to the class. Then he would show his dad how if you looked carefully at the big willow leaning over the pond, you could see the robin's nest there. You could watch the mama robin poke her head above the nest and fly a bit if the coast was clear. And if you sat very still, the ducks and the geese would not be scared any longer and they would come back over near where he and Daddy sat on the grass by the water. Maybe the ducks had a story to tell, or that pretty robin sitting on her nest, or the tree itself. Each one of them had a story, each creature, each life. The stories were everywhere just waiting to be heard, it seemed to Aiden.

Listen, Daddy, he'd say. All you have to do is listen.

AUTHOR'S NOTE

Though I might wish otherwise, my June Lake is a fictional place. However, Mount Adams, its supposed home, is one of several volcanic peaks that form the backbone of the very real Cascade Mountains. Mill Three is imaginary, while Hood River is not. The River City Saloon was a Hood River institution but was never owned by the descendants of the O'Neill clan. In this way, I've mixed fact and fiction to suit the needs of the story.

For the details of Frankie's crow research and various anecdotes about crow behavior, I am greatly indebted to Dr. John Marzluff at the University of Washington. I first learned about his study of crow facial recognition in a TEDx talk he gave, which led me to read the book he coauthored with Tony Angell called *Gifts of the Crow: How Perception, Emotion, and Thought Allow Smart Birds to Behave Like Humans*. For the purposes of my story, I shifted Dr. Marzluff's work to the 1990s. His well-known research with the caveman masks on the UW campus began in 2006.

The story of Charlie Crow's rescue was inspired by an episode in the book *Crow Planet: Essential Wisdom from the Urban Wilderness* by Lyanda Lynn Haupt.

Some of the details about crow behavior that I ascribed to *G. Gordon's Field Guide to the Birds of the Pacific Northwest* came from iBird Plus and *Peterson Field Guide to Birds*. *G. Gordon's Field Guide to the Birds of the Pacific Northwest* is my own invention.

For information about crow vocalizations—which I have not explored exhaustively—I drew directly from the work of Dwight Chamberlain and his 1971 publication in *The Auk* entitled "Selected Vocalizations of the Common Crow."

The fairy tales referenced in this story come from various sources, including Aesop's Fables, Hans Christian Andersen, and Grimms' Fairy Tales. Those who have not read those works may be surprised to find they are full of dangerous adults and neglected children. But they're also rife with magical helpers, surprising reversals, and unlikely heroes—the qualities of any good story.

ACKNOWLEDGMENTS

This book would not exist without the help of many extraordinary people.

To the wonderful Heather Carr and Molly Friedrich, thank you for your encouragement, enthusiasm, and guidance. I'm so grateful for your persistence and your belief in my work. You make it possible for me to keep doing this thing I love most. To Lucy Carson and Hannah Brattesani, my deepest gratitude for all the work you do in support of my writing and writing life.

Lindsey Rose, thank you for believing in this story and seeing its potential from the start. Your focused attention and keen edits helped burnish each draft and made the story so much stronger. Charlotte Peters, I'm grateful for your thoughts and support during the revision process.

To Emily Canders, Nicole Jarvis, and everyone on the Dutton marketing and publicity teams—huge thanks for all the work you've done on my behalf. I so appreciate your labors in garnering attention for my books in the competitive world of publishing.

Isaac LeFever, thank you for your gorgeous cover design, which so beautifully captures June Lake as I imagined it.

To everyone who is reading this book, thank you for taking the time to do so. To focus your attention on fiction in a busy, distracted world is a true gift to a writer. Though June Lake is not real, it exists in my heart and imagination as a place of refuge, and now, perhaps, in yours.

I'm eternally grateful to the private book clubs, libraries, community reads programs, and independent booksellers who hosted me while I was writing this book. Staying in conversation about writing kept me motivated to complete this story.

In creating the fictional world of Charlie Crow, I'm deeply indebted to the work of many writers and researchers, including Jennifer Ackerman, Tony Angell, Dwight Chamberlain, Lyanda Lynn Haupt, Helen Macdonald, and Sy Montgomery, but none so much as John Marzluff and Colleen Marzluff. Thank you for reading the manuscript and offering your insights on crow behavior to balance my fictional flights of fancy.

Developing the story of Aiden Magnusen, I drew on my life experience but also the work of many others, including Paul Collins, David Finch, Hannah Gadsby, Temple Grandin, Alicia Kopf, Jem Lester, Madeline Ryan, and Ron Suskind.

Matthew Lore, thank you for your friendship and continued support over the years. Your belief in my writing got me started and kept me going.

To (the OG) Jacqueline Wood Smith and Esther Lynn Brown, many thanks for your insights on academic programs as well as your intriguing thoughts on bird and human behavior.

Larry Garvin, thank you for fielding questions about fictional lawsuits and antique boats. Michael Garvin, I'm indebted to you for boat trivia and insights into academics.

Clarissa Pinkola Estés wrote, "Friends who love you and have warmth for your creative life are the very best suns in the world." Deepest gratitude to my far-flung clan for shining a light on me—especially Beth Award, Cory Jubitz, Amanda Lawrence, Michelle Nijhuis, Nicole Keim, Vanessa McRae Rice, Olivia Ullrich, Steve Zaro, and my Peishkas. And to Nancy Foley, thank you for your friendship, writerly insights, moral support, and fabulous book recommendations. I'd be lost without you.

Ann Modarelli, Margaret Garvin, Larry Garvin, and Michael Garvin—I love you more with each passing year.

To my parents, Lawrence and Patricia Garvin, my enduring gratitude for your decision to buy a house on a lake with a patch of woods behind. It changed our family forever in the best of ways.

And to Brendan Ramey, always and ever, thank you for your love, levity, and passion for life. My home with you and our creatures brings me so much joy.

ABOUT THE AUTHOR

Eileen Garvin is the national bestselling author of *The Music of Bees* and the author of the acclaimed memoir *How to Be a Sister*. Born and raised in eastern Washington State, Garvin lives in Oregon.